CHESAPEAKE BOUND

An Annapolis Novel

Sailing to Revolution Volume #1

THOMAS GUAY

McBooks
Press
Essex, Connecticut

McBooks Press

An imprint of The Globe Pequot Publishing Group, Inc.
64 South Main Street
Essex, CT 06426
www.GlobePequot.com

Distributed by NATIONAL BOOK NETWORK

British Library Cataloguing in Publication Information available

Library of Congress Cataloging-in-Publication Data

Names: Guay, Thomas, 1952– author.
Title: Chesapeake bound : an Annapolis novel / Thomas Guay.
Description: Essex : McBooks Press, 2025. | Series: Sailing to revolution ;
    volume # 1 | Summary: "Michael Shea is living rough after being
    blackballed from working as a surgeon's assistant and framed for murder.
    Out of options, he escapes the turmoil by shipping out for the colonies
    on the misnamed brig *The Delight* as a lowly indentured servant. But
    while on board, Michael realizes he has not yet escaped the murder for
    which he was framed"— Provided by publisher.
Identifiers: LCCN 2024030359 (print) | LCCN 2024030360 (ebook) | ISBN
    9781493088485 (paperback) | ISBN 9781493088492 (epub)
Subjects: LCSH: Indentured servants—Fiction. | LCGFT: Novels. | Detective
    and mystery stories.
Classification: LCC PS3607.U234 C47 2025 (print) | LCC PS3607.U234
    (ebook)
LC record available at https://lccn.loc.gov/2024030359
LC ebook record available at https://lccn.loc.gov/2024030360

For Elise

*When the Seven Years War ended in 1763, England took possession
of New France and was now master of North America.*

*However, wars are expensive, and Britannia found herself
nearly bankrupt. To pay off this heavy debt, Parliament
sought new revenues from her North American colonies.
But instead of securing a lasting peace, she unleased
a whirlwind of crises that inspired yet another war.*

Our story begins in London . . .

CHAPTER 1

THE SURGEON SPREAD HIS TOOLS ON A DUSTY TABLE BESIDE THE patient's bed. There was just space enough for a stack of dented silver bowls, some lengths of ragged cloth, and a silk tourniquet much streaked by repeated use. On top, he added a dirty lancet with two blood-stained blades. The room was stifling on a warm April day, yet he walked over to stoke the fire and bring it back to life.

The only light came in by way of a northern window, its velvet curtain yanked to the side. The southerly street-view window was shuttered behind a double-lined drapery, crimson framed with black dangling fringe in need of cleaning.

A layer of grey soot smothered the finer details of the room's richly appointed furniture. The patient's bed was under the exposed window, which allowed just enough light to keep the room flat and dreary. Above the bed, a fist-sized porthole had been cleared through the smoke-grimed panes to let some light in, or perhaps to look out. The window was ajar, and a hint of a breeze caught the surgeon's attention.

"Can't anyone follow instructions?" he grumbled as he walked over to close the gap.

The patient was barely conscious. That normally pleased Mr. Oliver. "So much easier to treat the sick when they ain't awares," he'd tell the loblollies when he served in the Royal Navy.

Shaving the sick man's head the day before had been a chore. The ordeal left more than a few nicks on the suffering and cursing patient. There would be help today, but it wouldn't come from the patient's servant. He refused to enter his master's room for fear of the pox. There'd be no assistance from the landlord either. He refused Oliver's request for help and barred any of his household from even going upstairs. He wanted the sick man on the street.

"Don't matter that he's got money," he told Oliver. "Pox kills a prince just as it kills us. Can't stay here, he's got to go."

"You do realize your tenant will return to reading law," Oliver pointed out. "If he survives." The landlord relented but still refused any assistance. And no help would come from Oliver's apprentice. He had died of smallpox three days earlier. A new assistant would come today.

After Oliver's eyes adjusted to the gloom, he nudged the sick man out of his sleep. "Mr. Carroll, time to attend."

Carroll groaned as he tried to throw off the multiple bed covers. Oliver stopped him.

"Sir, you must remain warm. Must keep warm, avoid drafts, and, above all, avoid night air." Oliver liked to repeat this instruction thinking that the more he said it, the more respect he'd get.

"So you've said," the young man mumbled. Being awake was a sad reminder of his raging fever, sweaty chills, and the festering pustules sprouting over his body. He held up his swollen hands to inspect an eruption of tiny volcanoes. "To choke on this foul air, lay about in a stifling room," he took a labored breath, "'tis as miserable as the pox. Am I to be disfigured? Will these remain on my face?"

"Too soon to know. The disease is just beginning to express itself. We'll know in a few days. If you're lucky, you may avoid the monstrous attacks that overwhelm some unfortunates, like myself. You have a small number of pustules at present. Not clear yet if they'll disfigure your countenance."

"You mean to comfort me?"

"The discomfort is necessary, Mr. Carroll. The fire and blankets are needed to induce sweating to purge the ill humours from your body."

"Well, sweating I am. Does this bring you joy?"

"Medically speaking, yes. It's a good sign."

Carroll noticed the instruments on the table. "Again?" His first encounter with bloodletting hadn't gone well. Oliver had been clumsy with his dull thumb lancet. It took four stabbings to open a wound. It wasn't enough to get a steady blood flow. The ordeal had sent Carroll into a faint, much to the relief of Oliver.

"We'll try the other arm today. I've sharpened my lancet."

"You humiliate me by shaving my head. I'm cold without my hair, even in this oven." This protest exhausted Carroll. He sank back in his bed from the effort. The hissing from the fireplace filled the room as Oliver reviewed his notes on the bleeding procedure. Violent shivering forced Carroll into a fetal position, but he had enough energy to complain. "On what grounds do you have the right," he let out a shaky breath, "to so mistreat the sick?"

With a muffled thump, the door creaked open. Light and fresh air accompanied the arrival of Oliver's new assistant, carrying a load of coal. He left the door ajar and headed for the fireplace. Oliver and patient squinted in the new light to inspect the newcomer, a young lad, roughly the same age as the patient. The assistant's expensive clothes had seen better days and were certainly not appropriate attire for carrying a load of coal.

"You're not in court, sir," Oliver said, turning back to Carroll and shutting the door behind the newcomer. The gloominess returned. Waiting for his eyes to adjust again, Oliver removed his faded green coat and hung it on the door. Months-old stains of perspiration spilled down the sides of his black waistcoat.

"This is not a legal proceeding, Mr. Carroll. You may find it amusing to challenge me as a barrister might. But I assure you, sir, you needs be more respectful of the disease. I've seen what it can do to the most robust. It has no mercy. Not for royalty. Not for paupers. Not for anyone. The pox be like the angry sea. It swallows and drowns at its pleasure . . . without remorse."

"Ah, the good surgeon is a poet, one who fears the sea. A wise man," said the new voice in the dim and dusty chamber. "I hope our patient can overlook that I bear more fuel for his misery." He dumped the coal into a tin-lined firebox and dusted himself. "A new chunk or two for the fire?" he asked as if serving tea. "It'll broil us all."

Carroll attempted to sit up, startled to hear the newcomer join the conversation as if he were a gentleman.

"Mr. Carroll, my assistant, Michael Shea. Mr. Charles Carroll, from the colonies. Maryland, I think it is."

"Good day," muttered Carroll. He returned his gaze to Oliver to create a social wall against inferiors.

Michael Shea ignored the game. "'Tis a glorious morning. Best not to dwell on your discomforts." He walked over to the patient's bedside. "These English think bleeding can cure any ill. It's the best they can offer. With Mother Mary's help, you'll rest comfortably again."

"I hardly call this comfortable," Carroll replied, and with a nod to the lancet and bowls added, "nor that."

"Bleeding'll be more bearable than head shaving. I see someone was in a hurry," Shea said inspecting Oliver's sloppy handiwork. "Mr. Oliver, how shall we proceed?"

"Best to have the patient sit up, arm bared, if he has the strength." Oliver handed the bowls to the newcomer.

Carroll tried to right himself. He fell back gasping. His head was spinning faster now. He was cold, yet sweating heavily and shivering.

"If you could possibly think of another time and place, Mr. Carroll," the assistant Shea said, rolling up his sleeves. "Breathe deeply." Carroll could only shiver. "Let me help you with the shirt, sir. If you'll just lean on me as I help you sit, we'll be ready for the procedure."

"Mr. Shea, if you could hold out the patient's arm," Oliver directed. "Mr. Carroll, it might be best if you'd look out the window as we proceed." As Shea started to remove the patient's shirt, Oliver barked, "Not so close to the pox. You risk the disease yourself."

"The saints will protect me."

"They didn't protect London," Oliver snapped. "What is it with you papists?" His assistant's indifference to the disease, and refusal to do as he was told, irritated Oliver. "How're yer damn 'saints' gonna keep you from the pox if ya gets too close?"

Shea ignored Oliver. He removed Carroll's sweat-drenched shirt and sat with him on the bed in full contact, arm to arm. Oliver handed him a length of silk. Shea wrapped it around Carroll's left arm just above the elbow and tied a loose knot. He inserted a stick into the knot and gave it an easy light turn.

"Must we do this again?" Carroll's breathing turned rapid and shallow.

"The discomfort ends soon enough," the surgeon said. "You may notice some warmth as the blood drains across your skin." Oliver opened yesterday's bandage and studied Carroll's wrist.

"Perhaps the lancet will be more kind today," Shea said observing yesterday's wound.

Oliver flashed a stabbing look at his assistant.

Carroll gritted his teeth. His muscles twitched. "I'm cold. My feet feel like ice."

"It's not as you are thinking," Shea suggested. He unfolded an apron and spread it under Carroll's arm and across his own lap. The patient felt the warmth of Shea's grasp on his wrist, then a throbbing in his arm as Shea gently tightened the tourniquet. The assistant stopped when a blue vein emerged in the patient's arm.

When Carroll felt the cold steel of the lancet touch his skin, his arm twitched, but he continued to start out through the dirty window.

Oliver fixed his gaze on the patient's wrist. The blade danced on the patient's arm as he hesitated. The surgeon shivered like a child in an ice bath.

Shea grabbed Oliver's wrist to steady the man and moved the blade to the vein bulging just in the nook of Carroll's elbow. "Inhale, sir, then forward. A sharp slice with authority should do the trick." Under Shea's firm grip, Oliver steadied and followed his direction. The patient inhaled sharply. Oliver sliced and quickly backed off.

Shea grabbed one of the bleeding bowls and maneuvered it to catch the blood.

"Nicely done," Shea said, not adding *"this time"* to the conversation. He relaxed the tourniquet.

"And you," Oliver replied. "You calmed the patient greatly. Most appreciative."

"The worst is over," Shea told the patient. "You'll do fine if you were to relax. Breathe slowly, deeply."

Oliver reasserted his position. "It's now a matter of measure. I think three bowls will suffice for today," he said wiping his lancet on one of the cloths from the table.

"Mr. Carroll, what do you notice?" Shea asked.

"Warmth," Carroll said, relaxing in Shea's hold. "Not what I remembered from yesterday."

"Thinking about it is worse than the procedure," Oliver said.

Carroll didn't reply. He was well aware of how smoothly the procedure had gone with Shea's assistance. He gave himself over to Shea and the bleeding. "You look familiar."

"This be our first meeting, sir," Shea replied with a smile. "We were just so introduced. Perhaps your fever brings on new memories."

Carroll studied Shea. "No. It's you who plays the violin in the garden."

"You've found me out, sir. Michael Shea, musicianer, at your pleasure."

"Your music is a sweet pleasure. It's the only thing that eases my misery," Carroll said. "I knew it would displease Mr. Oliver, but I opened the window to bathe in your melodies."

"You're too kind, sir, though 'tis nice to hear, especially from one suffering so. Will you have any . . ." Michael Shea didn't finish his thought. Carroll had dozed off, resting his head on Michael's shoulder as the bowls filled.

"Three bowls it is," Michael said handing the last to Oliver. Michael eased Carroll down on his pillow and bandaged the wounded arm.

"You deal with it." Oliver turned his back to his assistant. *"Papist bastard,"* he said to himself. As he refolded his lancet, he snipped the skin between his thumb and forefinger. "Christ," he hissed as he wrapped his wound in a dirty rag.

CHAPTER 2

THE ROOM WAS NO COOLER WHEN CHARLES CARROLL AWOKE, THOUGH it was gloomier. Evening was coming on. He checked his hands. Pox still there. His bedclothes damp with sweat. As his eyesight recovered, a vision of the medical assistant dozing in a chair by the fire emerged.

"Why aren't you afraid of the pox?" Carroll's whisper barely made it over the soft hissing of the dying coal fire. "Do you really rely on miracles?" His faint voice roused Michael Shea from his thoughts and worries.

"Miracles?" Michael turned towards the sound of Carroll's raspy breathing, the patient nearly invisible in the fading light.

"You called on the protection of saints and Mother Mary." Carroll took a breath. "You must be Catholic, as I am. Prayers didn't protect me. How do the saints keep you from the pox?"

"They don't. Merely a figure of speech."

"Oliver takes you seriously. We both did."

Michael stood to stretch his back. "Let him wonder." He added a couple of fresh coals. Darkness receded as a swirl of new sparks burst into flame. He poked at the fire, weighing how much to reveal. It was risky to admit to Catholicism in Protestant England. Yet since Carroll had volunteered he was a fellow Catholic, Michael was inclined to trust him. He walked over and sat on the edge of the patient's bed. "Don't worry, sir, the 'saints' will preserve you now," he said, "same as me. I survived the pox as a child. My family didn't."

Carroll considered this revelation. "Oliver doesn't know?"

"No, and I trust he'll remain so ignorant. 'Tis good to keep secrets from the English and their bloody 'majesty.' You never know when it will be useful."

7

"You risk much to disrespect your lawful sovereign."

"Lawful?" Michael jumped up and paced the room. "What have the English brought to the Irish? What have they brought to my family other than poverty and death? They steal our land, slaughter our families, burn our houses. The French welcome us. The English can only think to torture and kill us."

Carroll didn't know what to make of the outburst. Silence filled the room as Michael returned to the chair by the fire. The two men considered their own histories for some time.

Michael closed his eyes and remembered visions of his family home in Conlakilty, the smell of peat, his grandfather's scratchy chin, the feeling of damp air.

His mood lightened as he recalled the forbidden songs of his mother and grandmother, his father following them on what the young Michael called a trembling violin. The boy echoed his father's melodies on his own violin until his parents chased him and his sister to bed in the straw-lined loft. An earthy smell emerged along with memories of falling asleep to singing and muffled conversations. But that was before the fevers.

Carroll's rasp broke the stillness. "We Irish are persecuted in America as well, even in Maryland." He doubled over to get out a dry cough.

"You're Irish?"

"Aren't you?"

"I am, but I must have bled you too long. And just what county of Ireland was you to be born in then, Mr. Carroll?"

"I was born in my father's house in Annapolis."

"Then how can you claim to be Irish then? You're a Marylander."

"My family's Irish. My grandfather came from Aghagurty before he settled in Maryland."

"Ah, those Carrolls. Not even the Irish dared cross Ely O'Carroll uninvited."

"We were a proud family," Carroll said, "but landed there no more. The English stole the Ely. Grandfather came to Maryland for advancement, but persecution soon returned."

"I thought Maryland a haven for Catholics."

"It was, briefly." Carroll fidgeted, pushing the bed covers off, then pulling them back. "That freedom was short lived." He shifted into yet another uncomfortable prone position. "Once that damned Dutchman took the crown, he stripped all Catholics of our rights. We suffer under the same penal codes in Maryland as in all of England."

"I will concede then, Mr. Carroll, your forebearer was indeed a true Irishman," Michael said, "but you cannot lay claim to be Irish yourself if you was born in the Maryland colony."

"I must protest," Carroll huffed. His voice faltered as he gasped for air, "such a discourtesy. We Carrolls come from an ancient Irish lineage."

"That may be so, but 'tis where yer dear mother first meets an' kisses ya that determines what you are. Now, tell me sir," Michael asked with a smile, "where was this fine lady on the day she brought her son into the world?"

"In our home, in Annapolis," Carroll admitted with a heavy sigh. "But I'm Irish by parentage, heritage, religion, rebellion," another wheeze, "and persecution."

"By your reasoning then, sir, the English themselves are French because Guillaume le Conquérant took this damn island for himself and his Norman family."

Michael's polished accent took Carroll by surprise. *"Vous parlez français?"*

"Bien sûr," Michael answered in cultured French. *"J'ai vécu en France pour la plupart de ma vie, un peu plus de treize ans. Et vous?"*

In the genteel French of an aristocrat, Carroll replied. *"I too lived most of my life away from home, so far at least. I was eleven when Father shipped me off to school. Twelve years in France. First at St. Emer in Flanders. Then Paris, to the Court of St. James, to study law. These past three years, reading law here at the Inner Temple. I'm anxious to return to Annapolis."*

"I know those schools," Michael said returning to English, "havens for young gentlemen. I see you retain your clan's combative spirit, despite your unfortunate illness." He gave Carroll a wink.

Carroll gave Michael a curious look and, after a pause, smiled. "I concede, sir. I am indeed from Annapolis, a Marylander as you say, but you can't take away my heritage."

"You must be turning a corner, sir. A smile is a good sign."

"You have been teasing with me," Carroll grumbled. "Are servants all so bold in London to debate and torment their patients?" Confronting Michael's challenge had distracted Carroll from his fever. As Carroll realized what Michael was up to, his miseries returned. He shivered, sweated, and moaned in the darkness.

Michael wasn't sure if Carroll had mumbled a curse or a prayer. He rebuilt the fire. Flickering yellow flashes again painted the room. All was quiet except for Carroll's labored breathing and the hissing of coals giving up their souls.

CHAPTER 3

Snow was still falling when Michael reached Gracechurch Street and headed west. The flakes had been heavy and wet when he started his march to the White Lyon Tavern. The initial snow burst had covered the mud and filth of London streets, giving them a temporary sheen of purity and beauty. The snowfall also dampened the ceaseless barking of tradesmen, grinders, and beggars on their beats, and it forced the whores to cover up their wares.

But it didn't empty the street. Michael endured their desperate offers with a "Not tonight, dear," and wondered where he'd end up if he accepted an offer. There was nowhere for this class of ladies to go. When they found a client, they'd just brush off a spot under a doorway or edge into a shop entrance. The lucky ones crawled under a staircase. *At least I have a door on mine,* Michael thought, watching a working mother cradle her babe inside a stone stairway between customers.

How long even this wretched accommodation would last was in doubt. The worry weighed on Michael as he caught his reflection in an office window. Michael saw the same clothes he wore when he had assisted Oliver with the pox patient, Charles Carroll of Maryland.

Shouldn't have teased the old goat, he thought, *or was it that crack about barbers?*

It had been both. Oliver especially resented losing a rich patient to an upstart with lofty airs. As Michael looked again at his reflection, he remembered hearing from a former patient that Oliver would tell anyone who'd fill his mug, "That thievin' papist's a mere boy in his dead patron's clothes. Calls on saints for miracle cures." As most of London shared Oliver's antipathy towards Catholics, especially Irish ones, only foreigners and colonials like Carroll dared call on Michael Shea.

Now Michael had gambled away a precious shilling, foiled by a Ginger Red. The cockfighting season was in bloom, and he found it difficult to resist the itch. Maybe it was the way the barker touted the contest: "Ya can't lose on the Red," he'd yell, and then in a sing-song rhyme, "Bravest bird west o' Gravesend. Mean as piss an' the devil's sin." Michael crowded in close to the pit and made his bet. "'Tis easy to double-up on ye purse," the barker assured him.

To Michael's eye, this red champion, with its wing feathers clipped, comb and wattle cut, and sporting shining silver spurs, was dripping with ferocity. But games of chance weren't Michael's specialty. The loss still left a sour taste as he made his way down Bishopsgate in the snowstorm, worrying about where he'd sleep tonight. He was overdue with his bribes to the watchmen who "rented" illegal accommodations in abandoned warehouses along the Thames.

Halfway into his march, the big wet snowflakes turned into small dots of white ice. The wind blew harder. The snow squeaked and crunched under each footfall. He rewrapped his fiddle inside his dull red coat and held both tight, his right hand clutched over his heart. Shea ducked his chin into his scarf and breathed on his left hand to keep it warm enough to hold the coat closed against his throat. Gone was the rush of melodies he'd dreamed up earlier to mimic dancing snowflakes. Just reaching No. 3 Bishopsgate and the prospect of warmth and a hot meal were his only thoughts now. Crossing the Leadenhall intersection, he had to lean into the frigid northeast wind. The blast reddened his right cheek and howled into his ear.

Once he turned into White Lyon Court, he shook himself to warm up. He didn't want to appear the frozen and hungry waif he had become. *Your entrance makes a lasting impression. It sets the mood, says volumes about who you are. And*, he reminded himself, *it enhances your social standing.*

It was a lesson much harped upon during his time taking dance, grace, and music lessons with his patron's children during his previous life in Paris. The lessons served Michael well. Two years earlier when he first arrived, most of London mistook him for a young gentleman. Conversation didn't give him away either. It was the music. It was vulgar for gentlemen to perform in public, so once he took his place in a drawing room, mezzanine, or on a stone stage by the blackened hearth with his fiddle, he'd be dismissed as a servant, certainly not regarded as a gentleman.

Living the lesson, Michael brushed the snow carefully off his hat, coat, and shoes before entering the White Lyon Tavern. Once in, he traded secret glances with one of the barmaids, Emma Baker, eldest daughter of the tavern's owner.

Vintner Baker gave Michael a welcoming nod and motioned him over to the gracefully carved bar, its once-sharp edges dulled by decades of countless patrons tracing the Crusader King's fables. Emma found it convenient to wipe down the ancient wooden bar in front of her father as he greeted Michael.

"Good day to you, Michael. So glad you could brave this weather."

Michael didn't have a chance to exchange pleasantries. Vintner Baker let loose with his nervous assessment.

"We have a very full house tonight, and I fear there will be rather warm talk of politics. I'm hoping you and Emma can distract the hot-heads tonight with some dance. This Stamp Act business generates such ill talk in London. Bad for business when it gets out of hand." Turning towards his daughter, "Can you handle your minuets tonight, my dear?"

She nodded. "Sure Papa, hold this." She gave him the rag. "Which dress do you think is best to cool their tempers with? Mother always favors me in dark colors. Black or dark blue, tonight? Which do you favor, Michael?"

"And a good evening to you, Miss Emma," he said. "Perhaps the black? It brings more attention on your lovely smile."

She gave him a quick smile while she pulled out two ivory hairpins and shook out her pale red hair. "If only I had a black wig, like the Madams. That would certainly gain their attention." She pretended to breathe heavily.

"Something modest, Emma, we're not running a brothel," her father said. He puzzled over the rag as his daughter pretended to admire herself in an invisible mirror in which she could see Michael and her father watching her.

Vinter Baker renewed his nervous ramble. "Now, Michael, if you could wander around the tables for part of the evening instead of setting up in the mezzanine, it might help too. Or stand by the fireplace. Oh, and could you sing some of those lonely laments you like so well? But don't play from the Beggars Opera or that warbling Handel like you did last time. All those syllables overexcite a crowd. I don't want to excite anyone tonight. There's . . ."

"Mr. Baker, please, if you don't mind, take a breath or two. My frozen brain can't possibly hold all these directions at once. Perhaps we could share a mug and a chop by the fire? We have plenty of time to prepare. Perhaps a sit-down would ease your mind."

Without waiting for a reply, Michael walked over to the fire, sat down, and opened his fiddle case. He gave Baker a quizzical look, raising his brown eyebrows as an invitation.

The vintner turned to his daughter. "Small beer then, Emma." He ignored Shea's request for dinner and joined the musician by the fire, Emma's rag still in hand. He absently wiped Michael's table. Emma soon followed and handed her father a mug. Then she leaned across the table to give Michael a little peek, a wink, and his tankard. Michael kept his eye on Emma's hips as she returned to her station. Baker cleared his throat to gain Michael's attention.

The men toasted each other's health, not the king's. Michael savored his first sip and enjoyed a surprise, a good ale, not the small beer the vintner ordered. Baker had no reaction. Emma had given her father the common beverage.

"Now, Mr. Baker, if you could take things a bit slower, I'm sure we'll be just fine tonight." Michael savored his ale, watching Emma over the top of his mug. "My, your daughter 'tis a joy to behold, Mr. Baker." Then imitating a fop, he added, "absolutely enticing, her dancing is . . . so graceful. We'll have little challenge diverting their attentions from talk of stamp taxes to thoughts of nymphs alighting in a summer brook, to . . ."

Baker rolled his eyes. "To relieving their loins," he said breaking into Michael's commentary. Baker's honesty embarrassed Michael. "I'm not blind to my daughter's effect on men. I know what makes blood boil. Even the distracted gentlemen you imitate so well are drawn to her." Baker's voice was getting scratchy. He took a swig and nearly gagged. He turned to the bar. "Emma. Rum." There was no bustle to meet his request.

Baker sighed. He got up, served himself, and returned to Michael's table. "Where was I?"

"Something about Emma's effect on your customers."

"Ah, yes. You hear all types of talk keeping a tavern, especially from the jealous mistress or wife. Many come to fear, or perhaps resent, my dear Emma, in one way or another. She's the source of great discomfort for many of my best clients." Baker emptied his rum. "A glance too long during dinner turns into rather disquieting talk upstairs, even between fops, and much of it much too loud."

"Excuse me, I had no intention of . . ."

Baker waved his hand. "Not to worry, Michael. I'm used to the earthy talk, and it's not just about Emma. It's any of the barmaids, and the fairer they are, the more they're noticed. Even Moira attracts the same now that she has blossomed. Some mystical maleficent urge overtakes a man when a woman waits upon him. It's worse when they drink alone."

"To lust then," Michael said tipping his mug. "So back to why you want a dance tonight?"

"Where to start? Politics? Love? We have it all tonight. Most of it will surround that upstart tobacco trader, his 'highness,' Walter Broot." But Michael didn't react to the name, his attention stuck on Emma solo dancing behind her father.

"You've not 'eard of Walter Byron Broot? My god, laddie, where 'ave ye been?" As the rum took effect, Baker reverted to his country twang. His agitation caught Michael's ear.

"Practicin' upon me fiddle?" Michael replied, mimicking Baker's linguistic stumble.

Baker wondered if Michael was pulling his leg. After two years on Baker's stage, Michael knew the movers and shakers, but he offered half an explanation.

"I've been walking these miserable streets looking for advancement, which has done its best to hide itself from my inquiries. There's not much talk of fancy traders among the rabble. Don't give much thought to which patron you choose to fleece from one night to the next. Frankly, Mr. Baker, your employment is all that's keeping me alive. My association with that wretched barber, Oliver, has scared all of London away from my services."

"Can't help ya find patients. But I can offer a bonus for ya tonight if ye kin keep our Mr. Broot sanguine. He's me prime guest of late. Can't miss such a 'gentleman.' Gaudy, loud. A big man an' gettin' bigger by the day. Likes ta reserve our grand table and a suite upstairs. Has 'is eye on Emma, he does. She's the reason he graces us with hisself. I mean to profit from his entertainment."

"So, Emma's his prey?"

"Bait's more like it." Baker.

"He know about her 'dashing' husband, then?" Michael asked with the same scorn he had for Oliver.

"Don't be irreverent, Michael. Captain Longley be family now, sad is the fact." Baker spoke up in case anyone might overhear. "Proud we are, glad the captain serves his king in America." In a hush to Michael: "The longer he's there the better. An' yes, Broot knows about Emma's husband, but that ain't coolin' 'is pond while the man's in America. Walter Broot thinks he can buy anything these days. I'm not worried about Emma. She's a knack for feastin' off wolves an' keepin' 'em at bay." Baker returned to his small beer. "Now 'tis me hope, Michael, that you and Emma together kin help us lighten Walter Byron Broot's purse a bit. 'Twould ease me mind if ye could . . ."

Emma returned to deliver a plate of bread, boiled potatoes swimming in fresh butter, and two warm chops. "So kind of you, my dear," Michael said, accepting the gift.

Baker gulped at the sight of the chops. He wanted to scold Emma, but she anticipated his objection. "Now, father dear, if you want to hear those ballads sung loudly all night, you have to feed your musicians. You have no thought as to how difficult it is to perform on an empty stomach. And stroking that violin all night? Oh, I just don't know how our Mr. Shea lasts for so long. Oh, it takes my breath away just thinking about his exertions." She retrieved the dish rag from her father, twirled 'round, and left the two dumbfounded men staring at her as she danced back to the bar.

Neither man knew how to respond. "Just keep the fat man happy," Baker said to Michael, leaving him to his dinner.

The musicianer kept an eye on Emma and entertained a dream common among men in her wake. The fantasy faded as he turned his attention to a chop, some of the potatoes, and half the bread. Unlike most patrons, Michael unrolled the knife and fork and placed the napkin across his lap. He casually carved his chop into bite-sized pieces and savored each one. He wrapped the bone in a cloth and pocketed it. It might come in handy against stray dogs on Bishopsgate. He covered the remaining meal with the napkin and watched Emma rehearsed her dances, first a mix of clamouring hornpipe steps, then the quiet curtsies of the minuet. He watched in anticipation for a twirl and what it might reveal. But mostly he pictured himself on the receiving end of Emma's penetrating green-eyed stares as she paid honor to her pretend gentleman partner.

Daniel O'Mara broke Michael's trance. Danny had lumbered through the door with a hat full of snow and made straight for the fireplace, toting a trapezoid bag containing his hammered dulcimer and some flutes. No one mistook Danny for a gentleman, though he gave his instruments great respect, carefully placing them away from the fire before greeting Michael with a half a wink and a nod. Michael kicked out a chair and shoved his plate across the table as an offering to his friend.

The mass of wet wool and woven scarves sat down. A puddle soon formed under this reservoir of bad weather as Danny attacked the chop and wrestled with the bread. The back of his hand provided the occasional swipe to clear his lips. There was no recognition of the knife and fork Michael left on the plate. Michael watched with polite curiosity.

"You still cold there, Danny boy?" Michael asked as his friend gnawed the gristle from the bone. Great quantities of steam were rising from the thawing greatcoat. The question shook Danny out of his wolverine passion. He moved to unbutton his greatcoat.

"Before you wipe your hands on your coat, my friend, would you be interested in the remains of my chop? I had thought of offering it to Baker's mutt. He's got a hungry look in his eye, but you seem rather more famished." Michael unwrapped the dog's treat and let it fall onto Danny's plate.

"Ya leave a lot on the bone." Danny raked his chipped teeth along its length. "Dog can 'ave the marrow." He dropped the bone on the plate and fished out a couple of potatoes before wiping his hands on the sides of his greased coat. The coat was well used to the ill treatment. "We be up or down tonight?"

"Am thinking we stay by the fire," Michael said, watching Danny hang his coat by the hearth. "Emma's dancing for us tonight. Will be easier to follow her lead from down here."

Danny heard a mist in Michael voice. "Still dreamin' of a conquest, are ya?" Danny didn't expect any answer. "She don't even know yer name. Might happen, one day, if'in her husband don't turn up," the bigger man said. "Maybe ye'd 'ave a chance with such ladies if God 'ad blessed ya with more manly looks."

Michael had no reply to his friend's taunts, nor did he reveal who had manifested their dinner. Danny lost himself in the chore of tuning the fifty-eight strings on his dulcimer while Michael sized up the growing dinner crowd. Half an hour later, Danny returned to the table.

"Michael," he whispered, leaning in towards his friend, "'ave ye givin' more thought to me plan, the American adventure? 'Twould be grand if ya came. There be no future in England, not for the likes of us."

"Ah, my friend, and what would I be about in the wilds of Amerikay? Fighting off savages with a fiddle and bow? I need a patron. Someone with culture. I'm not made for the likes of farming and plowing. I don't have your skills for sawing and hammering."

"Ya learn 'em." Danny stretched to ease his frustration with his friend's resistance. "Listen, Michael, an indenture's better than any apprenticeship. Why can't ya see this? 'Tis only four or five years. Then we's free to make our own lives after the time's up. Yer time's never up in England."

"Perhaps, but a patronage in France still sounds more civilized."

"France clouds ye mind," Danny countered. "You're too spoilt my friend. Ya may 'ave their manners and graces, but that won't get back in their world. Ye patron's dead. His family cold in the ground, god bless them. They can't help ya no more. Can't ya see this? Ah, Michael, you may fool these English . . . what's Frenchie talk for a pretender?"

There was no answer. Danny shook his hands like he was emptying a bag of grain, gave up his lecture, and returned to his tuning.

CHAPTER 4

WHEN MOST OF THE DINERS HAD BEEN SEATED AND A COLLECTION OF boiled meats and stews served, the musicians sized up the crowd. Danny offered a set opener. "Michael, how 'bout a bit of 'O Sing Unto the Lord,' just to warm up?"

"Good choice." Michael started off first, as usual, standing and scanning the dining hall from the stumpy stone stage around the fireplace. Danny sat behind his dulcimer, his hammers bouncing, singing out tight arpeggios. Halfway into the tune, Danny switched to flute and found low harmonies to Michael's fiddle melody. The slight elevation from the hearth gave them an unimpeded view of their audience and helped propel their music over the clink and clunk of glass, pewter, and dining chatter.

The pair then eased into a mix of country tunes, familiar melodies and improvisations on ancient airs. Michael tended to sway side to side during the verses, a bit out of sync with the melody. Emma wasn't fond of his peculiar movements. She'd dismiss it as, "Our dear Mr. Shea thinks he's a willow tree." It just wasn't a dance to Emma unless there was fancy footwork to show off, either her own or other dancers'.

At key passages, Michael would dip to his right and pause in midsway as his fingers worked their way across the strings and up the neck. The flurry of notes and his rapid bow work never failed to attract attention. Conversation paused as diners absorbed the flourishes. Michael would then straighten up, arch his back, and sweetly finish with a long, high note. He liked to retard the melody and end a passage on a single trembling note.

This was a challenge to any accompanist. Danny had to keep an eye on Michael and wait for a smile, a raised eyebrow, or some subtle sign to time out the pause between chorus and verse. When Shea was in the back of a room, he'd be more obvious and wave his bow in a quick halo to get Danny's attention. Then the two were one again.

It was after one of these theatrical episodes that the duo brought the first part of the evening's entertainment to a close with a flurry of hammered notes on the dulcimer and a shimmering screech on the violin. Michael had meant the notes to be sweetly harmonized, but he was distracted by a familiar face, and his double stop didn't ring quite true. Last time he had seen it, the man's head sported a fuzz of brown hair replenishing itself after a clumsy shave. The fiddler approached his discovery with a wide-eyed smile.

"Charlie! So good to see you, my friend, and this time, with a glorious head of hair in full bloom. Now I see why you have no need of a wig. You're looking quite well."

"And you, Michael," Carroll said, pushing back his chair to stand. "My lord, time does fly. May I compliment you and your partner for such impressive musicianship?" He offered introductions to his four dinner guests. "May I present Mr. Michael Shea. Michael is as much a medical man as he is a musical marvel. He helped me survive the pox. Michael made it bearable. He most certainly has a healing touch." Three of the four guests exchanged pleasantries.

Leaning across the table to get the fourth's attention, Carroll spoke a bit louder. "Jonathan, you remember Mr. Shea, don't you? He sewed you up after your wound."

That snapped the man out of his thoughts. "Yes, of course, Charlie." Jonathan Clayborne, sporting London's latest fashion, jumped up out of his chair.

"You're looking well, sir." To himself, Michael mused, *Someone took prodigious pleasure in emptying his purse.*

"Indeed, I am much recovered." Jonathan bowed. "I still thank Providence for sending you after that butcher Oliver tried to ruin me." Jonathan wasn't a Londoner. His delicate drawl with its warm open vowels sang Virginia, not Kensington or Chelsea. "If you would but observe," he held out his arm, "I've regained my steady aim."

"Wonderful," Michael replied, "please spread the word about your recovery."

Overlooking Michael's frayed appearance, Carroll asked, "Have you continued your apprenticeship with medicine, Michael?"

"There's a long tale to tell, sir, but not time enough at present to start and finish. My medical work is greatly diminished of late. If you linger after dinner, I'll share my story."

"Alas, I cannot remain long. I've been recalled home. At last, Father has agreed to end my exile. I sail for Annapolis on the next tide. The captain allowed me this last earthly freedom to bid my friends here farewell." Carroll tugged on Michael's shirt sleeve to whisper a confidence. "I think the healthy gratuity helped ease his mind." He released Michael and continued. "Best that we find time now to review where we've been these past months. Otherwise, we must correspond by letter."

"A letter to the colonies?" Michael asked. "How long between exchanges?"

"Some of father's arrive within a month," Carroll replied. "Other letters seemed to take a more circuitous route. Have you an address, Michael? I'll write out instructions. I have a rather common name in Maryland, so you'll need some clues to make sure a letter reaches the proper CC in Annapolis. Could I offer you some wine while I prepare an introduction?"

"Very kind, but I have to organize our second entertainment. We have a minuet to prepare." Michael smiled. "Hmm, now as I remember Mr. Carroll, you're a student of dance. Perhaps you would like . . ."

Carroll held up a hand, shook his head, and wrote out his introduction.

Later, at the end of dinner, Vintner Baker and his barmaids removed the remains of the main meal. Emma followed filling patrons' raised glasses with claret.

At the main table, before Emma could refill any glasses, the gaudily dressed host, Walter Byron Broot, waved her close. She leaned in to face him head-on. She corked the bottle and scribbled a new order on her slate. He whispered a private comment. In reply, Emma ran her fingers seductively through Broot's wig and then flicked her fingers on it, creating an off-white sprinkle of starch. Broot's party hooted with laughter as she made this exit.

Michael was too far away to take in this conversation. He could only follow Broot's stare as Emma disappeared into the kitchen. Danny was watching the scene as well. "Like I said," he whispered to annoy his friend, "she don't know yer name."

"Let's get this going," Michael said, brushing the taunt aside. "Time for the dance Baker wants. If you could get them to clap along, then join in on the second turn. That would be grand." Michael ripped into a country reel in a blur of notes, digging his bow into the strings to create a crunching accent here and there.

Then Danny bellowed: "Ladies and gentlemen. Help us warm up this poor room on such a cold, cold night. Give us a beat!" He clapped his hands using his long arms to exaggerate the motion and make it clear it was time for the crowd to join in.

This was Emma's usual fanfare. But she emerged from behind the bar with three bottles of the tavern's best port. She made for the Broot party at the main table. Broot and guests welcomed the drink with a cheer as Emma poured rounds. She lingered, laughing, talking, smiling, and ignoring her other duties.

The crowd held their eyes on Emma, which provoked Michael's thought, *Taking your time, are you?* He jumped up on a table and let out a double-stopped fanfare to start a reel. Startled diners roared approval as Michael drew attention away from Emma. A surprised Danny picked up the melody on the dulcimer to cover any lapse in Michael's playing, but Michael didn't miss a note. The doubled-up melody of dulcimer and fiddle refocused the tavern's attention on them.

Vintner Baker ran out to clear the table of bottles, mugs, and plates. He didn't want Michael's antics to put a dent in the night's profit with broken bottles and wasted spirit. "Tame ye' passion, ya fool," Baker barked. Then he quietly added, "Keep ye' eye on Emma."

She was making a big show of pulling Broot out from behind his table, inviting him to dance. Broot was clearly uncomfortable. Gentlemen didn't behave so crudely, especially to barnyard reels. "Such a racket," he complained to Emma and his court at the table. "Not to a gentleman's taste at all." But his friends would have none of his complaints. They pushed him towards Emma. There was no retreat. Broot wrestled with what would look worse—clumsy dancing or refusing a beautiful woman.

Well aware of Broot's dilemma, Emma toyed with him. "Ah, my sweet Walter Byron Broot," she said for all to hear, "perhaps you'd be more comfortable with a different dance? A minuet?"

Broot was relieved, greatly relieved. The suggestion of a minuet offered an easy escape from a display that would tarnish his burgeoning reputation. "I'd love a minuet, especially to share with such an engaging creature as yourself, my dear," he bowed towards Emma, "but alas, we're in a tavern, not a great hall." With a nod towards Michael, he closed his argument. "Certainly this country fiddler don't have the breeding for such an intricate dance."

So you may think, she thought behind a sly smile. She twirled around Broot's table to give Michael a wink. She took Broot's hand and pulled him forward.

Michael was ready. He jumped back onto the stage all the while maintaining the rough and tumble momentum of "The High Reel." With a flourish, he and Danny brought the reel to a hard cold stop. The duo bowed and bathed in the crowd's enthusiasm.

Before the applause died away, Michael pulled his bow over the high string and introduced the elegant refrain of "Les Mademoiselles de Paris." A warm melody filled the room with a mix of beauty and a hint of melancholy, one that echoed a time long past, a love letter left unanswered. The diners settled down to appreciate a rare treat, a minuet performed right before their eyes. Most hoped it would be at Broot's expense as Emma maneuvered him to center stage.

She raised his hand to form the arch of the first curtsey, let go, and gracefully retreated to the ladies' corner and waited for Broot's return honor. Walter Broot had studied the complex steps, but he had to think and count his way through the routines, always half a step behind the triplets.

By contrast, Emma's movements radiated grace and poetry. Inwardly, she wasn't dancing; she was hunting. When they held hands a second time, they put on dancing smiles and began the intense face-to-face part of the dance, ignoring everything else in the room. Broot found this most difficult. It forced him to treat Emma as an equal. Emma returned

Broot's practiced stare with a Mona Lisa smile, thinking, *No longer can you treat me as the tart you'd like for dessert*. She wet her lips with long slow swipes of the tip of her tongue, like a serpent senses prey, slowly and deliberately, without breaking eye contact or exposing her teeth.

"You torment me," he whispered in French as they closed. "You dance as beautifully as the almighty has made you." They pressed their hands together, fingertips just touching, and rotated as if around a Maypole.

"You are too kind, sir," she answered in English. "Please remember," she whispered, "I do have a husband. This is, after all, only a dance. There's no need for your torment." But rather than disengage, Emma eased her fingers between his and then let her fingers twist in his warm grip before they separated to prepare for the next twirl. She took a deep, swelling breath before breaking eye contact.

When next they came together, Broot, his French exhausted, in English said, "My dear, Emma, you deserve more than a tavern can offer. Silk, satin, and lace. I have the means."

"You're free to give as you wish, Mr. Broot." She matched his turn to the left.

"For you, my dear, most gladly. But there might be," he said dropping his voice, "certain expectations."

"Ah," she hummed. "Now we get to the heart of the matter." Still smiling, she reversed her turn and resumed eye contact. "And what price are you suggesting for such luxuries, Mr. Broot?"

The audience heard not a word of these exchanges. But Michael did. He would've preferred to just concentrate on the complex textures of "Les Mademoiselles." He didn't want to hear a rival's lust, but he couldn't avoid it. The gods had given Michael a "gift" for eavesdropping while he performed. Unlike most musicians who are too absorbed in performance to notice the world about them, Michael couldn't stop himself from hearing what people said. For Danny, who was closer to Emma and Broot than Michael, the conversation didn't register. But for Michael, as he played, he heard, he remembered.

But he didn't get a chance to hear Broot's price. A ruckus broke out that diverted attention away from the dance.

CHAPTER 5

A CRASH OF UPTURNED CHAIRS AND SMASHED BOTTLES FILLED THE room. "You fiend. Unhand me," shrieked a large, corpulent figure. "Walter, help me!" His piercing voice echoed off the vaulted ceiling. Within seconds, stunned patrons watched two figures wrestling on the floor amid broken glass and pools of brandy in the space next to Charles Carroll's table.

Jonathan Clayborne, from the Carroll party, had launched an attack on the largest guest at the table hosted by Walter Byron Broot. While the Broot man remained sitting, Jonathan let loose with a burst of punches. The first one glanced off the bigger man's shoulder. The second smashed into the man's mouth, pinching his lower lip inside his teeth. Saliva splattered on the table. Blood oozed from his split lip. The rest of the blows missed their target, landing harmless on the big man's chest and shoulders, but they did succeed in dismounting his wig. It was the loss of the wig that had prompted the shriek as the big Broot man shoved his attacker away and rose to stake out higher ground.

The diminutive Jonathan didn't wait to be towered over. He slammed his head into the big man's stomach. The fighters bumped into the Broot table, upending the centerpiece, a large bowl of boiled calf's head soup. The two combatants slipped on the soup slick and ended up on the floor with Jonathan momentarily on top slapping away. There wasn't enough room to wind up a true punch, but the attacking Virginian did succeed in reddening the bigger man's cheeks.

The corpulent one didn't defend himself with fists. He wrapped his puffy arms around Jonathan and, using his superior weight, rolled over, pinning Jonathan in the puddle of calf's head soup. The big man grabbed

Jonathan by the lapels and bashed his head on the floor. Observers winced when they heard the loud crack as Jonathan's head splashed fatty gobbles of soup on nearby stockings and britches.

Victory was at hand for the bare-headed, bald man. "You impudent runt. How dare a colonial strike a superior." He spit this out as he held his attacker down with one arm across the colonial's throat, leveraging his considerable weight. But the bald one didn't know how to take further advantage or stop the squiggling underneath as the little man bounced his hips up and down, trying to shake off his heavy assailant.

"Ain't that a pretty sight," Danny snickered to Michael, "a mare in the saddle."

By now members of the Carroll and Broot tables were pulling the fighters apart, each wrangling them into protective corrals.

The commotion ended Broot's romantic trance. "You'll have to excuse me, my dear. My companions have run into some sort of trouble."

"Don't lose your top, Walter." She gave his powdered curls a sharp tug.

He offered Emma a quick closing honor, reset his wig, and walked, unhurried, to his table. She retreated to keep her father at a distance, as was her routine during such excitements.

Broot gave a puzzled look towards his table and then the Carroll table. His voice, a mix of agitation and reserve, filled the room. "What has become of my brother's peruke?" To his table, he admonished: "It wasn't that long ago I left you in such fine harmony. How could things have taken this sour turn?"

Carroll let his guests restrain Jonathan. "I was attempting to discover just that, sir."

"And you might be?"

"Charles Carroll, sir. And you?"

"This impudent mongrel attacked me," the corpulent one squeaked. "This is outrageous."

"I'll outrage you," Jonathan screeched, wiggling in the grip of his friends. He had lost all vestige of a gentleman's demeanor. The dregs from the floor were dripping off the back of his fancy coat and britches. Blood and snot dripped over his lips. Despite being restrained, he wiped his nose along his jacket sleeve and left a trail of maroon and white streaks across his face.

Broot gave each combatant an exasperated look. "Quite so, Marcellus. That you've been attacked is rather plain to see." To both tables he asked, "How is it that my brother and this diminutive 'gladiator' have come to ruin my dance tonight?"

"Sir, if I may," Carroll offered up in a flat tone as he stepped forward from his party. "The root of this disturbance lies in a disagreement over Parliament and this arrogant Stamp Tax."

"Taxes?" Broot tilted his head in puzzlement. "Such rude behavior, and a woman is not involved? Most curious." His comment generated polite chuckles and some smirks from other tables. The levity eased some of the tension.

Jonathan ignored Broot's quest for civility. "Why would a woman care for such a fop?"

"Please, that's enough, Jonathan," Carroll snapped.

"You dare insult a superior?" cried Marcellus.

"Superior, my arse," Jonathan sneered, "unless you're on a scale."

Marcellus's eyes widened at the insulting observation.

"Jonathan, let me speak," Carroll said before Marcellus could get another insult out, "or else we'll have to muzzle the both of you."

"Nice work quieting the back bench," Broot said to Carroll. "Perhaps we gentlemen can find a way to ease this disturbance." Then in a voice that other patrons, and Emma, could hear: "Let's not ruin such a promising evening." His eye found Emma leaning over the bar, chin in her hands and tapping a finger to her cheekbone.

Danny watched Broot's search for Emma as the musicianers took an unscheduled break. "This'll cost yer rival plenty," Danny said. "Yer Miss Emma don't like getting upstaged. Would ya look at the evil eye she's got on 'im?"

"She'll rewarm soon enough." Michael pretended to ignore the altercation. "You know, my friend, 'tis not polite to stare at those in crisis." He traded looks with Emma.

"Polite me arse," Danny said. "Should be instructive ta see how the highbrows deal with this. There, now the mare remounts his wig."

Michael gave in to curiosity to watch the spectacle as Carroll offered an explanation.

"My friends were discussing this this dreadful Stamp Act business when your man blurts out some obnoxiousness about colonials. He was rather rude in his opinions on tobacco planters. All of our families," Carroll motioned to include those at his table, "are in the tobacco trade in the colonies. We all felt your brother's commentary ill founded and most ungentlemanly."

"Do gentlemen brawl on tavern floors in the colonies?" Broot snapped.

"Certainly not. But Jonathan quite naturally felt obliged to defend his family's honor, however inequitably unbalanced the odds may seem."

"Certainly family honor is worth defending," Broot replied. "But one does question such a response from a man of obvious means."

"With pistols then," Jonathan challenged, quite unrepentant. "I'm ready, right now!"

Broot turned towards the tavern's door. "'Tis terribly cold for such vile business. However," he inhaled, "Marcellus could accommodate your request," he exhaled, "if pressed."

The dueling challenge triggered agitated murmuring throughout the tavern. It also triggered Michael's full attention. He gave his fiddle to Danny. "Be right back."

As the Broot brothers consulted, Michael circled around behind their table and hooked Walter Broot's arm. *"Monsieur, un mot, s'il vous plaît."* A startled Walter Broot found himself turned around as Michael in French warned, *"Unless your associate is an expert with the art of dueling, I would urge you to disengage. I am quite familiar with this colonial gentleman. He is most quick and, I must warn you, deadly accurate with pistols. I urge you to let cooler dispositions prevail."*

"Ah, merci." Broot returned to confer with his table guests, Michael to the fireplace.

Carroll also directed his discourse away from dueling. "My dear sir, might I assume that your associates have not traveled the colonies?" There was no reply. "Perhaps your friends do not appreciate how the issues of family, and honor, and taxes are intimately intertwined for Englishmen transplanted in America."

"I'm sure my party would like to know more," Broot said, taking Carroll's cue. "Perhaps my brother Marcellus was ignorant of your table's origins and your warm feelings on the matter." Broot gave his brother a "hold your tongue" look.

But Marcellus ignored this and spoke with a lisp exaggerated by his swollen lip to explain himself. "These colonial 'gentlemen' expressed the most unfounded view that factors do not deserve the commissions assessed for our services." Then, nodding towards Jonathan, he added, "not that this rube would understand. There's a reason the colonials are in America. They're not fit for England."

"You smoldering pile of shite," cried Jonathan.

"Jonathan," Carroll barked.

"Marcellus, please," said Broot, nearly nose to nose with his bruised brother. Carroll's and Broot's assertiveness broke the mood. Both combatants quieted down.

Carroll resumed. "Talk of money is a most inflammatory subject. There is a long history of our disputes with London factors over commissions imposed on colonial planters. And now, adding more fuel to this fire is this Stamp Act business. Surely you recognize that Parliament has no right to tax an Englishman without his consent. No man of honor would ever acquiesce to such an arrogant tax."

"But why, sir? Is it a surprise to colonials that England must pay her war debts?" Broot asked. "Especially when the money is to protect our dear colonial children from dreadful savages and the papist French! A small fee is necessary."

"The issue is not the tax itself, nor even how much," Carroll answered. "It's how the decision is made—without our consent—that flames the fire."

Broot watched Emma wander over to sit with the musicians. He had hoped to end the debate, but with Broot, politics trumped romance. "Parliament has every right to collect taxes," he insisted loud enough for all to hear. "Our glorious victory over the French comes with new responsibilities."

At that little speech, Emma turned her back to Broot and made a show of engaging Danny and Michael, laughing. Broot grimaced.

"Not without our consent," Carroll countered. "Every Englishman has the right to be heard. The colonies have had no voice. We have not been heard." Carroll's tablemates gave him a hearty, "Hear, hear!"

"At present, the parent must speak for the child," Broot countered. "Wars are costly, even when you win. Perhaps the news has yet to reach the wilderness, but the king's treasury is quite depleted. The burden has to be paid. It's only fitting," he paused for effect, "that those who benefit the most should help pay for His Majesty's sacrifice."

Jonathan slammed a fist on the table. "What benefit?" he shouted. "To be cheated by London merchants and factors? To let the king pick our pockets?" He tried to rush Walter Broot this time, but his friends grabbed him. Carroll stepped in front of his irate friend.

"You challenge the obvious?" Broot answered Jonathan. "You Americans no longer have the French to fear, but the savages remain. You enjoy the easy and prosperous life His Majesty has made possible. After all the kind attentions your generous parents have entrusted to you, you colonists behave like ungrateful children."

"Enough. Enough." A growling bark broke the debate. Vintner Baker arrived on the scene with a mop and bucket. "Ya can't change Parliament from 'ere. 'Tis not the place for such rhetoric. Take it outside."

Before Carroll or Broot could respond, Baker, his wife, and their daughter Moira crowded around the tables, creating confusion and distraction, mopping the floor, resetting the tables, and refreshing mugs. "Ya paid for good port, Mr. Broot," said Baker, "'tis a shame to let it go to waste. I'll trade this broken bottle for a fresh'n if you can return to lighter discussions."

"A splendid suggestion," Carroll jumped in. "May I offer to cover the bottle?" Carroll asked with a slight bow. Both sides welcomed Baker's intervention.

"Mr. Shea," Baker called out, "if you please."

"How do ya follow that?" Danny asked, looking at Emma.

"Well I'm certainly not going to curtsey and twirl with His Majesty's lap dog just yet." She turned to smile at Broot. "We need to reset the atmosphere."

"A bit of theater then," Michael suggested. "Emma, will your beau grasp the irony if you was to launch into 'Can Love Be Controlled?' It's a role well suited for you."

"Oh, Michael, you are a devious one," she said, "with pleasure." Emma took a moment to prepare for the role. She stepped to the edge of the little stage and waited for her cue.

Danny opened with a chorus that started faintly on the dulcimer, as if angels were singing far, far away, and then built to a pounding flourish. As Danny's hammers danced to their peak, Michael wove in the song's melody and the mood evolved. As he accented a shaking vibrato on the main theme, a sense of expectation filled the room. Emma took a slow step to center stage and presented a most serious face. Then her passionate voice roared:

Our Polly is a sad slut!
Nor heeds what we have taught her.
I wonder any man alive will ever rear a daughter . . .

Warm applause and cheers filled the White Lyon Tavern as patrons recognized what was coming. Tensions faded. The crowd alternatively cried, laughed, and snickered as Emma acted out key roles from the Beggar's Opera scene.

Walter Broot again fell under Emma's spell as his guests turned their attention towards the one-woman play. Marcellus nursed his bruised lip, and pride, and lost himself in Polly's story.

Jonathan pouted as he dabbed a blue-patterned handkerchief to his bloody nose. It stopped dripping, but not his anger.

CHAPTER 6

As the night closed in on midnight, the formal entertainment of popular songs, spoofs, and quadrilles evolved. The musicianers catered more to rowdy dances and bawdy songs as the wealthier patrons like the Broots retired for the evening and were replaced by a flood of younger drinkers. A noisy table of single men and two fine ladies right in front of the stone stage kept calling out for their favorites. Michael and Danny rattled through many of the requests. Then to clear the air and make room for the new arrivals, Michael gave Danny a nod. Daniel hammered away on his dulcimer a rapid-fire introduction of the familiar tune. A table of gentlemen immediately jumped up, clapping and stomping. Then Danny stopped playing, stood center stage, and belted out:

> Beauing, belling, dancing, drinking
> Breaking windows, cursing, sinking
> Ever raking, never thinking
> Live the Rakes of Mallow . . .

The lubricated patrons sang along, some adding sour harmonies to the punch line, *Live the Rakes of Mallow.* The men up front twirled their ladies while Danny's huge voice filled the hall.

For the closing stanza, Michael jumped up on his chair and raised his arms like a conductor, bow in his right hand, leading Danny through the final lines:

> Then to end this raking life,
> They get sober, take a wife,

Ever after live in strife,
And wish again for Mallow.

Michael dropped to the floor amid thunderous applause. They both offered exaggerated bows and collapsed in their chairs. "How I hate that tune," Michael grumbled, "such child's play."

"Why'dya play it, then?"

"Because, as you can see, it makes for a happy, busy tavern. And I've an eye on a free bed tonight. So much easier to call in a favor when the vinter's purse is weighted down."

Vintner Baker was indeed all smiles as he and his daughters hurried through the room to service constant demands for more drink. And there was a fresh group of newcomers just arriving, musicians and a mix of young gentlemen and ladies of dubious backgrounds. They gathered at the back of the bar and placed requests for drink.

Michael slumped in his chair. "Danny, could you find in yourself the energy to organize the players for our next session? I could use a moment's peace."

"I'll get 'em ready for ya. And ya may close yer eyes and end yer searchin'. She's gone."

Michael acknowledged with a nod as Carroll approached to say farewell. "Wonderful evening, Michael. This is our final meeting in London. If you ever venture to the colonies, ask for the home of my father, Charles Carroll of Annapolis. It's quite easy to find. Right next to the harbour. A brick house on a hill." Carroll handed Michael a carefully folded letter. "I've written you a letter of introduction. I'm sure Annapolis could use your medical and musical talents. My home city is quite cultured."

After the last of the revelers finally emptied out and headed home, Baker's youngest daughter, Moira, led Michael to a small attic room. "Mind your head, Michael. It's rather close for tall ones like us." She opened the door. "It's warmest of the rooms. Bed's beside the chimney."

"Thank you kindly, Miss Moira." A wind gust rattled the window.

"Will Danny be joining you?"

"I think not. He has, shall we say, an alternative arrangement. Ol' Danny's come under the spell of one of your customers. When he goes a-hunting like this, he don't want company."

"I know those ladies. 'Tis he who's hunted." There was an awkward pause. "I so enjoyed your performance tonight, Michael."

"Thank you, Moira, you're most kind."

"I added harmonies. Did you notice?"

"So you did, and very sweetly too. Your singing made Emma's Polly Peachum seem angelic. Not sure old John Gay intended for an angel to harmonize with Polly."

"I feel for Polly." She hoped Michael would discuss Polly's plight. He didn't. She fished for anything to keep the conversation going. "Would you say I sing as well as Emma?"

"In many ways better, but I wouldn't wish Polly's lot on you. Enjoy your innocence." He reached out his hand. "May I borrow your candle?" There was an awkward silence as he lit another by the chimney.

Moira fondled the bundle under her arm. "You can apply all these blankets for yourself then." When he didn't move to take them, she put them at the foot of the bed. "I'll be wishing you a good evening now."

"And you, my dear. May the saints keep your toes warm."

She gave a halfhearted curtsey and pulled the door closed.

Michael hung his candle from a hook on the chimney and folded his coat and waistcoat over the back of a small chair. He removed his shoes, the floor cold to his stocking feet. He visited the frosted window. With the heel of his hand he rubbed out a circle to view the city. Nothing. Only cold blackness and the whistling winter wind. On the inside of the window he watched the rippled reflection of his candle flare on an angle in the draft. Wax spilled over on the leeward side. He shut the drapery to cut the draft and counted two and a half small steps to the bed, and three short steps from bed to door. A night pot was under the bed. On a tiny dressing table by the door, he found the rump of another candle and a serviceable tinder box. He took a last survey of his quarters and snuffed the candle.

He waited for his eyes to adjust to the darkness before covering himself in blankets. Whenever the wind eased, he let the murmur of voices in rooms below lull him to sleep. Sometime later, the squeak of a hinge broke Michael's sleep.

"Damn you, Danny," he grumbled, his voice full of disappointment. "The slower you open that door, the more notice it makes. Floor's all yours."

The squeaking stopped. A bustling of heavy fabric fell to the floor. There was a hint of eau de parfum. "Warm me," whispered Emma in the blackness. She slid under the blankets.

"Am I in heaven?" he said, his voice now pleasant and joyful, his mind racing ahead.

Emma sidled up to him and pulled herself into a spooning ball. He mirrored her form, tentatively at first. Her shift was cold and damp. "Warm me, please, Michael."

He put his arms around her waist. She drew them up to her heart, holding his hands tightly in hers. She was shivering. Her feet found his. "You wear stockings to bed?" she asked.

"Wasn't expecting company. It is cold." He started to inch his hands inside her shift.

Emma stopped him and wiggled out of his arms. "There's been some ugliness, I'm scared." She sat up and crossed her arms against the cold. "A customer. Danny found him dead in the snow. He's all blue. Papa's taking care of it."

"Danny?"

"Danny's fine. He'd been with his lady 'friend.' Danny rousted Papa up to help carry the body in."

"What's going on?"

"Let me tell you." Emma pulled him back and slid back under the covers. Michael put his arms around her again. She turned to face him. "I was waiting on the Broots and their party."

"The Broot brothers?" He pulled his arms back.

"Don't be like that." Michael withdrew a bit more. It didn't faze her.

"So there I was, attending Walter's party. He had a private room arranged, as is his habit for gambling after hours. This time he had four 'guests.' Victims they was really, three of them anyway. The fourth was a business associate of theirs. What a sight. This fat man walking with canes escorts these gentlemen in. Then the show begins. At first it was just

Walter and his brother, Marcellus, you know, the one who lost the wig. They was playing backgammon. Walter lost and made a stink. 'Never in all these years have you bested me,' he said as he handed over several shillings. 'Me lady has surely abandoned me.' He said that over and over. Seemed he and Marcellus would come to blows, the way Walter was grumbling."

"Their fat man associate intervened, suggested a round of cards. He tells Walter, 'It'll calm your mind.' Now, I think that an odd sort of cure for anger, don't you? The guests thought so. They pegged Walter for an easy win, seeing as his luck had just run out. Then Marcellus says to the fat man, 'Cards is not my game. Perhaps I could use some air.' Then he and the fat man take their leave from the table." She giggled and then explained, "Such a strange couple they make, a pair of Italian gentlemen waddling hand in hand watching the cards."

"Emma, what about the dead man?"

"I'm coming round to that."

Ignoring the cold, she sat up again in the darkness. "At first, I believed them brothers was truly out of sorts over the game. Walter lost the first round of cards and ordered a fresh bottle of port, one of our finest, again. I knew Papa would welcome that order. I went to fetch and serve 'em so's I could keep my eye on things in case they kept going."

"Emma."

"Don't hurry me now, Michael. It was all I could do to keep their glasses full. Walter had me refill them after every sip. Walter started winning a hand or two. Then he'd lose one and reach for his glass, but before each sip, he'd complain about his lost luck, toast the players, and put his glass down. He never took a drop once the cards came out. Them guests did. That's when I realized it was all arranged. Marcellus came back to the game and left most of his drink in his glass. It was right there for these others to see. But they didn't take no notice. Walter's companions had their fill alright, and they lost more money than Papa could ever count, even on the best of nights. I kept up my part through it all. That is why I was there, you know, to sell drink. After all, it's what fuels our fireplace."

"So you've become an accomplice to this Walter Broot's scheming?"

"Don't put it that way, Michael. I was only pouring port and observing. It's my part in my family's business. That's how I discovered how he kept winning. Walter cheats. Sitting on his knee, I could see the color of his cards when I shouldn't have."

"Emma, what about the dead man?"

"Oh, yes. A young fellow. The odd little one who got into the fight with Marcellus, the one who ruined my dance."

Michael sat up. "I know him. Jonathan Clayborne. I attended to him several months ago. He survived a duel. The lead broke his rib. He was fortunate. The rib kept the wound on the surface, away from the heart. Nice enough fellow. Very touchy when you asked about trade and his family. He suspects all factors are in league against his family."

"Factors?"

"Men like your Walter Broot. Trading agents, mostly tobacco. Colonial planters do all the work. Factors get rich on commissions. That's why Jonathan was in London. He's hunting down the factors who cheated his family. He found one right away. Jonathan said he walked right up to the man, accused him of cheating. The factor challenged Jonathan to a duel, not thinking a colonial could be as skilled as a Londoner. Factor fired early, wounded Jonathan. Factor died."

"Rather bold action for such an odd little man." Emma shivered and slid under the covers.

"That's not all of it. We talked for days about it as he recovered. Jonathan and I got on well. I'd tweak his pride now and again, reminded him how the English will never treat a colonist as an equal. He didn't like hearing that."

"Michael, you're rude to your patients?"

Michael relaxed on his side, facing Emma. "Jonathan wasn't troubling with me. He was rather calm outside of business, even shy . . . didn't take well to being treated as a second-class Englishman. He'd get white hot over tobacco percentages, being cheated by factors. Said he aimed to put a stop to it. Aimed well, it turns out. Jonathan put the bullet straight in the man's heart. News travels quickly. When Jonathan found his next factor, the man quickly offered terms right away. A third disappeared. Jonathan was on a mission to discover the third factor."

"I should think so." Emma pulled the covers up to her nose.

"It wasn't long before Jonathan had a new problem. He couldn't find new associates with whom to trade. He didn't like it when I suggested killing your partners might not be a good way to run a business."

"You learn a lot about people you doctor."

"Just have to listen. Most are right grateful I can keep them out of the grave. Remember, Emma, I'm the one with needles and blades. Talking distracts 'em."

"Does it hurt to be stitched?"

"Oh yes, it hurts. Though by how much depends on the skill of the stitcher." Michael stared into the darkness. "I met Jonathan through another colonial, a friend of mine, Charles Carroll, a Marylander. He hosted the dinner party next to your Broot table. Carroll had referred Jonathan to me after a terrible barber, Oliver, made a mess attending to his wound. Pity any sailors in the Royal Navy who needed doctoring." He put his hands under his head. "Jonathan didn't take to him. No surprise. Oliver's clumsy, arrogant without any reason to be. Loves his drink."

"Why'd you apprentice with him?"

He turned to her. "Not an apprentice. I aided Oliver after the pox killed his apprentice. We were a poor match. I'm good and he's not. After a month or so, Oliver didn't appreciate his patients calling me, not him, for treatments. But Oliver has connections. He spread lies about. My services haven't been requested in months."

"Somebody's coming!"

"Must be Danny." Michael went to put a hand on her shoulder. But Emma jumped out of bed. She gasped as her bare feet hit the cold floor. The door opened.

"Michael, I need you." Vintner Baker called into the dark. A following candle revealed Emma wiggling into her dancing gown. Baker glared at his daughter and then the musicianer.

"Emma?" Broot entered with the candle.

"It's not as you think, Mr. Baker," Michael volunteered from the bed. "Emma was just informing me of the unfortunate demise of one of your customers."

"In bed?" Broot sneered.

"That would be a most indelicate interpretation," Michael answered. "We have no fire. It's cold. We merely huddled together for warmth to review the evening's unpleasantness." He rose to reveal his mostly clothed body. "As you can see."

Broot stiffened with indignation to replace the hurt. "You deceive me, Emma, for . . . for a musician?"

"Walter, it's as Michael says. We are dear friends, like brother and sister, nothing more." She calmly straightened the pleats in her gown.

"I thought we had," Broot hesitated, searching for the word, "an understanding."

"We do," she said, "when you pay me proper attention. But you was much too occupied with your gaming tonight. I won't play second to a stack of cards."

"That was business."

"A curious business indeed," Emma replied.

"No more curious than adultery? Or would this be incest?"

Emma deflected Broot's wounded arrow. "Perhaps we should ask your dear wife to explain the difference." She pulled up her hair, securing it with ivory pins as if readying herself for church.

"Enough!" Baker barked. "Sort this later. Michael, ye must attend in the hall. A customer, the little American. He were dead when we found 'im. But he's returned to this world. Gasped for air after we laid 'im out. Now he's breathin' and bleedin'."

"I'll see to him." Michael bolted from the room with Emma's "brother and sister" reverberating in his head. Baker followed.

Emma and Broot lingered. Their voices muffled, one pained, the other annoyed. "And why is it," she asked, "you're traipsing around with my father in the middle of the night?" She turned to check her hair in the murky mirror. "I have need of your candle."

Broot accepted the invitation, glad to come to Emma's assistance. "My brother has gone missing. I joined your father in the search for Mr. Shea, hoping to find Marcellus along the way."

CHAPTER 7

JONATHAN WAS LAID OUT ON THE TABLE THAT HAD EARLIER HOSTED Broot's dinner party. Bloody bubbles gurgled from his throat; panic filled his eyes. Michael leaned in to connect with him.

"Jonathan? Do you know me? Michael Shea?" He took Jonathan's hand.

Their eyes met. "Squeeze my hand if you understand me." Jonathan complied and didn't let go. Tears replaced some panic when he realized Michael was on hand. Jonathan tried to speak.

"No talk. Breathe through your nose," Michael commanded, "as easily as you can." With his free hand, Michael probed the blood-drenched neck cloth. "I'm sorry, Jonathan. I'll need both hands to remove your silk and discover what we have before us." Jonathan reluctantly let go. Michael peeled the blood-soaked silk away from Jonathan's throat. He stifled a scared breath when he saw the damage. He slipped his fingertips into the wound.

Michael took the colonial's hand again, looked him in the eye, and took a breath between every phrase. "Jonathan, you're most grievously wounded. Don't move. Squeeze my hand once for yes, a double squeeze for no. Do you understand?" A long slow squeeze. "Good. Are you in pain?" Two squeezes.

Michael became aware he had an audience, Vintner Baker, his wife, and Emma's younger sister, a very wide-eyed Moira. Looking at Baker, Michael issued orders.

"Mr. Baker, I need more light. Can you bring me four or five tapers? Close 'round his head. Jonathan needs a proper physician. You must send for one." Baker gave Michael a confused look. "Now, Mr. Baker, if you

40

don't mind. Don't delay. We haven't much time." Once Baker realized the task was meant for him, he hurried to the kitchen.

"Moira, I need hot water, clean, and cloth for bandages, clean as well. Ma'am, I have need of your best sewing needles and thread, the finest possible." That cleared the room.

"Jonathan, we have a few moments to ourselves." He picked up Jonathan's hand. "Your throat's cut. This is a terrible wound. You also have a severe trauma to the head. You've been unconscious. Do you understand?" Jonathan squeezed once. "I will try my best to stop the bleeding. We need a proper physician. Your injuries are deep, beyond my experience." Jonathan gave a squeeze of understanding.

Baker returned with several candles and started lighting them. "Arrange them, please, around the patient's head." Baker created a halo of warm light and then stood still, staring.

"The doctor, a real one, not a surgeon," Michael ordered. Baker was slow to respond. "Hurry!" Michael now found Vinter Baker's laconic demeanor irritating. "Your customer's life depends on your speed. He's 'your' customer you know."

"Right." Baker hurried to the door, grabbed his greatcoat and hat, and headed out.

Turning back to the patient, Michael whispered. "We're alone again. Would you like to see a priest? We are in a very dire time here, Jonathan." A double squeeze. "I understand. I'll pray with you if the time comes." One squeeze.

"Jonathan, I must inspect your wound more carefully." He let go of the patient's hand. "I can close external wounds, my friend, but I've never worked inside like this." As he took a closer look, Michael prayed that Baker would return quickly with a physician. He could feel his own pulse racing. He was shaking. So was his breathing.

Moira came to the foot of the table with cloths and a bucket of hot water. "If you can bear it, Moira, quickly now, here," he nodded to his left, "close by Jonathan's head." His mind was racing all around. "Please rip some small pieces of cloth. Hurry. Smaller!"

Mrs. Baker arrived with a large sewing basket. "Ma'am, most welcome. If you could take a position across from me, that would be most helpful."

"Moira, like this." Michael took the first piece, soaked it in the water, and wiped the blood from Jonathan's throat. "Come on, quick now!"

"You don't have to yell at me!" Her face flushed. "I've never done this." She was shaking.

Michael inhaled deeply to calm himself. "I'm sorry, Moira, neither have I." He exhaled. "I'm scared too. Now, please if you do as I just did as the blood collects." He demonstrated how to wipe away the blood.

She hesitated.

"You can do this." He put his arm around her shoulders. "Jonathan will welcome your warm touch. It can be soothing in a time of crisis." Moira reached her hands towards Jonathan's neck but stopped short. Michael held her hands and looked her in the eye. "I can't do this alone, Moira. I need you. Please, *comme ça*, little dabs. Let the cloth absorb the blood."

Moira took a breath and began dabbing at the blood. "Very nice. You have the touch of an angel." Jonathan weakly raised his right hand, thumb up even as blood spurted from his throat.

Michael probed deeper to take a closer look, but his own fingers blocked his view. He addressed Mrs. Baker, "Ma'am, could I borrow your knitting needles?" She offered two. "These will do nicely, thank you. I do hope Mr. Baker brings a proper physician, not a surgeon. Do you know who he might fetch at this hour?"

"The only medical men we know would be barbers," she said. "Am sure me husband will seek out who he knows."

That won't help. Michael bit his lip and straightened his back, lost in thought.

"Moira, could you possibly keep a cloth just here to draw the blood away from the wound?"

She leaned into Michael's ear. "I have no training," she whispered.

"N'ayez pas peur, ma petite," he replied. "Still, we must try. Just think of collecting the savory juices from a freshly roasted joint and you'll do just fine." She gave him a quizzical look but did as instructed.

This time, with the needles holding the flaps of skin back, Michael got a closer look at the interior damage. "Moira, as the blood collects just so, quickly wipe it away." As she huddled close to Michael, her hand steadied. She dabbed away as Michael probed.

"Ma'am, could you hold this flap of skin down just so?" Mrs. Baker complied with a delicacy unexpected for one with such large fingers. Mother and daughter watched with intense curiosity. All was quiet during Michael's further inspection, except for the gurgled breathing of the patient. Michael sucked air through his teeth and delivered his assessment.

"Jonathan, I'm close to it. I've found the main source of your bleeding. There's a big vein. It's been nicked by the blade, but not sliced through. Much blood escapes. I need to devise some way to stop the leak."

Jonathan turned his eyes to let Michael know he was understanding.

"Unfortunately," Michael continued, "I've never worked in such a confined area." Michael took Jonathan's hand and leaned closer to address him. "Would be best to have a physician attempt this repair." Jonathan squeezed his understanding. "I fear tearing it completely." Jonathan acknowledged with a single squeeze.

Michael raised his eyes towards the roof, searching for guidance, hoping Baker and doctor would arrive to come to his and Jonathan's rescue.

Suddenly, Jonathan's color drained away, his breathing slowed. Michael looked him in the eye. "Jonathan, we can't wait any longer. I'll attempt to repair the vein, then we can see about the gash across your throat."

Turning to Mrs. Baker, "Ma'am, could you run the thinnest thread through your smallest needle. My hands are too slippery." Michael took Mrs. Baker's needle. "No, no, this won't do, I need a curve on it." He tried but couldn't get the needle to bend.

"Allow me." Mrs. Baker struggled and fared no better.

"I have an idea," Moira offered. She took the needle and pressed it against the round table leg. "Mother Mary," she exclaimed when the needle pricked her finger instead of bending. She took off her shoe and hammered the needle against the rounded oak leg until it held the curve.

"Nicely done," Michael said when she handed him the needle.

Michael got to work closing the vein but poked his finger instead. He tried again and failed. His pulsed raced as Jonathan's grew weaker. Sweat poured out of Michael's temples, and his hands started shaking. He leaned on the table and spread his feet wider to steady himself to try again. The vein squiggled out of his fingers, blood obscuring his view.

"Moira, see my fingers? They're on his vein. Can you dab a cloth around there to clear some blood?" The patient lost consciousness.

Moira straightened up. "Michael, he's so still, is he . . . ?"

"Not yet . . . we haven't much time. Ma'am, I could use a finger to pressure this vein, quickly please." He took Mrs. Baker's hand and guided a finger to a spot just below the puncture. She hesitated. "You don't have to watch, just press like this. Good. Hold steady."

Michael waited for the pause in the spurting, then put the needle through the vein below the slice. It went the wrong way. He backed it up a little to free the point, then angled the needle to parallel the vein. He took new aim on the upper part of the cut vein and pushed the needle through the underside. The thread came out on top. He pulled the thread through to close the two sides together. It took some minutes to repeat the procedure three times more and tie a knot.

"You can retrieve your hand, ma'am." A surge of blood passed through. The bleeding was greatly diminished. "Scissors?" With a quick snip he cut the bitter end. "We've done all we can. He might survive should the doctor arrive in time."

The trio looked at the patient. He was ashen grey and struggling to breathe. "Perhaps that prayer you promised," Moira suggested.

"In the name of the Father," Michael led off. The three crossed themselves. "Father, your child, Jonathan, struggles to live. We have done all we can here to come to his assistance. If it is in Your heart to keep him in this world, he is now in Your hands. We await your judgment on his soul." The three stood silent, offering private prayers.

The front door swung open. Baker entered with a tall ramshackle man in tow. The newcomer came straight to the table. He dumped his greatcoat over a chair. "May I have a look?"

"By all means." Michael offered his observations and explained his procedure as the man started his inspection. The Baker women started to leave, but Michael motioned for them to stay close. He put an arm around Moira.

"Well done," said the man. "A practiced hand could do no better. His majesty could use a 'lolly of yer stripe. Many's a jack we put over the side for lack of such skill. Not much we can do other than close his throat."

Michael relinquished his place at the table.

The surgeon went to work with his own instruments. Moira and Mrs. Baker both noted how his rough needlework lacked the delicacy of Michael's hand. Jonathan was indeed fortunate to be unconscious. "If he lives, and that seems most unlikely, don't offer any food or drink for a few days. Then a bit of thin soup. Make sure it don't run down his shirt." The surgeon let out a chuckle. It wasn't echoed. He left the cleanup to Michael and sought out Vintner Baker and his brandy case.

CHAPTER 8

As Michael stood vigil, Emma and Walter Broot returned to the dining room and sought out the fireplace. Still in her breezy dancing dress, Emma now used a blanket from the bedroom as a shawl to cover her bare shoulders. She shivered. The dining room, hot and steamy when full of patrons, turned cold and drafty when empty. She stepped closer to the fire, but the embers released little warmth against the night's unpleasantness. Broot put his arm around Emma's shoulder. His touch startled her. She gave his hand a puzzled look and brushed at it with her fingers, as if chasing a spider away because killing it would leave a stain.

Vintner Baker observed the rebuff from the bar where he poured the surgeon a brandy. They talked in hushed tones, but Michael could make out their conversation.

"Remarkable steady hand your Mr. Shea has, Baker. Can't match what I've just seen with the stories Oliver tells." He gulped down his drink and pushed the glass towards the vintner for another. "Nice piece of work, threading that vein. Won't do no good, 'fraid to say. That's just the way it is with these wounds. Know who cut 'im?"

Baker shook his head. "We was closing down." Baker poured himself a brandy. "Had chased the last drinkers out when one comes a-bargin' back in state of excitement. Says 'e stumbled over a body face down in the snow, where 'e was 'bout to relief 'isself. We thought 'im dead as 'e were stiff and blue. Turned 'im over an' saw he were a customer."

"You'll have to answer to the magistrate, Baker, or one of his runners," the physician said. "They tend to get rather excited about murders. Am sure it'll be that by the time they arrive. They'll want somebody hanging at Tyburn. Better 'ave a good story."

"I sent for a constable," the vinter replied. "Would help to defend our reputation if you'd stand and offer your opinion." Baker made a show of slowly refilling the man's glass.

"I'm at your service."

"That would be most helpful, sir."

Baker turned his attention towards Emma, who was rubbing her shoulders with both hands. Broot was having trouble restarting the fire. Baker excused himself to join them, leaving the open bottle with the thirsty surgeon.

"Allow me, Mr. Broot," Baker said. He wedged the fire screen so it trapped Emma and Broot close together, added a small pile of coals, and rekindled the embers. Once the fire took hold, Baker added a full scoop and replaced the screen as the coals sparkled.

"A word, Mr. Baker?" Broot eyed the door to the kitchen.

"As you wish," he said to his most valued customer. He turned towards his daughter.

"Emma, if you could keep an eye on the fire. I expect more company soon. Would be good to warm the room for the interview." He retired with Broot into the kitchen.

Instead she walked over to the operating table. Michael had washed and dressed Jonathan's head wound. He was staring at his patient, his hands on Jonathan's. He didn't react to Emma even as she slipped a hand lightly under his forearm and placed the other over top of his bloodied sleeve. "Michael," she started to say before she took look at the patient. She gasped at the sight of the ragged stitching across Jonathan's throat.

"I'm but a brother to you, my sister?" Michael asked, keeping his gaze on Jonathan.

"What else could I say? It is rather awkward to have Papa and Walter discovering us in bed together. Was best I could dream up in a hurry."

Michael put a hand upon hers. "We've come to a time of decision, Emma. My heart aches. It cannot be eased hiding in your attic not knowing if or when you'll return. It's time to—"

She cut him off. "Oh, Michael, you have touched my heart." She pulled his hands to her chest, "deeply, very deeply. But there's no choosing to be made. Our affair can only abide in secret. Don't think of choices, my dear." She gave him a light kiss on his cheek with cold, dry lips. "Michael, you know what's at stake," she said softly. "You have to—"

She didn't finish. The front door swung open. Emma quickly withdrew her hands and stood aside as Danny and two bailiffs blustered in on a blast of icy wind.

With shoulders hunched and chins down, the city protectors marched straight to the fireplace to beat the cold from their coats and defrost their hands. They took no notice of the doctor at the bar. Danny trailed behind, scanning the room for Baker. Not finding the vintner, he gave Emma a look. She motioned Danny to the kitchen. The magistrate warmed himself by the fire.

Taking your sweet time, aren't we, your majesty? Michael thought as he lightly swabbed Jonathan's throat. When the magistrate finally approached Michael and Jonathan, Emma edged away and sat at a table nearby. "What have we 'ere?" he asked across the table from Michael. "Yet another dead 'un?"

"He still breathes," Michael corrected.

"And who might you be then, laddie?" he snorted. "What's your role in this affair?"

"Jonathan is a patient of mine. His throat was cut and a vein sliced. I stitched his vein to stop the bleeding. Now I'm standing vigil," Michael answered.

The magistrate studied the patient. "Curious stitching. Your needlework?"

"No. My work is inside the neck. The author of what you see is at the bar."

The magistrate turned to face the bar. By way of hello, the surgeon raised his glass.

"Who's in charge 'ere? Where's this Baker fellow?"

"Coming, coming," Baker cried, emerging from the kitchen. "So good of you, sir, to come so quickly." Baker bowed, then he turned to his daughter. "Emma, would you be so kind as to bring our guest a drink."

Baker escorted the officer to a table by the fire where they warmed themselves until Emma delivered a drink. The magistrate then questioned Baker about the evening, asking for names of customers, when they came, when they left, who dined with whom. "Did you hear any foul talk? See any signs of a threat?"

Baker overwhelmed the magistrate with each detail of the evening's planning and preparation: the menu, names of most of the diners, where they sat, and who ordered what.

"Just tell me how you found the body," the magistrate interrupted.

As Baker's detail-by-detail account rambled on, Broot inched his way towards the fire and, affecting disinterest, stood behind the magistrate and drilled his eyes into Baker's. The vintner skipped over Marcellus's insults and Jonathan's attack.

The magistrate nodded. "Let's review this, step by step, in the courtyard." Broot prepared to join, but the magistrate stopped him. He eyed Danny on the way outside. "All right lad, show us where you found the victim." Broot and Baker exchanged looks and disappeared into the kitchen.

As the group trudged out into the courtyard, a blast of frigid air filled the hall. It revived Jonathan. His eyes fluttered open. Michael took his hand. "Jonathan, can you hear me?"

The patient looked into Michael's eyes.

"Is there any way I can contact friends or family? Mr. Carroll?"

Two slow, faint squeezes. Jonathan pulled his hand away and reached for his breast pocket. He couldn't unbutton his coat, so he tapped on his coat. Michael reached in and pulled out a tall leather wallet with a wad of papers jammed inside.

"This?" Michael held the wallet so Jonathan could see it.

Jonathan managed a nod. With his left hand, he pantomimed a writing motion.

Michael pulled a pencil and a page from the wallet. "This?"

Jonathan blinked his yes. Feebly, he took them and tried to scribble a couple of words, but he hadn't the strength. His hands collapsed on his chest.

"I'll look after this for you," Michael said putting the wallet inside his shirt. Jonathan raised his hand. Michael took it and felt a slight squeeze as Jonathan's eyes stared at the ceiling. There was an exhale of breath. Then silence. Michael felt Jonathan's hand go cold.

Michael inhaled sharply, held the breath, and then hung his head in defeat. His throat tightened. He gently closed the unseeing eyes, folded Jonathan's hands over his heart, stood back, and bowed his head. Emma gasped from behind the bar. She crossed herself. Broot gave her a disapproving look. The surgeon followed Emma's stare towards Michael. He didn't get up. Michael smoothed Jonathan's clothes. He used the surgeon's coat to cover the body.

All was silent until the investigators returned, again clapping their hands together to beat out the cold. Now she joined Broot by the dying fire. She let him put his arm around her shoulders. "Where's Marcellus?" she whispered.

"Now's not the time." He made a show of consoling her. "Your father agrees it better to let the magistrate ask the questions. Your family is at risk. Best not attract attention."

The magistrate addressed the group around Jonathan's body. "As we expected, we now have a murder." He turned to Baker, "Not much more we can do from here now, is there? There's a trail of blood but it runs cold. We don't have a witness . . . yet. I'll leave the burial arrangements to you, Mr. Baker. Keep your ears open. Perhaps one of your customers will have more for us to ponder. I'll have my runners interview the ones you've listed." The two runners waited at the door as the magistrate looked at Baker. The awkward pause ended when Baker pressed some coins in the magistrate's hand. "Most kind, Mr. Baker." Then he and his companions were off into the frozen night.

Baker surveyed his dining hall. "Michael, Danny, let's move the departed to a quieter room." They made a litter out of the surgeon's coat and carried Jonathan into the room behind the kitchen where Danny had earlier entertained.

"Not on the floor," Michael said. "Let's have some respect."

Danny improvised a table across two wine barrels. They laid the body out. Michael rearranged Jonathan's neck cloth to hide his wound, then placed his patient's hands in prayerful repose. Baker rummaged out a dirty tablecloth to cover him. Before Michael could insist on a fresh cloth, Danny calmed his friend. "Don't worry, Michael, he won't mind."

Baker handed Michael the doctor's coat. "Best you return the surgeon's coat. Maybe 'e can help in yer search for employment."

Baker straightened his back. "I'll not be needin' yer services again, Mr. Shea. In light of events upstairs. Am sure ye understand."

Michael did and his posture summed up the night—slumped shoulders, head down staring at his feet, no words. He knew Baker had to eliminate any threat to his access to Broot's patronage.

But the dismissal startled Danny. "Are ye mad? Baker? You're cuttin' ye best meal ticket loose?" asked Danny. "I'm sure you tripled your receipts this night."

"An' good luck to ye too, Mr. O'Mara," Baker continued with a formal air. "Take yer music elsewhere. We kin manage without."

Danny's cheeks flushed red, ready to argue, but Michael cut him off. "It's no use, Danny. Our time is up." To Baker, Michael nodded farewell. "My best to Mrs. Baker and your gracious daughters." Michael held the door. "Danny, *allons-y.*"

CHAPTER 9

OUT IN THE COLD, MICHAEL TOOK OFF TOWARDS BISHOPSGATE WITHout a word. Danny took a couple of hesitant steps away from the door before speaking. "Wait on me now, Michael, wait!" Michael stopped in mid-step. "Why in the world are we out here?"

Michael half opened his mouth to reply. Breathy mist filled the air. The vapors floated in the still of the cold night. He didn't reply. He stared at his cold feet buried in the snow.

"Damn it, Michael! Ya try to save a man and Baker dismisses ya? What in God's name is going on? Not yer fault that fella up'n died."

Michael turned away and buried his chin inside the upright collar of his coat. His runny nose fouled the top button. When Danny caught up to him, Michael could only muster a broken, "Not now, Danny, please." He trudged out to the intersection. Danny turned to head down Bishopsgate, but Michael grabbed Danny's arm and pulled him instead towards the Thames.

"Where we off to, Michael?"

Michael paused in the whirl of snow on the empty street. He wanted to scream, *"for want of a fat purse, Emma abandons me,"* but his voice faltered, enraged by the image of Walter Broot comforting Emma by a cold fire.

Danny didn't see the rage. He only saw that it was tears, not snow, that Michael wiped from his eyes.

"Michael, I'm missin' something aren't I? Were ya close to Jonathan? Hadn't heard of him before tonight. I'm sorry you've lost a friend."

"If you don't mind, Danny, I need time to sort my mind," he said. He wiped his nose on his sleeve, where the mucus quickly froze. "For the present, I hope to report Jonathan's demise to Charles Carroll. He and his colonial circle were at the table where the fight broke out. If the tide is late, maybe he can bring the news to Jonathan's family in Virginia."

"Never 'eard of a tide being late," Danny grumbled, wrapping his stack of scarves around his neck. "Ya catch 'em or ya miss 'em."

"Nevertheless, we must try. This snow blew in from the east. Maybe it pushed the tide back a little."

"D'ya know what ship to call on?"

"He didn't mention a name. Said something about a dock near the Tower."

"Oh, a dock . . . on the Thames? That's a clue? Jesus, Michael, the Thames is awash with docks. How do you . . ."

"I don't know! We just have to try."

"Yer grasping at straws, Michael," Danny said, shifting his dulcimer and bag of flutes to his other shoulder. "Cold and frozen straws."

"Enough with the complaining. Where's your sense of duty? It'll be light soon. The sun'll warm ya."

Danny grumbled, but as there was nowhere else to go, he did his best to keep up.

At the river's edge, the bundled pair reconnoitered. The black and grey clouds of the night were fading in the western sky behind London Bridge. The first rays of morning were in the eastern sky. Flashes of yellow glistened off the Thames, hinting of warmth to come.

"Pretty sight, ain't it?" Michael said, taking in the half-revealed river.

Danny had more experience along the river. "Just wait, then tell me how pretty it is." As they surveyed the scene, the rising sun revealed the silhouetted outlines of scores of ships ghosting towards the sea. It was a grave disappointment for a tired, cold fiddler.

"Tide didn't wait," Danny muttered. The docks were virtually deserted, save for a few hands coiling dock lines. "We should be leaving with 'em, Michael. At least there we'd have a chance."

"There?" Michael questioned. "Where's there?" Michael's cheeks were bright red, his nose raw and dripping. His eyes were tearing again, but now from the cold breeze off the Thames.

"The colonies! Virginia, Canada, America. Anywhere but London. Can't ya feel it, Michael? There's nothing fer us 'ere, just muckin' in the mud and snow, beggin' for scraps or thievin'. Baker was our last chance."

Michael wasn't listening. "There are a few ships still about." He squinted as the morning sun crested the skyline. "We could ask these stragglers where they're bound."

"Really, Michael? Ya think these scows are destined for anywhere?" Danny unloaded his instruments in the snow and waved his arms over the docks below, like he was conducting a concerto. "D'ya see any sails on 'he trees?" His barking was just shy of a yell. "D'ya see any tars on board? D'ya see any baggage? D'ya not see their decks is clear? Not a one has any thought of a voyage."

Looking up and down the docks again, Michael let out long deep breath. Icy air screamed through his nostrils when he refilled his lungs to speak. "I concede to your most obvious argument, my friend," he said with a bit of a grin.

The pair watched the tide carry the flotilla of brigs, colliers, wherries, and barges, along with logs, trash, and the occasional carrion to the sea. A few dinghies dodged their way through the fleet on local errands.

As the sun rose, the river's filth asserted itself. "Now where?" asked Danny. "I'm not one ta see much joy in a riverbank, 'specially when the tide's out. The stench'll scare off ol' Satan hisself. He knows where not ta tread."

Michael changed the mood. "Well, my friend, Baker did pay us our due before he gave us the boot. We can stave off starvation for a few days. Let us find a bit of breakfast."

"Now yer talkin'," Danny replied.

They found a tavern among the warehouses on the river and dined silently on cold meat of questionable origin, stale dark bread, and finished it off with a mug of morning beer. Michael paid the reckoning and divided up their earnings from Baker. When he returned his purse to his coat, he remembered Jonathan's wallet. He gave it a quick look. A bundle of letters and other papers. No cash. He flipped through the pages.

"Looks like we have Jonathan's journal," Michael said after turning to the page with Jonathan's final scribble. "He started to write me a final note, but it was too much for him." Michael stared at the handwriting. "Lord, what a mess. Looks like the word 'father,' or 'further?' and a 'miss v.' His mother, perhaps?" He shared Jonathan's last scribble with Danny. "What do you think?"

Danny gave it a puzzled look. "How'm I supposed ta know? He have any lady friends?"

"No, ladies weren't Jonathan's interest. He mostly complains about tobacco commissions, London factors, and settling scores. He entrusted his papers to me."

"Not our family. Not our business. Send 'em back to Baker."

"No. Must be a reason." Michael stuffed the wallet in his waistcoat.

"Where now?" Danny asked.

"Been a long cold night. I know where we can find a warm room," Michael answered. "Jonathan stayed across the river, east of London Bridge. I doctored him there. If we slip in quietly, maybe we can stay a few days before the landlord starts wondering about Jonathan."

"Lead on."

Retracing their way back across the Thames, they wandered through the maze of streets and alleyways until Michael spotted the tenement where he had nursed Jonathan. Wasn't much to look at, a ramshackle affair with a cockeyed sign advertising rooms to let. The door had a faint tinge of red. "*Voila, mon ami*, Jonathan lives here."

"Not anymore."

"Indeed. The proprietor knows me as Jonathan's 'doctor.' He's used to me visiting. I turned him a favor when his wife came down with the pox. Same with that collier's child. Both were in a bad way when I first attended to Jonathan."

Danny took in the scene. A coal vendor was unloading a delivery from his wagon while his family milled about in front of a small platform that served as a porch, just a step above the street's muck. "Seen better days."

"Warmer than the street. That's Newell, the proprietor, welcoming the collier." A tall man in an open black coat was holding the door open when he noticed Michael and waved. He then nudged the collier.

"How we manage this?" Danny asked.

The collier dropped a bucket and waved as well.

"Not sure." Michael returned the greeting.

"You know the gypsy too?"

"Be nice, Danny, he's one of us. Name's Malloy. Lives with a wife and a kid or two in that wagon. Coal's his trade. He weren't born a tinker. Best he can manage in London. The proprietor Newell fancies he runs a respectable inn."

"Respectable?"

"It's warm." Michael rearranged his coat, stiffened his posture, and transformed his bearing to affect a gentleman's entrance. "*Allons-y*. Don't talk. No matter what's said, don't speak."

He marched right up to Newell and Malloy. "Good day to ya, gentlemen. I trust you've been well. Mr. Malloy, I see you survived this frightful storm in good order."

"Ah, Mr. Shea! Good ta see ya again," Malloy replied. He sported a crumpled cocked hat that had seen better days. His face was smudged with black coal dust. "Or kin I call ya Dr. Shea?" Malloy locked onto Michael's hand and forearm in a warm embrace. "Our dear Lucy responded so well to ya devoted attentions. She's back to 'er milkin'. The missus prays her thanks for yer deliverance this very day." He freed Michael's arm, leaving more traces of coal dust behind. "Dolores, we has us a visitor."

Mrs. Malloy emerged from the wagon and rushed to give Michael a kiss and hug. More coal dust on Michael's coat. "Oh, our dear savior," she cried. "Mother Mary surely sent you to us. We was so lost before you came, Dr. Michael Shea."

"Alas, Mrs. Malloy, I'm but a mere apprentice, not doctor, but 'tis very kind of you to think so." Michael wrapped his arm around her broad shoulders.

After the happy reunion, Michael addressed the proprietor. "And good day to you, Mr. Newell. You're looking well on this crisp morning. Might you have a spot by your fire before I call on my patient, your esteemed guest from Virginia?"

"I've neither seen nor heard from Mr. Clayborne this day." Newell ushered Michael to the door. "He favors late night rambles. Pays his rent he does, but too many late nights." As Michael stepped towards the door,

Newell gave a disapproving look at Danny. "And what have we here, Mr. Shea," Newell sneered, "a gypsy?"

"Ah, Mr. Newell, allow me to present my servant, Mr. Daniel Badilcocke. A joiner by trade. Sadly, the third son of a farmer. Not enough land to go around, you see, so our Mr. Badilcocke has come to London seeking his livelihood, as we all do. We are musicianers together. He now assists me with my patients."

Newell scowled at Danny's dark complexion, dark brown eyes, and thick and scraggly black hair. "Such a swarthy face," he sneered, "looks more tinker than farmer."

"Oh, not at all," Michael replied. "Daniel is most reliable. We've just come from a long night. A sad case of two brothers and sister, all down with the pox."

At the word *pox*, Newell stepped back from the door and away from the silent Daniel Badilcocke.

"Not to worry, Mr. Newell, Daniel is a rare treat. One willing to open his heart in aid to the afflicted. He's mute, but he plays such sweet melodies on these meager instruments. He gives the sick and dying, and their families, much needed comfort."

While Newell hesitated, Michael eased in between the proprietor and Danny. "Hurry along now, Daniel. Warm yourself."

Outmaneuvered, Newell put his discomfort aside long enough to settle his account with the coal vendor. Then he followed Michael inside.

"Mr. Shea, I am forever in your debt for restoring my wife against the smallpox. But your intimacies with Irish tinkers like Malloy greatly distress me," he looked right at Danny, "and others of his ilk. It's not good to associate too closely with their like."

Michael stepped on Danny's foot.

"Most curious, Mr. Newell. Are you disappointed with Malloy's services?" Michael brushed spots of coal dust from his coat, taking his time on one or two places. He applied only the lightest touch as he continued. "I remember your praise of Malloy's reliability," Michael said, as if commenting on a passing cloud formation. "As I recall, he was the only one to extend you credit for fuel when your business had taken a tumble. A case of smallpox does make it ever so difficult to attract new customers. Yet

Malloy knocked on your door and then his own daughter comes down with the pox."

"Well, yes, Malloy is reliable and, and . . ."

"Perhaps the word you're searching for is generous?" Michael suggested.

"Yes, one could say that," Newell admitted. "But I feel it proper to keep a respectable distance from these peddlers. There are certain," he took a breath, "appearances to maintain."

"Of course, appearances," Michael replied. "Now, if you don't mind, Mr. Newell, we'll go directly to Jonathan's room and wait for our patient and make sure he's on a proper mend. We wouldn't want a festering wound or a new fever to trouble an entire household." Michael put a deliberate stress on the words "fever" and "entire."

The memory of his wife's sickness gave Newell a shiver. "By all means." Talk of diseases made him eager to be left alone.

"Thank you, Mr. Newell. We'll find our way."

Michael made a show of tapping on Jonathan's door for Newell's benefit. After a second show, Michael let himself and Danny in. He put a hand up to warn Danny to keep his voice down.

"Jesus, Michael," came the whispered reply. "How kin we keep this masquerade going? An' now I'm yer bloody servant? Badilcocke? What sort of name is that?"

"You would prefer Monsieur Petitcoq instead?"

"An' what's wrong with O'Mara, then?"

Michael put an ear to the door before answering. "Had to dispel Newell's disdain of all things Irish. Thinks papists are the cause of all disease. He'd raise a stink and we'd be found out." Michael surveyed Jonathan's room. "We need to sort this through."

"Ya make me out to be some English twit and a mute at that?" Danny pantomimed a clumsy rube with heavy flat-footed steps.

"Patience, my friend, patience." Michael kept his voice low. "Best I could manage given our circumstances." He gave Danny a grin. "You saw Newell's aversion to Malloy. Think he'd let you pass his door if he heard that accent of yours?" Michael stretched out on the bed. "See to it that you don't talk. No matter what, don't speak. Practice humility," Michael counseled. "'T'would be good for ya," he said imitating Danny's accent.

Danny grimaced and affected his new role as mute servant. He pointed to the fireplace and fluttered his hands indicating rising flames.

"By all means, Mr. Badilcocke, see if you can get those coals to light for us." Michael rose from the bed. "Give us your coat and hat, now." Michael hung their things on the door and stowed their instruments in a corner away from the fire.

They sat facing each other, enjoying the warmth, pondering their situation, Michael remembering how he had removed the dueling bullet from Jonathan's rib. Danny sat in the room's only chair, a tall, padded affair.

"The question now arises," Michael said, "how long can Jonathan go missing?"

CHAPTER 10

Two mornings later, a pounding on the door broke their respite. "Mr. Shea." Three terse thumps. "Mr. Shea." A short pause then three harder knocks. "I must have a word." It was Newell.

Michael jumped out of bed and straightened his clothes. "Coming." He fumbled into his waistcoat and grabbed his cravat. Newell banged again. Michael let the silk dangle untied. The ends of the frayed white silk fluttered as he opened the door. "Greetings, Mr. Newell," he said with a bow. "'Tis good to receive you."

Newell didn't wait for Michael to close the door. "The master opens the door while his servant naps?" Newell snapped.

"It does seem incongruous at first blush," Michael said closing the door. "We have a rather casual arrangement. 'Servant' is probably an ill-chosen description. Daniel is more—"

Newell cut him off. "I've had enough of your fancy talk. I suspect, Mr. Shea," he said with a deliberate, flat tone, "you have not been straight with me about your whereabouts these last few days, nor your claim to check on my house guest from Virginia, one Mr. Jonathan Clayborne." Newell paced before the firebox. "Now, as I remember, Mr. Shea," he said drawing out the name, "you have occasion to perform at the White Lyon Tavern. Is this not so?" he demanded.

Newell's angry voice finally shook Danny from his sleeping place near the fire. Danny lost his place in Michael's play. "What's all this about?" he blurted out.

"As I suspected." Newell said. "The mute 'servant' speaks quite clearly."

A sleepy-eyed Danny looked at his friend. For once, he heard Michael stumbling for words. "My . . . apologies," he started to say, "perhaps I should . . ." he didn't finish. He stared out the window. Newell and Danny waited in the silence, their eyes on Michael, who was lost in the middle of a rewrite.

"Let's dispense with the scheming, Mr. Shea, and jump to the heart of the matter." Newell lowered his voice, his initial burst of anger now dissipated. "Out of deference to the services you've provided for my family, I'll tell you what I know, and what apparently you do not." He walked over the window and sat on the ledge. "Vintner Baker is well known to me through business. I frequently recommend the White Lyon when my boarders inquire about entertainments. Baker in turn sends customers to me when they need lodgings. We share many provisioners. Recently, I recommended the White Lyon to one of my boarders, Jonathan Clayborne. Said he needed a respite from his investigations. He seemed most agitated."

"Yes, Mr. Baker does run a fine establishment," Michael offered.

"Yes, indeed he does, Mr. Shea. And, as it would turn out, Mr. Jonathan Clayborne wasn't me only patron to inquire of entertainments. I sent three others trudging through the snow three days ago to the White Lyon. I hadn't seen them since, but do you know what they had to report this morning?" Newell asked. "What they witnessed?"

"I am at a loss, sir," Michael replied.

"Oh, I doubt that." Newell rose from his perch on the windowsill. "Your only loss is that you thought you could play me for a fool." He resumed pacing. "Imagine all the talk as they gathered at breakfast. They were remembering their most eventful recent evening. Grand tales of a beautiful lass performing a minuet with a lavish gentleman. How this beauty also sang and performed scenes from the Beggar's Opera."

Newell watched Danny button up his britches before resuming his taunting. "And how they were so soothed and excited by a fiddle player," Newell looked at Shea. "A fiddler who danced all around the dining hall 'whilst still playing so delicately,'" he said in a woman's voice. "They called him, Shea, a Mr. Michael Shea, as it turns out." Newell stopped in mid-step. "And, this wonderful Mr. Shea had a partner, a musician who not only sang with a," Newell paused, searching for the word, "with a ruggedness, oh, such an abandoned ruggedness," he said, again affecting a lady's breathless voice. "And he was hammering away on a rather unusual instrument, one with a trapezoidal shape. I suppose much like this shape here," he said, walking over to Danny's dulcimer. Newell ended his tirade and waited for a defense.

The three of them listened to footsteps in the hall before Michael broke the silence.

"Indeed, Mr. Newell. 'Twas us at the White Lyon," Michael said. "I most sincerely apologize for misleading. There was no malice intended, just . . ."

"No malice you say?" Newell jerked his hands up, fingers wide. "Whatever else could it be?" The room suddenly darkened as storm clouds rolled over the city.

"It's a complicated story, Mr. Newell," Michael said in the gloom.

"I'll say it's complicated." Newell's agitation returned. "Because as I mentioned, Baker and I share one or two provisioners. I went to Sharrad & Son this morning to order dry goods and fresh cloth. Do you know what other services Sharrad offers, Mr. Shea?"

"Again, sir, you have me at a lost."

"Funeral services, Mr. Shea. The talk was of a burial, a service ordered by one Mr. Baker, vintner at White Lyon Tavern. A burial for a dead patron, a colonial. A colonial, Mr. Shea, like my missing Virginian who has yet to return from said White Lyon Tavern." Newell stood with his hands clenched, staring alternatively at Danny and then Michael.

"Why has my trusted Mr. Shea lied to me? He was not dealing with no pox. Why create such a crock?" Newell took a breath. "So I asked meself, what could Mr. Shea be hiding? I can come to only one conclusion. You have made me an accomplice to murder! I'll not hang for harbouring you, Mr. Shea. How could you take a life when you try so hard to save others?" Newell had gotten himself in a nervous condition, breathing heavily. Sweat seeped from his brow.

"Mr. Newell, let me first assure you, sir, we are not murderers," Michael protested. "You cannot be made accomplice to any such misdeed as we ourselves have done nothing wrong. We are much saddened by Jonathan's demise. We have killed or harmed no one."

"Far from it," Danny said, no longer playing the servant's role. "It were Michael tryin' to save the fella, workin' 'is arse off for the poor man. I fetched a surgeon, at Baker's request, mind ya, to attend ta Jonathan." Danny was getting worked up. "That sot of a barber left all that careful work to Michael. Then Baker up an' dismisses Michael for 'is efforts, without so much as an 'ere's why. Not a thank you ta be given."

"So, you've been dismissed as well? That hardly bodes well." Newell let this sink in before renewing his outburst.

"Against your explanation, what can be true? A trusted business associate of mine gives you the sack. Why? Because you attend to his customer? Baker sacks the Good Samaritan? Hardly believable. Then you show up here, under false pretenses, to live in a dead man's stead? Am I to believe such incongruous stories?" Newell's fears produced a line of sweat along his forehead. "I'll not be accomplice to your scheming. There's a rotten smell to this sorry tale."

Newell stood staring at Michael, awaiting an explanation. When none came, Danny entered the disputation. "It's as Michael says, Mr. Newell. But I must admit, I'm in the same mist as ta why we was so rudely dismissed." He joined Newell in staring in silence at Michael.

Michael squirmed under their combined glare. He ran his hands through his hair, over each ear, and then down the back of his neck. He untied and retied his queue. He did this nervous maneuver a couple of times before folding his arms over his chest. Newell and Danny waited.

"There is a bit more to tell as to why Mr. Baker felt a need to discharge us, me in particular." Michael said this with an air of confession. "Danny," he said, looking at his friend, "is unfortunately a causality of my clandestine whereabouts. One that greatly pains my heart and has unsettled my mind." Again Michael paused. It was his turn to pace the floor. "If I could explain, I can assure you, there's no need to fear association with murder."

The anxious Newell wasn't interested in explanations. "You can explain on your way out if you don't mind, Mr. Shea. The story's about that you had a hand in Mr. Clayborne's demise, that rather than save him, you sped him on 'is way to meet the Lord. I'll not take a chance to have you here, in a dead man's room when the constables arrive." Newell moved to the door, opened it, and stood aside to usher the two musicians out. "They have already been sent for."

Michael persisted in trying to clear Newell's mind by explaining how Jonathan was discovered.

"An' where was you during all this?" Newell demanded.

Michael breathed slowly and looked Newell in the eye. "If you must know, sir, Miss Emma Baker can vouch for my narrative. We was together, in an attic bedroom. Innocently together, of course, but a most uncomfortable situation came when her father and a Mr. Broot walked in. Rather embarrassing for this Mr. Broot. He suffers from an intense infatuation for Baker's eldest daughter."

"Yes, an unpleasant business," said Newell after considering the implications, "especially as Emma has a husband away in the king's service." He gave it more thought, trying to make the circumstances add up.

Newell spoke with some caution, "Broot's intimate with Baker? I was unaware. Whatever was Broot doing there at such a late hour, I wonder, risking the wrath of the Lady Broot?"

"Profit and lust," Michael offered. He related Broot's gambling arrangement, Baker's reliance on Broot's continued patronage, and the gambler's lust for Emma's attention. "Emma knows how to twist a knot. But once Emma and I were discovered, Baker felt the need to eliminate a grave threat to the family business, myself that would be, when Broot realized he had a rival for Emma's attentions."

Newell opened the door to usher the two musicians out.

Michael made a last protest. "If your constable could but consult with Emma, you'll find my story true."

"I want no part of this sorry story."

Out of options, Michael and Danny grabbed their belongings. Danny peppered Michael with questions. In the hall, down the stairs, and out the front door, Michael flushed out the once-secret details of his relationship with Emma. It finally dawned on Danny why food and drink flowed so freely whenever he performed with Michael at White Lyon Tavern.

CHAPTER 11

IT WAS RAINING, COLD AND HARD. THE MUSICIANERS PAUSED UNDER THE inn's portico to consider the miserable day ahead. Newell's last point of farewell was to slam the door behind them. They heard the lock tumble.

"Hardly necessary," Michael muttered.

"Yet another barred door," was Danny's reply.

"Looks like my hovel or yours," Michael said watching rain drill holes through yesterday's snow. The sweet perfection of new fallen snow was now sullied by grey waves of coal ash and dust. In the street, a growing river of mud and slush was churned up by animals and wagon wheels. "How does yours stand up to rain and muck?"

"'Tis hopeless, Michael, just hopeless. We can't stay here. We 'ave ta leave. It's time ya realized this. I'm goin', with or without ya."

"With or without me, to where exactly?"

"Don't be thick, Michael. Amerikay, Virginia, Canada. Anywhere's that's not England. These bastards thrive on keepin' the likes of us down in this muck." Danny added his hat and braved the rain. Realizing he was alone, he turned and yelled back, "Come on. Newell ain't gonna unlock 'is door."

This time it was Michael following and complaining. "We can't make passage. I'll not be a servant."

"Ya'd rather sit in Newgate, Michael?" Danny's agitation enabled him to ignore the slush and rain. "Ya don't have a choice. Wake up. Think it through, Michael. Think ya 'kin explain to a magistrate what we was doin' in a dead man's room? They'll find something ya stole."

"We didn't steal anything!" Michael insisted from the portico. "We have nothing to fear. There's nothing to . . ." His voice trailed off when he traced the bulging outline of Jonathan's wallet tucked inside his waistcoat.

Danny ignored the protest. "If they can't find somethin' ya stole, they'll make it up. Look at how much trouble that Oliver caused ya. Ya knows the risk. Ya have no standin' in court. Yer Irish, yer guilty. Simple as that. English 'justice' don't need no other reason. They'll give ya a list of crimes as long as me arm, and ya can't stop 'em. Don't go a-thinkin' you can talk yer way out of that. Ya know this to be true, Michael."

There was no more conversation. Michael donned his hat, cinched up his cloak, and followed Danny's lead. It was a long, cold walk. They headed back to London Bridge, crossed the Thames, slogged past the slick and grimy wharves, heads down all the way in a forced march against waves of rain and a mounting stream of dung-tainted slush.

Finally, Danny stopped. "Point of no return." He pointed to the engraved sign on the imposing facade: "Royal Exchange."

"Odd time to go to market."

"Sufferin' Jesus, Michael, don't be such a twit. 'Tis where we find shipping news. Captains and agents announce their comings and goings. They's the one's who'll transport us to North America." He watched a river of rain roll off Michael's hat. "Look at yerself, now. It's only four years work. Then we're free, Michael. Free ta be anythin' we want. Ta enter any trade. Ta be somethin'. It's shorter than apprenticin' with the likes of Oliver. Not your patron's easy life 'tis true, but a dead man can't help ya now. Time to build yer own life. Start anew. Sleep in the London muck if ya prefer, but I'm leavin'." Lecture done, Danny jumped the first two stairs and pushed his way through the crowd.

Michael hesitated even though his feet were in a puddle of coffee-colored slush. His hat poured an icy stream down his neck. Still he resisted. He rubbed his chin with his right hand, scratching the emerging stubble.

It was the shivering that pushed Michael Shea up the stairs and in, out of the rain.

"Kin only git better from 'ere," Danny said when Michael caught up with him. "The shipping news. We only needs pick one." They faced a baffling mix of fares, destinations, and accommodations. They went notice to notice, studying offers. It was the first time Michael had seen the schedules that so excited Danny. After reading several departure posters, Michael gave up. He leaned against the wall. "Your turn."

As Danny stumbled through the next notice, an inquisitive voice accosted them. "Well, what have we here, now? A couple of likely lads looking for adventure, it seems. Perhaps I could be of some assistance in yer quest."

The friendly nature of the salutation startled Danny and Michael. They turned to find a dapper gentleman, a head shorter than most, carrying a large leather case.

"Best of greetings to ya on this most miserable morning," he began. "Eugene MacNeal, shipping agent. I kin see by yer study of the shipping news, ye 'ave interest in travel and adventure. 'T'ain't every day I spy fellows so carefully surveying the news."

The musicians acknowledged MacNeal with half-hearted bows.

MacNeal continued. "Yes, well then, perhaps it's in search of adventures to a foreign land yer after?" He rattled off the destinations in his power. "A trading life in India? Perhaps it's the Americas? His Majesty's colonies offer many's a welcoming port for gentlemen of yer circumstances."

"Good day ta ya, MacNeal," Danny answered finally. "Ya has a long way of sayin' hello." He introduced himself and Michael. "Indeed passage for the Americas 'tis our goal. Alas, fares such as these 'tis far beyond our meager means."

"Yes, yes. Quite understandable. But do not despair, lads. Many's a gentlemen like yourselves I've had the pleasure of doing business with," MacNeal tipped his hat, "and helping to reach their various destinations." He withdrew a packet from his case. "There are multitudinous ways of arriving at Amerikay. Some more luxurious and commodious than others, but all of them arrive safe and sound at the promised spot of His Majesty's soil. If you could but share a mug of beer with me, we could review the alternatives available to promising young gentlemen such as yerselves."

"Sure as it's rainin', I could enjoy a tankard with you, sir," Danny replied.

"I know a favored spot," MacNeal said, "just a few doors away."

True to his word, MacNeal ushered them to a table. They hung their coats on hooks by the side of the chimney. MacNeal excused himself to order their beer. He carved slices of bread and cold mutton from a joint featured on a side table.

Danny and Michael pulled their chairs close to the fire, removed their shoes, and soaked in the warmth. Wisps of water vapor rose from their dirty, drenched stockings. Three big toes popped through the frayed wool. They sat sideways to the table to keep their feet facing the fire. They let MacNeal wait upon them. They ate in peace before discussing business.

It was Michael who broached the topic at hand.

"'Tis rather simple actually," MacNeal answered. "I represent several masters bound for America. I recruit passengers who are bound for the colonies. There be a lot of jostling amongst captains for the indentured trade. They prefer cargoes, but when trade is slow, they make room for a passenger or two who is short on means. It's in the recouping of yer twelve-pound passage when they sells yer indenture that lures a captain to take on the extra freight." He gave a nod to correct himself, "My apologies. Passengers is the better expression."

"That's more earnings than we've made in three years," Michael complained after MacNeal's explanation sank in.

"How kin ya assist us in our voyage?" Danny chimed in, undeterred by financial obstacles.

"Ah, again, 'tis simple, sir," MacNeal replied. "First, we draws up an indenture of servitude. By such device, ya exchange the costs of passage for four years of service in America. Yer new master pays for yer passage. You provide labor in exchange, at the end of which, yer master provides a set of clothes and a small stipend to get you started in yer new world. Some of the colonies awards ten acres land from which industrious lads like yerselves can draw shelter and sustenance at yer pleasure."

"Land? We kin own land?" Danny asked.

"Such a wild promise," Michael muttered.

"Michael, think of it!" Danny said. "In four year's time, we be land-lords in our own right. Landowners of ten acres, free to properly marry . . . 'tis far better than I 'ad ever imagined."

"And how then does one go about interviewing prospective employ-ers for such a bounty?" Michael asked.

"Yes, as to the question of employments," MacNeal replied, "that does depend on who buys yer contract once you gets ta the new world. Ya have yer choice, from bustlin' Boston to charmin' Charleston in the Carolinas."

"Don't matter much where to me," Danny said. "Sign us up, a couple of Irish lads, me partner in music Mr. Michael Shea, County Cork, and me, Daniel O'Mara, late of Limerick. Where does we make a mark?"

"Oh no, them Irish names won't do, not at all. Papists ain't much welcome in the colonies."

"Maryland then," Danny said. "Catholics is welcomed there. Lord Baltimore's Act of Tolerance and all that."

"Oh, no, no, no. That was long, long ago, my friend. Not since the Glorious Revolution have papists been allowed in Maryland. The penal laws against Catholics apply to all the colonies."

"Then we're stuck in this pit of London?"

"Not at all, my friends. You just don't travel with them Irish names you're stuck with."

"Stuck, not on your life," Danny protested. "Am proud of the name me Da gave me."

"My apology, a poor choice of words." MacNeal adopted a concilia-tory tone. "Nevertheless, you can't go advertizin' yer religion."

Danny was itching for a debate, but Michael put an arm on his shoulder. "Not now, Danny. Our friend Mr. MacNeal here means no harm. He's merely stating the limitations, like 'em or not. Seems yer dear America's not as free as we've been led to believe."

"Oh, it be wonderfully free," MacNeal countered, "once you complete yer servitude. But you'll find life more convenient if you renounce yer papist ways. Many do and do quite well in the new world."

"We will not renounce," Michael said.

MacNeal sighed. "Gentlemen, some flexibility is in order to ease ourselves from this conundrum, which for me is that I cannot legally transport ye as Irish Catholics."

"What about New England, then?" Danny asked. "Might Boston have taverns and theaters to amuse musicianers like ourselves?"

"'Twould be even worse for ye. Boston's a severe place. Merchanting rules their lives. Not the place for music and theater, no not at all, I'm afraid. No, I think the Chesapeake best. We just need a temporary subterfuge. I've been through this before, gentlemen, many times. If you could but trust me for a few more minutes."

"You have a solution?" Danny asked.

"Aye, a simple one. We have to dispense with yer surnames. O' anything's too easy a giveaway to get past the customs at Gravesend."

"Danny Mara then."

"I was thinking perhaps something more subtle, more, shall I say, delicate. You have a middle name Mr. O'Mara?"

"Patrick."

"Oh, dear, no. Ya needs something more loyal soundin'. How's George suit ya? William's a long popular name." MacNeal let them ponder this for a moment before continuing. "Also, gentlemen, now I have to warn that once ye adopt new names, 'twill be bit hard for yer families to track where you're off to."

"Simple solution there," Michael said, "we don't have family."

"Ah, then you'll find it easy to evaporate, legally speaking."

"Yes, I'm warming to your subterfuge proposal," Michael said. *Could be to our advantage to disappear from our recent escapades.*

"And there's no need to ask too many questions."

"Simpler that way," Michael said. "Plus, for any friends and such that we do want to contact, we can let them know our whereabouts once we are on board."

"I'd suggest waiting until yer into yer servitude. Let the dust lie low."

"Agreed."

"Wonderful. Onto yer new names then."

Danny spoke up first. "I have cousins from Galway, relation on me mother's side, Costello. Most mistake it for Italian. I think it Spanish originally."

"Well if you're trying hide yer papism, Italian and Spanish names won't do now will they?" MacNeal let them both think for a minute.

Danny got on a roll. "How 'bout turning O'Mara, in'ta Mara, Moorah, maybe Mariner."

"Oh, Christ, ya make this harder than needs be," MacNeal scolded. "Williams will do fine for the crossing. Daniel P. Williams. Done."

"Now, Mr. Shea, what monicker shall we inscribe?"

"Saint something would do, make me a Huguenot."

"Really, do we need more theater?"

"Would be fun. Michael St. Clair."

"Done. Let's move on. Can you spell yer new names or will ya just make a mark?" MacNeal brought out two large contracts and started filling in the blanks. "Now, gentlemen, as to the question of which destination. I have three captains ready to sail."

"What about Annapolis?" Michael asked.

Chapter 12

"Welcome aboard *The Delight*, lads, a fine ship she." The creaking hello came from a grizzled older man at the top of a narrow bridge connecting the ship to the dock. He waved to Michael and Danny. "She offers every accommodation while ye study the sea. There's a dry place to sleep and three squares a day." He paused and gave the musicians a curious look. "T'ain't gots all day, lads. Ya can't git anywhere's with yer feets on the dock. De idea is ta put one foot in front of de' other. We sailors call it walkin', same as you lubbers."

"It's not the walkin' that's our concern," Michael replied. "It's the balancing. We have baggage and musical instruments. Seems a bit unsteady on so narrow a bridge."

"We calls it a gangway," the man said, swallowing the last syllable. "Try leavin' yer parcels on the dock and see if ya can make it up the gangway." He motioned to someone behind the baggage piled on deck. Two younger men appeared.

"Oh, I'll give it a go," said Danny. He dumped his baggage on the dock and started his assault on the gangway with hands out to either side. It looked like he was trying to find his way down a dark hallway where the walls were just out of reach. He planned every tedious step. He stopped halfway to admire his adventure. With his next step, he slipped on the slick walkway. He teetered, arms akimbo. But before he fell, one of the young sailors rushed to his aid. He grabbed Danny by the collar like a dog carries a helpless pup and hauled him safely on board. There was a howl of laughter from the old man.

As Danny recovered his composure, the rescuer scampered down the gangway to help Michael. "Don't mind the mate," the sandy-haired jack said, "'e's not a bad sort. The mate's likes ta 'ave a bit o' fun at a lubber's expense."

A net was lowered. "It's unseemly to go up in a net, sir," the lad said. "If ya want to give the gangway a go, I'd suggest gettin' a steady walk, not quite a run. Don't look down. Keep yer eyes on the entrance way. We'll take yer baggage."

When Michael arrived without incident, the mate addressed the two lubbers. "Weren't so bad were it now? Welcome aboard, lads. Where ya bound?" The mate seemed to be stuck in a leaning position, favoring his right shoulder. "Yer indentures, if'in ya please."

Michael spoke up first. "Annapolis. In the Chesapeake. Do you know the place?" He presented his papers. Danny did the same.

"Oh, we knows Annapolis just fine," the mate replied as he accepted the forms. He barely glanced at them. "A pleasant port if'in ya stays close to the water. Summers kin be most inhospitable once ye goes inland. Not fit for man or beast. Slaves don't like it neither, but they gots no choice now do they?" He expected a laugh but got none. "Chesapeake be tolerable once ya leave July behind."

Michael spoke up. "We intend to find employment with a certain Charles Carroll who resides in that city. My invitation is in his hand." Michael fished out Carroll's letter. "He specifically invited me to apply for employment in Annapolis."

"That may be yer plan, but I wouldn't count on it." The mate gave Carroll's letter a dismissive look and waved it back to Michael. "Since when does an indentured have a choice in the matter?" he scoffed. "We sells this contract to the highest bidder. If'in your Mr. Carroll shows up to buy yer contract, might bring a better price for ya. If not, we sells ya ta anyone that comes a callin'. Same for everyone below," he said motioning to a hatchway near the forward mast.

"But Mr. Carroll was most emphatic—"

The mate cut him off: "As I said, to the highest bidder, but we will make every effort to send your man a message when ya land."

"I see," Michael replied. "As to our accommodations?"

"Where ya find space. Mr. Farrell here will show ya the way. Might I suggest you stake yer belongings near as ye can by the mainmast. Be dryer there."

The curly blonde tapped a knuckle to the mate and led them to a hatch behind the mainmast. "Mind yer 'eads, lads. 'Tween deck be low to the ceiling. Keep a hand high." Down the ladder they went. At the bottom, Farrell warned, "Try not to step on the sleeping ones." He gave them a minute for their eyes to adjust to the dark.

They were at the rear end of a rectangular space with a low ceiling that left little more than a five-foot clearance. Farrell grabbed a hooded lantern and led the way through the darkness, crouched over. "How kin I find 'em if . . ." Danny let out a curse as his head bashed into a brace. The thunk was followed by chuckles from the massed bodies crouched in the gloom.

"Like I said, mind yer 'ead." Farrell scolded. He led them to a middle spot. "Secure your baggage to the mast here." He opened his lantern to light the spot. "Passengers stay down here for the voyage or," he motioned to the deck above, "between the two main masts on the top deck. "Beyond the bulkhead," he motioned towards a wall behind the hatch ladder, "is reserved for crew, galley, cook an' ship's officers."

"Can't see where ya pointing," Danny said.

Farrell nodded. "One gets used to the dark. You'll see better when hatches is open to load provisions," he explained. "We tends to keep the hatches open in fair weather, so there be times ta be graced with sunshine." He put the hood over the lantern. "There's room here to make accommodation."

"How we sleep here?" Danny asked.

"Ah, hammocks. Ya needs ta see Mr. Edmund-Tell. He's purser. He's also our supercargo."

"A what?" Danny asked.

"That's what we calls him. Means he's got power over cargo and 'tis Mr. Edmund-Tell who sells yer contracts. He handles all the financial talk. Leaves sailing to the captain. Yer future's in his hands, not the captain's. As pursuer, ol' Edmund-Tell kin sell each of ya hammocks. Keeps ya above the fray so ta speak. Makes for better sleepin' and it's dry."

"Dry?" asked Michael.

"Tends ta get wet and worse 'tween decks in weather, what with passengers not used'ta the sea an' all. Lot of sickness, especially in the early goings. Once them night buckets starts a-spillin' over, 'tis far more pleasant ta brave a storm swingin' sweetly above than be curled up on this deck. 'Tis the only privacy you'll have from now on. Be more obvious to ya when we takes on more passengers."

"More? Hard ta see where ya kin put 'em," Danny said, pausing searching for a place name, "down here."

"We calls it a 'tween deck. This time out, 'tis a cargo hold. Sailors store cargo in holds. You're the cargo."

"Cargo are we? Seems thick enough already for more cargo. Can't even see the far end of this cargo hold."

"Oh, twill be tighter than what ya sees now," Farrell said. "Safe ta wager that before we sails. Our indenturing agent, MacNeal, he'll find more lubbers like ya lads tryin' ta escape London." He repeated his advice. "Hammocks be a wise investment." He pointed to a few crescent curves with their occupants dozing in the darkness.

"Where do I conduct this transaction?" Michael asked.

"Edmund-Tell." Farrell motioned towards the quarterdeck. "Shares cabin with Captain MacNeal. Won't see him much once we sets sail. Sea don't agree with poor Edmund-Tell." Farrell lowered his voice. "If'in I kin offer ya some advice, lads, don't let 'im charge ya more than a pence or two. Pursers is born with a pirate streak in them and there's plenty o' pirate in Sylvester Edmund-Tell."

"Much obliged," Michael replied.

"There's time for a letter to yer families, if'in ya 'ave any," Farrell suggested. "Mate'll handle yer mail until we sails."

"T'ain't no one ta write," Danny said turning his attention to storing their instruments.

"I prefer to offer my farewells in person," Michael said.

"Best rethink that," Farrell replied. "Indenturered's can't leave the ship without postin' a bond equals to yer indenture."

"Are we prisoners?"

"'Tis extreme way to be lookin' at things. Jacks like me is used to livin' at Captain's pleasure. Best ta see yerself as valuable cargo. Captain don't like 'is passengers to warm their feet." Farrell gave the musicians a nod and left them in the dark.

"Well, Mr. St. Clair?" Danny asked.

"Well what?"

"What names do we use?"

"I think we can dispense with this charade. The mate didn't bother to read them. Who else are we to be living with?"

The two lubbers surveyed their new home. They could just make out groups nearby huddled around their belongings. Those at the far end of the 'tween deck were barely shadows in the dark. All in all, it was a sorry sight, anxious passengers staring back at each other. Mostly lads in their early twenties. The few ladies huddled together in a near corner, hidden inside capes, hoods, and shawls. They avoided eye contact outside their family circles.

"Perhaps I might give a letter a try," Michael said to the darkness. He made his way to the pool of light bathing the ladder that led back up to the main deck.

A sailor pointed towards the bow. "Yer most out of the way if ya stays in front of the foremast while we takes on freight and passengers. Any where's a'fore the mast, we calls the fo'c'sle. Ya's not allowed in quarter-deck," he pointed towards the stern. "Reserved for Captain an' the mate, unless and of course ya' be invited."

After surveying the fo'c'sle, Michael wedged himself between the mast and a pile of tarred line to collect his thoughts. The scratchy hemp provided a windbreak against the cold coming up the Thames. Memories of Emma's first flirtations, the escalation to intimacies, the various ways she'd secreted him away in the attic bedroom. He opened a ragged leather notebook.

My Dearest Emma,

My heart hurts and my hand shakes as I write. I wish could sketch a few lines of poetry, but the muses haven't seen fit to give me a strength in stanza and rhyme. Please know that our times together have brought me the warmest comforts since death stole my family and left me rootless on this earth. I'm sure you must know you made me feel loved in a way that can't be expressed.

I've spent the past days hiding tears from Danny since I wandered from you. I'm hiding them still in these days before we sail. Yes, sail away. In my desolation, I've done the unthinkable. I've signed an indenture for passage to the colonies. I am now bound for a place called Annapolis.

Is there any hope that you will join me on this adventure? Look deep into your heart, Emma. Do you still dream of the life you described in our tender moments?

I offer you my heart, Emma. You know my pledge is true. Where else will your love be returned so fully? Join me. Escape the emptiness that London holds. Can you give me hope, Emma, any sign, that we'll brave the Atlantic together?

We sail in two days' time, on the morning of the 24th. Please find your way to the merchant ship The Delight, *on the northernmost pier at Livermore, before that tide carries us away.*

I am always yours,
Michael

CHAPTER 13

THE SCREECH OF THE MATE'S VOICE COMING DOWN THE HATCH WOKE Danny. "Shea. A Mr. Michael Shea. Visitor on deck." Danny gave Michael a shove to roust him out. "Michael, my love," he said affecting a girl's singsong voice, "ya 'ave a visitor."

"Emma's come?" Michael bolted awake, his pulse racing. He tumbled out of the hammock and stumbled towards light in the hatchway. He poked his head through the deck and searched for a green velvet cape. Indeed, the cape was there. His breathing quickened. But then he noticed that the hem of the cape was muddied and draped on the deck. This cape was too tall for its occupant. His heart sank as he approached and found not Emma but Moira in her place, shivering in her older sister's wrap.

"Moria, is your sister not with you?"

"I come alone." She pushed back the oversized hood. She handed him a wax-sealed letter, heavily scented. "I fear it's not what you're wanting to hear."

"You are privileged to Emma's thoughts?"

"It is I who am here to wish you Godspeed, Michael." She fixed her green-blue eyes on his and used her fingertips to smooth away tears the winter wind blew across her reddened cheeks. "I had to help her with the spelling." She sniffled. "My dear sister can dance and sing, but she never gave attention to her schoolings. I could have written it in French, Dutch, or Latin. Emma can barely scratch a sentence in her native tongue. Mother used to say would be easier to teach a blackbird. They at least stand still when they sing."

Michael stared at the circle of red wax. His shoulders sagged.

Watching his disappointment take hold, Moira gathered her courage and sprang upon him, pinning his arms in an awkward embrace. "Michael, your love is so misplaced. It's wasted on my sister. There is another who'd . . ." Her words were lost in sobbing.

Michael freed an arm to unwrap his neckcloth. She used it to dry the edges of her eyes. She wiped her nose as well.

"I am touched, Moira, truly." He pulled away just enough to give her a soft kiss on her forehead. "May I humbly beg your sweet forgiveness? It was my sense you thought of me as one would a lost cousin. Are you yet sixteen?"

"A year ago I was." She stifled a sob. "Tell me about Annapolis. I've brought a bag. I have money."

Michael told her the little he knew and his and Danny's plan to indenture themselves. He asked about Jonathan.

"Papa had to pay for the burial. There's rumor Jonathan had money somewhere, but it's not turned up. An undertaker showed up next morning with his wagon, that was the end of it. At least we hope so."

"No prayer for his soul?"

"I said a prayer for you. Something's not right with Papa. One of the Bow Street Runners returned asking more questions. Papa left out a lot. He made no mention of the Broot brothers. He made up a story about Danny leaving early and how you disappeared later. I don't like what Papa's up to."

In the silence that followed, Michael worried over this news. He felt Jonathan's wallet and thought, *"How do I explain this?"*

Moira kept a cheek against his jacket and used the ends of his silk to dab tears. He drew soft circles on the back of her shoulder. Michael buried his chin in her light brown hair. The frizzly strands tickled his nose. He resisted the urge to scratch and escape the petty torment.

"I have more news," she said. "Captain Longley has returned from North America. It's an awkward reunion."

This revelation got his twitching nose out of Moira's hair. "Has he now. Was Emma glad to see her husband again?"

"Hardly. She lost interest in him when it was clear he wouldn't inherit as promised before she married him. Papa was right all along.

Now Captain Longley talks of a post in India, of riches, of advancement. Been a most cold hello. And Papa's already fretting on the loss of business. It's barely a week and we've already lost the crowds you draw. They don't stay as long. And the Broots and their associates now dine and gamble elsewhere. Walter certainly don't like competing for Emma when her husband's about. Business will be terribly slow without his patronage and your entertainments. One hopes Captain Longley's stay will be a short one."

Michael became aware that they had an audience. The morning watch was listening, waiting for the next scene in the unfolding drama. As Michael looked about, two sailors and the mate busied themselves with idle chores.

"Come, my dear, the fox ears are very much awake." He led Moira to the gangway. The mate moved to block Michael's path.

"Some space to talk privately, if you please," Michael said. Then leaning into the mate's ear, he whispered, "unless you prefer to risk stretching your neck on charge of kidnapping this innocent child." The mate backed off.

"Thank you," Michael said, returning to a normal voice. "Would you be so kind as to arrange a coach for the lady? The White Lyon Tavern."

He led Moira by the hand down the gangway. The mate gave a wave to one of the sailors who followed at a respectable distance.

On the dock, Moira composed herself. She appeared taller. "Why won't you take me with you?"

"Out of respect for you and your parents. They've been most kind to me."

"But Father dismissed you."

"In any event, I could not return their past kindness by secreting you away."

"Hardly seems they notice me."

"*Ils seraient désolé sans toi.*"

"Only because they'd be burdened with my chores. Emma certainly won't do the scrubbing and washing. Life's hard work's left to me and Momma."

"Cruel words. *Ta famille t'aime profondément.*"

"Why then does Papa's world revolve around Emma? All I am to him is a scrub maid, a servant. I'm invisible to Papa."

Michael let that complaint drift with the breeze. Moira shivered. He put his arm around her and drew her close.

"I can sing better than Emma," she said into his coat. "And I can harmonize. She's always stuck on the melody."

"You do have wonderful gift, *mon petit chou.*"

"I am not a cabbage!"

"It is an expression of endearment."

"To the French maybe, but rather you say nothing than spout such a confounding expression."

"As you wish." Michael observed *The Delight*'s sailor walking up the wharf not with a hackney but with a tinker leading a donkey cart. "Seems some transport has been arranged."

Moira dried her eyes again. "Do you think lowly of me, Michael? Is that why you won't take me with you?"

"Not at all. It's just premature to fly the nest. As for my part, as an indentured servant, I'll be powerless to protect and serve you. I'm no longer in charge of my own life. I may soon rue the morning I went to the Exchange. I should blame it on Danny, but it's my own doing."

"I don't care. I'd take that chance to be with you."

"Brave words, but there's no guarantee we'd be in the same city. Families are dispersed and flung apart like handfuls of seed. There are severe limitations upon this sort of life. We are not free to move about or change masters. We're not even allowed to marry. Unless you have twenty pounds to lend, a slave I'll be."

"Then how could you have begged Emma to join you?"

"Beg?" Michael blurted out before remembering his letter. "Perhaps in my passion, I wasn't thinking as clearly as I should."

"In four years, I'd be free to marry. You'd be free to choose too."

He took her hands and smiled. "Much will change in a few years' time. There's every chance a deserving lad will shower you with the attentions you so deserve."

Moira's watery eyes searched his face.

"Excuse me, Moira. Let me attend to a detail or two."

Michael approached the tinker to negotiate a rate he could barely afford. After a bit of conversation, the tinker nodded. Michael returned and took Moira's gloved hands. With faux-formal ceremony, he helped her into the back of the cart and put her bag at her side.

She dabbed her eyes with his silk cravat. With both hands, she toyed with the ends and slowly drew him close. Then she pounced, kissing him hard on the mouth. He froze. She repeated the kiss, softer this time. He returned it. There was a third and fourth before the cart pulled away.

Savoring Moira's kiss, Michael felt his lower lip swell. He watched the cart carry her down the wharf. Her white-laced fingers waved a heart-broken farewell. He removed his hat and returned this with a proper bow. Then she was gone around a corner.

He lingered a bit, to taste his swollen lip, the mix of Moira's moisture with his, and to retrace the embrace with his tongue.

"Mr. Shea," the mate bellowed from the ship.

Michale acknowledged, but before climbing the gangway, he rested by a barrel and opened Emma's heavily scented letter.

My Dear Michael,

Please forgive me for sending you these lines of farewell under my sister's hand. I must decline your invitation to join you on your adventure to America. You must understand it is easier this way than to put ourselves through a discomforting fare-thee-well in full view of gawking sailors on a public landing stage.

I am truly touched by your most intriguing proposal, though I had thought you understood the limitations of our tender situation. Our liaisons, though tender and warm, could only by nature be secretively enjoyed.

You must understand, I have obligations to my husband, and responsibilities that cannot be lightly abandoned, even if I were free to leave my home and family. I wish you well, Michael, and please

know the memory of our performances will linger in my thoughts always. I am yours,
   Emma

Michael drew the note to his face to savor Emma's fragrance. In turning it over to refold it, he noticed a few more lines, these in a sloppy scribble Emma had added in her own hand:

My Deare,
   I tell you seperetly what I cant share with my swete sifter. My Hufbend has reterned to reclame his bride. I am much relieved. It is clofe enouf to our enconter that he will believe a childe, if one were to come, will be his owne.
   Take caree Michael, you are for ever with me. Emma.

CHAPTER 14

As Farrell predicted, MacNeal sent more desperate souls to *The Delight*. The latest indentureds entered at the far end of the 'tween deck hold, through the forward hatch. Though Michael couldn't hear Farrell's now familiar instructions, he knew what was next: the thump of a head cracking against a brace and the resulting curse. While the hatch was open, Michael could just make out forms in the distance. Few opted for the expense of a hammock. Most set up makeshift cots, using their baggage to establish a perimeter. The bunks along the hull had been long ago claimed by earlier arrivals.

After each settled in, it was their turn to discover the open-air joys of the privies at the head of the ship. The lads didn't mind, but the ladies did. Michael could just make out the occasional family man screen his missus and children as they squatted over the ubiquitous night buckets. Once the hatch was closed, the new arrivals disappeared in the darkness.

"Danny, care to see if the moon'll show herself?" Michael whispered. "I know our Mr. Farrell's little speech word for word. I'd appreciate a change of scenery."

Danny didn't stir.

"Sleep tight, then." Michael wriggled out of his hammock. He nearly fell the three feet to the deck. Crouching under the low ceiling, he headed for the hatch for the chance to stand upright and escape the thick smell of huddled humanity. Farrell greeted him in the night air.

"Pleasant evening is it not, Mr. Farrell?" Michael replied.

"Aye, 'tis a rare one for a winter's night."

"Might I inquire of you, Mr. Farrell, will we sail by morning?"

"Maybe a day, maybe two. I expect we'll take on more cargo."

"More? How could that be? We be toe to toe down there already."

"We sailors pack tight, but not ta worry, ain't likely. Too late for more indentures ta be signin' at this hour." He stretched his back. "Most, like yerself an' yer friend, come direct after signin.' No reason ta delay comin' aboard. Yer out of options, aren't ya? Otherwise, why'd ya signin' yer lifes aways?" He rolled his shoulders to work out the kinks in his back. "No offense, sir, 'tis a familiar story we hears in this trade."

"None taken, Mr. Farrell. Indeed, it is our lot. A hard one to be sure, but it is, nonetheless, of our own making. We are, as you say, out of options."

Farrell pulled out the remains of a tobacco prick and a knife and proceeded to slice a plug. "Share a chew?"

"Another time perhaps. Enjoy your masticating."

"If I may offer yea's a piece of advice, sir."

"By all means."

"Ya won't be a needin' dem fancy words on this ship or any. Kin be off puttin' during a long voyage on a small ship."

"I'll be takin' yer suggestion ta heart," Michael said imitating Farrell. "No needs ta create troubles where none is needed."

"Much better."

Michael replied with a tilt of his head and winked.

"You're a curious one, if I may be so bold ta speak plain," Farrell said. "What's yer story then? Ya don't quite fancy the look of most indentures. Ya seems to have proper schoolin'. And from what we jacks observed this morn', ya be blessed with affections of a comely lass. Don't make much sense ta be runnin' aways from such a lovely sight."

"If we are to trade stories, Mr. Farrell, perhaps an introduction is in order. Michael Shea, medical apprentice, musicianer."

"Ordinary seaman, Liam Farrell." The words were garbled as he maneuvered his chew into one cheek. "Previous to me sailorin', I was ta be apprentice at clock making. But I longed for a more adventurous life."

"Ordinary? Liam's a grand name, nothing ordinary about it."

"Lots of learnin' for ya, Michael. Ordinary's a jack's ratin'. Means I'm new ta sailin'. I'm to be rated able-bodied this voyage. Means better wages."

"I thank you for the terminologies, Liam."

"Crew calls me Billy. Became a Billy when me family came ta England. I'm only Liam to me devoted parents, an even then, only in private. They said best ta assume English names once we came to London. Me ma's word for it was 'similate.' She tried to part on me some of her book learnin', but I were a restless one. Not one for readin' and writin'."

"How is it you came to London then?"

"Me dad were lookin' for advancement. 'Weren't enough work in Ireland ta keep us clothed and fed. Saw no profit in breakin' ground 'n toilin' for his brother after plantin' their parents in the churchyard. Next thing I knew I was learnin' the streets of London, glad to be on solid ground after all the sickness. It was a wretched trip. Usually is, I've found."

"Yet you're a sailor after such a journey?"

"Short memory. The mate an' Captain MacNeal were persuasive when they spotted me wanderin' tavern to tavern like, singin' 'n dancin' for a fresh mug. Assured me I'd come to like sailorin'. By and large, they was right."

"With your parent's blessing then?"

"They knew the sea 'twas for me. Shared us many a farewell tear."

Farrell scooted to the gunnel for a good spit. Brown spittle sprinkled on his chin when he returned to his story. "London never offered the employments me da' sought. If'in he were lucky, 'e might work for a month or so." He wiped his chin with his sleeve.

"But then he'd idle for months. There'd be dozens or more clock makers scramblin' about for work that 'tweren't there. Only enough work to keep three or four busy." He took another break to spit over the side.

"Me ma took ta cleanin', but 'weren't never enough work. Livin' were hard. Me da'd wander all of London lookin', beggin' for scraps of work. A day's labor, anything. As a lad, I could easily tap a fancy dance. Eventually 'e was draggin' me ta taverns 'n sawin' away on 'is fiddle. One night the mate and Captain introduced themselves. By the time me da woke next day, I were cabin boy on *The Delight*. Captain MacNeal and the mate taught me sailin'. Five years on, I'm now Mr. Farrell, spillin' me story ta Mr. Michael Shea."

"I'm honored to share your adventure."

The two sat for a while soaking up the night air.

"So 'tis yer turn, Michael. How's it a lad with such a lovely lass at his heels bound for Annapolis? How could ya turn 'er down?"

"This day has indeed been a curious mix." Michael replied. "I had to return her to her family. I could not in good conscience let her descend into an indentured's lot with me. As your mate made clear, we are indebted, bound for the Chesapeake as servants, bound for the cost of this passage. How could I put such an innocent at the mercy of some hungry master?"

"'Tis true you're bound, but still, Michael, how could ya resist her? I knows I wouldn't."

"I'm turning that very question meself. At the day's start, my heart belonged to another. I thought the sentiment returned. I was mistaken. How could I quickly change affection to her younger sister?"

Farrell motioned him to the river side of the ship. He spit, but it didn't make it to the Thames. A brown glob of goo landed on the side of the ship, the remains dribbled over his lip. After Farrell transferred the dribble to his sleeve, Michael continued.

"I worked for their father at the White Lyon for these past three years."

"Ah, the White Lyon. Renowned for prodigious dinners."

"Quite so," Michael replied. "I was engaged as musicianer with my friend Danny. The vintner's elder daughter, Emma, joined us to dance and sing. Emma and I would perform bits of theater. At first we acted out the parts of doomed lovers." Michael put his hand over his heart in a bit of mock acting. "Was just part of the show . . . at the beginning. We achieved much celebrity with our performances. Then life became sticky."

"Sticky?"

"Little by little, those fanciful lives extended off stage as well. Was necessary, of course, to keep our amours unbeknownst to her family. I kept Danny in the dark too. And she had to appear interested in the patrons who shed many a quid in vain hope. And there is the uncomfortable matter that the lady in question does have a husband."

"A husband? Illicit suitors? 'Tis some lady. Yer tale 'tis fraught with hazards." Farrell put a sloppy spout of brown chew over the side.

"That is truly disgusting," Michael said. "Little wonder your desire for a relationship with a lady remains unrequited. Do you really enjoy the flavor?"

"Flavor? Nah. Mostly burns. I've seen many a gentleman doing the same in taverns. They're not accosted so rudely."

"My apologies, Billy. But it is my recollection that the only 'ladies' drawn to those who chew are for hire. If you have designs for a lady standing, some reform would be necessary."

"'T'aint gonna happen out on the ocean." Billy relieved his mouth again. "Who's there to care? But I'll take yer admonition to heart when next in port." He spit again, then faced Michael. "A taste for tobacco's no sin. But, how kin' I put this lightly . . . aren't adulteries frowned upon in society and church life?"

Michael smiled. "I take your point. Love has a way of overlooking certain, shall I say, inconveniences. I thought it was love. Seems now I was but *'un divertissement'* to Emma Baker."

"There ya go again, Michael, fancy words."

"I was a toy for her affections."

"You rake! Double dippin' in the family. 'Tis a dream ta be toyed with by a lovely lass like the one you just chased away."

Michael looked out across the river. "Until today, I was unaware of Miss Moira's affection. I had thought of her merely as the promising younger sister. I assure you in all confidence, never was there any thought of 'dipping,' as you so eloquently put it, with Miss Moira."

"Difficult ta believe, Michael. A priest be hard pressed not ta notice such a beauty. He'd be sore tempted ta break 'is vows."

"Indeed, she has her charms," Michael mused. "In any case, I'd rephrase your sense of admiration, was you to attempt a hello, into a more respectable fashion when such an opportunity presents itself."

"No 'fense intended 'to the honor of yer admirer, Michael. We sailors have a saltier way of expressing our thoughts than ya lubbers 'ave need of sayin'. I would, o' course, choose milder words 'twere I to have the pleasure of an introduction. I might even sing a verse or two, maybe try a hornpipe with 'er."

"You sing and dance, then? That's a good sign. Do you have an instrument in your repertoire as well?"

"Alas, no. You?"

"Fiddle is my avocation. It brings great solace. I only wish it could bring steady meals."

"Music 'tis a joy, certainly, but do ya 'ave any useful skills ta offer yer new masters in Maryland? I take it you're no farmer."

"I have been apprenticed to a physician."

"Doctoring is it then? How is it there are no employments for ya?"

"I briefly assisted a Naval surgeon, a most incompetent scoundrel. A mere barber and not a good one at that. His skills were quite diminished, but his patronage in London well entrenched. I sense he be jealous of my abilities, and he detested my religion. Trouble started right from the first patient. I was falsely accused of thievery. A silver knife mysteriously appeared in my jacket after we had attended to a smallpox patient. Fortunately, the suffering gentleman vouched for my integrity. But I couldn't outrun the maliciousness my employer spread. It's why I was reduced to tavern performances for my daily bread."

"That led you to sign papers with MacNeal then?"

"Was overwhelmed by my friend's dreams about the colonies. He was always going on about what a new life we'd find there. 'A few years servitude 'tis an easy price ta pay for freedom,' he likes to say. In a moment of dissipation, I succumbed to his dream."

Farrell considered Michael's story for a bit. "Well, we'll deliver ya across the sea to Annapolis. Then you'll see what fate has in store for ya."

CHAPTER 15

THE NEXT MORNING PROVED FARRELL WRONG. MICHAEL AND DANNY awoke to the pounding of feet hurrying every which way on the deck above. They scooted up the rear hatch and found *The Delight* loading more cargo. The last of the cargo came with the clucked cries coming from caged chickens. They provided an odd harmony to the plaintive bleating of a pair of goats already on deck.

Piercing through this chaos came a tall, grizzled man's voice berating the mate. He apparently had repeated his demands without receiving the consideration he expected. The stiff-backed man, in elegant preacher's attire, led a flock of disheveled souls huddled at the entrance way. Michael counted five men and nine women. They all wore dark brown coats, long and plain but of good quality wool. The men wore matching hats with wide circular brims. When the women in the group realized Danny was sizing them up, they huddled together like penguins and hid themselves in oversized hoods.

"Can't you read what's under your nose?" the agitated leader demanded.

The shock of this public rebuke of the mate caused Farrell and his crew to freeze for a moment in mid-haul, leaving the chickens swaying overhead.

"We are not servants! We are farmers. We are Palatines."

Farrell nodded to his crew. They resumed their loading, but in slow motion to eavesdrop.

"Our brethren will honor our passage in Maryland. And, I must emphasize to you, sir, we will not accept accommodation in a cargo hold with indentured servants."

The mate didn't take this well. Leaving the newcomers to cool their heels, he stomped towards the quarterdeck and disappeared into the ship's galley and captain's quarters. He reappeared helping the purser, Edmund-Tell, cross the deck. The purser needed a cane in each hand to wobble on gout-swollen ankles. Everyone could feel Edmund-Tell's pain as he waddled across the deck. Without introduction, the purser grabbed the document from the man's hand and jabbed a fat finger at a section at the bottom. "Read here, if you can," Edmund-Tell stifled a sneeze, "as you should have before you signed."

The man's head jerked slightly as he read the passage. His shoulders sagged on the second read and sagged even more on the third.

"So you see, Mr. Brouchard," Edmund-Tell sneered, "you owe our mate an apology."

"I am a man of God. The proper salutation is Elder. I shall speak with your mate."

"As you should, Mr. 'Elder' Brouchard. You and your congregation will indeed bunk with the indentured. How you are redeemed depends on how quickly your brethren make good on yer passage," he paused to count Brouchard's followers, "and fourteen of your flock." Edmund-Tell signaled to the jack by the entrance, who slammed the gate shut behind the group. "The mate will show you the way."

On the quarterdeck, Captain MacNeal's attention was on stowing livestock. The squawking of the incoming barnyard created a stark contrast to the silent shuffling of the Palatines to the forward hatch.

"What a ya make of this bunch?" Danny asked Michael.

"They look the way I feel . . . regretting ever stepping foot on this boat. Why'd I ever let you talk me into this misadventure?"

"How kin ya complain? We be eatin' steady now. When's last time ya ate three a day?" Danny continued as Farrell walked by. "An egg or two now and again will be most welcome. Maybe a fresh bit of goat's milk?"

Farrell broke Danny's daydream. "Not on yer life. Don't give no effort to such a thought. They be for Captain and his guests. An' don't go thinkin' no servants'll be invited to his table." Then he whispered, "Cook claims we get beef and pork, but could be horse. Hard to tell by the time he stews it all down. Good eatin' compared ta starvin'." He winked and walked off.

Danny realized that Michael wasn't listening but staring at the dock. "What-ya pinin' away for?"

"A fare-thee-well, a final adieu."

"Jesus, man! Let go o' the past. Keep yer thoughts on the real future."

"Future? To be a servant? What sort of life is that? Even these common sailors look down on us. I'm to be grateful feasting on horse?" Michael's outburst was too much for Danny. He left his friend to his lost boy brooding.

Why am I doing this? Michael was thinking. *How could Emma abandon me?*

A bit later a bosun's whistle screeched. The captain consulted with the mate, who let loose with a volley of commands. The ship's crew was everywhere at once as *The Delight* nudged away from the wharf on the ebb tide.

Danny put his back to the gunnel, mesmerized by the crew's flurry of preparations. "Wouldn't ya love ta join 'em up there, Michael? Flyin' about in that tangle of rope? Like spiders dancin' along their webs." He faced the docks with Michael. "Ain't it grand, Michael? There's adventure in the air."

Michael refused to break his sour mood. *Adventure? To be a slave?* He remained transfixed on the empty wharf. Danny put a hand on Michael's shoulder.

CHAPTER 16

Two days later, a lively stomping of feet pounded the top deck while Michael on fiddle, Danny on flute, and a sailor called Knob on concertina struck up a set of quadrilles. Captain MacNeal ordered out extra rations of rum to celebrate their first night on the open sea, becalmed in the Channel just south of the English coast. The dancing and rum worked their magic to ward off the cold and anxiety that haunted the indentureds. Not so for the Palatines. They kept to themselves and threw forlorn frowns at the dancers because Elder Brouchard disdained such blasphemous behavior.

The crew and some of the indentured lads provided most of the dancing. The ladies who braved the dance had all the attentions they could want. It was a refreshing break from hovering husbands. As the musicians played, bits of conversation found their way to Michael's ear. When Farrell, standing close by the musicians, made a move to horn in on a dancing lady, the mate held him back. "'Tis bad luck to have women on board."

Farrell dismissed the warning. "Luck's what ya make of an opportunity, sir, and we has 'ere an opportunity." He joined the braver sailors who were beside themselves, jostling about for a chance to bow and twirl with a female.

After hearing Farrell's raw wisdom, Michael started rooting for the sailor's success in the dance. As one set of tunes led to another, Danny leaned into his friend's ear. "There ya go Michael my boy, good ta hear yer coming alive."

Michael's fiddle lines danced on top of the concertina's melody, much as the sailors seemed to dance along the ship's tangle of rope to set sails.

These improvisations were new to Knob. It was all he could do to stay true to the melody and not be distracted by the antics of fiddle and flute.

"Again, my friend," Michael would say to Knob during the turnaround to encourage him to elongate the dance, "from the first." The trio fired away, speeding up the pace.

At this point Captain MacNeal left his perch on the quarterdeck to join the dancers. The crew reveled at the sight of the captain's participation. They started pounding their hands and stomping their feet to egg him on. Michael thought he noticed some Palatine feet tapping along when their elder wasn't watching. It was a grand release for all on a calm night under a mountain of limp sails. Then there was a slight breeze.

Michael might not have even noticed it but for the sweat dripping down his forehead. The sudden chill caused by light puffs of air caught his attention. It also caught the captain's attention. He made a discreet exit from the dance line to reclaim his place on the quarterdeck.

Michael could hear bits of their conversation. "Weather, just a breeze? Gale? It'll come on quick like."

The mate turned MacNeal's whispered commands into steady action. One by one, the crew slipped out to attend to their duties and left the passengers to revel in their innocence. It took another set of jigs before the change was noticed by everyone. Knob was the last sailor to join the exodus. "Duty calls, lads. It's been a pleasure." The passengers gazed about, curious about the sudden burst of activity.

"What'ya think Michael?" Danny asked packing away his flutes.

"We're in for a rough ride."

"You've crossed the Channel, what kin we expect from the great Poseidon?"

"He'll make it a bumpy ride, most unpleasant. Cold and wet. Worse than any storming on land, I'll tell ya that."

As the winds increased, Farrell and a couple of sailors hurried the passengers below. He ran over to Michael and Danny. "Better get below, gentlemen. Tie down yer instruments as best ya can. Anythin' not tied down will be thrown about. I'll join ya presently."

Farrell stood still in the rear hatch area in the dark hold with a hooded lantern, which illuminated only him. He made a racket pounding a belaying pin on the bottom of a night bucket to get the passengers attention. "If'in I kin get yer silence. Please, I needs yer attentions." He pounded again. "Some weather's comin' on. Let me assure ya that storms like this is natural ta us sailors, so we'll be working the ship normal like, but you needs to keep clear of the decks. Much safer ta ride out down here." He let the news spread to the far end of the hold before continuing.

"One 'vantage of a good storm is we kin quicken our exit from the Channel. Once we reaches the Atlantic, we'll bear south for Portugal and Spain. When we hits the tropics, we turns due west for the Leewards, and ultimately, land you nice and safe like in Amerikay."

A murmuring built to a barrage of questions about the weather. Farrell tried to reassure them.

"A storm's a storm. Nothin' more. Time now ta secure yer belongings. I urge ya ta secure all boxes, chests, cots, beds and whatnots to the deck, bunks, or bulkhead. Partitions can stay for now."

"Ya kin rely on yer candles and lanterns for a bit more, but once we closes the hatch," he pointed to the opening above the ladder, "we must insist on lights out, 'cept for this hooded lantern." He hung the lamp above the ladder. "Best ta see if'in ya can get some sleep while it's dark and stormy." Farrell didn't wait around for more questions.

Michael and Danny did their best to secure their clothes in the foot of their hammocks, which hung in the space between the mainmast and the rear hatch. Danny hung his dulcimer between his hammock and the mast. Michael lashed his fiddle case inside his hammock.

The ship started to roll and pitch as it picked up speed. First up and down as the hull plowed through the Channel's swells, and then random rolls sideways. Michael and Danny wiggled into their hammocks, butts three feet off the deck.

Michael thanked Mother Mary and any saint who'd listen for Farrell's advice to invest in a hammock. They were indeed dry, but not dry as Farrell had implied. The humidity created by the breathing of forty-eight souls in close quarters, nearly shoulder to shoulder, made it impossible for anything to be actually dry. Dry just meant not soaking wet.

And they weren't sick. At least, not at first.

Chapter 17

At first, their swaying hammocks insulated Michael and Danny from seasickness. The indentureds camped out on the deck were the first victims, followed by those packed into the double-decked bunks along the hulls.

"How ya feelin' Michael?" Danny asked in the dim.

"Unsettled. Don't like the dark."

"Was more thinkin' of yer insides."

"Too soon to say."

"Wish I could say the same. Thinkin' I'll befriend one of them buckets. Maybe if I could get some air on deck." Danny headed for a bucket lashed to the ladder in the dimly lit hatchway. He just made it without stepping on the dark forms of fellow sufferers camped out on the deck. Doubled over on his knees, he vomited. His groans mingled with the chorus of passengers moaning in the darkness.

Michael hunched his way out of the blackness to keep his friend company.

Danny planted himself at the foot of the hatch ladder. He gulped for fresh air, one hand holding on to the ladder, the other against the bulkhead to prop himself upright. Another bout of vomiting. Danny missed the bucket, his bile mixed with a steady stream of the sea cascading down the ladder and spreading throughout the 'tween deck. He grabbed the ladder to right himself. Danny was sweating, his thick black hair matted to his forehead and temples.

"Thinking of climbing those stairs are we now, Danny?" Michael asked to let his friend know he was there.

"God no. How could I? It's like . . ." He didn't finish. He was on his knees again, cramping and dehydrating himself. When finished, Danny lingered in his kneeling position. "Tell me why, Michael," Danny asked, "why's a merciful God do this to his beloved creatures?"

"Maybe if you had chosen the priesthood, like your dear mother would have liked, God would've graced you with immunity."

"Tough price ta pay, I'd say, ta forsake a-tumblin' with a lass."

"Perhaps you should call on St. Augustine for some guidance."

"Hope my prayers reach him before he turned saint."

The boys chuckled. "Glad to see your humour returns, perhaps you'll survive. Mind would ya, Danny, if I left you to your prayers for a bit? There are other unfortunate creatures who may need some attention. Will you be safe while I crawl about to see what needs to be done?"

"Off with ya. Kin be sick all by meself. Cold air helps. I'll stay put an' commune with Augustine."

Michael turned to face an epidemic of sickness. The victims in various states of crouching, mostly on their knees, heads over bucket, trying to hold still while the deck rocked. Adding to the stench, night buckets overturned into a sea of filth that sloshed across the planked flooring.

There weren't enough buckets to go around. Many never made it to a bucket. They'd kneel in the stinking sea to spill their guts again and again. Those in bunks could get their heads over the side. The less fortunate in cots found themselves overturned as the ship lurched sideways. Others were stuck sitting in the filth, which added an extra layer of humiliation to their misery.

Michael braved the filth to wait upon some of the more helpless. He could barely make out faces in the gloom under the lone hooded lantern left by the hatchway. All he could do was offer encouraging words. He'd hold a hand when possible or soothe a forehead. He'd offer them "Will pass soon enough," or "It's but a bad moment," and other such pleasantries. Some uttered a thank you, others just managed a squeeze of the hand.

As he worked his way down the larboard side, he found a young lady laid out in a cot groaning with her hands in folded in prayer. Her husband knelt beside, one hand in the muck, bracing himself much as Danny was, in preparation for his next eruption. His other hand tried to keep a bucket ready for his wife. Michael rubbed the man's shoulder. "This'll be just a memory in a day or two, my friend."

The man nodded. Michael took a closer look at him. "I remember you steppin' right lively before this weather came up."

"Can't think on dancin' just now."

"Never fear. You'll be ready for another hornpipe soon enough. How's the missus?"

"I be doin' better than Mr. Rawlings," came her reply before her husband could answer. "Kind of you t'inquire." She half raised her head to address the shadow that was Michael. "Ain't as troubling for me as 'tis for others. Have other thoughts on me mind at present." She rubbed a hand over her belly. "Prayin' the child will wait out the storm. Don't want the babe a-borne in this hell." She reached out to cover her husband's hand, but instead Mrs. Rawlings was jolted out of her cot by a violent sideways rocking. The collision of ship and waves was followed by a thundering on the deck above and the sound of canvass ripping.

Despite his weakness, Mr. Rawlings caught his wife and returned her safely to her cot. "Maybe a prayer, my dear? Ask our Lord to ease his temper?"

After their prayer, Michael said, "Sir, Mrs. Rawlings is welcome to my hammock if she might be more comfortable. It's just there, not three feet from your encampment."

Mrs. Rawlings answered, "Kind of you to offer, but in my condition, climbing into a hammock puts me to worry. How could I ever clamour out of such a contraption, and in the dark mind you, when the time arrives?"

Before Michael could answer, there was a howl at the hatch. Farrell had stepped on Danny's fingers as he bounded down the ladder to address the passengers.

"Any mens not sick are needed on deck." Farrell's bellow filled the 'tween deck area. "Captain MacNeal has requested assistance of all able bodies. Be lively now!"

Chapter 18

Only three men, Michael included, were fit enough to answer the call. Danny was one of many lads who tried to step forward despite their sickness, but Farrell refused them. "Brave of ya lads, but we needs strong hands not weakened by sickness. There will be other times for ya t'assist."

Farrell opened a locker by the hatch and handed out tarpaulin jackets to his three new sailors. His briefing was direct. "We've lost some yards and sail. Lots of tackle to untangle. We've lost two of the crew. One's unconscious, the other seems to have broken his leg. We needs yer help on the lines as me mates bend on a new canvas. Yer job's ta pull for all yer's worth when the time comes. I'll be telling yas when and wheres. Up we go now lads."

Out on the lurching deck, a cold spray spouting over the bow and sides instantly drenched the raw recruits as *The Delight* plunged into the valleys between waves. Michael and his new mates stumbled around in the dark, unsure of footing. In the lull as the ship started to climb the next wave, they righted themselves, crouching with their feet wide apart.

"Lesson one," Farrell yelled over the storm's roar. "Always, always, keep a hand on the ship. That's what lifelines is for." He pointed to the ropes running lengthwise along the deck. He picked one up to demonstrate. The recruits followed him forward. Farrell then pointed skyward at two ghostly shadows riding a yard on the foremast. The top third of the mast was missing. Its wreckage had become an obstacle course on deck for the rookie crew to navigate. The apparitions above were stationed along a yardarm perpendicular to the remaining mast. Two heavy lines hung from the yard to either side of the deck through blocks attached to the the sides of the ship.

"Mates," Farrell yelled pointing to the ghosts, "yer ta hoist a new sail so the lads can bend it on the yard. Two to a side." He gave a rough line to Michael and motioned for one of the passengers pair up with Michael. He introduced himself. "Edwin Hoecker, weaver," his partner offered.

"When I gives the word," Farrell yelled across the deck, "we hauls the halyards tight and walks the deck to the stern." He motioned to the back where the captain and helmsmen stood on the quarterdeck. "Put the line o'er yer shoulders, like so, when ya pull."

Farrell took the largest recruit with him to far side of the deck and waited for a sign from the ghosts in the rigging. When it came, Farrell was all action. "Okay, now heave it, lads. Put yer backs to it."

"Jesus and Mary," Michael said to his rope mate, "Never expected a damn piece of canvass could be so heavy."

Farrell kept up a stream of encouragements. "Pull! Pull! Pull!"

Eventually the wet canvass sail made its way up the mast. "Tie 'er off, Mr. Shea," Farrell hollered over the wind.

"Where we supposed to do that?" he yelled back. Before there was answer, Hoecker and Michael were pulled backward towards the bow.

"Jesus, pull, man, pull!" screamed Farrell.

Michael and Hoecker redoubled their efforts, but they only slowed their reversal against the slick deck and the weight of the sail as the ship careened down an ocean swell. "Me frickin' fingers is bleedin'," Hoecker grunted, but he held on.

Farrell and his conscript rushed to join them. With Farrell in the lead, the four regained the lost ground. Farrell got the line around a belaying pin.

"Thank you, lads, and my apologies. I forgot ta give ya a critical instruction. Wait here 'til we've set the sail. Then we'll await Captain's orders." Farrell left to attend to the sailors in the foremast.

The newbies huddled by the quarterdeck until the biggest of the group spoke up. "Certainly a wild sight, is it not gents?" asked the burly fellow who had worked with Farrell on the rope pull. He was near twice the size of Michael and Hoecker.

"Indeed it is, sir. Might we have the benefit of your acquaintance?" asked Michael.

"Martin Tombler, smith, at yer service."

The ship rocked sideways. Michael grabbed the lifeline to steady himself, his partner used the gunnel. Tombler couldn't reach either. To keep from falling over, he clamped on Michael's right hand. Michael winced in the grip.

"Sorry," Tombler said when recovered. "God gave me strength." Michael and Hoecker made their hellos.

Tombler echoed what they all felt. "A frightful sight, ain't it? The sea, its power. I must admit I'm more than a bit worried seeing how easy we're tossed about. I thought the ship so steady when we was on the Thames. Our situation's far more fragile than I'd imagined."

"Aye, 'tis," Hoecker piped in. "Don't mind sayin, I have a new respect for prayin' jest now. Prayed to escape London. But have I given up weavin' only to be drowned in the cold dark Atlantic?"

"That remains to be seen," Michael replied. "We're still in the Channel."

"Would ya look at that," Tombler said, watching *The Delight*'s crew wrestling with the new foremast sail as the ship careened side to side.

A different sight caught Michael's attention. Behind Tombler, two sailors were struggling to steady the helm. They were draped in long black slickers and both sported blue-trimmed, white scarves wrapped around their necks and over their heads to hold their hats on. The bitter ends trailed in the wild wind.

"Quite a sight, Mr. Tombler, behind you," Michael yelled over the storm. "We've got two monks driving us. Hope they're not taking us to their heavenly paradise."

"Hardly reassuring is it?" Tombler asked after a quick glance, "to see such a sight driving us through a gale."

"Gale? Hardly," said Farrell just returning to relieve the new crew. "This ain't got no gale. Just a bit of weather. In a gale, we'd hammer the hatch shut and put four men at the helm. If'in ya think this was adventurous, wait 'til ya has the Atlantic to deal with."

As the recruits pondered this, Michael spoke up. "How does your doctor attend to the injured when we're rocking so wildly?"

"Doctor? We have no surgeon. Mr. Cain or one of us does the best we can, when we can. They'll have ta wait 'til we have time to attend to 'em."

"Perhaps I could be of some assistance, Mr. Farrell."

"Can ya mend bones?"

"I once returned a cow to mobility. She didn't mind the limp. I was, unfortunately, not successful with a beloved mare."

"'Tis better 'n we has. Captain'll appreciate any help ya can offer." There was a shrill whistle from the quarterdeck. Farrell acknowledged. "But for now, your attention is needed on deck."

After hours of sorting tangled lines, Farrell sent Tombler and Hoecker below to the 'tween deck. He took Michael down another companionway to the crew's quarters under the quarterdeck.

CHAPTER 19

FOLLOWING FARRELL DOWN THE LADDER, MICHAEL HEARD A MAN moaning, "Jesus, sweet Jesus." It wasn't a prayer and its meaning was clear—much pain ahead. There were two injured sailors, one needing immediate attention.

In the same instant, Michael noticed something more remarkable. The mess, galley, and crew quarters stood in marked contrast to the murky accommodation for the indentureds in the 'tween deck. In this area under the quarterdeck, two lanterns provided sufficient light to reveal a spartan, well-ordered state of affairs. There was even a bit of warmth provided by the small galley firebox on the starboard side. There was plenty of headroom too. He didn't have to hunch over as in the hold.

Michael headed straight to the groaning man's side. It was Knob, the concertina player from the ship's dance just a night ago. He lay half-covered under a blanket on the deck, wedged up against the hull between a bulkhead and a secured bench in the crew's mess to serve as a makeshift sickbay. An unconscious sailor was lashed to a bench under the forward table.

Farrell assumed a formal tone. "Mr. Knob, I leave ya in the care of Mr. Michael Shea. Seems our fiddler has some medical experience."

"Mr. Knob, good to see you again. Sorry it's under this unpleasant circumstance. Now, what have we here?"

"Me leg's broken, badly, Mr. Shea. Hurts to no end, even to the slightest touch. Afraid to look at it."

"Mind if I take a look?"

"Aye, tenderly if ya can."

Michael turned to the cook who was busy behind a stew pot. "Sir, we need some assistance with a candle or lantern. Could you oblige?"

The cook gave Michael a wrinkled, gruff look. "Ain't me job, and I don't take no orders from no servant."

"It is a humble request, sir, not an order, to assist your shipmate in distress. And I'm not yet a servant. I am your passenger and therefore your ship's legal responsibility, and one who is directly responsible for making sure the captain has largess enough to pay your wages upon successful completion of this voyage."

Unable to comprehend this blur of wordage, the cranky cook complied. He hovered behind Michael, holding the lantern above Knob's knee area.

As Michael went to remove the blanket, Knob's whole body tensed. He expected the gruff treatment he had witnessed during his days on His Majesty's warships.

Instead Michael waited for Knob to relax. "Mr. Knob, please breathe long and slow." Michael waited. "Very good, Mr. Knob. Best if you can resist tensing up."

"How'm I supposed to do that?"

"Just think yourself through one of those new jigs we threw at ya." Michael half turned towards the cook. "If you don't mind, sir, the light would be better if you hold it closer." The light improved. "Much better, thank you, sir."

Returning to Knob, Michael made another request. "It might help if you could explain what happened on deck while I appraise the situation we have here. Just how did this calamity come about? Start from when we played that last set of quadrilles."

"After the dance, I jumped below to stow my concertina. Ran back on deck without me slicker. Didn't think it'd blow hard enough just then. Was following Farrell's orders to adjust sail. We was hurrying about cause if we could get 'er ta run 'head o' the storm, we'd be outta the Channel by daybreak."

As Knob recounted the minutia of sailing the ship, Michael got a closer look at the sailor's leg. The gentlest of probes sent pains ricocheting up Knob's leg. Knob stifled a yell. "Keep talking," Michael instructed.

"Ya, well then I was drenched by the sea and the cold startled me. It usually don't, but today were different. Was more than I'd expected. I was slow to jump when the mast cracked 'cause I ran into Cane." He nodded towards the unconscious sailor. "Cane weren't in no hurry like he should-a be. I pushed 'im hard ta get him out of me way, but took too long t'escape the wreckage. Don't seem fair. All 'e got were a bump on 'is head."

"Do I detect a bit of humour there?" Michael asked while continuing his inspection. "Light, please."

"Gallows humour," Knob answered. "Cane's a lucky one. 'e don't know what 'it 'im. Least not yet." There was a hint of a sardonic laugh in his voice. "That'll be some throbbin' headache."

"We'll see how lucky your Mr. Cane was in due course. First I must resolve how to address your wound. Am most interested right now in hearing your story. Please continue."

"Yes, *The Delight*'s sailing condition. Well, we should've spent more time refitting. But the owners don't care about a sailor's lot and quibblin' about repairs, do they, Cook? All they wants is fer us ta make port earlier than the next ship."

"Was unaware that the ship was unfit for sailing," Michael replied.

"Unfit? That's a stretch, we's just in need of repairs. Jesus! Do you have to do that?"

"My apologies, but I need to expose the area to study the break. I count three loose sections of bone. Two breaks below your knee. There's a lot of bleeding near your ankle."

Curiosity got the better of the cook. He took a look. The leg was a zigzag. He went woozy.

"Light, sir, light, if you please," Michael demanded. Cook returned to his illuminating duty.

The news devastated Knob. "Oh sweet Jesus. I'm done for."

"Premature to panic. I'm sure you'll be playing upon your concertina again. Please continue your narrative. Something about repairs?"

Knob's words escaped through clenched teeth, punctuated with short, sharp inhales. "Yes, the repairs. I know. Captain MacNeal had the same opinion, I 'eard. I 'eard 'im meself. Was raisin' a bulkhead, outside

Captain's cabin. I'm ship's carpenter and me duty were there at the time. Anyways, I heard 'im plain. Captain was much worried about the masts. Ow! Damn tender there, Mr. Shea."

"Thanks for letting me know. Please continue."

"Yes, the masts, 'e were sayin' both was suspect. Captain arguing with the owners, them Broot brothers. Captain wanted more time for repairs but dem Broots said ta repair them at sea, and Captain keeps tellin' dem ya needs good weather an' that ain't likely in a winter voyage. To wit, they dismisses his concerns. 'Just repair on the run,' they tells the captain.'" Knob inhaled and stifled a groan.

"Walter Broot?" asked Michael, "I've heard of a factor in London with that name."

"The same. Gots 'is own fleet, 'e 'as. Three, maybe four ships, but 'e keeps ownership under a-hush. It's why 'e only visits at night. Broot don't care 'bout sailin' or ships, just the profits. That behemoth of a brother always in tow. Devil's a-brewin' in that one, I'll tells ya that."

"Indeed," Michael said. "What were you saying about the repairs and running away?"

"Ah, ye lubber! Not runnin' away. Means wind's behind ya, pushing ya forward. Broot meant ta repair at sea. That's what I overheard his 'lordship' tellin' the captain, 'No more delays!' Precious few secrets on board, but dem Broots don't seem to remember that. I kept up a steady hammerin' during this so's not ta rouse suspicion I were listenin' in."

"You double as carpenter, quite handy, I'd say. Is there an extra pay ration for you then?"

"That's a laugh. We all does what we can."

"I see. Anyone double as surgeon?"

"Hardly. The only medicine man we 'as is unconscious behind ya. Cane's no better'in a barber. Yer on yer own. God, have mercy on me."

"Mercy is always welcome, Mr. Knob, but this does not have to become a mortal wound if we can address it properly. Still, prayer would be most helpful. Would you mind asking if the Almighty has it in his heart to fill us both with courage?"

"Now, sir?"

"As soon as you are able would be good."

Michael half turned to address the cook. "Sir, I will need some assistance in this operation. There are some sturdy lads among the passengers that would be most useful. Could you fetch them? I need, in particular, Danny O'Mara, Martin Tombler, and Edwin Hoecker."

The cook resisted. "Ain't my place to be a-minglin' with the servant class."

Michael stood up to face the cook nose to nose. "Sir, your shipmates are in a critical state. It will be on your shoulders if we don't come to their assistance quickly. I'm sure your captain will consider any inaction on your part as a dereliction of your duty."

Cook acquiesced. "I'll relay your concerns to Mr. Farrell."

"Much obliged. Please insist upon O'Mara, Tombler, and Hoecker."

Chapter 20

When the cook returned with the recruits, Michael greeted them. "Gentlemen, thanks for answering the call." He grabbed Danny's shoulder. "Good to see you, Danny. Feeling any better than you look?"

"Barely. Vomitin's eased, still woozy. Droppin' by to visit 'tis sure a welcome break from the filth we're bathing in. Stuck on that ladder, I were wishin' ta be back on land."

"On land is it now, Danny? And after all your dreams of sailing to America?" Michael chided.

"Don't get me started, I'll use ya for a bucket."

"Keep your humour fired, Danny boy. You're gonna need it."

Michael turned his attention to all three huddled at the foot of the stairway. "Gentlemen, I need your assistance with Mr. Knob's broken leg." He lowered his voice to just reach their ears. "He has a most severe wound. With your help, we may yet save his leg and return him to duty. The other fellow got a nasty knock on the head. Don't know what we can do for him. For the present, we'll leave him wrapped in that blanket."

When they saw the moaning Knob, their own miseries faded.

"As you can see, gentlemen, we can expect much resistance when I put his bones in order. No way to avoid the pain if we're to save him. Have any assisted in a bone repair before?"

None responded. In the pause, Knob realized he was on display. He yelled at them. "Stop yer gawking. Them wide eyes ain't helpin' me none."

Michael persisted in directing his comments away from Knob. "It will hurt him greatly until we get it right." He looked each man in the eye. "You have to ignore his agony, lads. No matter what happens. It's the only way to help him."

"Mr. Shea," Knob roared. "I knows it's gonna hurt. It already hurts. Get on with it."

As Michael led his crew, they too inspected the galley, mesmerized by the space, light, and warmth and the smell of a cooked stew.

"A fine set of loblollies" was Knob's greeting. "I trust you'll do yer best, lads. Don't let me howls get under yer skin. Just get it done. I thank ye now for your help. Share a laugh tomorrow."

Michael got to work. "Danny, could you roust up strips of wood, three feet long would be best. We'll need it to bind Knob's leg once his bones are in order. Anything solid will do, and cloth, rope, yarn. Something to tie altogether. Needle and thread too."

Knob half-righted himself and barked. "Cook, take this lad to the sail room. Help 'im gather what 'e needs."

Cook defied Knob. "I answer not to servants or crew, only to the captain."

Danny took the initiative. He untied an iron kettle from an overhead brace and slammed it against the galley bulkhead, just missing the cook's head. When the startled cook turned around, Danny muscled the kettle into the cook's chest.

"Ya ready?" Danny barked. The cook froze. "Weren't a question." The cook gave up his resistance and led Danny away.

During this drama, Michael directed Tombler and Hoecker. "Mr. Tombler, could you lash Knob's left leg to the bench. Tightly. Don't want him kicking away while I set the leg. Mr. Hoecker, his arms too if you please."

"Mr. Knob, are there any medicines available? Laudanum is what I'm after."

"Jimmy Cane there keeps the key. Should be 'round 'is neck. First cabin outside the captain's, larboard." He nodded towards the dim passageway.

Michael returned empty handed. "Only empty vials. Appears your Mr. Cane has a taste for laudanum. Would explain why his being slow on deck. All we have for you is the leather. Bite on that. Better than grinding your remaining teeth."

When Danny returned, they got underway. The powerful Tombler's task was to sit behind Knob, wrap his arms around him, and hold him steady as Michael worked. Knob did his best, but his agony filled the cabin as Michael guided the bones up, down, and sideways. It took Michael multiple attempts to realign each fragment. Not one made it back into its proper place on the first attempt. Knob passed out.

"Thank God for that," Michael said as he aligned the last part of the leg, splinted it, and studied the open wound.

"Danny could you round me up some thread through one of those needles? Quick now before he revives."

It took a few minutes for Danny to get his thick fingers to do the work. Michael dressed the area around the broken skin, wiped out as much blood as he could, gathered up the skin, and threaded it together. He bandaged the leg with strips of a red calico shirt that the cook supplied.

"Gentlemen, now would be a good time to get Knob off the floor and into a bed," Michael said, surveying the galley and mess area, "or whatever these sailors use when they're hurting."

"Sick bay's under the fo'c'sle," Cook grunted. "Rough work fer lubbers getting''im there in a storm. Best leave 'im 'til the watch is relieved."

"Why don't we just lower these tables?"

Cook shook his head in disgust. "How ya think they kin manage on top of a table rollin' about in their state? Hard enough for a live jack ta hold 'is dinner down."

Michael reinspected the mess. Cook extended his lecture. "Even if it could work, which it won't, crew won't take kindly to the loss of their mess. When their watch is done, and they're looking for supper, they don't like no surprises."

Michael deferred to Cook's experience. "Gentlemen, into the hammocks with Cane for now. We'll leave Knob where he is. Can't see how that leg'll fit in a hammock."

As they stuffed Cane into a hammock, Farrell bounded out of the companionway. "Lads, time to clear out if you don't mind. Double watch is ending. The boys is cold and hungry. Makes 'em unpleasant until proper fed."

Farrell gave Knob a look. "This won't do. We must remove Knob."

"With pleasure, sir," Michael answered. "Just where would you suggest? Hammock won't do. As you can see, we need to keep his leg laid out."

Farrell pondered. "Remove him to Cain's cabin? Lash him in the bunk?"

"Danny, you heard the man," Michael said. He didn't want Farrell to reconsider. "Mr. Tombler, could you and Danny carry Mr. Knob to the cabin? Follow Mr. Farrell. Mr. Hoecker and I will deal with Cane."

A bell rang. "Double watch's over," Farrell said. "We be done none too soon." His words were obscured by the bustle of sailors crowding into the galley, four to a table, and jabbering all at once. One by one they made a visit to the cook's kettle to get a stewy glop and chucks of hard bread. They helped themselves to a beer keg, filling their squat mugs only halfway to limit spills as the ship bounced, swayed, and rolled.

"See what I mean about getting a move on?" Farrell said. "All the best manners, too."

After getting Knob and Cane settled, Farrell waved towards the other end of the mess area. It was his way of breaking the news to them that they were expected to return to the 'tween deck.

Michael grabbed Danny's arm and pushed him inside the cabin. "Danny, keep yer eye on the patient," he said so the others could hear. "Mr. Farrell, we need to make arrangements to prevent any spread of fever, should that arise."

Farrell gave a start at "fever." He gave Michael a worried look.

"Now don't you go a-worrying just yet, Mr. Farrell. It's a routine caution when a bone breaks the skin like that. Infection is Knob's next concern. We must keep an eye on him." He put an arm around Farrell's shoulder and picked up his pace down the passageway with Farrell in tow. Michael kept up the chatter.

"Seeing as Daniel has survived the pox already, he'll be safe while he's on watch. I think it best if we sling another hammock for Daniel's vigil. Would that be all right, Mr. Farrell? He'll have to share the fever watch with me. But first, I'd like to attend to this Mr. Cane. Can you give me a hand here?"

Farrell stood by, not sure whether to question what just transpired or lend a hand with Cane.

Michael kept the patter going. "Ah, good, see here, Mr. Farrell?" Michael made a show of putting his ear close to Cane's mouth. "He still breathes, and by the smell of him, it's clear where your laudanum disappeared to." Without pausing Michael motioned to Cane's head. He parted the thick grey hair above the right ear. "See how he has received this massive contusion. Must have been quite a blow. I'd be quite surprised if his skull were not broken. Have you seen this type of injury before?"

Farrell looked uneasy, almost noxious. Farrell followed Michael's fingers as they probed the swollen area.

"See where Cane's skull bulges? Watch," Michael said laying it on thick to keep Farrell's attention away from Danny in the cabin with Knob. He gave Cane's skull a slight push so it would flex.

Farrell shivered at the sight.

"As I feared. Cracked skull. Not sure what we can do for him, other than pray."

"If I may be frank, Mr. Shea," Farrell whispered across Cane's body, "I find it most distressing ta see me once vigorous mates laid out so helpless. Storms, gales, and hurricanes, I knows what to do. But medical repairs? I'm afraid I have no idea of where to begin. Makes me feel helpless. 'Tis a frightful feelin', not knowin' what ta do. 'Tis reassurin' you're here."

"Very kind of you to say, Mr. Farrell. I felt the same before I studied. Spent several years assisting me patron on his rounds, attending the sick, watching, listening, observing, practicing, dissecting."

"Dissecting?"

"Sometimes on people. My patron lectured on medicine at Faculté des Arts, in Paris. He was quite renowned. Fond of bringing students to his manor. We'd set up in a barn to study anatomy, cut a few things out, that kind of work, when cadavers weren't available in town."

"You cut up real people?"

"Of course. But not like we was butchering like cannibals. They were quite dead, I assure you, Mr. Farrell. There is a formal procedure, out of respect for the contribution the dead make for the living."

Michael gave Farrell an intent look. He whispered to create an intimate conversation. "Mostly we dissected criminals. They didn't mind. A simple penance for the grief they caused during their time on earth."

Farrell appeared disturbed, so Michael laid it on thicker.

"I practiced along with my patron's students. Dr. DeSuigny harped on the importance of skin-mending skills. Like I just did on Knob's leg. It's a lot like tailoring. The better the skill, the smaller and tighter the stitching." Michael kept talking as they lashed Cane into the hammock. "Instead of wool and linen, it's skin. Human or animal, the skin does amazing things, Mr. Farrell. With care, you can limit the scarring. I learned how to turn a bladder into all manner of useful items. Odd texture at first, but then one does get used to odd things."

The mate's squeak interrupted. "Mr. Farrell. On the quarterdeck."

"That be the captain a-calling. He'll be wanting 'n appraisal of Knob and Cane."

"I'd be glad to assist in any way, Mr. Farrell."

"Join me then. Wait outside the quarterdeck until yer called."

CHAPTER 21

ONCE ON DECK, MICHAEL REALIZED THE ROLLICKING STORM HAD GIVEN way to a crescent moon peeking through the black and grey clouds and a few stars twinkled to keep it company. No longer tossing about, *The Delight* sailed steady with a slight lean south towards France. Michael soon learned that in nautical talk, the ship "were heelin' ta larboard." Michael watched the wind whip the tops of channel swells into a creamy froth. They sparkled white in the occasional moonlight and then colorless when the cloud cover returned.

At the foot of the quarterdeck, Farrell waved him over. "We wait here for Captain's call."

"Rather an intriguing evening, Mr. Farrell, almost pleasant." He savored the predawn air. "How is it that the sea can be so agitated while we enjoy this soft breeze?"

"Breeze only seems soft whilst we enjoy this great run." He pointed towards the stern. "Wind's behind, pushin' us. Don't feel it sailin' like this. The mate says we'll make our turn south by morning if this breeze keeps up. Not so pleasant if we was beatin' against the wind, like them poor buggers." He pointed to a white set of sails heeling very sharply. "When close hauled like that, ya make great speed, but ya ain't really goin' nowhere, what with all the back an' forth ya have ta do to beat up the Channel."

Michael was also surprised to find several indentureds milling about on deck, taking in the cold air. He nodded hello to his new friends, Tombler and Hoecker. Then he spied the Rawlings couple. He couldn't see Mrs. Rawlings's or any of the ladies' faces. Above and below deck, they hid themselves in oversized shawls and hoods. But it was clear it was

Mrs. Rawlings, her full belly pushing out her cloak as she leaned back against the weight to stretch her back for relief. Her husband held her arm to provide support as they shuffled around the main mast.

"I see your prayers have been answered," Michael called out.

The couple turned. Mr. Rawlings gave him a quizzical look.

"Your child to be, sir. When last we spoke, we were making a prayer the babe would wait out the storm."

"Our prayer was indeed answered," the husband replied. "We thank you for your concern."

"Mr. Farrell," the mate called from the quarterdeck, "Captain awaits."

During Michael's presentation, Captain MacNeal paced while listening, shaking his head at the news that he had lost two of his crew and was now even more shorthanded.

"A tough loss isn't it, Mr. Farrell?"

"Aye, sir, 'tis."

"Your thoughts then, on making up the loss?"

Being asked to take part in strategic planning was a new opportunity for Farrell. He didn't hesitate. "Sir. First, I'd suggest Mr. Shea here be asked to take over Cane's sick bay duties. He showed a steady hand when he were fixin' an' stichin' Knob's leg."

"Has he now? Agreed." MacNeal eyed Michael. "We are lucky to draw upon your services, Mr. Shea. I hope you'll be able to familiarize yourself with our medical tools and supplies."

"A most kind offer, Captain. Might I inquire then as—"

MacNeal cut him off. "Mr. Shea, this is not a discussion of an offer of employment. It is an order! It was presented politely considering you landsmen are unused to the necessities of the sea. In the future, you will be mindful not to offer an opinion unless asked. There is no room for idle chatter on this quarterdeck."

Michael started to back away. "Mr. Shea," MacNeal commanded. "As ship's doctor, you have not been dismissed."

Michael froze at this second reprimand and stiffened in imitation of Farrell while before the captain.

In a calmer voice, MacNeal addressed the sailor. "And now, what about the forward watch, Mr. Farrell?"

"Sir. I'd recruit from the indentureds. There be some lads who'd make passable sailors if'in they was of a mind ta learn. Two performed quite well after the trouble with the foremast, sir."

"A sound plan, Mr. Farrell. Add 'em to your foredeck. However, do not invite them to mess with the crew right away. Their help is welcomed, but equal status must be earned. They are not yet rated. Test 'em first, then report to me when they're ready to be rated."

"Sir."

After the mate whispered in MacNeal's ear, he added another order: "And a carpenter. See what you can find 'til Mr. Knob recovers."

"Will inquire amongst the passengers, Sir."

"Thank you, Mr. Farrell. Gentlemen, you may take your leave." MacNeal paced to windward. The mate gave Farrell a smile and flicked his finger across his nose.

CHAPTER 22

"MICHAEL, MY FRIEND, YOU'RE A MIRACLE TA BEHOLD!" DANNY COULDN'T contain his joy. "Ta be outta that stink hole and luxuriatin' in a cabin? With a door? Privacy?"

"At your service, as always." Michael was all smiles, jammed in the cabin with Danny leaning on the edge of the bunk next to the unconscious Knob. The comatose Cain hung in a hammock at Knob's feet. Michael wedged himself next to a small desk with its medical chest. A small lantern, gimbaled over the desk, was bright enough to read under, and it provided a veneer of warmth.

"The real thanks goes to the storm Poseidon brought upon us." Michael warmed his hands over the top of the lantern. "Give him credit for breaking Knob's leg and smashing Cane's skull." Michael gave Knob a quick look. "I have no idea if Knob will walk again. He's in a serious way. Am most anxious about infection. He'll lose the leg if the gangrene sets in."

"Jest put yer healing hands on him, Michael. Yer magic's worked before."

"It's not magic, Danny."

"There be somethin' ya do that heals. I've seen it happen. Yer patients calm down when you're 'round 'em. They usually gits better."

Michael let Danny's comment settle in. He took Danny's arm and whispered, "If asked, let it be thought I'm worried about fever. Knob does risk and infection, maybe gangrene, but let's call it fever. And by fever I mean the pox. Any mention of fever seems to scare these sailors to the marrow. Don't say more. Let their imaginations wander. Hopefully, a bit of fear'll keep 'em from prying too close about our cabin arrangement."

"How long do ya think we kin hide out here?"

Michael waved a hand at Cain. "Depends on his recovery. MacNeal has appointed me ship's doctor 'til Cane recovers. Until then, we get access to this fine accommodation."

"All four of us?"

"Better than that filthy hold."

Danny stretched out on the floor to see if it might suit for sleeping. "I could build us a bunk if you can get me some tools. Would be much better than the floor."

The idea of Danny building things sparked an idea in Michael. "Danny, I'm curious, what's three times five?"

"Fifteen."

"Fifteen times six?"

"Ninety. Stop, Michael. I know numbering." He sat up, fingers tapping his head. "'Tis all in me 'ead. Me da' drilled it in'ta me. I apprenticed with him. Had us a great system. Like when we make a cabinet for a fancy house or cuttin' in a staircase. Dad would plan out the dimensions. He'd call out a perimeter. I'd give him the boardage ta make it. 'T'ain't hard, Michael."

"Braggart."

"Why ya so curious about me numbering?"

"Might mean a job for you. Knob here was ship's carpenter. He won't be sawing or hammering anytime soon. Captain MacNeal asked our friend Farrell to find a replacement. I'm thinking you should make yourself known."

"What's the pay?"

"Better accommodation, I should think. Better food than what we're offered in steerage. Haven't you noticed the crew gets something hot to eat? You'd have to answer to Farrell. Think you can do that without arguing?"

"Anythin' ta' stay outta that stink hole."

Michael took a close look at his friend's face. "Danny, your color's returning. You don't have that grey look of death about ya anymore."

"Am feelin' a bit improved, now that ya mention it. Not so bad with the ship's sailin steady like. Perhaps I kin make it to America after all without—"

The clanging of the ship's bell interrupted them.

"How many was that?" Michael asked.

"Who knows. Six or seven at least. Why?"

Michael poked his head out the door. "Crew change. I'm thinking it's dinner or supper or whatever they call a meal at sea. Let's join 'em. Better play nice to that cook this time. He was none too happy with us earlier."

"That'll take some doin'."

"I'll say. Maybe smart of ya to kiss and make up."

The Delight suddenly lurched to starboard. Danny fell back against the bunk and bulkhead. Michael had to grab the desk to avoid falling over. "Danny. We've made the turn. We're in the Atlantic. Farrell said we'd head south once we cleared the Channel. Let's take us a look."

CHAPTER 23

THEIR EXCITEMENT DIMMED AS THEY STUMBLED DOWN AN UNSTEADY passageway. The ship's disjointed rocking had returned and intensified. The crew had already scrambled on deck, their respite short lived. The cook dosed his fire and was securing his pots and equipment.

On deck, instead of a beautiful ocean vista, the musicianers found an angry ocean, waves breaking over the bow, the deck awash, scuppers overwhelmed. On the quarterdeck, Captain MacNeal stood to windward holding on to the taffrail with his right hand, yelling commands at two men struggling with the helm. Michael and Danny were not three feet away from the captain, yet MacNeal's commands were lost in the screaming wind and the crunch of waves exploding over the sides. The mate orchestrated action high in the mainmast with a speaking trumpet jammed against his mouth, yelling commands to sailors aloft. Whether they heard him or not, work progressed as the sailors knew their task.

Danny grabbed Michael's arm and pointed towards Farrell, who was at the foremast directing his crew. Danny leaned right into Michael's ear to yell, "How da ya do that?" They marveled at the sight of sailors high in the rigging, their bare feet balanced on a thin line with their stomachs gripping the yardarm as they wrestled with heavy wet canvas. As the crew started their descent, the mate noticed Danny and Michael. He yelled into his trumpet but couldn't make himself heard over the screaming wind. He scrambled over to shout in Michael's ear. "Get yerselves below. Deck's no place for lubbers."

Michael acknowledged him with nod and headed towards the crew's mess.

The mate grabbed Michael's arm. "Mr. Shea. Yer duty's 'tween decks. We're in for a blow! Reassure the indentureds, calm 'em best ya can. Knob and Cain 'ave ta wait."

Michel and Danny hesitated at the thought of returning to the vile hold. But Michael could see Captain MacNeal scowling. "Aye, sir," Michael answered as he heard Farrell do. He grabbed Danny's arm. "Come on. We can bear it." He led Danny by the arm down the ladder into the hold. The mate slammed the hatch shut behind them. In the darkness, Michael and Danny cringed to the squeal of rope against iron as the mate lashed the hatch, locking them below.

The stench of sickness overcame them both. It forced them both to sit at the foot of the ladder to let their senses acclimate to the smell and sound of incessant vomiting. Children's voices added a plaintive chorus of "mother," "mamma," "father," and "papa" all at once. The men voiced their anxieties as bass and baritones. The women added alto and soprano lines. The tenors tied them all together. It was a choir of suffering.

One lad, whose family had set up camp near the hatchway, was spared the sickness. He weathered the rocking secured in a bowline his father had tied to keep the boy from wandering from his clan. Farrell had taught the men three basic knots before they had left London. This father had practiced his lessons on his son.

The boy wasn't at all concerned with the storm. "Did ya see, did ya see *The Black Cloud?*" he asked like a hungry chick peeping for attention, his wide-eyed inquisitiveness in stark contrast to the sounds of the sick.

"Ya mean the pirate *Black Cloud?*" Danny asked.

"The same. Did you see her?"

"Why ya worrying 'bout pirates, lad?" Danny asked. "'T'aint nobody gonna be boardin' in such a dreadful storm."

"We're McMahon, from Ballycory. Me brother told me ta keep me eyes open for Gráinne Ní Mháille. She's mad 'cause our family killed Hugh deLacy."

"Ya mean the pirate Grace O'Malley?" Danny asked. "Me Irish fails me much these days."

"The same," the boy replied. "I'm a scared. She'll seek her revenge. Conor says they'll turn me in ta a monkey slave and make me pour their grog."

Danny chuckled and poked Michael. "Not likely, lad. Gráinne Ní Mháille sails no more, nor any of her clan. Ya kin be sure of that. They're all sleepin' safe in Tír na nÓg. It's been one hundred years or more since they last sailed. We've nothing ta fear from Gracie O'Malley."

"Ya sure?"

"Never could I lie to a fine Irishman such as yerself." Danny extended his hand to the boy. "Danny O'Mara, at your service, laddie."

The boy put his tiny hand in Danny's. "Your hand's scratchy."

"Aye, laddie, 'tis. I'm a carpenter. Been batterin' me hands on wood and nails for ten years now. How is it now that we meet on this grand adventure?"

"Bailiffs came, took all our corn. Walked off with Nobly 'n Molly."

"Yer sisters?"

"Milk cows," said the boy's father, rousing the energy to enter the conversation. "That's enough, Jimmy." To Danny, he introduced himself. "James McMahon, farmer, blacksmith, farrier. Ain't no work fer the likes of us. English turned me family out in '41, during the Frost. I were no more 'n Jimmy's size. Farmers we was. Next breath, we're payin' rent to starve on our own land. Me dad apprenticed me to a blacksmith in Dublin so's I could send wages ta supplement me parents."

"How'd ya end up on *The Delight* then?" Danny asked.

"Hoped to find work smithin'. But London's like Dublin. No work, too many workers."

"Familiar story," Danny replied. "'T'ain't never enough work for the Irish. Not enough for the English neither. Don't matter where we're born, there just ain't enough work."

"Aye, ya speak a truth. Where ya away to?"

"Mary's Land. You?"

"Anywhere's there's work. Don't matter where, long as there's work, steady wages. I'm bound seven years so's I kin keep me family intact. How long for you lads?"

"Four years," Danny answered. "I'm a joiner. Michael here's been apprenticed to a physician."

Michael changed the conversation. "How are your fellow passengers? Are any in need?"

"Hard to say. When I'm not spillin' me own guts, I mostly stays an' tends ta the missus. She tends ta me. Little Jimmy's the only one fit. His brother Conor's in a bad way, with his mother." He indicated the cot next to his. "None of us kin keep food down."

"Might I have a look?" Michael asked, sidling over to the cot.

"Care for a visit with the apprentice doctor, Julia?"

Mrs. McMahon took her time to respond and then only turned her head towards her husband.

Mr. McMahon rambled on. "Been laid low like this since we left the Thames. 'Tis why we didn't join the dance. Was a lovely sound down here, all them feets a tappin' and slidin'. Just us and the Palatines back there." In the cold darkness, not even shadows were discernible in the far corner McMahon was pointing to. "Can't see nobody now, but we could hear them. They've hung drapery for privacy. None of us down here is fit for socializing, but them ladies do sing pretty."

"Ladies?" Danny inquired. "Thought they was nuns in them cloaks."

"Could be a disguise," Michael chimed in, "to protect themselves from the likes of you."

Danny ignored the ribbing. "Any chance ya got a peek at their faces?"

"None as yet," McMahon replied. "Can't vouch for their fairness, but I will tell ya that there's beautiful music in 'em. Had ourselves a fine concert when the first storm eased. When the ladies sang their prayers, at least I think were prayers, they turned that gruff Hessian talk in'ta somethin' heavenly. There was even a bit of 'Over the Hills' from one of the girls. I was longing for her to let loose with it, but the elder one put a hush on her."

"Perhaps I should offer our services to accompany them. What d'ya say, Michael, ya game?"

"By all . . ." His reply was lost in a deafening roar. *The Delight* shuddered and pitched violently towards starboard as a giant wall of ocean slammed into the opposite side of the ship. The force of the wave opened cracks in the seams of the hull and let the black sea pour. Another flood cascaded in from under the lashed hatch.

The Delight let loose a nerve-rattling creaking as the hull stretched towards its breaking point. This was joined by a menacing, low-pitched moan from the mast as it twisted up through the decks and into the storm. The groaning gained in volume and pitch as the seams, lines, timbers, blocks, and joints fought to restrain the mast.

The wave's assault threw Mrs. McMahon and child, still in their cot, onto Michael as he reeled backward into Mr. McMahon. Danny was thrown clear across the hold into a jumble of bedding now strewn about in the mix of filth and sea water two feet deep.

The passengers beyond all jolted to starboard and found themselves dislodged from their camps and into their neighbors'. Little Jimmy was one of the few who held his ground. He straddled the ship's center line in the hatchway, secured in his bowline, grabbing for the hatchway bulkhead.

Then, in a blink, *The Delight* righted herself, reversing the dislocation. The hull's timbers realigned, once again locking out the sea. The mast steadied. The stunned passengers sat still and silent in a collective attempt to understand what had just happened.

At first, everyone was holding their breath, afraid any exhale would again topple the ship. Then, one by one, sounds of breathing and wheezing. Despite her weakness, Mrs. McMahon rose out of her cot to kneel in the stench and darkness, "Hail Mail, full of grace . . ." Mr. McMahon joined her at "the Lord is with thee." He then moved to help her back into her cot. She could barely move without his aid.

Once she was resettled with Michael's help, Mr. McMahon sang out a mournful verse. "My Lord is my refuge and my fortress, in him will I trust." When he repeated his refrain three more times, Michael added a harmony. Prayer ended, McMahon wrapped Little Jimmy in a bear hug.

"How you holding up, my brave lad?"

"I asked Jesus to help mamma."

"I'm sure he's listening to ya, Jimmy." He gave his son a hug. "Work in a word or two for all of us if'in ya could."

As Jimmy mumbled his prayer, the indentureds offered their own private pleas for salvation as they listened to the groaning of the ship and the crew's battle against the angry ocean. Michael wasn't alone in thinking that the rapid *tap tap tap* of their feet sounded like a carpenter's steady hammering of nails into a coffin lid.

CHAPTER 24

Later, with the storm still raging, Farrell squeezed through the hatch, lantern in hand. A flood of seawater accompanied him. Halfway down the ladder he started barking into the cavernous dark hold: "Tombler, Shea, Hoecker, O'Mara. On deck." He yelled his command a second time before the ship rocked and he was knocked from the ladder. His landing was softened by the sea in the 'tween deck. Farrell hung the lantern and used his hands as a megaphone to repeat his command.

"Jesus, we're coming." Tombler was the only one to answer Farrell's shadowy outline.

"Hands on deck," Farrell yelled. "Move it. Can't leave the hatch unlashed."

"Where you been, Farrell, whilst we've been drownin' down here?" It was Hoecker who braved a complaint.

"You'll see, soon enough."

"What's our status, Mr. Farrell?" Michael called out of the darkness. Danny swayed in his hammock, snoring away.

"Mr. Shea, report to the captain. Tombler to the helm. O'Mara, Hoecker with me to start the pumps."

Michael pushed Danny to roust him. "Come on, Danny, it's a chance to get outta this stye." He rolled out of his hammock and found his feet underwater. "And get our feet out the damn ocean." As he leaned across his hammock to give Danny a poke, there was a thundering crash, infinitely louder than the last.

Michael found himself in a free fall towards starboard along with everybody and everything loose in the hold: cots, baggage, stools, blankets, clothes, and tools. It was a waterfall of bodies, some headfirst, some sideways, others sliding feet first through the inboard sea and crashing into a tangled pile of bodies and debris.

Those who had set up their camps along the starboard hull were buried and held underwater by the weight of their fellow passengers, all crushed into a wretched heap of human ballast.

Another monster wave had slammed into *The Delight*'s larboard side, throwing her sideways into the sea, her starboard side now underwater, her keel out of the water ready to slice into the next rogue wave. The Atlantic had the ship laying sideways. In such a death grip, it's only a matter of seconds before any ship, no matter how stout, will flounder and sink.

Everybody in the 'tween deck faced their final agony in a cold wet panic, in the dark, all writhing and struggling against the sea and the weight of their fellow passengers.

Danny was still in his hammock suspended above the melee. "Michael!" No answer. His voice was lost in a cacophony of gurgling screams, the ship's groaning and the crunching of baggage and equipment. Like Danny, Little Jimmy McMahon swung above the pileup secured in his bowline. He kicked about wildly in mid-air and screamed for his parents.

It seemed like an eternity, but only a second or two later, the ship reverberated with the tearing sound of breaking timber. The main mast snapped somewhere above deck. An instant later, the sea swept away the foremast as well. Relieved of this weight, *The Delight* wrestled loose from the ocean's death grip and righted herself, sending the pile of bodies and possessions tumbling back across the 'tween deck. The indentureds gasped for breath as they rose out of their watery graves.

This was followed by a mad scramble of frantic passengers searching for their loved ones. Against a sloshing backdrop of debris and bodies rose terrified screams. All manner of replies echoed back and forth as loved ones tried to relocate each other.

Most were reunited. But not all happily. A man shrieking, "Marta, Marta dear, breathe! Please my dear, breathe!" was Michael's first memory when he surfaced. In the darkness, he pushed himself out of the black water up on his knees, his hands on the deck as he coughed and wheezed the sea out of his lungs, the mix of sea and sewage dripped from his hair. He shook his head to get the mess off his face.

"Oh Jesus, sweet Jesus, Marta, breathe!"

The voice was right next to Michael. He could barely make out a lifeless form wrapped in a drenched winter cape. He grabbed the man's arm to right himself. "Get her on her knees, head down."

"Danny," Michael called out in the darkness. "You alive?"

"Been better," came a hoarse reply.

The man couldn't manage his wife's limp frame. Desperation set in. "My wife, she won't move." He was panting, shivering, and crying all at once.

"Danny, find me," Michael yelled. "Farrell? Mr. Farrell? Bring us your lamp."

To the man wrestling with the woman, Michael ordered: "On her side now, face in your lap. Head out of the water." Michael found the woman's body in the dark and got his arms around her waist and with effort, turned the lifeless form sideways, facing her husband. "Any response?" he yelled over the commotion.

"None."

"Damn." Michael tried to maneuver the woman's knees together. He couldn't manage it, as her legs were wrapped in her cape. "Get this cape off," he yelled, but the man was frozen in fear. Michael tried to wrestle the cape away but couldn't get the head free.

"Danny, quickly."

"Already here, direct me."

"Lift her arse up in the air. I'll wedge her knees together, you lift. Get yer hands under her stomach."

Danny straddled his legs on either side of the lifeless woman and did as instructed. Together they raised her rear up as if she were prostrating herself before a god. This forced her head into the man's gut, her mouth barely above the water. The man held her head between his hands. He was shaking uncontrollably.

"Pry her mouth open. See if we can drain any water."

The man tried to obey. Michael inched his grip forward, his hands now joined at the bottom of the woman's rib cage. He started pressing up and down pulling against her sternum.

"Anything?"

"Nothin'."

"Why can't we raise her any higher?"

Farrell arrived. His light revealed why. Two men recovering from their own near drowning were kneeling on the cape, holding Marta down. Danny pushed them off. Still the cape wouldn't budge. It was snagged under a pile of debris.

"Knife. I need a knife."

Farrell offered Michael his. Michael ripped through the cape, separating it from the hood. Michael traced the hood's closing ribbon to the lady's mouth. She had swallowed the ends while gasping for breath underwater. Michael gently eased the material out. Air passage cleared, he backed up and again jammed his strength against her sternum.

"Anything?"

"No."

Michael renewed his attack on her chest, his hands on the inside of each breast. Still no breathing. Michael pried open her mouth and appeared to be giving her an awkward kiss. The husband was appalled but couldn't speak. Michael parted lips with the girl and took a deep breath and covered her mouth with his, blowing air into her mouth. He did this several more times. When he stopped to recover his own breath, the girl twitched and gagged. Her legs kicked. Michael rolled her on her right shoulder. She vomited in her husband's lap.

"Marta? Breathe girl, breathe," the man begged.

She gulped for air and convulsed another shot of vomit all at once. Then she spit on her own and started coughing. Her breathing, at first shallow, became deeper as she shivered under her slime-drenched nightshirt.

Scared and exhausted, the group lingered in the black water. Farrell's light revealed Marta as one of the Palatines, indeed a delicate girl, not yet twenty Michael guessed, reclining in the bosom of her husband. Her eyelids fluttered as she tried to return to the living. Her gloved hands, clenched in fists, crossed across her chest to fight the shivering.

"If you don't mind, sir, sit her upright. We want her to vomit and spit as much as she will."

The man complied, still holding his dear Marta. "Such sweet breathing. I've never so welcomed such a sound, my love."

"May I?" Michael didn't wait for permission. He removed Marta's head scarf and used it to wipe the vomit from the girl's face. He freed a matted mess of curly, straw-colored hair that had been tied up in twin ponytails, now mostly undone. Farrell's light also revealed a bloodied nose, deep scratches on her forehead, a swelling right eye, and more of her bosom than a lady would like. Michael covered her with his jacket.

Marta revived enough to stare at Michael, confused as to her situation. He held his hand in front of her face and watched her focus on it. He moved his hand. She followed it with both eyes. Michael smiled.

"Danke," barely escaped her lips.

Farrell didn't wait to witness other reunions and rescues. "Tombler, Hoecker, O'Mara," he bellowed. "If you ain't drowned, get yerselves on deck. Mr. Shea, Captain'll need a count of dead an' injured. No dallyin', report as soon as you know. Tend to 'em later."

Chapter 25

It was well into daylight when Michael wiggled through the half-opened hatch. Sheets of sideways rain from the black cloud cover pelted him and the ship. He instantly lost his footing and had to crawl on the slick deck to prop himself up against the hatch. There he hung on as *The Delight* lurched this way and that, taking a new direction from every wave.

"Lifelines," Farrell yelled over the storm, handing one to Michael and pulling him up. He led the way up the ladder, having collected Michael for his audience with the captain. Farrell grabbed Michael's shoulder and pointed to the rumps of two masts poking through the deck and wreckage.

"We're adrift," he yelled. "Helpless. Can't set no sail. Can't rig none neither in this wind. Lost the mate when we broached, God rest his soul."

Michael nodded and crossed himself.

"Mate had just untethered himself ta go below when the wave hit. Had gone to get more hands on the helm." Farrell pointed this time to the quarterdeck where Tombler and Hoecker had joined the helmsman struggling to hold a course. "They're puttin' their backs to it best they kin, but ta no avail. We're at the mercy of wind and wave. Not much we kin do, other than hold on," he lashed the hatch shut, "and pray they kin keep us in front of the next wave."

Farrell sidled up to Michael, crouching low against the closed hatch.

"Captain's in a bad, bad way. He watched the mate go down. He'd a-gone down with 'im, weren't for the lifelines. Captain and the helmsmen was hanging on for dear life 'til the ship righted herself. Mate was swept aways. Captain says the mate was clinging to the maintop when he last saw 'im. Mate waved him a goodbye, knowing his fate. Captain's very dark about it. Mate and he was close. Very close. Ten years or more at sea they was. Survived many a misadventure, they did." After a pause, "Any dead below?"

"Two. A lad and his mum. Found 'em too late," Michael's voice faltered, "drowned in the wash of water. They was held under too long by the weight of the loose baggage." Michael throat tightened. He stifled tears. "Danny and I did best we could, same as with Marta." Michael composed himself. "The lad seemed to revive at first. We got some of the sea out, but there was no strength left in him. Been sick all this time. He joined his mum for the trip to heaven."

"Injuries?"

"Lot of scrapes, cuts, bruised ribs. Some black eyes, a broken nose. Stitched three wounds. I tended best I could, except for the Palatines. They wouldn't let me in their world. Marta's husband's English, recently married. He's the only English in the group. Says they likes to keep unto themselves."

"Captain'll want the dead overboard, right away."

"How do we organize a funeral for Mrs. McMahon and her boy in this weather?"

"Ain't no time for services, mate. Too dangerous. It's over the side with 'em. Pray for 'em later."

"I can't tell Little Jimmy we'll dump his mum and brother over the side without ceremony."

"I will. 'Tis me duty now." He got up to open the hatch.

Michael tugged on Farrell's arm. "Have some respect, man. We are not used to your ways of the sea. A family needs time to grieve and prepare for their parting. We all do."

"They kin grieve all the way to America. May sound cruel to ya, Mr. Shea, but 'tis the way it has ta be at sea. Captain'll say the same when you make yer report, which you should be about this moment. He's in his cabin. Yer duty's with the livin', Mr. Shea. 'Tis me duty to dispense with the dead."

He wedged the hatch open and climbed over the edge. Before pulling the hatch closed behind him, Farrell promised, "Will do best I kin ta break the news soft like." He pulled the hatch closed behind him.

Michael made his wobbly way through the crew's mess, arms outstretched on both walls to brace himself from the jagged swaying of the ship. He looked in to check on Knob and Cane.

"Mr. Knob? You awake in here?"

"Aye," returned a gruff but weak voice from the dim.

Michael pushed his way past Cane. "How's the leg?"

"Hurts somethin' awful. Not as bad as when you was messin' with it."

"I'll take that to mean you're better than yesterday."

"By that measure, aye."

"Have you eaten? Any drink?"

"Grog, bit of cold stew. Can't light no fires in this weather."

"More than we get." Michael loosened the bandages to inspect Knob's leg in the grey light and talked as he inspected. "Forty-eight desperate souls crammed into that foul place, locked in the dark, swimming in piss and vomit. We're all scared and anxious."

Knob let out a sharp groan.

"Sorry."

Michael turned to check on Cane. He laid two fingers against the man's throat. "Oh dear," he muttered. He pulled the blanket over Cane's face. There was a loud angry pounding on the bulkhead that interrupted his concentration.

"Mr. Shea." The drawn-out name came from Captain MacNeal. "I have been awaiting your report on the passengers. Why is it that instead I find you here reporting to the crew ahead of me?"

"Was checking on their health, Captain. I thought it my duty to see to your crew. Knob's recovering." He stepped away from the hammock. "But we've lost Cane, sir, to his head wounds. Two passengers, as well, drowned below. Several injured. They'll recover."

"Most lamentable. Let Mr. Farrell know. He'll organize a detail to get them overboard."

"He's aware, sir. He inquired as soon as he retrieved me from the hold."

"Add Cane to the list. I want this done now. I can't take no chances with the dead lingering on board."

"Might I inquire about funeral services, sir? The family needs some . . ."

"You may not inquire, Mr. Shea."

"Captain, sir." It was Farrell. He knew why MacNeal's voice was heated. "We may need to make some accommodation."

"What on earth are you suggesting?"

"I sought men ta form a burial detail. I explained the necessity of quick-like puttin' the dead over the side. But I met with a most agitated revolt, sir. A pregnant woman, very pregnant she is, resisted me every effort to explain. Wouldn't listen ta no reasonin', sir. Passengers rallied behind 'er an' refused all manner of persuasion. None answered my call, sir."

"Who ya takin' orders from Mr. Farrell? A pregnant woman and bunch of scared lubbers or yer captain?"

"Was only seekin' advice, sir, on how ta proceed. There was such a foul mood in the hold."

"Captain MacNeal," interrupted Michael, "perhaps, if I could present your case for you. It might be easier for them to accept the need for the expediency. If I could only let them know there is some flexibility in your timeline."

CHAPTER 26

DESOLATION SURROUNDED MR. MCMAHON AND LITTLE JIMMY WHEN Michael and Farrell returned to the 'tween deck. Jimmy sat in his father's lap next to the cots where his mother and older brother were laid out. Two or three inches of water still sloshed across the deck, but nobody paid it much mind—as long as *The Delight* was mostly upright, it was far better than what they had just experienced.

Mrs. Rawlings, the pregnant woman who had accosted Farrell earlier, knelt in the water combing Mrs. McMahon's hair. A lantern cast amber shadows over the pale bodies. Her Pietà sorrow vanished when Farrell approached, hunched over under the low clearance. Baring her teeth, she stood fully upright and held the brush as if it was club, ready to bash Farrell. At a hair or two over five feet, her head didn't quite touch the deck above. She was ready to restoke her fiery disapproval of all things Farrell. The sight of him rallied several passengers to her side. They crowded into a tight semicircle around Farrell and Michael, blocking their way back to the hatchway and trapping them in the McMahon's grieving world.

But Mrs. Rawlings held her tongue when Michael acknowledged her with a nod and raised a palm to signal forbearance. He did the same to calm the gathering mourners. Farrell leaned against the bulkhead and, like all the men, kept his head and shoulders sharply bowed under the low ceiling.

All eyes followed Michael. He put a hand on Mr. McMahon's slumped shoulder. The widower covered it with his own while keeping his gaze on wife and son.

"We have no favors to share," McMahon said to no one in particular, "for the service."

Michael kept to his agenda. "Mr. McMahon, we all join you in lamenting the loss to your family. I wish, with all my heart, I had been successful. 'Twas not for want of effort."

"'Tis hard to understand the ways of the Lord," McMahon said.

"Life is a mystery," Michael answered. "We are asked to respond to difficult circumstances, ones that defy explanation. Hard for any of us to know what to do in times like these."

"I can only think of prayer for their departed souls," McMahon said. "But you have more on your mind, don't you, sir?"

"Indeed there is, Mr. McMahon," Michael said, but with his eyes on Mrs. Rawlings, pleading for restraint. "As we are at sea, battered about in this terrible tempest, we are at the mercy of the ways of the sailor. Strange and odd customs apply. Difficult circumstances force us to consider," he paused, "require us to embrace," he paused again, "to accept unfamiliar ways."

Michael's speech didn't seem to register with McMahon, but his intended audience listened. Mrs. Rawlings laid the brush down. Tension eased. Farrell sensed resolution. He pulled Danny with him towards the hatchway. The crowd let them pass.

McMahon watched them leave. He didn't address Michael's comments directly. Instead he voiced inner thoughts, as if answering a confessor's inquiries. "Perhaps the saints have answered her innermost prayer." He wasn't talking to anyone in particular. "My wife did not approve of this adventure."

"It's a risk we've all accepted," Mrs. Rawlings said. "The road to salvation is not an easy one."

But McMahon didn't seem to hear her any better than he had Michael. He kept up his own narrative.

"She did not want to go to America. We argued 'bout it often. Many harsh words. 'There's no work, no place in England for the hard workin',' I'd say, 'Unless ya wants to be a slave to merchants an' royalty. They not be concerned for our daily bread.' But she weren't never in a mood ta listen ta me, she kept sayin, 'it be too dangerous for the children.' But I couldn't hear her pleadings. I only saw what we all saw, no future in the land of our birth. Back and forth we'd argue like this. Now I've lost half me family."

He tightened his hug on Little Jimmy. "I were wrong. She were right. It's come ta pass, just like she always says, it'll come ta no good end."

"But you was right," Mrs. Rawlings said, "no disrespect intended to yer missus' views. I share her fears for me own child ta be. But surely she knew, in 'er heart, there weren't no future fer you, in England, only hunger and misery. We have no alternative, 'cept do the thing and survive."

"Still, I'm haunted." He started sobbing.

Little Jimmy took his father's hand. "It's okay papa, momma stills love us. She and Johnny will watch out for us."

When his papa didn't reply, Mrs. Rawlings filled the uncomfortable void. She put her hand on the boy's knee. "Yes, child, she will always be with you." She turned to her husband. "Perhaps, Mr. Rawlings, a prayer or a hymn to soothe our souls?"

Before the prayer began, McMahon revealed he had read through Michael's ramblings about the strange ways of the sea. "How long do we have, Mr. Shea, before the burial?"

"As soon as the storm above abates, however slightly. Best to prepare yourself now."

"Perhaps we could have a hymn now, then," McMahon said.

Mr. Rawlings motioned for all to close ranks. Most of the forty-six remaining indentures bunched together, shoulder to shoulder, in the dim light. The Palatines at the far end of the hold stood in solidarity, respecting the chance to pray. Mr. Rawlings recited the Shepherd's Psalm. Mrs. Rawlings's alto filled the room as she sang: "My Shepherd, you supply my need, most holy is your name."

Some men joined her, filling in a resonate bottom. Michael hummed along. The melody came quickly enough to his ear, but he was unfamiliar with the Presbyterian hymn.

When Mrs. Rawlings continued into the second verse, "When through the shades of death I walk, your presence is my stay," Michael took notice of a sweet soprano voice from the Palatine quarters. In the darkness, Michael could just make out the hint of seven or eight dark-cloaked shadows at the far end of the hold but couldn't distinguish which shrouded form was the sweet source. At first the voice echoed the melody, then it added a harmony that wove in and out of the melody with a mix of long-held vowels.

Danny returned with arms full of sailcloth as the third verse began. He too heard the soprano winging around Mrs. Rawlings's lead. He stretched his neck to look through the darkness but couldn't find the singer. He caught Michael's eye, raised an eyebrow. Michael acknowledged with a curious look. After the final verse, a deep silence filled the hold.

"Wow," Danny blurted out, "that were somethin'."

His remark startled many, mostly as it was the first sound to break the silence. Many who felt the same way turned their heads towards him as a thank you for voicing their reaction to the Palatine ladies, who, though they shunned attention, felt called to song in times of sorrow.

"Indeed it were," answered John McMahon. He faced the gathering and acknowledged the Palatines in the far end of the hold. "As you all surely know, our Lord said that whenever we pray together, he's with us to comfort and guide us. I believe this true, but never have I felt so close to heaven. I thank you ladies for your sweet song."

Chapter 27

The next morning, John McMahon and Little Jimmy stood vigil while Mrs. Rawlings attended to final preparations. Michael helped her wrap mother and child in sail cloth, taking care to fold the hands in prayer across their chests before smoothing the sails and lashing the shrouds tight around the chest, waist, and knees. Michael double-stitched the canvass along the sides, leaving the shrouds open at the feet. Farrell would add ballast and thread them shut after the bodies were carried up to the top deck for burial.

Likewise, Farrell and crew in their quarters prepared Cane's body. Unlike the McMahons, they added a final stitch through Cane's nostril to make sure he was dead, as is customary for sailors, and to make sure Cane's ghost wouldn't haunt them for an improper burial.

When the gale eased enough to allow for the burial, most of the indentureds braved the upper deck out of respect for the McMahons and for the chance to stretch their legs on deck and breathe in fresh air.

The Palatines made the climb as well, their first venture out of the hold since London. Hooded and hulking together, the brown-cloaked Palatines formed a tight circle amidships, facing the burial detail. The ship's crew formed a loose circle around the bodies. Spits of freezing rain swept across the deck.

After nine days of storm with no reference to sun, moon, or stars, MacNeal didn't know where *The Delight* was on the ocean, only that the disfigured ship's compass pointed in a southerly direction. This was important to help ease the sailors' superstitions, to make sure the bodies, going over the starboard side, would fall towards their destination, the American colonies.

Farrell's crew had rigged a platform to raise the bodies over the gunnel one by one. Captain MacNeal read a short prayer that named each of the dead. His voice broke when he said the mate's name. Shaking, he motioned to his new mate. It was Farrell's duty to make sure each body sank before launching the next. He sang out, "by the mark," waited for each splash, and watched each body sink before signaling for the next. Those closest to the ocean could hear each splash.

Michael heard them too and he shuddered each time, as if cold water was dripping on the back of his neck. *What's it like*, he wondered after Cane went over the side, *to sink into an icy black grave? Could've been any of us, or all of us.* An image of bodies crushing each other, thrashing about 'til their breath gave out came to mind. He shivered at the thought.

When Mrs. McMahon went over, he thought of his mother's face, not the pale visage of fevered death, but the rosy face, the bright smile. He could hear her sing-song voice, *"Night my dearest, sleep well, there be kisses for you in the morning."*

After Little Jimmy's brother joined his mother, Michael's mind was a jumble. *Why'd I ever get on this damn boat? I hate the cold. I hate the wet. To be a servant? In the wilds of America? No wonder Emma refused me. I've failed this child. I failed his mother.*

When MacNeal barked, "Thank you, Mr. Farrell," it signaled that the service had ended.

But the Palatine ladies weren't satisfied with a sailor's closure. They launched into a song. MacNeal stiffened. He didn't appreciate his charges ignoring what to him was a clear and obvious signal to clear the deck.

Farrell intervened. "Sir, aren't there times when it be best not to start a fight ya can't win?"

MacNeal let the perceived challenge go. "Perhaps so, Mr. Farrell, we shall respect their concert." He welcomed the respite from command so he could grieve the loss of the mate.

Even from the back of the group, Marta stood out from the wall of dark brown cloaks, the only female without a hood. Two days removed from near death, she now refused to don any head covering at all. Straight backed and shoulders squared, she shook her head to scatter her locks in the wind. She enjoyed the feeling.

Her newly wedded husband, Simon, was the first of her brethren to realize she relished this freedom. Before the funeral procession, Marta's accented and angry broken English had filled the hold. Everyone heard her defiance. "No more for me a bonnet, Simon! It near killed me once. No more! I decide now what to wear." Simon had quickly given in and later put his arm around her as she refused the collective admonition of the Palatine flock and the Elder Brouchard himself when he tried to correct her.

Admiring the loose-haired Marta, Danny and Michael stood at attention out of respect for the ladies' willingness to sing during such duress and to enjoy what they hoped would be another extraordinary vocal performance.

"Ya think Marta's the soprano?" Danny asked. "That Mr. Marta lad sure be a lucky one ta be fetchin' such a fair young lass."

"Most fair indeed, but she seems more the alto to me, judging from her outburst this morning."

The ladies sang a Latin hymn, then despite the cold, added another, this time a German folk song. The passengers faded away in twos and threes to seek shelter in the 'tween deck. Michael and Danny remained to listen and to guess which hood hid the artist underneath, the one who graced the melodies with harmony. Clearly, it wasn't Marta. She had a soft, rich tone, not the powerful voice that intrigued the musicianers.

"Damn. I wish I had my fiddle. Can't you just hear how we could accompany this one?"

"Have ya spotted 'er yet? Could be a boy. That tone has a young lad's clarity."

"A boy? Certainly possible."

Michael surveyed the Palatines. "Danny boy, you've been too long at sea. Now tell me, seriously, do ya see any britches in the choir? Seems all cloaks and dresses to me." Danny nudged his friend as the choir finished. They were the last of the audience. They applauded as loud as four hands could allow.

The ladies returned the honor with curtsies before the group broke up. A small group lingered by the severed mast. Marta wandered off with her husband. Danny trailed after Marta, scheming against the obvious hurdles for a private meeting.

Finally, one stood alone. Michael waited for her to exit. *Would it be stage larboard or stage starboard?* He allowed himself to smile at his nautical joke even as he shivered.

But the lady didn't exit. She remained head down, fidgeting with her hands, her slender fingers within woolen gloves. It was then that Michael noticed that under the heavy overcloak, which was a tad too short for its occupant, there was a ribbon of green circling her feet. The fabric was sagging and torn, filthy and wet, but clearly green, and it was velvet.

Michael took a step closer.

The lady's fingers toyed with the ribbon holding the hood under her chin. With eyes transfixed on the deck, the hands untied the ribbon. The wind blew wisps of frizzy brown hair across the figure's face.

He took another step, and when the hood was finally removed, Michael came face to face with a misty-eyed Moira Baker.

CHAPTER 28

UNLIKE THEIR PREVIOUS ENCOUNTER, IT WAS MICHAEL WHO FELT THE urge to embrace Moira. He took a step forward, but Moira didn't run to him as he expected her to. He hesitated in mid-step, stunned to see Emma's younger sister magically appear in the middle of the Atlantic Ocean.

"Just what are we waiting for over there, Mr. Michael Shea? I've not traveled all this way just to watch you staring at me, not knowing what you're about." Moira smiled and folded her hands against the cold, arms parallel with the deck. She let her bonnet dangle and twirl in the breeze.

Am I outta my head? Michael asked himself. He abandoned his hesitation and reached out to her. They kissed, hers full of romantic energy. Michael wasn't sure if his kiss was greeting a long-lost sister, a cousin, or something deeper.

Moira had no doubts. She initiated another gentle kiss. This time, she didn't bruise Michael's lip. Both warmed in the glow of the moment. When *The Delight* slid down a watery mountain, they braced themselves for the crash without breaking eye contact.

"I don't understand. How? Why are you here?" he asked.

Moira put her back to the mast, facing windward. Michael, with his collar up high over his neck, moved to shield her from the icy blasts. His right arm was along the mast to hold himself in place. Wispy strands of his hair, powered by the swirling wind, danced in the air. Moira brushed back his hair and held it behind his ear so she could return his gaze.

"'Tis grand to see you, Michael, grand, truly grand."

He said the same, but his mind filled with worry. *What do I do with this girl? What will Emma think? Her family? How can I protect her if I can't protect myself?*

Curiosity overtook his worry. "Well, my dear, how is it you are here?"

She snuggled into his shoulder before explaining. "I found the indenturing agent, MacNeal, at the Exchange, same as you had done. I feared the thought of losing you, Michael. Never seeing you again was intolerable." She held his gaze, nearly eye to eye, waiting to hear the same.

It took him a moment to realize what was expected. "I am overjoyed to see you too." But this fell a bit flat. He'd been pining for Emma, not for the younger Moira. "I just can't believe you're here at all. What in the world did you tell your family?"

"Not much. When you sent me home on that wretched donkey cart, no one knew I had even left. I walked in, holding my bag, draped in Emma's mantle, and it was just like I had never left. 'Moira, clean this. Moira, fetch me water.' I put my bag on a table and all the while, Emma's humming away, working on a dance, lost in her own world, oblivious to the work that needs taking care of." She paused to breathe. "She didn't even notice what I was wearing."

Michael tried to lighten her mood. "Ah, Moira, *ma chère, votre histoire me rappelle de la belle créature de M. Perrault dans son histoire* Cinderella."

"Stop it, Michael." She wiggled in his grasp but didn't try to escape. "I'm not in the mood for frivolous comments. I'm serious. Listen to me. I felt ignored, abandoned. I couldn't bear the thought of playing second to Emma anymore, invisible to Papa. I told Papa I'd bring his water as soon as I could, gathered up my bag, turned right around, and went directly to the Exchange."

"You just disappeared on them?"

"I certainly couldn't ask for permission, now could I? I left a note."

This weighed heavy on his mind. Emma, her parents, they'd all blame him for Moira's disappearance. But he didn't share this worry. Instead, he asked "The Palatines? How did you come to join with them?"

Taking his hand, Moira paced before answering. "Simon Carrington was there, in the Exchange. He'd been apprenticed to his uncle, a brewer. He made early morning deliveries to the White Lyon. You'd never see him at that hour. I fancied him a bit. He always spoke pleasant when it were just us. I let him steal a kiss or two. He ran off after the Cider riots. Said London weren't for him on account of how the tax had ruined his family. Found his way to Amsterdam. 'Twas there, he says, he up and found himself a religious conversion. Joined up with this Palatine sect, and what a different lot they are. Between us, Michael, I doubt any religious conviction on his part. I think Marta had more to do with it than the Lord. He is so infatuated, more so than she in him. But she likes him tolerably enough."

"She has certainly caught Danny's eye," Michael observed.

"He's one of many," she replied. "But she agreed to marry Simon. He were just the better of some pathetic options the elders were fostering on her."

Michael stopped their walk. "Really?"

"Oh, Michael, how can you be so blind? Have you seen the old men in Marta's party? There's a reason men become hermits. It's good for the rest of us not to have to look at them."

"I hadn't given the Palatines any thought at all. Anyway, how am I supposed to divine all this? My first sight of Marta was trying to get the sea out of her lungs. Even then, it wasn't until I heard their psalmist choir at the funeral service that I took notice of this sect. I'm no owl, Moira, I can't see in the dark."

"Oh dear, men are so blind to what's right before their eyes."

"You mean to melt my heart with insults?" he asked.

She stopped pacing and faced Michael. "Is there a chance it will beat for me?"

"You certainly have my attention, my dear." He took her arm to ward off the cold.

"Well then, I'll let you in on a little secret," Moira said, putting her hand under his so they could walk arm in arm. "Marta and I became fast friends as soon as we came on this sorry boat. In less than a fortnight, we're like sisters, not like Emma and me, but loving sisters. Living with rats in this horrible ship has brought us together. She teaches me bits of German, I help polish her English. Her elders won't let us mingle with anybody."

"Have you joined this Palatine sect?"

"Never," she answered. "They don't own me, though they certainly try to. They were ahead of me at the Exchange negotiating with MacNeal for passage. He was most anxious to sign up more souls for this horrible journey. I prevailed upon Simon to hide me amongst his pilgrim family. He introduced me as his cousin in search of salvation. That were a temptation the elders couldn't escape." She pulled his cloak around her. "Why is it, Michael, these zealots think they need only dictate and women must follow?" She stomped a foot on the deck to warm it up. "Do they not think God gave us a brain so we can think our own thoughts?"

"I have no answer for you. 'Tis a mystery how religion excites the mind of an acolyte."

It's more than religious zealots, she thought, *it's all manner of men.*

They toured in silence, each savoring different joys of rediscovery, but Michael's joy was offset with worry as he ruminated. *How can I protect her? Where will we end up?*

Moira broke the silence. "I know you came to Marta's rescue, Michael, and the others. Never have I been so afraid and so scared, and so grateful, in such quick succession. Where did you learn to revive the drowned? Simon said you breathed life into the dead. I've never heard of such a thing."

"From my uncle. I'd listen as my uncle and his physician friends debated whether it might work. How to drain water out of a lung and how to use a bellows to force air in. There being no bellows about, I did the next best thing. Wasn't enough for the McMahons. Why does God let some live and others not?"

"It was enough to save Marta, and for that, I am forever grateful, as are Simon and Marta herself. I don't see how I could continue this dreadful voyage without her."

They returned to the main mast and snuggled in its lee to get a tiny break from the wind. She toyed with his hair. The wind kept blowing it back into her face. She grabbed a handful and jammed it behind his ear.

"Ah, Michael, never could I have imagined such vile conditions." She released his ear. "I just can't believe the filth, the stench, the appalling food. How could MacNeal mislead us so?"

He didn't have a ready reply.

She renewed her agitation. "It is criminal, and most certainly a sin against God himself how we women are so mistreated." She separated from Michael to emphasize her anger but took his hand and walked him to the windward side to stare at the sea. "Ooh, Michael, how I resent the way men treat their wives and daughters. These cloven-headed brutes," she made a face as she took a breath, "they think they're better than my sex, as if God didn't give a lady the power of thought. How is it men can lie, steal, and cheat as they do, and then pontificate about morality and prayer? What is this disease that overtakes men, Michael? Will it ruin you as well?"

All he could muster was an arm around her shoulder. She resisted his first outreach where only moments earlier she had wrapped herself in his embrace. But she then accepted his second attempt. There they remained, facing the wind, two saplings woven together, bending and swaying with the storm.

"What will happen to us, Michael? What has MacNeal promised you?"

"Only that my indenture lists Annapolis as my port of delivery. I hope to call on a former patient of mine."

"Can we stay together, Michael?"

Michael sighed. "Will be difficult. If there are no buyers in Annapolis, *The Delight* can sell our contracts anywhere in the Chesapeake."

"What about families?" She wigged out from under his coat as her anxiety simmered. "They can't separate Simon and Marta, can they?"

"I woudn't think so."

"Then, if we was married, they couldn't separate us, could they?"

"Alas, there is no priest about." He waved his hand towards the emptiness of the Atlantic.

"Would you then, if there was?"

"If I were the one asking, I'd be needing your father's blessing," he replied, "and as we can see, he's not about to answer such a request."

"Don't play with me, Michael. I know you don't love me. In time, I pray your heart will melt, at least a little."

"But what if you first find a match among the Palatines?"

"I'd rather take to a convent. It be one thing to hide amongst them to follow you, but I have no intention of following them to Philadelphia."

"Philadelphia?" Michael mused. "Wherever did that idea come from?"

"Elder Brouchard says they'll redeem themselves in Philadelphia."

He turned to put his back against the gunnel. "I hadn't heard any mention of Philadelphia when Farrell rattled off the ports of call on this voyage." He turned to look at Moira. "It were my recollection that our new mate fully expects *The Delight* to return to London after visiting the Chesapeake."

"Well, it would serve Brouchard right to be outwitted," she said. "Won't be the first time, nor I suspect will it be the last."

CHAPTER 29

REPAIRING THE WRECK OF *THE DELIGHT* WAS THE FIRST ORDER OF BUSI-
ness as soon as the storm eased. Everybody was enlisted to perform using
whatever skills God gave them. Danny joined the carpenter ranks, taking
direction from Knob's bedside. Farrell directed his foremast crew to do
what they could to raise a spar and rig a sail. MacNeal took charge of
main mast repairs, though the best they could do was to rig a main that
was anything but straight and true. Tombler lent his muscle to raising
sail. Hoecker alternated at the helm to free up experienced hands. Moira,
Mrs. Rawlings, and Mr. McMahon mended sails. Marta, Simon, and
some Palatine men learned how to weave new standing and running
rigging.

As the weather eased, crew and passengers alike found reasons to
spend more of their days on deck to escape the foul air below. And as the
sea settled, rumors circulated that MacNeal's reclusive cabin mate, a Mr.
Edmond-Tell, had finally left his bed and braved the deck in the hours
before dawn.

"'Tis true, Michael, I've laid me eyes on him," Danny said one morning at the starboard head.

Michael wasn't convinced. "I hear this purser fellow never leaves his
cabin on the open ocean. He only comes on deck when it's time to sell
our contracts."

Cook, on the seat next to Michael, came to Danny's defense. "'Tis as
yer friend says. He were indeed walkin' the deck. And Mr. Edmond-Tell
be much more than a mere purser. Supercargo's what we calls him cause
he's the one who makes all money. Once we's in port, that is. He don't
show hisself much while we's at sea. Mostly in bed in Captain's cabin. I

brings 'em meals. They plays cards at night, talk a bit. He don't do well with the sea despite his years on it. But once we's in port, he takes charge of trading and sellin' your services."

"I stand corrected. Danny, my apology," Michael said. "I thought yer story a foul tale and now I realize you're smellin' fresh as roses."

"Speaking of smells, Mr. Shea," Cook said, "I fear you needs take a closer look at Knob's leg. Smelt sour just now as I brought him a bite."

Michael noticed the fetid odor right away. "Good day to you, Mr. Knob. Are you able to receive me?"

"Aye, Mr. Shea, come in. Knew it wouldn't be long before you'd get wind of this. Cook gave me a worried face just now. I knew his mind. Tell me it ain't so, will ya, Mr. Shea. Will ya have ta cut me leg off? Ain't there anythin' ya kin do fer me?"

Michael rubbed the man's shoulder. "Let's not jump ahead before I've had a chance to take a closer look."

Michael unraveled the bandages that kept the splinted leg straight. He gently pried the bandage, now caked in dried blood, from the skin. Knob flinched as Michael probed the wounds. There was substantial bruising under the thigh break. "A good sign," Michael said, "you're on the mend here." The break below the knee had blackened the skin, but it was also on the mend.

It was the break above the ankle that was infected. The smell intensified when Michael removed this bandage. The first whiff of the wound forced Michael to crinkle his entire face, hold his breath, and squint. Knob covered his nose with his hand. The wound revealed a circle of greenish-black skin on nob's calf.

"When did you notice the . . ." Michael paused, "peculiar odor?"

Knob pushed himself up by his elbows to get a better look. "Don't need no fancy words with me, Mr. Shea. Gettin' to the point is fine by me." He grimaced when he saw the spot on his calf. He let himself down, re-covered his nose.

"Yesterday? Weren't sure at first. Hoped it were Cook's cooking." Knob gave a nervous laugh. "But by today, I was sure it was me leg. There's no more hidin' from that."

"Why didn't you send for me?"

"Ah, ya spent so much time with me already, thought ya needed a change of air."

"Mr. Knob, it's my pleasure to attend to you. Am most hopeful we'll run through some jigs and hornpipes again."

"With or without me leg?"

"I'm not sure. But in any case, it won't affect your concertina playing."

"Aye, that is a joy I'd hate to lose." They both smiled. Then Knob broke the mood. "Do I have to lose me leg, Mr. Shea? It's the only cure sailors have. 'Tis a frightful thought."

"I wish we had a proper physician to guide us." Michael sat on the stool by Knob's bunk inspecting the dirty bedding, looking for traces of lice. "Am rather curious, Mr. Knob, why is it that you sailors have such an aversion to bathing? We've been at sea for near a month and I have not noticed anyone as much as washing their hands, much less making any strides to remove salt and sweat."

"'Tis bad luck to bathe at sea. No jack worth his salt would risk the devastation ta follows was he to break the rules of the sea."

"Ah, I see," Michael replied. "Then let me pose this question to you, Mr. Knob. How is it then that we are better off in this misadventure by not bathing? As I look about, we've lost two masts, *The Delight* nearly sank with all hands, your mate was swept overboard, three more are dead and over the side, we're low on food and water, and your leg may have to come off. This is the reward for keeping to your superstitions?"

"Do not with chide me, Mr. Shea. It's our way, our rules. 'Tis not to be tampered with."

"Well, I have been washing my hands," Michael said as he stood up. "Am I to blame for our misfortunes?"

"Misfortunes? Who said we've had misfortunes?" Knob asked leaning on an elbow to face Michael. "So far as I kin see, there's nothing out of the ordinary in our passage, excepting the loss of the mate, of course. The mate were a good sort, a reliable sailor he was."

Michael returned his attention to Knob's worst wound. He probed around the edges of the gangrenous area and the inflamed but still living skin. "Can you tell me what hurts more or less?" he asked as he applied pressure around the area.

Sharp inhales through the nostrils let Michael know where the most painful areas were.

"How about now?" Michael asked as he probed the middle of the green-black area. Knob didn't respond.

"Curious," Michael said, pondering the area. Then he walked over to the desk, opened a drawer, and pulled out a musty book bloated by years of humidity and neglect. "If you'll excuse me, Mr. Knob, I need to make my report to your captain. Then I'd like to review what Mr. Woodall here has to say on the matter." He raised the book for Knob to see. "Then we'll consider our options."

MacNeal muttered an "I see" after Michael reported on Knob's leg. He let out a long slow breath and let his shoulders slump a bit as he scanned the cloud-streaked sky. "Most disappointing news for Knob. Have you amputated before, Mr. Shea?"

"Not like this would require, sir."

"Mr. Knob's loss, I'm sure."

"And the ship's loss, too, sir. Many don't survive."

The captain opened the binnacle to no purpose other than to open it as he absorbed the news. "Perhaps our cook can do the job." He closed the binnacle cover. "He is a good man with a knife. I'm sure he can handle it. He was a smith before turning cook. He knows how to get a fire hot for the cauterizing."

"Perhaps, but we'll need a saw, not a knife, to cut through the bone, sir. A strong sharp saw."

"Mr. Knob will have to lend you his."

"If we get to that."

"You'll not amputate?"

"I'm hoping to kill the gangrene and thereby save Mr. Knob's leg, sir."

MacNeal gave Michael a puzzled look. "You can defeat gangrene?"

"Been reading Dr. John Woodall's medical book, sir. I found it in Cane's cabinet."

"What book?"

"*The Surgion's Mate*, sir. An excellent narrative on medical treatments, especially for use at sea. He suggests some cures for gangrene."

"Cane had such a book?"

"It's all that's in the medicine cabinet, sir. Doesn't look like he used it much."

"I dare say he didn't. What other treatments? You will blister and bleed him?"

"Woodall suggests some treatments that don't involve torturing the patient, sir."

"Torturing the patient? It's standard treatment in the Royal Navy. Blisterin' and bleedin's been standard treatment since Roman times. They learnt it from the Greeks."

"Indeed they did. But that won't help Knob keep his leg, sir."

"So what does your Woodall suggest for our Mr. Knob?"

"A series of treatments offer some promise. However, as we have no medicines to work with, I'll start with bathing, sir."

"That will never do, Mr. Shea. Am sure Mr. Knob would prefer bleedin' and blisterin' to bathing."

"Aye, so he says," Michael paused to gather his argument. "Mr. Woodall emphasizes a novel treatment. He insists on constant bathing of the wound and removal of the dead skin. He suggests that cleanliness helps retard the spread of the gangrene."

"Nonsense. What's bathing got to do with it?"

"He doesn't make that clear, sir," Michael admitted. Then he leaned in towards MacNeal to share a private comment. "But it would seem rather logical, considering that finer gentlemen like yourself do wash their hands and face most days and can be rather particular about their attire."

"Knob's a sailor. Tars like him don't concern themselves with such niceties."

"All the more reason why I need your support, sir, to convince him to let us attempt Woodall's treatment."

"Fine, do as you suggest. You're excused from the quarterdeck."

"There's a bit more, sir."

"Mr. Shea, I do have a ship to sail."

"Indeed, but it would be of tremendous assistance if you was to order Knob directly to follow my direction and let us treat him with a regime of bathing and scrapings."

"Who is this 'us' you speak of?"

"Ah, that's another approval I shall need from you, sir. I intend to enlist one of the lady passengers to assist with the treatment."

"A woman? In the crew's quarters? That will never do."

"We could move him to the filth of the 'tween deck, sir, to be amongst your passengers, but that would defeat Woodall's emphasis on clean conditions. And, unless you want to devote one of your crew to the task instead of sailing the ship, we have not many other options. As you may remember, Mr. O'Mara was assisting me, but since you have reassigned him as ship's carpenter, he has no time for this."

"We are short on crew," MacNeal acknowledged.

Michael continued to press. "Knob will need constant attention to some medical details, sir, if he's to continue training Mr. O'Mara. It's to save your carpenter's leg, sir. And, I might emphasize again, sir, I've no experience with amputations and most amputations end with fatality. Do you want to risk Knob if another approach might save him?"

MacNeal scanned the sky looking for guidance. He seemed to find it in the low grey clouds.

"As you wish, Mr. Shea. And who, might I ask, will become your assistant?"

"One of the Palatines, sir, the lass with the most wonderful singing voice. She has a steady hand for such procedures. She has assisted me before in London. And, if I may say so, sir, she's rather easy on the eye. I'm sure you won't mind a glance or two, sir."

CHAPTER 30

"Ya be dreamin', Michael. As much as I'd love to spend time together, this is not what I carry around in my mind. I'm not going to get anywhere near his poisoned leg. I will keep the poor man in my prayers, nothing more."

"Moira, please," he countered. "I was favorably impressed with how well you came to Jonathan's assistance. You were not squeamish then. Why now?"

"Because these sailors are so filthy. They should be the ones living in this dank hold, not us. I can't stand them near me. Near a month at sea and I've never seen any as much as any of them wipe his hands. They leave food bits in their beards. Oh, they comb and grease their pigtails often enough, but nothing else."

"It's tar, not grease. Keeps their hair from getting caught in the rigging," he said.

"What's the difference? It's so queer."

Her outburst attracted the attention of passengers nearby. Michael put a finger to his lips. She lowered her voice, but not her tone. "They're disgusting, Michael."

Michael decided on another tack. He leaned across his hammock so only she'd hear. "Would the prospect of a hot meal, a hearty stew instead of cold biscuit mush, change your mind? And I will bathe Knob to get us off on a clean start."

"Bathe him?" She shivered at the thought. "Hot food? How?"

"Knob's in a cabin near the galley. I'll make sure you get the cook's hot meals."

"Hot water?"

"Of course, twice a day."

"Promise?"

"You have my word. Hot food, hot water." He let that sink in. "Let me show you the way."

Michael led the way up the ladder and held Moira's hand as they walked across the deck. "Captain, sir." Michael yelled at the foot of the quarterdeck.

MacNeal had been expecting one of the Palatine ladies shrouded in their plain brown, oversized hoods. Instead he found Moira's brown curls swirling in the breeze and her bright green eyes blinking out of the pewter grey mist rolling across *The Delight*. The shock of a lively young woman, nearly as tall as he, staring back caused his posture to hiccup as Michael made the introductions. MacNeal lost his sea legs for a moment before he put his clothes in order and recovered his commanding posture.

"Many thanks for your offer to assist, miss. I must warn you that you may find some of the crew's habits a bit unusual, but they're good lads, miss. You must understand that the sea forces 'em to adopt ways that appear rather strange to ladies of quality." MacNeal bowed in a most gentile fashion.

Moira answered with a curtsey. "I will do my best to help your most unfortunate carpenter, Captain."

"I'm sure Mr. Knob will be most appreciative." MacNeal took Moira's gloved hand and mimed a kiss. He paused and looked her over. "Might I suggest, Miss . . . I'm not sure quite how to suggest this delicately . . . but would you consider a change in clothing, something less flowing than your lovely attire?"

"Flowing, Captain?"

"Such a pretty dress is most appropriate for the drawing room where you have the room for all that fabric, miss. But on-board ship, we live in tight quarters. Am concerned that it would be all too easy for my crew to be tripping on the hem of your gown."

"It's all I have, Captain. Two dresses and a nightgown. I must wear something."

"I'm trying to suggest . . . ," he paused, "to inquire as to whether you might wear something more like what a sailor wears."

"You mean a man's britches?"

"Precisely."

"May I have a hand in their making?"

"By all means, something you approve."

"I will need fabric, needle, thread, scissors."

"At once, then. Thank you, miss." He turned to the mate. "Mr. Farrell, make it happen."

Returning his attention to Moira and Michael, MacNeal was in command. "We will visit with Mr. Knob to tell him the good news and to let the crew be aware that you shall work among them. Prepare yourself, miss, for the oddities of sailoring." He led the way to the galley.

CHAPTER 31

THE NEXT MORNING *THE DELIGHT'S* MEDICAL TEAM MADE ITS WAY TO the theater of operation. Knob grumbled as Michael, Farrell, Danny, and Tombler assembled in the tiny cabin. "Was thinkin' it be just you and the misses, Mr. Shea. But I sees ya brought along some muscle." The sight of Tombler particularly darkened Knob's expression. "Ya intend to saws me leg off after all?"

"No, Mr. Knob, much worse than that." Michael replied as the lads snickered. "You're to get fresh bedding, and the worst part of all, I'm afraid to say, is that you're about to have a bath."

Knob turned pale. "Whoever 'eard of bathin' at sea? Brings back luck. What's bathin' have ta do with a broken leg anyways? No good kin come from bathin'."

"I beg to disagree," Michael answered with a slight smirk. "It's all here in Sir John Woodall's monumental work on medical procedures for seafarers." He dropped the book on Knob's lap for emphasis. "His careful analysis on combating gangrene starts on page 213. See for yerself."

The team stood in silence, staring back and forth between Knob and the book on his lap. They held their tongues waiting for a reaction, knowing that Knob couldn't read. He could barely tell whether the book was upside down or not. Under their glare, Knob wanted to put up more than a verbal struggle, but with all their weight against him, it was hopeless.

The next distraction was even more overpowering.

Moira entered carrying a large bucket of hot water, cloth, and a scrub brush tucked under arm, and she was sporting her latest fashion creation— canvas britches, cinched with a rope belt, high on her waist, and blue ribbons holding the leg ends fast below her knee. Pale red stockings led down to her black leather shoes. To this she added a blue sailor's shirt, buttoned to the neck, loose fitting, but tailored enough to track a young woman's curves. Moira had added a black sailor's jacket. It was oversized for her frame, so she wore it as a cloak over her shoulders. She hadn't had time yet to make her mark on it. She had also pulled her hair back tightly in imitation of a sailor's pigtail.

"That be some transfamatin', miss," Knob offered as a compliment. "Ya aim to torture me clean?"

"Alas, Mr. Knob, I leave the intimate details of bathing to your handsome shipmates. An innocent such as myself is not ready to behold what God has allotted to the male of our species." She gave him a wink and left Knob to his fate.

After a half hour, Michael fetched Moira. "We are ready, Miss Moira. Not only do we have a bathed carpenter, but a vinegared bunk and a rather tidy cabin as well. And, might I say, you made quite an impression. Wherever did you get the inspiration for such an intriguing outfit?"

"Why thank you, Mr. Shea, if you are attempting to flatter me." She gave him a man's bow instead of a curtsey.

"I am. You make the most alluring sailor I've ever laid me eyes upon."

"Some compliment." She exaggerated a frown.

"You are indeed most appealing in whatever outfit you inhabit."

"That's better." She pretended to be stern. "You need more practice. Perhaps a compliment every day would be best."

"As you wish. Time—" The cleaning crew interrupted him as they made their exit. Each tipped hands to foreheads to bid Moira good day. "Time to get to work."

"I'm ready, and I must say, I do thank you for getting Knob bathed. Why haven't others adopted this man Woodall's teachings on cleanliness and bathing?"

Michael put finger over his lips. "If truth be told, there's nothing about bathing on page 213 or on any other page in that book. Knob could have easily uncovered my lie had he turned to the page. But he don't read."

"You devil, to tell such a tale."

"A minor indiscretion, wouldn't you agree? Thought it easier this way, to rely on such an august expert as Sir John Woodall instead of myself." Michael led Moira to the patient's bedside.

"Mr. Knob, Miss Baker and I will remove the gangrenous skin. It's a small area. If we can remove it, quickly, you may yet keep this leg. Now, as it appears dead to the touch, you shouldn't notice as we scrape away the skin. Try to be patient with us. If you fidget too much when we hit live tissue, we'll have to enlist crew to immobilize you. Understood?"

"Aye, git on with it."

Michael unwrapped a bundle of tools stored in the medicine cabinet and placed them on Knob's bunk and washed each item. When ready to attack the gangrene, he put his back to Knob to block his view. He placed Moira at the patient's feet. "Moira, as I remove bits of black skin here . . ." he poked at it with the end of a long skinny knife and scraped off flakes of crinkled tissue. Both recoiled as the fresh puncture released more stench and puss underneath. Michael handed Knob and Moira silk cloths. "For your nose and mouth as necessary."

After this first effort, Michael resumed explaining the procedure. "Notice how Mr. Knob doesn't respond when I poke here. The skin is dead. There is no feeling. I'll start in the center of the black and work towards the edges to the white skin. I will need you to wipe the bleeding and remove the debris so I can see."

"Aye, aye, Dr. Shea." She watched in fascination as Michael peeled off layers of skin. "This is most disconcerting, and riveting, all at the same time."

"Aye, miss, 'tis," Knob agreed, "be glad you're not the one receiving your kind assistance."

Michael sliced into the center again and scraping out another layer of blackened tissue. Knob started twitching as Michael dug his blade deeper into the leg. "Stings like a thousand bees," he groaned. But somehow Knob kept a lid on his leg's twitching. The debris collected in a pile at Michael's feet. When most of the black skin was removed, Michael kept trimming until the live skin started bleeding. Moira's hands followed every cut line, dabbing and soaking up the blood with bits of cloth that ended up in the gory accumulation. Knob grimaced and wiggled more and more as Michael cut into the live skin. Michael paused now and again to put his hand on Knob's calf. This helped soothe the carpenter to hold still long enough for Michael to continue without calling for restraining help.

Over an hour later, Michael summed up the morning's work. "Mr. Knob, I've removed all I can see." Michael stood as tall as he could in the low overhead. Moira put a hand on the ceiling to curve her back and roll her shoulders to get the kinks out. Her stretching was a welcome sight to the patient as Michael continued. "Your recovery now depends on repeated cleaning of your wound. We shall return three times day to refresh the dressing, clean your wound, and pray you're out of the woods."

Dots of sweat covered Knob's forehead. "Aye" was all he could muster. He nodded off.

"What about that hole in his leg?" Moira asked, unable to stop staring at the disturbing sight.

"It's too big a gap to stitch. I'm hoping if we keep it clean, the skin will return. It'll be your job to keep the wound clean until then."

CHAPTER 32

THE NEXT EVENING, AFTER THIRTEEN DAYS OF STORM, THE MOON AND stars reappeared, sparkling in the crisp cold of a winter's night. Sailors treated them as familiar signposts, quickly taking note of their reassuring presence, while the passengers stood in awe of the heavens and traded hushed tales of constellation mythology. In the morning, the dawn's rosy fingers slowly warmed the eastern sky.

However, without the mate's mathematical skills, MacNeal was unable to use the stars to estimate how far off the coast they were or how far south. Despite MacNeal's years of service in the Royal Navy, he had never mastered the math needed for navigation, and as a result, his career stalled. MacNeal inquired among the passengers for any who might be familiar with maths, but to no avail until Michael volunteered that Danny had a head for figuring.

At MacNeal's request, Michael escorted Danny to the great cabin. It was an awkward interview as they gathered around the captain's table. Michael tried to appear involved in the discussion, but he was as lost as MacNeal. Michael put more of his energy in trying to get a peek at the supercargo, Edmond-Tell, who breathed heavily behind a bedchamber curtain on his side of the cabin. The smell of vomit very much filled the cabin.

It didn't take long for the great navigation summit to unwind. Mac-Neal's propositions left Danny scratching his backsides after wrestling with the captain's readings. Danny could add up the numbers MacNeal rattled off, but MacNeal wasn't sure of the angle of his course, or from where they started measuring, much to MacNeal's embarrassment. "Seems we're somewhere near the table's edge and halfway down the center table leg," he'd say with a smirk, poking fun at his own expense. He'd try again and again and Danny spit out his sums nearly as fast as MacNeal rattled off his list of readings and estimated daily runs. "You'd stand well as a purser, Mr. O'Mara, if you gave thought to a career at sea," MacNeal said by way of thanking Danny for the effort.

"Best if I reckon our way. Head south 'til the weather warms. Then west. I'm sure we'll find our way to North America."

That Michael and Danny had a private moment in the captain's cabin was of great interest to Farrell, who approached Michael when MacNeal took his next noon reading. Appearing nonchalant, Farrell asked, "Was yer mate of any help to the captain with his navigating?"

"We're near lost," Michael answered. "Your captain's trying to locate a longitude. Danny may have an easy way with numbering, but what the captain were asking for is beyond Danny's ability to resolve. None of Danny's calculating gave the captain the bearing he's so anxious to find. Said he'd just recognize where we was going. What's out here to recognize other than water?"

"Means dead reckonin'," Farrell said. "Most captains is pretty good at that. Just means measuring our speed with the log every hour, estimating a distance, and running that against a compass bearing."

"Ah, well in that, Danny was of some help then," Michael replied. "The two of them think we've made some five hundred miles since the storm. But where we was when we started seems to be a mystery. Captain wouldn't come out and say it, but 'tis clear he has no idea where we are after we lost yer mate."

"We'll end up somewheres," Farrell said, "always do. We should soon sight land to larboard. Galicia. That's what Captain says. Expects us ta dip in and to take a proper bearing. But if you asks me, the captain's trying to find his way with Paddies' candles. The more he tries ta make his figures add up, the more lost we really is. Just look at him there fumblin' with the sextant, takin' his readings."

"Isn't that what a navigator's supposed to do, mark the sun at noon?" Michael asked, turning to watch MacNeal.

"Aye, navigators do. Captain's a lot of things, but without the mate, we don't have us a proper navigator. Captain just collects a list of bearings he can't make no sense of. That's why Captain left His Majesty's service. MacNeal's a fighter, but the Admiralty refused to give him command. A fall from grace, if you will, from warship to collier."

"So this is just for show?"

"Captain likes us ta think he's got everything under his hat. Crew knows better."

"And would you two handsome gentlemen hazard yer own guess if we might be closer to Spain, or is it the Azores?" Moira had drifted into the conversation with Marta, arm in arm.

When Farrell turned towards her, his cheeks reddened when he made eye contact. He stammered, "Good day, ma'am." Then corrected himself, "I mean, miss, misses." He adjusted his posture, jerked a bit left and then right, unsure of what to do with his hands.

"Ah, Ladies Moira and Marta, so pleasant you could join us," Michael said with a slight bow. "May I have the pleasure of introducing Mr. Liam Farrell, recently appointed second-in-command of the good ship *Delight*. Mr. Farrell, you are now in the presence of Misses Marta Carrington and Moira Baker, late of London."

"Delighted," Moira said, speaking for the both of them. Marta brought a hand up to cover her grin. Moira held her hand out for Farrell to take. She expected the novice officer to kiss it. But he didn't know how.

Michael leaned towards Farrell. "A gentleman takes a lady's hand when offered, even when they're dressed as a lad, gently if you can. There's very much a lady hiding in sailor's britches."

"As am I," Farrell answered Moira. He took Michael's advice, but he grabbed Moira's hand as if it were a belaying pin. He raised it as he lowered his head in a too-steep bow. Michael turned away to hide his mirth at the clumsiness. Marta giggled.

As Moira retrieved her crunched hand, Farrell straightened up. Then with a creak in his voice, Farrell stumbled over his words, "Captain, he says we's 'bout ta touch Galacia. Should makes a landfall ta larboard right soon." He pointed towards the eastern horizon.

"I certainly hope we don't touch too hard," she replied, massaging her gloved hand. She waited for clarification. None came. She didn't let the silence linger. "Mr. Farrell, I'd be willing to wager that we'll make a landfall over there," she said pointing to starboard, "on that side of the boat, in the west."

"*Delight*'s a ship, miss, not a boat." He slid his hands in and out of his jacket. "A boat's somethin' ya row about with oars, like the one we lost in the gale, and 'taint possible in any case, Miss Baker. Galacia kin only be ta starboard if'in we was to be sailing north."

"I see, Mr. Farrell," she replied, "but could you tell me then, why is there a mountain rising out of the sea on the wrong side of your dear ship?" She pointed across the deck.

Farrell stretched his neck, put his hand over his brow, and squinted to study the other horizon. "Ah, miss, 'tis only Cape Fly Away."

"Cape where?" Michael asked following Farrell's line of sight.

"Only a cloud bank, no land," he replied. "They rises up like that and then flies away like birds. Common for lubbers, I mean ladies, to be mistakin' clouds for a landfall."

"How about that wager then, Mr. Farrell?" Moira repeated. "How about you, Michael?"

Farrell let the challenge go unanswered.

Michael didn't. "My dear Moira, where did you gain such confidence to offer a bold wager?"

"We ladies have our ways." She gave each a smile before turning to watch Cape Fly Away. "Come Marta, let's see if these clouds fly away as our Mr. Farrell expects."

Farrell took a longer look at the clouds. "Just clouds on the 'orizon, miss. 'Ave you 'eard other speculation?"

"Just my own thoughts about that *horizon*," she said emphasizing proper pronunciation. "But seeing as you gentlemen don't have the back to risk a wager, I'll add that we spotted some gulls sunning themselves along this side just this morning."

"We've had lots of birds of late." Farrell spoke carefully following Moira's rebuke of his tendency to drop all his *h* sounds. "I've seen them fly off every which way."

"I see," Moira said. "I might add that this morning we also watched a lonely turtle lazily swim in the direction of those clouds. He would make a tremendous soup if this ship had any fishermen aboard. Now just where would he be swimming to if it weren't to rest on a sandy shore on your Cape Fly Away?"

"If I may add to me defense, miss," Farrell answered, "tortoises is known ta swim entire oceans. Matters little which direction they goin'."

"Just the same then, gentlemen, are either of you bold enough to risk your pocketbooks? Make it a shilling if you're so sure?"

"Alas, I haven't a shilling to risk," Michael said, "even if I knew where we were."

"I too must decline the wager, miss. Captain MacNeal would frown upon one of his ship's officers takin' easy advantage of such a comely lady as yourself. And if I may, I'm most glad you and Miss Marta have abandoned your hoods to let the sun be warm upon yer faces."

"Well, you may not know where you are, Mr. Farrell, but we do welcome your flatteries." Moira smiled. "If only other lads would be so generous with their compliments." She gave Michael a raised eyebrow.

"I wish you well in your new duties, Mr. Farrell. And if we may have your leave, we'll continue our promenade. We'll soon see who gets to spend their money, you in Galacia or me on your Cape Fly Away."

CHAPTER 33

BY SUNRISE, CREW AND PASSENGERS ALIKE WERE ALL ABUZZ AS THEY crowded the starboard side watching "Cape Fly Away" turn into an island with two mountains. The smell of land was heavy in the air. Storm clouds hid the top of the bigger mountain.

Like the others, Michael and Danny remained transfixed at the prospect of walking on solid ground when Moira joined them. "It's just as I said, Michael, we're nowhere near Spain. I believe we've found the Azores, though our captain can only claim credit for stumbling upon them. Oh, how I wish you and William had taken my wager."

"Mornin', Moira," Danny said with a nod. "I share yer surprise at Michael's restraint. Rare's the day he passes a chance to lose his money."

"Was sore tempted," Michael admitted, "but as I count only two pence in my purse, I had not the nerve to meet Moira's high stakes, nor did Mr. Farrell."

"Oh, Michael, it seems silly to call such a lad 'Mister.' I was beside myself yesterday trying not to laugh. He's such an awkward one, handsome, a bit rough, but fine features, don't you agree?" Despite her sailor's gear, she assumed the airs of a lady in waiting. "Can't see how he'll ever improve his social graces plying the seas on *The Delight*."

Danny changed the topic. "Might yer lovely companion, Miss Marta, join us this morn?"

"Alas, Danny, or am I to call you Mr. O'Mara now that we're both in the ship's employ?"

"We're not real sailors, but the britches suit ya. Any news of Marta?"

"Alas, she's not one for the early side of the morning," Moira answered, "and unfortunately for yourself, Marta's husband, as you must remember, insists on staking his claim with his wife. I had to rise early to leave them to their fidgeting."

Lucky man was Danny's thought.

"When do you think we'll call on our island?" Moira asked.

"Sometime today, I'd say," Danny answered, "I sure could use a proper meal, anything that ain't been salted."

"Could this be true?" Moira asked. "Oh, how wonderful. Marta and I would just love a chance to visit a shop together." She turned to look for Farrell on the quarterdeck and called out to him, "Mr. Farrell, sir, is it true we could make landfall soon?"

"Mornin' miss, 'tis a pleasure to see ya so excitable." He walked over to them and lowered his voice to address the trio. "I have news, but it won't be to yer likin'. There won't be no landfall for *The Delight*."

"What?" Moira's shriek attracted the notice of nearby passengers. "How can we not visit this lovely place?"

The other passengers drew near.

"We have dire need of proper medicines. We must make a landing," Michael insisted.

Danny chimed in. "How kin your captain let such a chance pass by? Them farms seems overflowing with livestock. I kin almost smell 'em."

"Regrettably, we cannot put a foot on Graciosa." Farrell's news produced a wave of discontent that traveled ear to ear. He faced a wall of disappointed and sour faces. "Our best hope is ta 'eave-to and wait for the islanders to put in a boat to visit us."

"What's to prevent us from landing?" Mrs. Rawlings demanded, wiggling into the circle.

"Pirates," Farrell replied, "they are . . ." He was drowned out by a chorus of indignation.

"You cannot be serious," said McMahon. "Them days of Jolly Roger is long gone."

"Mr. Farrell," Captain MacNeal bellowed from the quarterdeck seeing his novice officer losing control. "If you could bring our passengers hither." He stood by the helm with his hands folded behind his back. When the group regathered, MacNeal addressed them.

"We are presently offshore of Graciosa in the Azores," he began, keeping his voice neutral. "As you may know, the Azores is owned by the King of Portugal, and His Majesty King Joseph has made a treaty with the Bey of Algeria to protect his countrymen and their vessels from seizure by Barbary corsairs, which ply these waters most regular." He evidently thought this was enough of an explanation. "Let us hope the local boats will wait upon us. They are free to sail in their coastal waters."

"Beggin' yer pardon, Captain," McMahon called from the crowd, "that don't explain why we can't make a landing. We are sorely in need of fresh provision."

"I take your point, sir," MacNeal replied, but didn't offer any explanation.

"Then what be yer point?" McMahon asked. His question triggered an explosion of mutterings that gave him strength to again challenge the captain. "No Barbary would dare molest one of His Majesty's ships. Don't matter what the King of Portugal signs or don't signs."

The murmuring among the passengers increased, just as a pot of water starts to bubble before boiling. Surveying this threat, MacNeal got to the heart of the matter. "These seas are infested with Barbary raiders. They rule all the waters off these shores. If we attempt a landing, we'd be trapped in the harbour and in danger of easy capture. These Barbaries sell captives in a most despicable slave trade, and they especially like trading in Christian slaves. Considering our situation, there's little reason to suspect any possibility of a ransom. We'd all be sold and lost forever on the shores of North Africa."

The grumbling continued. MacNeal raised his voice. "Christian men are in much demand by their Beys as galley slaves. You'd be chained at the oars until you die or drown. Women go to the Beys' bedrooms at night and haul water day by day."

"How can this be?" McMahon asked. "We are British subjects, protected by the Royal Navy."

"Captain, sir," Mrs. Rawlings called out. All eyes shifted to the pugnacious pregnant woman. "'Tis me recollection the Admiralty long ago signed the same treaty with the Barbaries as King Joseph. We can sail unmolested when you present our Mediterranean pass."

All eyes were back on the captain. "Alas, therein lies the problem. Our owners did not deem it necessary to obtain this document." He let that sink in. "We sail without the required pass. And as there are no warships about to come to our rescue, we are, therefore, very much at risk of capture."

CHAPTER 34

NO BOAT VENTURED OUT WHILE *THE DELIGHT* LINGERED IN THE OFFING. "It pains me so deeply to watch this slip away," Moira said. She nudged into Michael's side as she stifled a sniffle. He wrapped his arm around her. She dabbed her watery eyes.

"Aye, 'tis disappointing, but ya don't have sound so downtrodden," Danny observed. "Aye, 'tis a lovely sight, but hardly worth the risk. Wonder if'in they has any women left. Care ta wager if they been taken to harem service?"

"Danny, do not give credence to such a thought," Moira said, thinking, *Those poor ladies.*

Michael's attention was on the quarterdeck where MacNeal and Farrell held a whispered conference. "The Barbaries are not to be trifled with, Mr. Farrell. His Majesty lost near four hundred sailors to 'em last year. Every Christian's a target. They wreak havoc all along these coasts. Barbaries have enslaved entire villages, taking hundreds in a single raid in Ireland. A lonely vessel such as ourselves is easy prey . . . with or without a pass."

MacNeal surveyed the harbour. "This is a puzzle, won't you say, Mr. Farrell?"

"Sir?"

"That no boat is in the water. Surely, they've seen us by now. One would think these islanders would welcome a chance to trade. Do you see any sign of activity?" MacNeal asked.

"None that I can make out, sir."

"My glass, Mr. Farrell." After a pause, "Curious."

"Sir?"

MacNeal handed him the glass. "Just there inside the little cove."

Farrell struggled to control the bouncing circle of shore. "Lanteen rig, I'd say, judgin' by how forward the mast. Be more clear once they gets that yard in place. A coastal fisher?"

"Anything else? The flag for example."

"Don't recognize it, sir. Certainly not Portugal or Spain."

"Algiers. Most unwelcome company. Doesn't appear to be a watch on deck." MacNeal called to the helmsman. "Mr. Clarke. Two points west by southwest."

"Skirting Faial are we?" Clarke asked.

"Aye, best not loiter about, Mr. Clarke. We're in no state to defend ourselves. We can make do 'til we reach King's Station in Antigua."

Michael took his leave to check on Knob. "Miss Moira was just here an hour ago, Mr. Shea. She be one pleasant one to be 'round."

"Indeed she is."

"She may have an eye now for Mr. Farrell. The lad's found one reason or another ta be visitin' me when Miss Moira's here."

"I see," Michael muttered. "Still, I'd like to see your leg."

"Ya doubtin' her work?"

"Not at all. But I haven't seen your progress this day." Michael smiled when he saw the wound healing. "Have you ever had such a—" A knock interrupted Michael. It was Farrell. "Captain want's ya on deck. A special request ta be puttin' to ya."

Michael alternated glances between his patient, the wound, and the officer. "Can it wait?"

An uncertain friction filled the room.

"Go on, Mr. Shea. A sailor don't keep Captain waitin'," Knob said.

"I'll be up presently," Michael said, "soon as I close this binding."

Farrell stomped off knowing Michael was taking his sweet time.

Knob was displeased. "Why the rudeness, Mr. Shea? He's jest relaying Captain's orders. That's not how ya treat a mate and a friend."

"I don't like distraction when I've got my mind on a thing and getting it done," Michael lied. "Perhaps I'm sore our medicine supplies is empty," he lied again. "I have nothing to work with and now, no chance to refresh at Graciosa."

"That be MacNeal's doin', not Farrell's."

Once on deck, Michael waited outside the quarterdeck while Mac-Neal paced with Farrell. MacNeal was aware two young men failed to acknowledge each other as had become their custom. *Jealous suitors?* popped into his head. As payback for Michael's tardiness, MacNeal let Michael cool his heels for some time. "Ah, Mr. Shea, finally, were you indisposed?"

"Was assessing Mr. Knob's progress."

"And how is our patient?"

"Better, sir. Could walk soon with a crutch, but I still worry about infection."

MacNeal considered this for a moment, then asked, "How's the mood with our indentureds?"

"Sour, sir."

"Most unfortunate, but unavoidable."

"Aye, sir," was Michael's terse reply.

MacNeal leaned in to create an air of familiarity. "Mr. Shea, I have a proposition for you." He smiled. "We have the ocean to ourselves. Am hoping you might orchestrate some music and a dance for us. What ya say, aye? Help lift the ship's spirits once these squalls pass?"

"If so ordered, sir," Michael pouted.

"I hope you can help to dispel the mood. Get our minds off the Azores."

"If I may be frank, sir," Michael answered.

"By all means."

"Perhaps some time to grieve would be appropriate. The lost sight of land is still fresh. Feelings is raw."

"Grieve?" MacNeal replied. "It'll only be a fortnight or two before we sees land again." The cold line squall and low-lying clouds started to break up behind MacNeal. "A sailor knows the best way to forget what's behind. Look forward, is what I recommend, always."

"Sound advice, sir. Might I suggest a look behind yourself?"

MacNeal and Farrell turned to face the bow. Both gasped when they saw a lush green island in the distance emerge from the passing squall. "Oh Lord," Farrell exclaimed. "What's this? Have we circled back to Graciosa?"

"Faial's more like it, Mr. Farrell," answered Clarke at the helm. "That volcano's much bigger than the sleepy ones on Graciosa."

MacNeal studied the island. "My glass, Mr. Farrell." After a quick survey, MacNeal confirmed. "It's Faial alright. That'll be Horta." He snapped the glass shut. "Mr. Farrell, do we have power dry enough to fire the gun?"

"Enough for a salute, maybe two. That'll pick our spirits up, sir, to land at Horta."

MacNeal called to his helmsman. "Mr. Clarke, hard to port, bring 'er due south towards that squall line."

"Due south it is," Clarke sang out.

"Sir?" Farrell asked.

"We're not entering Horta, Mr. Farrell, far from it. There are two Barbary dhows riding anchor and a galley run up on the beach. They're not here on a fishing expedition. Am hoping our gun will discourage them should they attempt to board us."

"Will they give chase, sir?"

"I expect they will." MacNeal put his glass to the harbour. "There it is." A second later, the retort of a gun reached *The Delight*. "They're gathering crew."

MacNeal snapped his glass shut and turned to face the quarterdeck. "Gentlemen, we have a head start, let's make the best of it. Mr. Farrell, set all the sail we can. Then go below to organize a defense from the ranks of our passengers. Collect anyone who knows a firearm. You must turn 'em into marines with the muskets in the arms chest. You'll also need a gun boy or two to help 'em reload. Can't spare any crew. Need 'em to sail as sharp as she can be." He turned to address Michael. "Mr. Shea, collect a stout lad or two to help Cook man the gun."

"Sir, it's no more than a signal gun," Farrell observed.

"It'll have to do. Fill it with nails, any metal bits you can find. We'll have a nasty hello for the Suleimans if they venture close."

"Sir, I have no idea how to operate it," Michael said.

"Cook'll prime and fire. You will assist him. Quick now."

Forgetting his jealousy, Michael imitated Farrell's knuckle to the forehead to acknowledge the order. Now partners again, they bounded down the ladder into the 'tween deck. Their sudden agitated appearance filled the hold with apprehension. Farrell explained the situation.

Little Jimmy McMahon spoke first. "Pirates! I knew they'd come for us." He turned to his father. "See, I told you so."

"Now lad, hush," McMahon said, putting his arm around the boy.

Farrell got to the point. "Anyone know how to handle firearms?"

Mrs. Rawlings got the ball rolling. "Mr. Farrell, me husband were good enough to get 'isself arrested for poaching. Not that we ever ate much venison, but we did enjoy us rabbit and squirrel now and again." Horace Rawlings stepped forward with a mix of embarrassment and excitement. He made a show of bowing and blowing a kiss her way.

McMahon and Hoecker also professed experience, though Farrell was dismayed to realize their "experience" was assisting rural gentlemen with fouling pieces on bird hunts. Tombler joined them. Something about the way Tombler stood calm, feet apart, reassured Farrell. He didn't feel a need to inquire. He turned to the assembled. "I could use a lad or two t'assist with powder and shot."

"I'll give it a go," Simon called out. He was at once accosted by his elders for speaking up.

Marta grabbed Simon's arm. "Not to worry, my dearest," he said loud enough for all to hear, "am sure this'll come to naught. We kin share a laugh about pretending ta be soldiers after dinner." He gave her a kiss on the forehead. It did not appease his beloved. In a softer voice, Simon asked Moira, "Could you comfort my dear wife, just for the short while we're topside?"

"You're a dunderhead, Simon," Moira answered, "you know nothing about this business."

"True," he said, "but one must protect the ones they love."

She glared at him. When he stepped forward, two other Palatine lads joined him.

Farrell addressed them again. "Ladies, gentlemen. None of us is soldiers. But as we have no marines, we must do what we kin ta keep them scimitars at bay."

"How long 'til we know?" Mrs. Rawlings asked.

"Could be an hour or more. Wind, weather, and wave be in our favor. All passengers must remain below. That understood?"

Moira spoke up. "Let me pass, Liam, I must attend to Mr. Knob while I can."

After Farrell led his marines up on deck, Michael asked for help with the ship's signal gun. Danny quickly volunteered. He gave Jimmy a pat on the head and mussed his hair. "Not ta worry, lad. We'll scare 'dem pirates away for ya."

Michael wasn't surprised at Danny's eagerness. But he felt an urge to chide him nonetheless. "You don't have a wink of an idea how to shoot these things."

"No more than you," he said, "but I'd rather fight than wait here in the dark, hiding with the women." Danny eyes were bursting with excitement. "Let's go, quickly now, before the excitement's over."

On deck, the recruits observed MacNeal in action, pacing the deck, at one point up on the taffrail, the next barking orders to raise more sail to maximize speed on a run. "Navigatin' may not be our captain's game," Danny whispered to his battlemates, "but he sure seems ready for a fight."

"That he does," Tombler said. "He's got blood in his eye. I likes that in an officer."

"Thought you was a blacksmith."

"That too."

Michael and Danny looked at him, expecting more, but Tombler didn't elaborate.

Danny grabbed a ratline and jumped up on the gunnel for a better view. "Looks like two boats. One setting sail. One's a galley. Don't think they has trading on their minds."

"Indeed they don't," Farrell said. "Vessels is coastal raiders. Barbaries use 'em to hop from island to island. They're meant for shallow water. Galley will try to ram and board us. Can't sees how many's in 'em at this point. Will be ugly if'in they catch us."

"Can they?" Michael asked.

"Depends on the wind," Farrell answered, "if we work it right. But with this rig," he raised a hand towards the half-repaired masts, "the galley's got speed on us in a light breeze. Expect Captain to test how they sails, see which points gives 'em a weakness."

"Have you been in sea fight?"

"Never fired no gun in action. Only in practice."

"I'm betting the captain has," Tombler said.

"That he has," Farrell replied, "on the North American station."

"What's our plan then?" Michael asked.

"Simple, Captain means to run away."

"And if that fails?" Danny asked.

"Fight," Farrell replied. "We have four men to fire muskets, twelve muskets, and a signal gun loaded with nails and bits. Enough powder for few volleys, assumin' we reload in time."

"An' if we're boarded?" Danny asked.

"Best not think about bein' boarded."

Chapter 35

MacNeal was a whirlwind. After setting sails and course, he instructed Farrell and his musket crew how to load powder and shot, dry runs at first. Simon and two Palatines were assigned to reload for the shooters. For the gun crew, Cook divided up roles. Michael prepared powder and wads of metal bits rolled up in thin cloth. Ramrod went to Danny. Cook would aim and fire. MacNeal brought the firing crews together.

"Gentlemen, the Barbaries will catch us in an hour or so. When they do, we will wait until the very last moment before we volley. I want you to see their teeth, if they have any, before ya fire. Not a shot's ta be fired without my direct order. Is that understood?"

All nodded, eyes riveted on MacNeal.

"We will unleash our first volley just as they spring upon us. Close range. All four at once. Aim for the lead man in the bow. Fire. They'll expect a reloading lull, so grab a second musket and on my order, we hit 'em with a second volley. Again, aim for the lead man. Then it's Cook's turn to hit 'em with the grape. Then marines, ready your next volley. Again, no one fires except on my command. And you are to remain here at this larboard station. This is your only battle station. Is that clear?"

"Aye, sir," was the collective reply.

"We repeat until we're out of powder," MacNeal said.

"An' then?" Rawlings asked.

"Grab a cutlass." MacNeal opened the lid to the arms chest. "Do as much damage as you can. You have nothing to lose. Death's better than capture." The prospect of hand-to-hand fighting sobered the recruits. They listened to the ship's groaning before the captain spoke again. "Our plan is to avoid the sword. Make your shots count. If we kin make it hot enough to give them hesitation, we may have a chance. Let's give this a bit of practice."

Hoecker, Rawlings, and McMahon stumbled through the procedure. In their experience gentlemen took their time. There was plenty of time to reload. MacNeal noticed that Tombler knew the drill.

After four practices, MacNeal ordered out powder and shot. At his command, "Fire!" two shots rang out, and a second later, a third. The fourth came when McMahon remembered to cock the hammer. "Again," MacNeal ordered. The procedure took nearly six minutes. "Mr. Tombler, assist Mr. Farrell to drill these men on reloading. Must be faster. When we're ready for action, load all the muskets, three to each man."

"Aye, sir."

"Cook, two musket volleys, then it's your turn."

"Aye, sir."

"Now gentlemen, if you could join me in a prayer." The crew drew tight around MacNeal as he invoked the Almighty.

"Dear Lord, if it be in your power to save your devoted Christian brethren from the torments of everlasting slavery at the hands of these Algerian buggers, may you steady our hands and sharpen our minds, and forgive us from having to break your most sacred commandment. Amen." MacNeal left them as they echoed "Amen!"

"An odd sort of prayer, don't you think?" Hoecker said to no one in particular.

"Aye, 'tis," Danny answered, "but it does have a practical ring to it."

CHAPTER 36

Once *The Delight* fully escaped the influence of Faial's headlands, her sails filled and she gained momentum. MacNeal ordered more sail. Once these were set, he eased his pacing. "Gentlemen, we'll soon have a chance to see how our Barbary sails." He put *The Delight* on a reach to sail west. *The Delight* edged away slightly from the galley. The Barbary dhow was stuck in the harbour's dead air. Its sails slack, the crew put in a longboat to tow their ship to the wind.

MacNeal and crew knew the real threat was the galley. Once its oarsmen hit their stride, the needle-nosed craft could knife through a calm ocean. In light air, any galley can easily overtake a ship in full sail. MacNeal relaxed a little when the galley hit the rougher waters of the open ocean. It slowed a bit, but it was still faster than *The Delight* as MacNeal ordered a more southerly course. *He certainly takes his time making a turn,* the captain mused. He ordered a series of zigzags.

"What's with all this back and forth?" Hoecker asked.

"Lookin' for a weakness," Farrell answered. "The galley likes runnin' best. They struggle when wind's to their starboard. Hopefully, Captain'll think of somethin' them Barbaries has overlooked, like that bit o' weather ahead." Farrell nodded to the storm line in the distance. "Them squalls kin help us if'in we gets there before they gets here."

Despite the zigzag turns, the galley gained on them. MacNeal got his battle plan underway. He put his ship before the wind for the last part of the chase. "Mr. Farrell, let the men ready themselves. I need your attention now. We will reach westerly to gain momentum. Then be prepared to wear ship. Cook, O'Mara, Shea, stand by with the gun."

"Make yer preparations obvious and sloppy, lads, and be slack about it," MacNeal said. "Galley intends to ram and board us. We will let him think he easily can. I aim to draw him to the squall line. When the squall hits, we wear 'round, sharp as possible. I intend to bring our broadside against her to run down and disable them sweeps."

"Sir, ta wear in a squall? Don't we risk broachin'?" Farrell asked.

"Precisely what I want this Barbary to worry about. 'Tis far more dangerous for him than us. Our sloppiness should make him think we'd never attempt to wear in this sea. But we'll be ready. We know what we're about. He'll have ta guess our intent. I'm hoping it'll linger on his mind enough to distract him, force him to hesitate."

Michael surveyed the situation and interrupted MacNeal. "Sir, they're about ta attack on the larboard side. Shouldn't we get our marines to larboard?"

"Do not question me, Mr. Shea," MacNeal snapped. "You will fire from this position." Michael stiffened up at MacNeal's bite. "You'll see soon enough. Stand steady. Be ready."

In the anticipatory silence, *The Delight* could hear the steady thump, thump, thump of a drum beating the rhythmic cadence, and the snap of a whip as rowing master urged his slaves to greater effort on the oars. As the galley closed in, *The Delight's* crew could hear each drumbeat answered by grunts from the rowers. Thump-grunt, thump-grunt—as steady as a timepiece.

"Let's give him a show, Mr. Farrell," MacNeal said. "Make him think we're tryin' to run and hide in the squall. Let's see how well he sails on a reach in this sea. Prepare to tack." Farrell relayed the orders. To the helmsman, MacNeal ordered, "Mr. Clarke, bring her more south on a broad reach. Steady. Steady."

The tempo of the attacker's drum increased sharply as the galley closed in.

"He's drooling now," MacNeal said to the quarterdeck, "thinks he kin ram us. Hear how he's tryin' to pick up speed? Steady, lads, steady."

Then he gave the key command. "Prepare to wear ship."

Farrell barked out the orders.

"Bring 'er round, Mr. Clarke. Sharply, now, very sharply."

Clarke pushed the helm down hard. *The Delight* threw her stern across the wind. The ship spun sharply around as if riding on a whirlwind. The makeshift spanker came across the quarterdeck, slowly at first and then it slammed across the deck with an enormous crunch and snapped full in the wind. Rigging groaned under the intense burst of pressure. *The Delight* was now sailing parallel to the galley in the opposite direction.

"Hard starboard," MacNeal yelled, "harder, harder. Run down them sweeps."

The galley captain hadn't anticipated the maneuver. Caught off guard, he ordered a hasty turn but forgot to reset his sail. The fresh breeze hit the sail and quickly overpowered the galley. The galley heeled sharply to larboard, oars too deep in the ocean, her starboard oars caught in mid-air. Her captain had to pause to ease his sail to regain control, but he wasn't fast enough. *The Delight* crashed through the galley's line of larboard oars, cracking and splintering them like dry twigs.

The Barbaries heaved grappling lines. Three lines landed amidships. *The Delight* groaned under the weight of the galley in tow.

"Mr. Farrell, sail us to weather."

MacNeal turned his attention to his firing line. "Marines, ready." He raced to join them. "Steady lads." As the grappling lines squeezed taut, the first wave of boarders crouched on the galley's bow.

"Mr. Clarke, two points starboard."

The galley came into full view as *The Delight* turned. When the first Barbary stood up, MacNeal hissed, "He's the one, boys. You kin almost feel the devil ready to burst outta that one." The lead raider was color-ful. Maroon silk pantaloons tied off below the knee, a broad yellow and green striped belt with an unbuttoned brown leather vest over his bare muscular chest. When the second stood, MacNeal whispered, "Hold on, hold on." Finally, when the third and fourth raiders stood, MacNeal gave the order. "Fire!"

Battle-hardened Barbaries aren't intimidated by musket fire. But as they hadn't expected gun play from a cargo ship, the surprise resistance caused them to hesitate even though the shots missed. They regrouped behind their lead man. He sneered at the Christians and sliced the air with his glimmering sword.

The Delight's marines handed off the discharged weapons and readied their second volley.

"Ready lads," MacNeal called. "Mr. Clarke, another point if you please." He let the lead man get a hand on *The Delight*. "Fire!" Two balls found their mark. The would-be boarder crumpled over, his bearded face grimacing in surprise. Blood oozed from his dark brown chest and seeped over his belt and down his loose-fitting trousers.

The Barbaries hesitated before renewing their attack. This time a taller man with slender but chiseled features under a sharply trimmed beard and mustache took the lead. He wore the same colorful regalia as his predecessor and sported a red leather skull cap.

"Mr. Cook, ready your gun."

As the Barbaries made another attempt, they met the roar of the signal gun. The spray of shrapnel at close range produced an explosion of blood and bits of skin that splattered across the galley's bow. The Barbaries hesitated as the leader and two others fell. A third leader emerged, dressed in the same red-capped attire. But this one sported a white blouse trimmed with European-style ruffles. No shots greeted them. *The Delight*'s marines weren't ready.

MacNeal grabbed two boarding cutlasses from the arms chest and gave one to Simon, the other to Tombler. "Come on lads, we've got to cut their lines! Hop to it, now. Chop as hard and quick as ya can!"

Simon hacked away at the first line while Tombler worked at the second. While they hacked, the lead Barbary jumped over the gunnel and onto the deck of *The Delight*. MacNeal drew his sword and raced to take on the boarder. Simon hit the first line again and again before it finally snapped. Tombler, despite his strength, needed as much time to sever the second line. Simon turned for the third line but hesitated at the sight of the Barbary and MacNeal sizing each other up, swords at the ready. MacNeal surprised the Barbary with a charge and wrestled him to the deck.

A second boarder jumped on board. Rawlings grabbed the cutlass but his advance did little to scare the boarder. The Barbary scoffed at the sight of such puny resistance. He gave a toothy smile from his perch on the gunnel, like a hawk ready to pounce on a mouse. He drilled his eyes into Rawlings's. Rawlings froze, his cutlass wavering. Briefly, the boarder enjoyed gloating over an easy kill. But Tombler didn't hesitate. He put all his energy into his cutlass swing. The blade buried itself in the raider's gut. Blood splashed. Tombler couldn't withdraw the cutlass, so he thrust it deeper and pushed the boarder overboard. "Give me that," he said, taking Rawlings's cutlass. Tombler turned his attention to aiding MacNeal.

"Cut the line!" MacNeal roared. "Cut the line!"

Simon was ready to jump at MacNeal's order, but Tombler waved him off, as it was too dangerous to try to slip behind the Barbary and the captain. Tombler hacked through the line. Three Barbaries fell into the sea as *The Delight* pulled away from the galley.

The effort to yell that command distracted MacNeal's attention just long enough for the red-capped attacker to break out of the captain's grasp. He regained his feet, backed away, and drew his scimitar, his legs spread wide in a crouch, not sure which enemy to attack. *Renew with leader? Challenge the giant?* He studied their feet. Widespread stance, *experienced seaman.* The other held his feet close together. *Not a sailor. Dispatch the giant first.*

To hold off MacNeal, the raider made a threatening show, waving his boarding sword high in his right hand while simultaneously slashing his scimitar in his left for a lunge at Tombler.

Simon was just behind the Barbary close to where he had severed the second boarding line. He turned to track MacNeal and Tombler's movements. It was in his turn towards MacNeal that the Barbary's scimitar windup, meant for Tombler, caught Simon across his throat in a downward slash. Simon fell back in shock, a flood of blood pouring out.

The raider now had both arms extended, one weapon behind, wedged in Simon's collarbone, the other waving a sword towards MacNeal. As the Barbary turned to see why his scimitar was stuck, Tombler pounced, cleaving his cutlass into the raider's gut, just under the ribcage. There was a loud walloping sound as the cutlass hit.

The blow forced the raider to release his weapons. He doubled over, his hands trying to hold his sliced gut together as he fell to his knees in disbelief. He sat back on his heels, wordlessly watching his slayers. His complexion turned grey. MacNeal ran him through. The corsair crumpled over. MacNeal sneered at him, put a foot on the bloodied chest, and used both hands to retrieve his sword.

Michael ran to Simon's side.

CHAPTER 37

LIKE A COCK ABOUT TO CROW, MACNEAL JUMPED ON THE GUNNEL TO watch the crippled galley slip astern and founder when a swell hit her broadside. The galley raiders found themselves in a free for all, thrashing desperately about for broken oars and other debris for flotation. None gave a thought to the screaming men chained at the oars, straining against their shackles as the galley slipped beneath the swells. The sight unnerved the once cocky MacNeal.

"Mr. Farrell, quick as you can, into the squall." To his marines, "Well done lads. God chose to answer our prayers. We won't be so fortunate if that dhow catches us." Then he remembered that victory came with a price.

MacNeal walked over to a desolate Michael, who cradled Simon's blood-soaked body in his arms. "Nothing I can do." Michael barely got the words out. "No time to . . ."

MacNeal put hand on Michael's shoulder. "Nothing you could do, lad, 'twas God's will." He started a prayer. "Dear God, have—" He was interrupted by a scream.

"Let go of me!"

"Moira!" Michael shouted. He laid Simon down and rushed towards the hatchway just ahead of MacNeal, Danny, and Tombler. But Michael fell back as a bearded Barbary raider in red skull cap charged up the ladder, wielding boarding sword and scimitar. Michael dodged the first two swings of the sword, but the smaller scimitar sliced across his back. He collapsed to his knees. The raider, eyes blazing, turned his attention to the other *Delights*. Michael crawled across the deck to the arms chest. The ship's defenders backed into a semicircle around the companionway and the invader. MacNeal took center position with his bloodied steel blade.

"Marines," yelled MacNeal, "prepare to fire." His order was followed by the rattling of ramming rods stuffing powder and shot into muskets.

The second figure up the ladder was Moira, who was held as a shield by another corsair. He was powerful enough to hold her above the deck with his left arm as she squirmed and kicked to no avail. He flung her around, left and right, as he waved his sword in tight circles, sizing up his opponents.

The lead Barbary did the same as he directed a short speech towards MacNeal. Battle commanders can spot each other instantly. The burly armed Barbary holding Moira threatened her throat with his sword hand, confident with his bargaining chip. The leader waving towards the approaching dhow.

MacNeal pointed to his line of gunners and his line of swordsmen, indicating the difficult odds. "Steady on, Mr. Farrell," MacNeal called out. *The Delight* was just ahead of a squall line that was coming up fast behind the Barbaries. The crew and defenders could see the violent swirling sea approaching. The raiders could not. MacNeal yelled out his battle plan. "When she shutters, we fall on these bastards."

The lead Barbary repeated his speech, his voice more intense, and he sized up his European opponents.

Meanwhile, Michael crawled behind the invaders to reach the arms chest. He grabbed the first weapon he saw. The cutlass was heavier than he had expected. He could barely lift it.

MacNeal anticipated what Michael was up to. Keeping his eye on the lead attacker, the captain called out, "Mr. Shea, patience. Stand down." MacNeal repeated himself, louder the second time, and made faces as he spoke to make it seem he was trying to communicate with the Barbaries. "You don't have a chance. They are experienced killers. You are not, Mr. Shea."

Moira got into the yelling game as she wiggled this way and that. "Michael, listen to the captain. They've killed Knob and the supercargo."

Danny inched up behind Michael, put a hand on his shoulder, and quietly took the cutlass.

A sudden pressure drop swept cold across the deck. The Barbaries couldn't risk turning around to see when the storm would strike. *The Delight* defenders could. The stalemate was short lived.

When the squall slammed into the stern with a roar of wind and rain, it forced the attackers off their mark for just a moment. As they wobbled off balance, Michael ran at the man holding Moira, tackling him inside the knees. The Barbary fell backward, rolled over Michael, and landed on the deck still holding Moira. This forced him to roll right and use his fighting arm to push off the deck to regain his feet. But with Moira weighing him down, he was slower than he expected. As he started to push up from the deck, Danny swung his cutlass down hard on the man's right arm and severed hand and sword from the arm. The man screamed. Moira wiggled free and crawled to safety by the quarterdeck. In disbelief, the Barbary grabbed his bloody stump and curled it over his heart. He watched his right hand, still clutching his sword, slide across the rain-swept deck. It left a bloody trail all the way to the gunnel.

Michael and Danny rushed to Moira. She sat with her back to the bulkhead, chin on her knees, eyes closed, shivering. Michael sidled next to her, put an arm around her. Danny crouched, feet wide apart, cutlass in hand, standing guard against a possible counterattack.

In the same instant, before the lead Barbary could regain his stance, MacNeal and the other *Delight* defenders swarmed over him. MacNeal drove his sword into the man's right side. The other *Delights* secured the warrior.

"Mr. Farrell, any sign of that dhow?"

"None, sir."

"The ship is yours." MacNeal bounded down hatch. "Mr. Shea!"

They found the supercargo face down in the passageway outside Knob's cabin. MacNeal rolled him over. His face was a bloody mess, his nose broken, and he had a huge welt on his forehead. Severe slash marks across his forearms. When he moaned, MacNeal and Michael turned their attention to Knob. He lay still in his bunk, slash marks over his face, arms, and chest. Michael was first to his side.

"Is he?" MacNeal asked from the door.

Michael held his breath as he put his head to Knob's chest. "He breathes."

"Save them, Mr. Shea. That's an order."

MacNeal raced back to the deck to resume command, bumping into Moira on his way out. His "Beg your pardon, Miss," alerted Michael that he had company. Moira's arms were crossed, her hands pulling her jacket tight. Michael held her in the darkness of Knob's cabin. Both were cold, soaked through, dripping, and shivering.

"I can't stop shaking."

"I'm glad you're . . ." He pulled her close. They held each other for warmth and comfort. The creaking of the ship and the chattering of teeth punctuated their sense of sanctuary from the screaming squall above.

"We heard a crash, glass breaking. They came in through Captain's window." Moira shivered as she spoke. "Saw me peeking out Knob's door. I made for the ladder to warn you. The big one grabbed me. The other one went after Knob. Would've killed me outright but the supercargo surprised him from behind yelling something. That's when that brute threw me against the door. Ripped my blouse open. Such a loathsome look, like he'd never seen a woman before. Ain't no wonder if he hadn't. Such ugliness. Supercargo had a pistol and was yelling something. My captor jabbered back at him and then laughed as the other one jumped out of the cabin and beat him most brutally. That's when they dragged me up the ladder."

"How do you fare now, Moira? Anything broken or amiss that might need attention?"

"Can you just hold me?"

He hugged her tighter before he broke the news. "I'm sorry to have to tell you, we've lost a brave lad. Simon's gone."

"Simon? No, can't be!" Forgetting that she was cold, wet, and exposed, Moira turned to face him. "What happened? Does Marta know?"

"Not yet." He related Simon's bravery.

"Hold me, Michael. I'm scared."

He did for a few moments. "Moira, I must check on our supercargo. If you can, keep an eye on Knob, hold his hand, and get him to talking. His wounds look survivable."

"What about Marta?"

"We're needed here first." He held her hand as he walked away, not wanting to let go. She smiled at the gesture and realized she wasn't shivering.

Outside Knob's cabin, Edmund-Tell was breathing heavy, trying to roll himself into a kneeling position.

"Sir, let me assist," Michael said.

"Is the girl safe? Knob? The ship?"

"They are."

Edmund-Tell replied: "Heard her and Knob talking, laughing these past days." He vomited. It took him a few minutes to recover as Michael softly rubbed the man's fleshy shoulder. "She's a godsend to Knob. Haven't heard him so lively since we lost the mate. Methinks cupid nicked our carpenter. Mr. Farrell, too, from what I hear."

"Can you rise, sir?"

"If you can lend a hand." He wobbled to his feet, bracing himself against the bulkhead.

Michael studied the man. "Much bruising and swelling and bleeding. I can stitch these gashes. Most of the bleeding's from a nasty cut above your nose. Appears broken."

"Endured worse," he said, rising full upright and leaning against the bulkhead. He let Michael wipe and inspect the gash. "I'd trade this beating any day if it would end the sickness."

"You've been a long time at sea, doesn't the sickness ease?"

"Eases when we hit the tropics." He patted his body, searched the deck. "Would you mind kindly retrieving my pistol there?"

When Michael stooped to reclaim the weapon, the supercargo took note of Michael's wound but kept quiet as he inspected the pistol. Satisfied, Edmund-Tell stuffed it into the waist of his britches. He produced a second pistol from his coat pocket and made the same inspection. Then pirate-like, he stuck the weapon in the other side of his britches.

"Mostly for show. Will you keep my secret?" he smirked. "Mr. Shea, it appears you have your own wounds to attend to." He called into Knob's cabin, "Miss, our young doctor needs your attention." Moira popped out. Edmund-Tell pointed to Michael's bloodied back.

"Michael, you're hurt!" She ran to his side.

"I'm all right," he lied.

"Don't be a hero, lad. We need you alive. Let the miss bandage ya. Now, if you'll excuse me, I feel compelled to visit with the captain."

"In this storm, sir?" Michael asked as Moira started to open his shirt to inspect the wound.

"Just a squall." He climbed up on deck.

"It can wait, Moira."

"No it can't, Michael. I can almost put my fingers in, like you did with Jonathan."

"Can you wrap me up tight for the moment? There's cloth in the chest. Let's comfort Marta, see if there's anything we can do before addressing this."

She wrapped a long piece of worn sailcloth around his chest and tied it with a line of cord from Knob's chest. He hissed and groaned as she pulled the knot tight. She helped him back into his bloodied shirt and jacket and they followed the supercargo into the storm.

CHAPTER 38

STILL SLUMPED BY THE SIDE, SIMON WAS SURROUNDED BY HIS PALATINE brethren. Marta, with strands of her hair plastered to her tear-stained cheeks, held his cold hand, trying to rub warmth and life back into it. She had tied her scarf around his neck to hide the horrible wound. Elder Brouchard muttered prayers. Moira pushed through the Palatines to be with Marta. They were both inconsolable.

Michael stood in the Palatines's circle as they mourned their loss. Danny joined him. "Yer bleeding, mate. Let me help ya."

"Some respect for our brave friend." They crossed themselves. Michael broke the silence. "I can't believe it, how life can extinguish so quickly, so suddenly. I've seen death before, Danny. Each is painful. With the sick, there's a sense of forewarning," he hunched over due to the pain of his injury, "of preparation. With Simon, so brave one instant, then gone the next. I didn't know what to do."

"Ya did more than ya realize, Michael. Ya gave him comfort as he left our world. 'Tis far better than goin' it alone."

They stood together awhile, grieving with Marta, hypnotized by the dolorous murmur of Palatine prayers, the rolling sea, the whistling wind, and the moaning *Delight* as the Palatines prepared his body.

Slowly, Michael's attention was diverted towards the quarterdeck where MacNeal and Edmund-Tell interrogated the captured corsairs. The raiders were sitting on the deck, backs against the hatch. At their feet, the body of the raider Tombler had slain. The leader's hands were bound behind him. The handless warrior wasn't bound, a small act of mercy so he could hold his left hand over his right stump. No effort had been offered to help him stem the bleeding.

"Again, would you please." MacNeal put the question he wanted answered to Edmund-Tell. "How many men on the dhow?" No reply.

"There be no medical treatment if they refuse my questions," he barked at his prisoners. "I'm of a mind to put them right over the side and be done with 'em. Let them know that."

The supercargo, pale and struggling with sickness, tried once again. "It's no use, James." He managed to stand up to face the captain. "I know their type. Fear, threats, death have little sway. They have much disdain for Christians. They seek revenge for the loss of Spain. It's why they enslave us."

"That was three hundred years ago," MacNeal noted.

"They still grieve the loss," the supercargo replied, "they harbour an everlasting resentment, nay, I should say, a deep, very deep hatred."

"But that was Spain's doing, not England's."

"Makes no difference. To them, all Christians are a plague on this earth, a scourge to be lanced. We are all infidels, invaders, Crusaders. Their distain has no end, and as you can see, it puts a lock on their tongues. Let me conduct my own interview if you please."

MacNeal left the inquisition to the supercargo. After a few minutes, a grudging back and forth emerged between the portly, pail Edmund-Tell and his muscular, dark brown prisoners. At one point, the supercargo pointed towards Michael, seeming to indicate that the skinny, disheveled lad could address the issue of the bleeding stump. The prisoner snarled and spit out some invective that turned the supercargo's pallid face blood red. The other prisoner hissed a few more words that further inflamed Edmund-Tell.

Danny also took notice of the interview. "What ya think they're jawin' about?" Danny asked.

The question broke Michael's fascination with the rhythm and sound of the foreign tongue. "Can't make any sense of it, but our Mr. Supercargo has a fluency with their language."

As neither could follow the interview, they turned away to look across the sea towards the wreckage of the galley and the dhow in the distance. "You think they'll rescue their comrades?" Danny asked.

"I should—" Michael's reply was interrupted by the sharp report of two pistols fired in close order by the supercargo, who was now enveloped by the smoke and smell of gunpowder. Before him, the one-handed prisoner fell back dead, blood oozing from his chest. The other sat twitching, wounded in the gut. The supercargo dropped his weapons, walked behind the wounded raider, and retrieved something long and thin from his waistcoat. With a flick of his wrist, a shaving razor opened and locked. With a single slash, he slit the Barbary's throat. A fountain of red blood poured onto the deck.

Standing tall, Edmund-Tell watched the blood drain into the scuppers as he calmly wiped the blade with a handkerchief, refolded it, and returned it to the waistcoat pocket. His nose wrinkled as if he had come across a pile of ripe refuse.

MacNeal bounded towards the supercargo, red faced with anger. "You have no right. Only I have power to command life and death."

"Legally correct," the supercargo replied, unfazed by his action. He stared at his victims as blood seeped from the gash over his nose. He tried to blink the blood out of his eyes.

Instinctively, Michael rushed over to assist the wounded, but both were gone. He closed their lifeless eyes. Then he studied the dead man's opened throat. The cut reminded him of Jonathan's, the way it sliced across the right side of the man's throat and neck, only this one had cleanly severed the artery.

The supercargo bent over the rail and let a stream of bile go over the side. Then he collapsed to his knees. MacNeal half-knelt with Michael beside him. "What the hell?"

Edmund-Tell's voice lost the polished edge it had when he was grilling the prisoners. "They recognized me," he paused, "I mean recognized who I was, what I was, how I'd been treated in Algiers. I were taken," he gulped for air, "as a lad. Was just ten. Mother sold to harem. I went with her and learned their ways and language. Took five years for Mother's family to pay the ransom. But Father was chained to a galley, like those poor souls who attacked us. Didn't last a year. Men like these . . ." he trailed off to stifle a vomit urge. "I don't speak coarse like they do. My accent's from the harem. They resented my upper-class language, especially that it was coming from an infidel. They turned to insults. I saw no need to let them remind me of my past."

MacNeal realized that Michael was listening. "Mr. Shea, not a word of this can be repeated."

"Aye, sir."

"Could you help our supercargo to his cabin? He and Knob need your attention. You are dismissed from the deck."

Michael tried but couldn't. MacNeal realized why. "My god, man, you're bleeding." He helped Michael up. "O'Mara, help our supercargo get below."

"Aye, sir."

MacNeal stood to acknowledge the looks from the rest of the crew and passengers. "Mr. Farrell!" He walked over to the bodies of the invaders. "Over the side with this garbage."

His order met with no hesitation.

CHAPTER 39

Michael grimaced at the foot of the companionway ladder. It was his first attempt to stand fully upright after a sleepless night in Knob's cabin. His slightly scabbed skin separated like the splintering of a sapling. The pain kept him hunched as he waited for Simon's funeral to proceed.

Danny joined him on the outskirts of the crew. "How's it feel to be the patient for once?"

"Like I slept in a briar patch. Moving terribly slow this morning." Michael paused to rest and breathe. "Cook stitches tolerably well. Never do I want to go through that again."

A bell tolled. Elder Brouchard led the way. Mute passengers climbed the ladder one by one. The deck was full of the sounds of shuffling feet, rustling fabric, grieved weeping, and the creaking of the ship's rigging. Tombler and Hoecker helped two Palatine lads carry the shrouded Simon. Moira and Marta were last up.

MacNeal took his place to lead the service. Having lost one of their own, the Palatines would not form a choir as they had for the Rawlings family. Instead Brouchard prepared a sermon on the ephemeral nature of life. As MacNeal ended his opening prayer, Michael whispered, "Danny, if you could pop down and retrieve my fiddle and your flute, we could provide some solace. Give Simon a proper farewell after Brouchard lectures us."

"Gladly." Danny raced away.

They waited until Brouchard had run out of scripture to recite. Michael winced when he first put bow to string. His back screamed "stop" as he stretched bow arm to see how much movement the stitches would allow. "Something easy and mournful?"

"'Brian Boru's' then?" Danny suggested.

"Ah, most appropriate." Danny took the lead. Michael eased into the tune with long slow pulls of his bow, leaving Danny on the haunting melody. On the third rendition, as his arm loosened, Michael wove in harmonies and echoed the main melody. After their final notes, the creaking of the ship and splash of waves on the hull served as the tune's coda.

Brouchard let the silence linger before he bowed to thank the musicians for their inspiration. He invited MacNeal to close the service. The captain offered his best memory of a verse from Lamentations:

> *For the Lord will not cast us forever, about these seas.*
> *Though He causes us to grieve*
> *whenever He calls His children home,*
> *He will have compassion to ease our torments,*
> *according to the multitudes of His mercy.*

MacNeal nodded to Farrell as he closed his prayer. "Dear Lord, we commend our brother to your eternal care."

In the solemn silence, Farrell grunted the order. The funeral detail hoisted the mess table holding Simon to the rail's edge. They gave a quick push to raise the inboard side high. Simon slid into the sea . . . then a sobering splash. Marta let out a desolate cry and buried her face in her hands. Moira held her close and led the young widow to the hatch. The funeral circle opened a path for them. As the Palatines and passengers lingered on deck, Michael asked, "Another?"

"Lead on."

Michael's bow drew out a long, low note to introduce mournful air. By the second verse, Danny's flute doubled the melody. By the third reading, he added a harmony line that lent strength to the tune. They continued as the mourners dispersed, each lost in thought.

"Nice tune there, Michael. Where d'ya find that one?"

"'He Chose a Mournful Muse.' One of Handel's. Always liked the title. Best I could remember it. The muses must have loved that man. Such a lovely way of revealing a melody."

"Not bad for a German."

"Ah, Danny-boy, don't be so proud. The muses inspire any artist, regardless of his birth."

"Or her birth?" Mrs. Rawlings broke into the conversation. "Aren't the muses all daughters of Zeus? Cupid certainly vexes both the sexes." She rubbed her ample belly.

"Of course we agree." Michael gave her a nod. "'Twas indeed the work of the muse to create the lovely voice we know as Moira. And there's an equally wonderful singer in the form of Moira's older sister. She's the one who opened my ears to the Handel. Quite the actress as well."

"Our Miss Moira has an actress for a sister?" Mrs. Rawlings asked.

"Quite so," he replied. "Her sister, Emma, graced the London stages. Broke many a suitor's heart. I accompanied her rehearsals. Moira sang the other roles so Emma could learn her cues."

"There's another with a voice as fair as our sweet Moira? And they're sisters?" Mrs. Rawlings asked. "My, my, must have been quite a dilemma betwixt such talents. I wonder, could a young lad such as yerself avoid the mistake Paris made with his apple." She gave him a smile.

"The stage did land the sister a husband, an Army officer."

"And what of our Miss Moira?" she asked. "Have you given thought to what fortunes might await her in the Chesapeake?"

"I've heard Annapolis compares to Athens, ripe with culture and wealth. Should be many an opportunity in a new city on the rise."

"And what of employments, Mr. Shea?"

"Maybe a theater will redeem my contract. Danny here promises plenty of opportunity."

"Theatrics?" she scoffed. "A dubious aspiration, Mr. Shea, for one looking for a home. Music and theater certainly do not resonate as employment." She soothed her belly. "Come on, Horace," she took her husband's hand, "let's complete our walkabout while the air's pleasant."

"What's all that about?" Danny asked.

Michael shrugged.

CHAPTER 40

THE CLANG OF THE DINNER BELL BROKE THE SOMBER MOOD FOLLOWING Simon's burial, at least for the crew. They hustled into the mess with their usual enthusiasm, oblivious to the memory that their table had just said a final farewell to Simon.

Danny savored the smell. "What you think, Michael, kin we get a taste of hot supper?"

"Worth try," Michael said, "come on, time to change Knob's bandage."

They followed the crew through the galley and into Knob's cabin. After his inspection, Michael offered an update. "So far, so good, Mr. Knob, Miss Moira's tender care is keeping the black at bay. You may walk again one day."

"Not too soon, I hope," Knob said. "'Twould be a shame to give Miss Moira reason not ta visit once 'er grieving's done."

"Be assured she'll return. She enjoys scrounging at the hot meals your mates leave behind."

"Ya couldn't say it better," Danny said. "Such a different story for the crew. Ain't been no hot meal in the hold since we was in the Channel."

Farrell stuck his head in the cabin. "Well, misery likes its company they says."

"How d'ya mean there, Mr. Farrell?" Knob asked.

"Ain't likely they'll be much joy for the crew soon."

"How kin that be?" Knob righted himself. "We ain't been two months at sea. Can't 'ave ate everything yet."

"We didn't eat our share, Mr. Knob, sea 'as. The storms took the chickens and goats. We've lost more to spoilage than usual. Wouldn't of mattered if'in we'd secured provision in the Azores. Cook and me just

197

took inventory of our beef and pork. Most casks is spoilt. Bilge an' sea soakin's doing their best ta starve us."

"Can't we soak 'em?" Disappointment added fresh lines to Knob's grizzled face.

"Cook tried," the young mate replied. "Even the rats won't eat what's left. Much of our water's goin' as well. Best ta see if'in the sea can provide a meal. We needs a rain to collect some fresh drops."

"I saw Cook put porks o'er the side this morning," Danny said.

"Aye, he did. Sharks got 'em," Farrell answered. "Cook's all in a tizzy about it. He don't want to risk soaking the last precious few porks we have. You'll hear crew cryin' soon enough. It's pea porridge and biscuit tonight, not stew. No potatoes neither. Most is gone black."

"Most disappointing," Michael said. "I fear I'll crack a tooth on those damn biscuits."

"Mr. Shea, ya don't eat 'em dry, ya soak 'em, in the stew."

"Stew? Now there's a debate," Danny grunted, "with all that crawls from 'em clumps of sawdust."

"Best not to dwell on eatin'." Farrell answered. "Things'll improve."

"Perhaps there is an alternative," Michael said, "one that involves some just revenge."

"Tread carefully, Mr. Shea, sailors don't like to go against the Lord. He warns us plain, 'avenge not by yerselves, for 'tis written "vengeance *is* me own," 'tis I who'll repay,' saith the Lord."

"Interesting translation, but fear not, am sure the Lord weren't talking about fishing."

As the weather warmed, the seas calmed, and *The Delight* drifted lazily under cloudless skies across the Atlantic. Life was pleasant by most accounts, except biscuit was all they had to float in constantly thinning soup. Michael called on the cook.

"I likes the way ya put it," Cook said after mulling Michael's proposal. "'Twould be a tasty revenge on them sharks for stealin' me porks."

"Can you offer us something to bait the fish?" Michael asked.

Cook offered a foul piece of meat the rats had refused. "Crew won't touch it." Michael recoiled when the cook uncovered the joint. "Doubt you indentures will want it."

"No, they won't," Michael agreed.

"Then let's ready yer fishin' crew." He showed Michael how to fit hooks and fashion the bait on the ends of three stout lines. Knowing Michael's injury, Cook hauled the gear up on deck. "Let me remind ya," Cook said after Michael recruited Danny and Tombler, "fishin' shark outta the sea's no mean business. They won't take kindly ta leavin' their domain. If ya's lucky, ya snags a young one. Lord help ya if ya put a hook into his daddy. And, I warn ya, gettin' them monsters out of the ocean's the easy part. Am sure I needs not tell ya ta keep yer distance from the mouth. He'll take an arm or leg off faster than a jack kin say, 'God help me.'" Cook looked the team in the eye, one by one. "Pay extra mind. Avoid the creature's tail. Expect the most vigorous thrashin' about. One swipe of the tail kin batter a man to the deck an' break his bones."

"Then how, exactly, do we subdue this creature?" Danny asked.

"That's where the ax comes in handy," Cook replied. He picked up the long-handled blade he brought with him and gave it to Tombler. "Needs a big strong hand ta wield it quick like."

"I ain't no woodsman," Tombler said.

"Don't matter. Them meat hooks of yers is what counts," Cook replied. "Soon as the creature's on deck, remove the tail." He pantomimed the chopping action. "'Tis an easier chop than trying to behead the thing. Do it quick like, one chop, like Henry did to Queen Anne." Turning to Michael and Danny, Cook continued. "Now, while yer man Tombler's tryin' ta disengage the tail, you two have the honor of keepin' the creature's attention by pullin' on the hook an' line. He'll be right angry an' seek his revenge for tryin' to turn him in'ta dinner. 'Taint a pretty business, that's for sure. Once the shark gives up his ghost, we'll gut him straight away and make ready for a most bountiful stew. Ready?"

Michael leaned over the side trying to envision the procedure. "How do we haul up one of these monsters?"

"Takes a bit of muscle," Cook answered. "We run the lines over the gunnel through these blocks here and then round the capstan. We'll get a few hands to put their backs to it. It'll be yer duty, Danny, to get a line about his tail and guide the monster over the side. Once on deck, ya orchestrate his final agony, assumin' yer man Tombler can quickly dispatch the tail."

"Right, then let's get 'er done." Danny started coiling up the lines.

"Good luck to ya," Cook said. "Call if ya gets a nibble. Meantime, I've gots ta prepare something I can call dinner, *zee biscuit* à *la hot water*." It was the first time Michael had heard the cook express humour.

Danny and Michael made for the quarterdeck to drag the lines behind the ship. However, he was stopped by Farrell. "Hold on, there, Mr. O'Mara." Farrell adopted a more careful speech. "Officers only on the quarterdeck, unless Captain specifically invites ya, or if it's yer turn at the helm. You'll have to set yer lines forward. I'd suggest just there," he pointed to the leeward side, "where the cook used to set lines to freshen his meats."

"For the love of God," Danny protested, "Who made you Lord of the sea?"

Michael intervened. "Let's just focus on what we can do." Michael got his hands around the coiled lines. "Don't blame our mate. It's not in Liam's power to rewrite the rules of the sea." Michael gave the lines a tug to get Danny walking towards mid-ship.

They unraveled the lines and played them out as the cook had explained. "What's with his new fancy talk?" Danny grumbled as they stretched their necks to watch the lines disappear under their wake, "Who put a stick up his arse?"

"I don't think its his arse we're talkin about," Michael said, pulling a line to see if the bait was still there. "I'd say Moira and Marta have something to do with his new attitude." He jabbed Danny's arm. "Open yer eyes, Danny boy. Our mate is love struck. Keep an eye on him when Moira and Marta mourn on their promenade. See how long he takes before he finds reason to inspect the deck."

"Got his eye on Marta, has he? Can't blame him, though I don't welcome the competition. I'll make me play, once Mrs. Carrington's past grievin' her husband."

"Rather considerate of you," Michael said. "But I don't think you have to worry about our mate. I'm thinking our Mr. Farrell's got his eye the taller of our lovelies."

"Moira? Your child admirer? Well, well, well. That makes life more lively for ya, don't it?"

"It does," Michael mused. "Our Mr. Farrell's not thinking of Moira as the child we know."

"Do I detect jealousy?"

"I'm not sure." Michael let his fishing line breathe.

"Better make up yer mind, my friend, and make yer case while love is fresh on the bloom. Ya won't get a second chance if she gets use to Farrell's attentions. Now that I study the situation, seems he's taken a keener interest in how his clothes fit."

"I had thought Moira would favor someone with a bit more polish."

"Don't underestimate a challenger, Michael. Unless ya have a fortune, ya never kin know what really warms a lady's heart."

"You've talked with Moira?"

"Just a bit of advice, Michael. Which side of the purse was it your dear Emma found favor for when she had ta make a choice?"

CHAPTER 41

MICHAEL SPENT THE REST OF THE MORNING STARING OFF TO THE HORIzon, transfixed by the infinite emptiness. Here and there he gave his lines a jerk or two without purpose. He was still at his post when the captain made his appearance, sextant in hand, on the quarterdeck. "Any luck with our dinner there?" MacNeal called out. The captain's call shook the fisherman out of his daydream.

"Not as yet."

"It's been near four hours. Ya think they'd be hungry by now," Cook said, emerging from the galley. "Ya wants ta see what's left on them hooks?"

Michael reeled the bait in until it bounced in the ship's wake. "Mostly still there. Oh lord!" He and Cook quickly turned to face the wind, backs to the bait. "Do sharks like rancid meat?" Michael let the line go to hide the smell under the waterline.

"Fish stew don't seem so likely, do it?" Cook said.

Michael wasn't listening. He had his eyes on Moira. "Would you mind terribly if you could spell me a moment? I feel a need to pay my respects to a couple of ladies while I have a chance." He handed the lines to the cook and hobbled away.

Cook found himself holding the lines, flipping them from hand to hand. "Hold on, here, Mr. Shea. It's not me place ta be idle on—" He let out a yell that filled the entire deck as one of the lines yanked him against the side, leaving a rope burn in his hand.

"Ya bastard, I'll get you for this," Cook snarled. He let go the line and secured the bitter end to a belaying pin before the line snapped taut. Turning aft, he announced for all to hear, "Captain, sir, we may have ourselves a stew tonight!" Then to Michael, he ordered, "Mr. Shea, round yer fishing crew. I needs ta run below and get me knives."

"Come on, Michael," Danny said with a fire in his eyes, "what you waitin' for? Let's get this bugger on deck."

It was Michael's turn to yell at the quarterdeck. "Captain MacNeal, sir, might we have a few hands to pull our dinner out of the sea?"

Glad to give up his charade with the sextant, MacNeal released Farrell to take charge. Farrell tied a block on taut line and ran another line through it. He then had a sailor run up the rump main mast with a block, run the new line through, and lead the line back to the capstan. A half hour later, 250 pounds of thrashing shark was lowered tail first onto the deck to the cheers of the passengers. Three of Farrell's sailors secured a line around the tail and struggled to control it as Tombler turned it into a tailless shark. Cook shook his head. "Only a mako," he observed, "but good for a couple of meals."

The shark lasted three days. Then it was back to thin soup and bug-filled biscuit. But complaints were few as everyone knew that within a fortnight, they'd find the Leeward Islands. They smelled land for two days before Antigua was sighted.

Within minutes of anchoring off Navy Dockyard, MacNeal and Farrell put ashore to attend to repairs, Cook and Supercargo Edmund-Tell to resupply provisions. That first meal: beef for the crew, hot goat stew for the indentureds.

By day's end, the main and foremasts had been stripped and readied to sprout again. There was relentless hammering everywhere. Most of this seemed to be right above Knob's cabin when Michael checked on his patient.

"Speak up, lad, I can't hear with this incessant clamour."

"Tryin' to say, Mr. Knob, two breaks are mending. Bruising looks good." Michael turned back to inspect Knob's lower leg. "Moira might have saved your leg."

"Can't 'ear ya."

There was a pause in the hammering. Michael found himself shouting, "We must find proper medicines on the island," before speaking normally, "Captain about?"

"Aye, but he's got company, merchants." Knob pointed towards the bulkhead that separated his cabin from MacNeal's.

"Will the captain replenish our medicine chest?"

"Ya kin ask. Put yer ear to the bulkhead, see where they's at."

Michael didn't need any prompting to eavesdrop. Once he got his ear against a seam in the bulkhead, his eyes widened when he heard the captain's voice.

"We have more than sufficient funds on draft with our banks in London."

Michael couldn't hear the quieter voices. Then there was a loud thud as someone slammed a hand on a table and MacNeal cried, "This is piracy!" Several voices growled at once. Michael could make out another voice, ". . . nothing of the sort." He gave Knob a puzzled look. The sailor put a finger to his lips and motioned for Michael to stay put.

"My dear Captain, you must realize an opportunity when one presents itself." Edmund-Tell, the supercargo, was talking as if to a child.

"This is not what we have promised," MacNeal snapped.

"Nor was the gale that stole our masts, nor the pirates that nearly killed us," Edmund-Tell countered. "We are overdue. That makes every transaction more costly."

"No voyage is without risk . . ." MacNeal started to say something else, but he was cut off.

"Nevertheless, we are in need of hurried repairs."

There was a silence. Michael couldn't hear more than his own breathing. There was the clink of glass and decanter. He gave Knob an I-don't-know look.

"Really now, Captain," it was the supercargo again, "you think you have a choice in the matter?" There was no reply. Edmund-Tell continued. "These kind gentlemen are prepared to handle all of the arrangements for us to continue our journey. But as they have made quite plain, they desire cash, not letters of credit. And they're willing to pay a premium on the one item of cargo we can readily sell to raise the capital we need."

MacNeal renewed his first defense. "We have contracted to deliver these souls to the Chesapeake. I am obliged by their indentures, as is spelled out in my brother's own hand, to deliver them to Annapolis."

"Well, Captain, my dear man," said the supercargo, who must have had his back to the bulkhead because Michael could hear his gurgled breathing between phrases. Michael could picture tobacco smoke hanging heavy in the cabin. "You certainly are master of Mr. Broot's vessel as it traverses this vast ocean. I applaud your seamanship and your success over the Algerians. Our employers are most grateful for the rescue of their ship. But you have not had a chance to read law at the Temple? Have you?"

The breathing ceased. Michael pictured the supercargo leaving his perch on the wall to pace the cabin, his voice softer and then louder.

"No, I don't recollect a naval officer to have that opportunity. But as I have, I feel it my duty to explain the contracts that your dear brother so eagerly sells for us at the Exchange. You see, Captain, I've had a rather heavy hand in formulating the said terms and conditions, so I know of what I speak. We have no legal obligation to deliver any servant to any specific landing stage."

Edmund-Tell was against the wall again. "Unless the indentured clearly inscribes a precise port of call, we have, as our first and primary obligation to our employer, the obligation to take profits as the chances present themselves. Yes, the forms that your brother so eagerly flashes about do hold places for the guileless to write in a destination. But most can't write their own names, much less spell out 'Maryland.' It is left to us to decipher their undefined and illiterate requests. I'm sure most don't even appreciate the difference between one colony and the next or where they are on a chart. We can treat such discussion as mere suggestion, legally speaking, because buried in the text, which I must admit is purposefully circular in nature, and I take personal credit for that, is the real meat of the contract, which clearly gives me, as the supercargo of this vessel, the right to choose the when and where of any sale."

The harangue seemed to tire him. He paused, apparently to drink something. "Alas, my dear captain, your responsibilities are limited only to the safe delivery of *The Delight* to ports of my choosing."

Michael kept his ear flat to the wood as he whispered to Knob. "Sounds ugly. Supercargo's pulling rank. Captain's angry. There's a struggle. Would MacNeal strike him?"

Knob was about to answer, but Michael waved him off as the sounds of struggle eased. Awkward silence. Edmund-Tell spoke.

"Perhaps you should enjoy some of this fine port, Captain. I will handle the sale of the young ladies' indentures. I'm sure with time, they'll warm to the bedrooms awaiting them. All you have to do is mix the young ladies into a general parade on deck so our guests can make their choices. And make sure Ms. Baker's in a dress, not that sailor's kit."

Chapter 42

Michael bolted out of Knob's cabin and up the hatchway. Moira and Marta weren't on deck. Michael jumped jumbles of cordage and dropped down into the 'tween deck before a distraught captain, a smiling supercargo, and the eager merchants assembled on the quarterdeck.

Michael found the girls in the Palatine quarter sewing in the dim light and grumbling about it in their mix of German and English. In a sharp whisper, Michael raised the alarm. "Moira, they're planning to sell your contract, right here, in Antigua."

It took a moment for the warning to set in. "Can't be," she said, "I'm bound for Annapolis, same as you. Marta's going to . . ."

Farrell's voice filled the hold. "All hands. All hands. On deck for assembly."

Moira finished her thought, ". . . to join family, and . . ."

"Moira, they're not shopping for cooks. It's Covent Garden they're after."

"What? We escape a Barbary harem to be sold as whores? It's not . . ."

Michael cut her off. "Did they specifically write a destination into your indentures? Did you insist on Annapolis? Where exactly does your indenture say you'll be landed?"

"Don't remember one way or the other. I just asked to be on the same ship as you."

"Marta, where you bound? What port did you sign for?" Michael asked. Moira translated.

She shook her head. "Simon put marks next to agent's finger, like others do."

"All hands," Farrell repeated.

"Moira, get yourself and Marta in your cots. Cover yourselves, shiver as fast as you can. Make me believe you have a fever."

Michael walked over to the hatchway to acknowledge Farrell. He mussed his hair to appear tired and haggard. He looked directly into sunlight to enhance his squinting and made a mess of clearing his throat.

"Good day to ya, Mr. Farrell, might I inquire as to what's on yer mind up there?"

"Collecting passengers." Farrell took a closer look at Michael. "Are you alright, Mr. Shea, you don't look well."

"Feeling a bit woozy. Touch of fever. What's on deck?"

"Sale of indentureds. I need ya on deck. Captain in particular insists on Moira and Marta." There was disappointment in his voice.

Michael could hear Captain MacNeal yelling, "Mr. Farrell," to hurry him up.

Michael persisted in seeming unconcerned. "A sale? We're not in the Chesapeake."

"Captain's orders. Everyone on deck, yerself included, quick like."

"Would seem rather pointless to drag me on deck for this, Mr. Farrell. Needs I remind the captain my contract specifies delivery in Annapolis, not Antigua."

"I needs ya assembled on deck."

"As you wish, Mr. Farrell, I shall join you presently. However, we do have some new sickness in the ranks." Michael backed out of the sunlight and lowered his voice so Farrell wouldn't be able to hear him clearly. "There may be fever, Mr. Farrell, in the Palatine ranks."

Farrell fell for the bait. "Speak up, man, we don't have all day."

Michael reentered the shaft of light pouring down the hatch and took a step up the ladder to make sure his voice would carry past Farrell. "Fever," he bellowed. And even louder, "Could be the pox." Then he lowered his voice so only Farrell would hear, "at least it could be."

In an instant, the murmur of "pox" spread throughout the ship. Crew, visitors, and passengers all gave Michael a wide berth as he made his way to the quarterdeck. When he heard one merchant mutter to another, "Sorry sight for a 'doctor' ain't he?" Michael added a dry cough and made a show of itching himself. In threadbare clothes that were now too big for his famished frame, Michael looked like the stick frame propping up a scarecrow. No one wanted to breathe as he sauntered by. Conversations stopped. People froze in place. After Michael passed, the merchants made for the gangway for a barge to return to shore.

"In my cabin," MacNeal ordered. Once below and after the captain's door banged shut, he said, "What's this about fever?"

"Three fevers still in sick bay, sir, two responding well to the fresh provisions since yesterday. One is not, I'm afraid. However, I may have to move two more forward if my suspicion proves correct."

"A suspicion, Mr. Shea?"

"I found two more Palatines shivering in their cots just now, sir. Could be typhus, maybe even the pox. It's too early to know which, and in the darkness, 'twas hard to see the condition of their skins."

"So then you're not really sure what their status is. Is that your report to Captain MacNeal?" Edmund-Tell's gurgling voice emerged from behind a canvas curtain covering his berth. "Tell us about your 'suspicion.' I am most interested." He flopped his legs out of the bunk. It was a painful procedure. He wobbled on grossly swollen ankles to lean on the captain's table.

"Two ladies, sweaty and warm to the touch," Michael said. "Glad to see your nose on the mend, sir, but am I right to observe you're hampered by gout? I would advise rest, sir. Keep those legs elevated."

"That is neither here nor there." The supercargo ignored the advice and stood, in obvious agony. "The issue now is a fever allegation?"

"It was the shivering of ladies in question, sir," Michael said, "a growing itchiness, some swelling, complaints of bloating and some nausea. I need a closer inspection to confirm their ailments. Unfortunately, sir, their modesty prevents me."

"Yes, I'm sure a lad would love to have a closer look," Edmund-Tell replied. "Now if you were a proper doctor, perhaps these ladies would overcome their modesty. Who's to say where true interests lie?"

"Was endeavoring to gain their trust, sir, when Mr. Farrell called to assemble."

"Captain," the supercargo inquired, "have our guests heard about this allegation?"

"Indeed, they have." MacNeal put his hands flat on the table and scowled at Michael.

"What?"

"Everyone heard, quite clearly."

"Damn it all!" Edmund-Tell fell back from the table as if hit by a cannonball. He flopped his butt on his bunk. There was a knock.

"Yes," MacNeal answered.

It was Farrell. "Sir, about the promenade, there's a crowd at the gangway demanding to return to shore. Some have already departed."

"Damn," MacNeal said. "Tell them it's safe, a false report."

"Aye, sir." Farrell scurried down the companionway.

MacNeal turned to the supercargo. "We need to respond. Have you any idea?" Edmund-Tell simmered. To Michael he asked, "Can we say this with confidence, there's no risk?"

"Certainly, sir. Anyone on deck is quite safe as long as they stay on deck while I remove the patients to sick bay."

Captain's taking this well, Michael was thinking.

"Sly, can you make it on deck?" MacNeal had jumped to familiar speech with his cabin mate. "Perhaps we can salvage something."

"If there be any business to attend, send for me; otherwise, I haven't the strength. I don't see the point, now."

MacNeal stepped into the passageway. "Mr. Shea, come with me. You will have to recast your story, diminish fears, if asked, but let me do the explaining."

"Aye, sir, am confident there's no threat to any on deck."

MacNeal appeared relaxed, even nonchalant, as he endeavored to staunch the merchants' exit. "Gentlemen, our young medical apprentice here may have confused the ladies' indisposition with fever. Not unusual for a young lad unaccustomed to the fairer sex and their monthly ways." He rubbed Michael's head and mussed his hair as one does to a small child. "Please be assured we have none of the pox aboard. We are quite safe here."

Turning to Michael, MacNeal ordered so that all could hear. "Be a good lad now, son, and attend to the broken bones. Leave Mrs. Rawlings to attend to the young ladies during their time."

Turning back to the remaining merchants, MacNeal smiled. "'Tis the first time for some of our blossoming flowers." He forced a laugh, but the merchants didn't join him. They didn't budge either. They were heading for shore.

Upon hearing her name, Mrs. Rawlings perked up, ready to respond. But Michael scurried over before she could upset the captain's charade. "I can better explain below," he whispered." She hesitated. "Please, Mrs. Rawlings, we don't have much time." He took her arm and waddled with her across the deck and down into the 'tween deck.

Chapter 43

Convincing Moira to move to sick bay wasn't easy. Plus, for the first time in her life, she was angry and upset with Michael, because in the rush to get the girls to move into sick bay, Mrs. Rawlings had confused Michael's and MacNeal's competing narratives.

"Not on your life, Michael Shea, will I go live in that disgusting sick bay and waste away just to protect your petty lies."

Michael and Mrs. Rawlings stumbled over each other to quiet her, but Moira was in full voice. "Whoever gave you permission to speculate about my person? And, in public no less, for all to hear? 'Tis no business of yours to know if'in there was a reason for any indisposition of my person."

Marta didn't know why Moira was so aggravated with her rumpled knight, but she gave Michael evil looks out of respect for her constant companion.

Mrs. Rawlings tried again. "Moira, my dear girl, Mr. Shea had nothing to do with the disposition tale. 'Twas the captain's invention. He were tryin' ta counter Michael's report about you and Marta suffering from fever. Supercargo plans was to sell yer indentures here, not in Maryland. They ain't a-lookin' for no serving girls. They's buyin' harlots, miss. 'Tis Mr. Shea's scheme to subvert the sale and protect ya from these lecherous islanders."

Moira gasped and opened her eyes wide.

"So that's your intention, Mr. Shea? To interfere with the running of my ship?" MacNeal's howl forced Michael to spin around. He found himself heeling backward under the force of MacNeal's blistering glare. "How dare you challenge my command of *The Delight*."

"I have . . . I thought . . . I mean, there's more to explain, sir."

"Don't need to hear no more."

"Was my intention to protect a loved one, sir."

"I don't care what your intentions." MacNeal was in full sail. "You have disgraced yourself. Your deception has put my ship in jeopardy. We can land no passengers, not even myself. Nor can we linger and take on new provisions. We will be ordered out of port or face quarantine."

MacNeal breathing heavy, struggled to contain himself. He opposed this sale. He resented Edmund-Tell pulling rank to order it. Michael's fever subterfuge had given him a moral victory. But now he saw Michael's interference as a direct challenge, a mutiny, to his command of his ship. He hollered for the first mate.

By the time Farrell appeared, MacNeal was livid. "Bring a detail this instant. You are to confine Mr. Shea to the brig, in irons, for mutiny. I'll not have such a villain roaming free on my ship."

"Sir?"

"You heard me, Mr. Farrell, do your duty."

Farrell soon returned with five confused crew. Standing at the foot of the ladder, Farrell fidgeted, hesitant to be the bearer of bad news. "Sir, there is no brig, nor irons, on *The Delight*."

This reality fueled MacNeal's temper. "Don't bother me with damn details. In the hold, then, as far forward as ye can. Whatever needs to be done to confine the prisoner." MacNeal turned beet red. "Now, Mr. Farrell. Get it done." The captain stomped up the ladder.

Farrell broke the dark silence. "'Tis me duty to obey an order, Michael, I am sorry."

As his crew bound Michael, Danny jumped down the ladder. "What in the world, Liam? 'ave ye lost yer mind?"

"Hold on, Danny." Michael explained his plight for all to hear. The revelation led to resentful grumbling as the crew led Michael below. Now everyone knew about the aborted sale as a breach of contract. Trust was lost.

Moira's eyes welled up, her only comfort was the echo of Michael's justification for his scheme.

When Farrell and his detail reemerged from the hold, tension was heavy in the 'tween deck air. He could feel the passengers' evil eyes. "We've made him as comfortable as we is able. I will attempt to ease Captain's mind. Have seen his temper before. It'll play out."

He pulled Danny aside. "I left his knots as loose as can be considered bound." He swiped his nose with his index finger. "Mr. Shea asks for his papers." He quietly, almost tenderly, shut the hatch. "He'll need a lantern. Don't ask me if such is allowed."

After the detail climbed up to the deck. Mrs. Rawlings broke the silence that lingered: "Oh dear, Horace, it's time."

CHAPTER 44

DARKNESS ENTOMBED MICHAEL, A TOTAL DARKNESS, AND HE HATED the dark. It scared him. He blinked, blinked again, harder and slower. Pitch black, no hope for any night vision. He settled down as best he could, swamped by the sickening sweet smell of bilge below. Later, he knew it was dinner by the hustle of feet overhead. Much later, after the evening watches were set, the hatch opened; a candle approached. The ghostly apparition with the light was Farrell.

"You alive there, Michael?"

"Barely."

"I bring you dinner." He handed Michael a rare treat, fresh bread from shore. Michael accepted it with his bound hands.

Farrell let Michael devour it in peace.

"Captain brushed off me efforts to seek ya clemency. No chance, right now. We've been quarantined. Must admit, we are a frightful sight. Didn't help with Moira and Marta groaning and carrying on on deck as if they has the kiss o' death on them. They kept pretending sick long past it was clear they weren't. Captain were livid. Supercargo even more so."

"Liam, could you do me a favor?"

"If I can."

"Leave me your candle?"

"I can't, I'm sorry."

"'Tis only a stump as it is. You'll not miss it."

"Supercargo was specific about leaving you in the dark."

"He's in command, then?"

"'Til we sail. Next tide."

Michael watched the light fade with Farrell. The dark is darkest just after a light is extinguished. He closed his eyes. Not as scary with eyes closed. He felt like it was a benevolent darkness that way, like praying. His anxiety eased. Restless memories swirled about. The attic bedroom. Emma. Warm, perfumed skin, soft, smooth. He lingered with that memory.

Then Jonathan intruded. Michael prayed: *I tried my friend, did what I could. What else could I do?*

Michael wasn't sure if he was awake or asleep. His skin tingled and itched. The hairs of the coarse hemp binding his wrists seemed to give birth to a thousand spiders creeping over his skin. Was that something crawling down his spine? He shivered at the thought, tried to shake the phantoms off.

He awoke to noise of the crew raising anchor and the ship slowly gaining way. The familiar groans of timber and twine were reassuring. He let the familiar sounds envelop him. He searched for musical patterns in the rhythm of sailing.

He dozed off. He was nine in the Clonakilty cottage, reliving a nightmare, one that plagued him as his family, one by one, succumbed to fever. A coffin closing on him. The *tap tap tap* of his father nailing the ill-fitting lid shut, his mother crying, his little fists pounding on the inside of the cover, crying, *"Momma, don't leave me. Don't put me in here!"* A crucifix on the inside of the lid, to keep him company in the grave. *"I don't wanna be alone. Jesus, help me!"* the boy cried out. Darkness upon more darkness, then he's floating, drifting towards sky.

But there are no clouds and harps in heaven. A dead man glaring at him. The corpse floats closer, pointing to his neck. It's the Barbary pirate. *"I didn't do it!"* Michael runs away. *"I tried, I tried."* Michael wipes his eyes. For a moment, it's Jonathan. Michael relaxes. Then it's the Barbary again. He can't escape the spirit. *"It wasn't me! Supercargo killed you!"* he yells. *"Go haunt him!"* The phantom shakes his head, keeps closing in. Michael runs, but the specter sticks to him like a shadow. Now he's on a frozen lake. He's slipping, his feet are running but he's not moving. Nowhere to hide. Nowhere to go. *"It's not my fault!"*

Out of the mists, the faces of Jonathan, Simon, Mrs. McMahon, her boy, all flash by like comets across the sky. His own mother. His father. His patron. *"I tried to save you,"* he cries to them all. *"What could I do?"* A hole in the ice. It moves towards him. He can't move, can't retreat. He falls through, trapped under the ice.

Then a woman's screams and grunts. Michael bolts awake, breathing hard, covered in sweat. The wailing of a baby's cry. It took him a moment to realize he wasn't being tormented by the dreadful parade of the dead. *Is that the Rawlings's child?* The crying subsided. *Thank God . . . no ghosts about.*

CHAPTER 45

A FORTNIGHT LATER, THE CRY OF "LAND HO!" WAS WEARING THIN. Nobody wanted to ponder the low coastal smudges of British America. But when Cape Hatteras was sighted, anxiety ensued. Everyone knew they were sailing over a graveyard. The notorious shoals weighed heavily on their minds. Barrier islands were to be avoided, and Raleigh's Lost Colony could only be a harbinger of trouble.

"Just a shadow," Danny said, squinting into the setting sun. "Was expectin' a sea of forest, not this desolate place. D'ya have the strength, Michael, ta look for the Lost Colony?"

"Not worth the trouble." Michael returned to puzzling over one of Jonathan Clayborne's letters. He'd been preoccupied with them after his ordeal in the hold. Danny had smuggled in a lantern and Michael busied his mind studying Jonathan's jumbled cyphered letterbook.

Three days after leaving the Caribbean, MacNeal had agreed to let Michael roam the decks. MacNeal's change of heart was induced when Horace Rawlings, prodded by Mrs. Rawlings, the Elder Brouchard, and Danny, organized a protest over Michael's incarceration. The passengers had refused to participate in any way with the details of operating the ship until Michael was released. Their work stoppage forced MacNeal to negotiate. Michael heard Horace Rawlings demanding a pardon. Michael was impressed with his assertiveness. *How does a poacher know so much legal talk?* he wondered.

MacNeal tried to sound reasonable. "Mr. Rawlings, as I have explained, I consider Mr. Shea's actions mutiny. It is within my rights to do whatever's necessary for the safety of my ship."

Rawlings raised the key argument. "As we understand definitions, sir, mutiny's an attempt to replace a captain. Nothing of the sort were contemplated, and none of us below would ever agree with such an accusation, if we was forced to testify about this misappropriation of justice in a court of law. May I remind you that servants have rights in court?"

"Mr. Shea was interfering with my command of this ship."

"Hardly, sir," Danny butted in. "Michael were attempting to stop an illegal sale of our contracts." His argument raised a chorus of ayes from the indentureds.

"We are all in agreement," Rawlings summed up. "None of us will provide assistance, nor aid your diminished crew, unless and until you reconsider your harsh judgment. The missus and I speak for all the passengers, sir, that upon reflection, you might come to realize how yer decision were made in the heat of a passion."

"Which means, Captain MacNeal," Mrs. Rawlings called out from her bunk with her newborn, "yer sailin' even more shorthanded than ya should be, unless you release our Mr. Shea. We needs his care for the fever-stricken ones in that stye you calls a sick bay."

Brouchard picked up the drumbeat. "Mrs. Rawlings raises a direct point, sir. Our sick brethren are surely lost without his aid. Their untimely demise will be a heavy burden upon your judgment. 'Twill be their souls at our Lord's right hand when He pronounces His eternal judgment on your piteous soul for denying our brothers and sisters a chance at life. Is eternal damnation worth such a risk, Captain?"

"What's it to be, Captain, sir?" Mr. Rawlings asked. "Punishin' an innocent? Saving the lives of the sick? You can't profit off the dead. Even the supercargo can figure that out."

MacNeal cut off discussion before the pot got closer to a boil. He needed time, everyone suspected, to negotiate with Edmund-Tell and keep the incident under wraps from the owner syndicate. Two days later, he released Michael, on his promise not to interfere in future contract sales. MacNeal's antagonists answered with three "Huzzah's" and "Hurray for the captain."

Later that night, when he was summoned to the captain's cabin, Michael realized the real reason he was being released. A severe attack of gout was crippling Supercargo Edmund-Tell. "Started last night. He's been calling for you."

CHAPTER 46

THE DELIGHT SAILED INTO THE CHESAPEAKE ON A MISTY MORNING, leaving the dark low outline of Cape Henry to larboard. She followed a pilot boat and chased the storm clouds rolling up the bay. Excitement grew as they closed in on Annapolis. Many indentureds remained on deck for final landfall. They'd cat nap to the lullaby of creaking lines and luffing sails.

The next morning, *The Delight* hit a rough patch once they left the pilot behind and crossed the mouth of a broad river. The rocking and jostling sparked a wave of sea sickness most hadn't seen since the wild gales of the Atlantic. The turbulence made itself especially known to Michael who was helping Knob practice walking with the aid of a crutch. "Come now, Mr. Knob, you'll enjoy this bit of freedom, ya just need . . ."

Michael couldn't finish. His throat clamped down. He fought a losing battle with his unsettled gut and raced for the rail, his cheeks puffed trying to contain the vile acid taste.

"Always a troubled spot," Farrell said after he noticed Michael's woozy, desperate look. "Potomac's a nasty one all right. Not like Virginia's gentle streams."

"Why's the water boiling so?" Michael gulped cool air as he wiped vomit on his sleeve.

"Always a fight between these two," Farrell philosophized. "Chesapeake never willin' t'accept this river. Other streams makes it just fine, not the Potomac. 'Tis a rude hello to Maryland, ain't it? You'll be better once we're outta this chop."

The Delight didn't like the Potomac passage any better than Michael did. She jolted side to side as the river roughed its way into the bay. There was a loud crack as a yard snapped. Half of the foremast yard and sail now dangled above the deck. "Damn this river," Farrell cursed, "like the devil's waiting here ta torment us." He ran off to organize repairs.

Michael gulped air. A cold sweat covered his face as he knelt down. He dropped his forehead to the deck and tried to wipe the foul taste from his lips. The only water nearby was in a sailor's scrub bucket. He used it to douse his face, the salty taste a welcome antidote to vomit. He gave himself three splashes and used his hair to dry his hands as he pushed his fingers along his head and pulled his hair back into a ponytail.

He surveyed the crowd on deck. He wasn't the only one made sick by the Potomac. He found Marta and Moira farther up the rail near the bow. They weren't sick. Marta held the Rawlings's babe, giving the new mom a break while she attended to her morning routines. Mr. Rawlings hovered by his wife's side.

Michael braved a step to join them but was humbled by sickness. Head over the side, his main thought, *glad they don't see me like this.*

But Danny found him. "I must say, Michael, yer lookin' rather green this fine day. At least you're not on yer knees, that's a good sign."

"Was just there." He slid into a sitting position.

Once the ship left the Potomac behind, she steadied and sailed smooth. Clearing skies in the west revealed a lush coast.

"Don't give up so easy, Michael. 'Twould be a shame for ya to miss this grand procession of forest. Jesus, this place is green. Far grander than anythin' I could imagine."

"Wish I could enjoy it with you Danny. I'm still wondering why I let you talk me into this scheme of yours."

"Ain't no future in England, ya knows that, but here," he said waving his hand towards the pockets of dense forest, "betterment awaits, it beckons, I feel it in me bones, Michael. We have a chance. Possibilities await in Annapolis!

Once past the Potomac, Michael's spirits recovered. He shared in the burgeoning excitement as *The Delight* eased past a gentle river and a line of tall sandy cliffs, each topped by dense forest cap. In the morning sun, they gleamed light brown, warm and welcoming, not at all like the stark white cliffs in Dover. Tidy farms sprouted from the wilderness. Each touted rows of an unfamiliar crop. The smell of chimney smoke was in the air.

"Can you smell that, Michael? That ain't no peat or coal. They've got wood! Imagine that now would ya? Wood for a cook fire?"

Michael just nodded.

"Just imagine how big is this place is," Danny continued. 'Tis an endless ocean of forest. Certainly nothin' like the damn Thames."

"Takes a while ta get used to it, the bigness of it all," Farrell said, strolling by after managing the latest repair detail. He had more on his mind than pleasantries with the boys. To be within eye and earshot of Moira was his true aim. Lately whenever she was on deck, Farrell stood as tall as possible, minded his elocution, and kept one eye on his ship, the other on Moira. "Took Captain Smith two years to survey this bay."

Moira left her station with Marta and walked back to join the boys. She gave Farrell a smile but sidled up to Michael and put her arm through his. Farrell didn't hide his disappointment but stayed with the group.

Hoecker talked to no one in particular. "'Tis what a man kin only dream 'bout in England. To be left alone to 'is own devices."

Moira squeezed Michael's arm. "What now, Michael? This place is so remote, so wild. How can we find one another? Are there no roads? Are there no towns or cities? What awaits us? I can't be sentenced to a life milking cows or churning butter. I'm no farm girl."

He pulled her close, keeping her hand under his arm, holding it to his body. "The indenturing agent assured me there'd be employments in Annapolis. There is a reason he filled *The Delight* with skilled trades, not field hands. MacNeal stands to make a much better profit selling our services in a city than turning us into sot-weed gardeners."

"'Tis true, Moira," Danny piped in. "Our skills are needed in town."

"You're right about that, Danny," Farrell added. He gave Moira a nod. "Yer carpenter skills will be in much demand in a city on the grow like Annapolis. Captain and Supercargo are not ones ta waste yer skills on a planter if'in they can avoids it. In the first instance, farmers lack the cash to bid on yer services, and in the second, the supercargo don't believe in no credits. And at any rate, farm work is better suited to the convict and slave trades, if'in they can keep 'em from runnin' away."

"Where in the world would one run away to?" Moira asked. "Hide in the forest like Robin Hood?"

"Runaways usually is caught by manhunters. They're punished and their time is increased," Farrell answered. "Some kin buy their way out of servitude if they're lucky. Better than a slave's lot. There's no escape for them. I've seen slavers. Gruesome. They pack 'em like cord wood 'tween decks. Animals get better treatment."

"What about servants?" Moira asked. "Aren't we to be slaves by another name?"

"Yer life'll be far better," he answered.

"Certain 'tis," Danny insisted, "Our servitude is limited by law and contract. And we gets land upon our release, I remember that promise made by our indenturing agent. 'Tis a far shorter path to liberty than an apprentice in London's got."

"Aye, that's what I hear as well," Tombler said, "We are freeborn Englishmen with God-given rights and liberties. We are merely bartering our skills and service for food and shelter, and a start. Ain't that right Mr. Farrell?"

"You kin petition courts to enforce liberties against harsh masters." He interrupted the conversation to relay an order from MacNeal to increase sail as the breeze slackened. He scratched his chin in imitation of his captain in thought before resuming. "It's as Danny says. Four years is a brief servitude compared to apprenticing in London."

He looked at Danny directly. "But as this be me fifth trip deliverin' servants to Annapolis, I never heard of no promise of land."

"No land?"

"'T'aint heard bones about no free land." He let Danny grumble. "More than likely, you'll set yerself up in a trade where it suits ya."

"When do we get started then?" Michael asked.

"Soon as Captain and Supercargo pass muster at the Customs House. They'll place adverts. Once word spreads, there's a bit of meet and greet on board as buyers consider skills. Once arrangements is made, you be leavin' *The Delight* for dry land."

"Where do we stay in meantime?" Elder Brouchard asked from back of the pack. "What's our accommodation?"

"Right here. Supercargo won't let any disembark until debts is settled and contracts bought."

"What about redemptorists?" Brouchard pressed.

"As soon as your family present themselves, Mr. Brouchard, they can redeem ya."

"Ya mean we're held prisoner on this ship?" Tombler jumped into the discussion.

"Be a harsh way of puttin' it. We keeps indentureds on board 'til we settles terms. Same with convicts an' slaves. Reduces risk of those who gets ideas of tryin' to light foot it out of town. Ya can't leave before contracts is signed."

"But why, Liam?" Moira asked. "There must be an inn wherein we can prepare ourselves proper."

"Ah, Miss Moira, if you 'ad the resources, you'd be a stayin' at Mrs. Middleton's Tavern, then you wouldn't have come across in the indentured trade now, would ya? You'd have yer own cabin and been feasted at Captain's table."

"Sounds to me like we're on a prison ship."

"I didn't make the rules. Until a buyer covers the costs of crossin', indentureds will stay on board. Could be only be a day or two more, maybe a week 'til Supercargo finds buyers."

It was Michael's turn. "What happens if no one shows to purchase our services?" He was thinking, *What if Carroll's indisposed? Working his farms? Died even?*

"We'll take the unsold to other ports. A last resort is the plantations direct an' see if'in they'll take on field hands. If'in we git there before slavers, we might make a sale. If takers is thin, Supercargo sells the stragglers to wholesalers. They'll take ya overland to inland farms."

"I'm not suited for farm work," Michael replied.

"I'm yer blackbird," Hoecker yelled with an eager smile, "Take me to yer plantation." His enthusiasm warmed the mood.

Farrell had a last bit of news. "Now to ease yer disappointment overstayin' another night or two on *Delight*, I have news. You'll find real food tonight. Captain'll make his investment in fresh provisions to fatten ya's up a bit. We're all a bit thinned after this tiresome voyage."

"Oh, what's that?" Moira cried pointing off the bow. The crowd followed her finger and squinted into the mid-day sun.

"Miss Moira wins the prize," Farrell yelled out for all to hear. "Yonder lies the Athens of the colonies. Welcome to Annapolis."

The Delight took a wide turn westward into the mouth of a river that Farrell identified as the Severn River, named after England's Severn. Forest and farmland all around. Sailors scampered aloft to furl sail as they glided into a lazy creek and dropped anchor in Annapolis harbour.

"You call this a city?" Danny's comment carried across the deck. "Ain't no more than village, an' barely that. How can you call this an Athens?"

"Don't be concerned with size, Mr. O'Mara." Captain MacNeal said from the quarterdeck. "Plenty o' wealth in this harbour. Many as rich as any in London. An' far better entertainments here than you'll get in Boston."

Farrell pointed out another landmark dead ahead. "That fine brick house just ahead belongs to Charles Carroll, one of the wealthiest men in the colonies. Many calls this Carroll's Creek."

As *The Delight* eased into the harbour, he added, "And see, they have a bustlin' port o' entry." He gave Danny a nod and pointed to the shipyard. Farrell pointed out a few landmarks. "Middleton Tavern is the red brick building beside the shipyard. The tobacco trading's done in them brick warehouses. They calls it Factor's Row. That ramshackle affair is their market house, open two, maybe three days a week. The Customs House is the little building by all these wharfs."

Moira whispered to Michael, "Could that be the same Carroll who knew your friend Jonathan?"

"Must be. He said it was near the harbour. Had no idea he'd live in such a fine castle."

CHAPTER 47

A<small>S TWO SAILORS ROWED THE CAPTAIN AND THE SUPERCARGO ACROSS</small> the harbour, anxious immigrants exchanged endless questions and conjectures about what lay ahead. They made straight for the Customs House to register *The Delight's* cargo. Then they met with a group of chandlers on the dock to arrange for provisions and refitting.

The chandlers didn't hesitate and Farrell was ready for them. Standing tall, the mate relished his new authority to place orders for fresh provisions, water, cloth, thread, naval stores, and shipwright services. He recruited Michael and Danny to help: Michael to order medical supplies and record the transactions as Farrell was uncomfortable with the art of writing. Danny kept a running tally of prices.

Farrell opened the bidding by letting Michael rattle off what he wanted in his medicine cabinet. He didn't finish his list.

"Hold on there, lad," interrupted one chandler. "That's far too much Latin. If I was to speak directly with the ship's doctor, perhaps I could make an arrangement."

Farrell made the introduction. "Sir, you are indeed addressing our ship's doctor, Mr. Michael Shea. Many's a life he did save on our rough crossin'. May we have the pleasure, sir, of yer own name and establishment?"

The young man acknowledged Farrell and Michael. "Jacob Tolinger. I represent me family's dry goods and supplies. Rope walk's just beyond the state's house there." He waved towards the top of the city's only hill. Inspecting the masts, he added, "Looks like you're in need of a bit of repair, sir. Our great city is well suited to supplying all you need. Dry goods and such I can supply. As for medicines," he said looking at

Michael, "I would be glad take you to young Dr. Warfield's home. I'm sure he'd be well disposed to be of assistance."

Michael gave Farrell a longing look, hoping to join Tolinger.

"Alas, Mr. Tolinger, none of the crew and passengers can leave *The Delight* until Captain MacNeal makes his return. Mr. Shea will scratch out a list."

Farrell moved on to his main business with the chandlers. During the negotiating, Tombler yelled out. "Will the local brewers be making their wares known to us, Mr. Farrell? 'Twould make mending our clothes go ever so much faster."

"Aye that it would, Mr. Tombler," Farrell replied from behind the wall of eager merchants. "But first we concentrate on the necessities. Captain's afraid ya might put yer buttons on backwards if'in ya got the taste of fresh rum in ya. Sooner we finish this business, Mr. Tombler, sooner we can visit the taverns."

A round merchant leaned towards Farrell's ear. "You're Farrell, are ye not, behind them scrawny whiskers?"

"Aye, 'tis me. Is it you, Mr. Royce, growin' out of your waistcoat?"

"Aye, growing good, as is our fair city. Wish I could say the same for *The Delight*. Your scow's barely afloat, Farrell."

Knob butted in. "Sir, you're addressing our mate, Mr. Farrell. Some respect is in order."

"Is he indeed? Was not aware of your rise in station," he paused before adding, "Mr. Farrell. My congratulations." He tapped the edge of his hat. Royce lowered his voice. "Need I remind you, Mr. Farrell, servants ain't allowed in taverns, not without their masters."

"If you could indulge me, Mr. Royce, now's not time ta break the man's 'eart."

"If you insist."

"Would pain me greatly to explain yer queer customs. They have the idea they'll find more liberty, not less, in the colonies."

"Are servants permitted to drink with their betters in London?"

"Indeed they are. You should visit London an' see for yerself if'in ya hopes ta join the ranks of English gentlemen." Farrell awarded his orders to Royce's competitors, who undercut Royce's price every time.

"Gentlemen, I am also in dire need of fresh water. Are there any who could deliver this day?"

"That would be me," yelled a lad at the entrance way. "James Diamond at yer service. I'll get ya two fresh barrels before nightfall and two more by morning. I offers a fair price. All you have to do is crease me hand and have your men ready at the capstan."

"How you gonna keep such a promise?" griped Royce. "You can't move that much water in that scow of yours." To Farrell the rotund one explained, "You can't make no deal with Diamond, Farrell, he ain't got no slaves to get it done. I'll get 'em workin' it. That's them lounging by my crane on the wharf. They'll get you a water barrel loaded up by noon tomorrow."

"Don't need no slaves, don't need no cranes, Willy Loo, we uses our brains," Diamond countered. He gave everyone a grin.

Royce bristled at the nickname. "We're not children anymore, Diamond."

"If you say so."

"You need muscle for this job, not the vague promise of a river squawk," Royce said to Farrell. "It'll take two, maybe three of my slaves to get enough water to suit your need," he paused before adding, "Mr. Farrell." A short pause, "sir."

"How's about a race then," Diamond suggested. "Whoever gets here first? Simple, hey? See which of us makes good on the promise, my esteemed colleague and his slaves, or me and my boat. I'll deliver four barrels of the sweetest water culled from just up river. You decide if you likes the taste of my fresh water or the piss they'll sell ya in town."

The competitors glared at each other while Farrell mulled the challenge. "As ya wish gentleman, first to deliver." He creased both their hands, then addressed all the merchants. "Gentlemen, I thank you for visiting. We'll resume business in the morning."

CHAPTER 48

FARRELL'S CALL TO ORDER IN THE 'TWEEN DECK WAS DROWNED OUT BY anticipatory industry. It took a few moments for the indentures to focus on the mate. For the first time since London, both hatches were latched open. Sunlight flooded into the 'tween deck. As they all turned to face the mate, their faces crinkled, their eyelids pinched.

"Ladies and gentlemen, yer attention." When all quieted down, he shared the provisioning news and added, "Captain has also arranged for a shipment of fresh water for bathing and drinking. With luck, you can start this evening. Now's yer time to make yer farewells to yerselves and our dear *Delight*. We have a day to freshen up, bathe, and clean as ye like. Supercargo expects ta commence yer business in the next day or two." He turned to leave but a wobbly Brouchard blocked his exit. Sweating profusely, the Palatine raised an outstretched palm to Farrell. He leaned on the ladder for support. The hold fell silent knowing Brouchard had lost his preachy voice.

"Mr. Farrell, where might all this transacting take place?" Brouchard stifled a deep wet cough. He wiped his sweaty brow with a shaky hand. "And when," he wheezed, "can we make arrangements for our redemption?"

"I am not familiar with Palatine arrangements."

"We are not to be sold one by one." Everyone could hear Brouchard wheezing. He couldn't keep standing without help. Danny slid over to prop him up. "Please remind Captain MacNeal about our redemption." He tried to raise his voice. "We are not to be sold as chattel." An ugly cough. Nobody dared breathe while he wheezed. "We are smiths, tanners, millers. All of my party, minus our poor brother Simon, o' course."

"I will make yer request known."

"'Tis not a request, Mr. Farrell." He wheezed. "'Tis our right of contract."

Several passengers then shouted out a barrage of questions. They ignored the mate's repeated reminder that he wasn't privy to any answers regarding a servant's redemption.

Michael caught Moira's eye. She was easy to spot, her canvass britches and coat a sharp contrast to the wall of dark brown Palatine gowns and hoods. She eased over to the relative privacy around Michael's hammock. She grabbed his arm to talk directly into his ear.

"Michael, you must talk to MacNeal. Brouchard's counting me as his, but I'm not one of them. I didn't come all this way to milk no cows and haul water. I came to be with you! You have to make MacNeal understand."

"MacNeal distrusts me."

"Michael."

"What about the rest of us, then?" McMahon called out from the semidarkness as Brouchard fell silent. "What becomes of me and Little Jimmy? Did we survive the Algerians just to be auctioned here, on a slaver's block?"

"And us?" Horace Rawlings barked. "Where will the babe and me missus end up?"

The usually quiet Quigley joined in: "Make sure my indenture goes to a farm. I knows livestock." His demand triggered a cacophony of distressed demands.

Farrell waited for the frenzy to die out. "I kin only explain the little what I knows."

"Well, what do ya know then?" Mrs. Rawlings called out.

"I cannot enlighten yer requests 'bout terms of yer contracts. 'Tis the business of the supercargo." He let a wave of grumbling pass. "First of all, I can assure you," he looked at McMahon, "there won't be no auction block." That met with some relief.

"Once we tie up, we'll conduct business from the deck." He motioned with his hand to the deck above. "You'll present yourselves and Supercargo will do his best ta negotiate skills to master as close as is possible. Be ready to state your skills and health as quick ya can."

"Will we all be sold in this little town?" Danny asked.

"Some will. Those that don't will travel to the next port."

"An' if'in there's no takers for me service and me boy?" asked McMahon.

Farrell avoided McMahon's gaze. He pursed his lips, stared at his feet. "Such details I cannot give answer to," Farrell replied. "Yer situation's complicated owing to the loss of yer wife and child. Supercargo will address your particulars."

"What's the loss of me wife have ta do with anything?" He put an arm around his son.

Farrell had said too much. He shrugged. But Mrs. Rawlings wouldn't let him off the hook. "Aye there Mr. Farrell, you didn't answer the man's question, did ya, now?"

"Better answered by the supercargo."

Mrs. Rawlings's challenge renewed a wave of grumbling. She didn't move to quench the fire she had started. All eyes were on Farrell squirming in the sunlight, his every twitch amplified.

Marta walked up to Farrell. She pulled off her hood and shook out her hair with a few twists of her head. The flood of sun sparking on her straw-colored hair gave the impression of a halo. She took his hands in hers and looked him in the eye. "Please, Liam, to us, tell a truth." She didn't budge. She kept his hands in hers and her eyes in his, waiting for an explanation. He didn't try to escape.

"Family arrangements kin be cruel," he said just to Marta. The passengers pressed close to hear. "Families is usually broken up. 'Tis hard ta find buyers who kin afford more than one servant in one bite, even if they has enough work for 'em all." He paused, unwilling to break off the intimacy. Marta lightly massaged his hands as if it would draw out hidden details.

"Is more?" she asked still holding his hands.

He answered now loud so all could hear. "Mr. McMahon will have to make good on passage for his departed wife and son, as to Little Jimmy, there, truth be told, he owes passage for four, so his servitude will be extended. Likely Mr. McMahon will have to give the boy over to a master until he reaches his majority."

At this, McMahon hugged his son, pulling Jimmy's head into his stomach. His eyes teared. "How could ya tear us apart after the trials we've suffered?"

"It's how they keeps servants from absconding."

"You mean Little Jimmy's a hostage?" Mrs. Rawlings called out.

"Harsh way of putting it, ma'am."

She hugged her babe as Farrell spilled more news. "As to the Rawlings family, they have to cover passage for the newborn. One or the other, usually the father, gets his servitude extended ta cover the extra passage."

"He ain't ate but the milk I give . . ." Mrs. Rawlings's protest was drowned out Captain MacNeal above.

"Mr. Farrell, that will be enough," MacNeal barked. "On deck this instant. Hoecker, O'Mara, Tombler. Shea as well."

Farrell scampered up the ladder like a puppy with his tail between his legs. Moira grabbed Michael's arm as he made his way for the ladder.

"I know."

"Now."

"Of course."

After Michael followed his mates up the ladder, MacNeal latched the hatch shut.

CHAPTER 49

MACNEAL CALLED FOR THE SHIP'S DOCTOR, "MR. SHEA, A WORD IF YOU please." Michael scurried to the quarterdeck. He adopted his best sailor-like attitude, even putting a knuckle to his forehead as he gave his, "Aye, sir," the way Farrell did it. Michael had been doing this since his release from the hold.

Both men fidgeted, uncomfortable with the rickety truce that was in play. MacNeal had released the errant doctor based on his word, "as a gentleman," not to hinder any negotiations. Releasing Michael still felt like a public countermanding of his authority even though the passengers had cheered him. Now he had to rely on Michael to conduct these negotiations.

"Mr. Shea, if I'm not mistaken, we still have fevers in sick bay," he drawled. "Any chance of a speedy recovery?"

"Hardly, sir, not whilst they're imprisoned in sick bay."

MacNeal's face reddened at the comparison.

"There are five, sir. Could be six soon if Brouchard can't rally. Your man Chalmerson's the worst, sir. He's puckered out like a pin cushion." He dropped his voice to add, "I think it syphilis, sir. Certainly not the pox." He paused to let this sink in. "He's in a bad way. The other fevers may recover with proper food and clean air."

"Might I also prescribe bathing for our sick, sir? They're carrying filth from months at sea." He bowed towards MacNeal. "Nothing I can do for yer man's," he leaned even closer to the captain and whispered, "social disease. It's well advanced, sir." He returned to a normal tone. "Chalmerson needs treatment if he hopes to see London again. Best if he could be attended to by a proper physician, best for all sick bay, sir."

"And cover a physician's invoice? Supercargo would hardly approve."

Michael whispered. "Sir, if I may, you risk losing all chance for return on their passage. Ain't it a captain's responsibility," a pause before "sir," before continuing, "to care for yer charges? Perhaps, sir, you could prevail upon Mr. Edmund-Tell, let him know your fears, that it will be his responsibility to be stuck with the contracts of four or five dead," he paused and added another "sir," for good measure.

"Are you telling me how to command my ship?

"Is it not my duty, sir, as ship's doctor, to tell you straight how best to care for your sick crew?"

"You're no doctor." MacNeal's snapped.

"I am serving in that role, sir, under your orders," a pause, "sir." Michael kept his tone calm and neutral. "I have done my best to serve at your kind pleasure. And it is most unbecoming for gentlemen to argue if our mutual goal is to return our sick to profitable health." An emphasis on "profitable."

MacNeal's mood began to ease as he weighed the implications. Michael continued, sensing a chance to slip in his request. "At your pleasure, sir, I'll continue to be of service. And I humbly reiterate my vow to avoid any misadventure. Though I would appreciate a word about the contracts for Moira Baker and Danny O'Mara, as we agreed, sir."

Farrell returned to the quarterdeck, much deflated following his one on one with the irate supercargo. The presence of the mate underscored the need for a captain to control his emotions. Bad form for a gentleman to lose control in front of his officers and crew. MacNeal crinkled his forehead as he weighed options, trying to calculate the loss of four contracts against the costs of preserving them. Losing a sailor was a routine hazard, but cargo losses would weigh most unpleasant when *The Delight*'s owners settled their captain's contract.

"I am familiar with our agreement, Mr. Shea. Short of putting our sick ashore, is there anything we can do to ease their sufferings and encourage their recoveries?"

"They need air, water, and food, sir, in equal amount. Could we rig a cabin for them like Knob enjoys?"

"That would never do. Can't be having fevers near crew's mess. I'd face mutiny for sure, deservedly so. 'Tween deck, then."

"We risk the rest of the indentureds, sir."

"Of course." After some reflection, MacNeal made his offer. "Best I can do right now is fresh food and water. We can leave the forward hatch open to allow better air until we are docked. However unseemly it may be, perhaps we could tent our sick on the foredeck until we have suitable space below."

"That would be wonderful, sir, and it would demonstrate to buyers the sincerity of your care. When might we expect refreshments?"

"Tonight. Perhaps even fresh water. Apparently, there be some sort of friendly competition between the local chandlers."

"Aye, sir. A young lad made what another merchant thought an unreasonable promise."

"We shall see. I will give your fevers first access to water rights, whenever it may appear."

"Thank you, sir, I will endeavor to . . ."

The screech of a bo's'n whistle and Farrell yelling, "All hands, all hands," was a welcome interruption. "Hands to capstan. Fresh water's on hand."

The prospect of receiving anything fresh sent everyone to the rail. A single-handed sailor in an oddly shaped boat hailed "ahoy" and waved a floppy hat. He came into the harbour breeze and dropped his only sail, directing it with one hand to lay alongside a barrel that was near the size of a hogshead. He glided the last few feet. His craft just kissed *The Delight*'s hull.

"Lo and behold, sir," Farrell explained, "the upstart chandler. He's handily beat our old friend Mr. Royce with a water delivery."

"Seems a sprightly lad, indeed," MacNeal said watching the newcomer handle his craft. He turned to face his mate. "And just how is our Mr. Royce faring? Is he still the pompous lout of last year?"

"Aye, sir," Farrell laughed. "Fairly described. I seen him yellin' at his slaves even before he put ashore."

"A volatile one he is. Such a temperament is ill suited for a merchant."

"Precisely, sir. Royce weren't there but a minute when I saw him a saunter over ta Mrs. Middleton's. He sent two men runnin' up the street. Ain't been no activity since. That makes a lost day for Royce in this race. Pity them slaves when Royce sees he's been bested. Seems those that does the heavy work gets the worst of the deal in America."

MacNeal took this in without comment as he watched the water man work his boat. *What an odd boat. She's near wide as she is long.* "Ahoy, skipper, what manner of boat?"

"Me own design, sir. One part barge with a bit o' keel," Diamond yelled up the side, "to steady her against the weight. Ain't pretty, but she kin carry a load."

"A strange boat, is it not, to have 'er mast so far forward?"

"Strange indeed." Diamond grabbed a line from *Delight* and slipped it over a foredeck cleat. He ran another line to his stern, all the while explaining. "Bit of an accident really. Was tryin' to build me a rowin' barge, but I couldn't manage the oars meself on account of too much beam. Rather than start over, I stuck a stick on her and well, there you are. Now, if yer crew could oblige me, I kin get the first of two barrels transferred before sundown."

Farrell sent two sailors over the side to help Diamond secure the water and arranged a derrick to haul the water up. At the last moment, Diamond jumped on the barrel and rode it up. As the crew pulled the barrel over the side, Diamond swung himself from barrel to ratline to deck, landing next to Michael.

"G'day to ya, Jim Diamond."

"Nice entrance." Michael said. The newcomer was a head taller than Michael, rivaling the height of MacNeal. "Watch out, lad," he whispered, "our captain may try to press you into service."

MacNeal approached. "Nicely done, sir, nicely done. A deft bit of sailoring. Sea must be in your blood."

"Aye, she is. Ma says I were born a water spider. Spent me whole life, so far anyways, sailing these waters. Been all over the Chesapeake, sellin', buyin', tradin', fishin'. Done just 'bout everything but courtin'." He smiled. "Been as far south as the 'Ginny Capes. Thought I'd make for the Indies once, but it were too stormy for me little boat to test the Atlantic.

Suppose I'm just a bayman." He grinned at Michael. "I sees you knows yer captain's mind."

MacNeal pressed his case. "There be plenty of opportunity and adventure for a jack with yer skills. We can show you how to deal with the Atlantic. I'm in need of crew. We're London bound."

"Tempting, depending on the wages, and if you have a good cook." Again he turned to Michael, "How's the vittles? You're looking a bit ragged, if I may say."

"Cook's tolerable good, when there's food to be cooked." Michael gave himself a look before adding, "crew eats better than its indentured cargo."

"Ah, a servant ship. How many survived passage?"

When MacNeal hesitated, Michael jumped right in.

"Forty-five of forty-eight survived, plus one newborn. Lost two crew. Nearly lost a leg. That's him hobbling around," Michael said pointing to Knob. "Ship's carpenter and a good one at that."

MacNeal offered a defense. "We had a most unusually long passage."

"I'm sure, I'm sure. Tell ya what, captain," Diamond said, giving him a nudge with his elbow. "I'll cogitate on the offer once we transfers your water. I'll be needing my barrel back so I can fetch your second shipment."

Once the transfer was made, Diamond jumped on his barrel, held on with one hand, and gave a wave with the other as the crew lowered him onto the strange squat boat with its mast set too far forward. He scurried around to secure his barrel, dropped the lines, and gave himself a shove. In a wink, he raised his sail and caught the southern breeze for an easy run out of the harbour.

Michael let MacNeal study his prospect's sailing skills before he pressed what was on his mind. "When, sir?"

"When what?"

"When can I transfer sick bay? There's a fine breeze building."

"Hold on, Mr. Shea. Can't be having no sick on deck whiles we dock. Make preparations, get them their water and food. We shall move your charges once we're alongside the dock."

CHAPTER 50

MICHAEL, DANNY, AND KNOB WERE ON DECK EARLY THE NEXT MORN-ing when a shout came up from the water. "Ahoy, Farrell, Mr. Farrell," Royce bellowed, "yer water has arrived as promised."

"Oh, this'll be sweet," Michael said.

"Morning, Mr. Royce," Farrell answered, "I fear you're two barrels behind already. Your dear friend, Mr. Diamond, delivered two yesterday. He were as good as his word. A most sweet drink he has brought us."

"That so?" came a defeated voice from below. Then it perked up. "As I remember, Mr. Farrell, you was ordering four barrels."

"Aye, sir, that we are. We'll accept your offering here, but not another as I expect another from Diamond shortly. Come aboard."

Unlike the spry Diamond, Royce lumbered up the ship's ladder, his puffing getting more intense the higher he climbed. He left it to his slaves to arrange for the transfer. He reached the deck on a big sweat and still huffing when Farrell brought out the paperwork to seal the deal. Michael, Danny, and Knob kept watch over the transaction.

"What ya lookin' at?" Royce growled.

They shook their heads and pretended to be working on Knob's crutch. The sour merchant wanted to growl some more but stopped himself. Instead, in one smooth motion, Royce bowed, tipped his hat, and advanced his left leg. "Morning, ladies." When he righted himself, he pulled at the ends of his waistcoat to advertise his paunch.

"And a lovely day to yerself," Moira replied for herself and Marta, just starting their morning walkabout. Against the chill of the morning, Moira draped her green velvet cape over her sailor's outfit; Marta wore her Palatine wrap.

Royce forgot all about the water. He oozed politeness. "I trust an introduction might be arranged? I would be most honored to introduce you to our fair city once you've disembarked."

Neither Michael nor Danny felt compelled to oblige, but Knob had no entanglement. "Mr. Royce, may I present our fair and tender ladies, Miss Moira Baker and Mrs. Marta Carrington." Each curtsied at the sound of her name.

"The honor is all mine." Royce continued oozing. "Annapolis boasts of the best music, balls, and theater in the Chesapeake."

"I'm most impressed," Moira replied. "Can one enjoy a Handel operetta here?"

"As of yet, we haven't had that pleasure, but we have had a Shakespeare and John Gay returns to the stage regularly. Our performances come tolerably close to those of London, or so I'm told by Mr. Eden's secretary, Mr. William Eddis." He bowed again. "Whenever you are situated, it would be my honor to call if you would but indicate such an interest."

Knob butted in. "Ah, sadly mate, our lovelies won't be ready to take up no visitin'. Unless 'n o'course ye was to negotiate for their indentures. Servants be our cargo this trip."

"I see." Nevertheless, Royce stayed true to honoring the girls as debutantes. "Ladies, the pleasure is all mine. 'Til we meet again." He tipped his hat and then was over the side. He put in his best to appear graceful on the way down.

When Royce was out of hearing, Danny got in Knob's face. "What ye tryin' ta do, man, makin' an introduction to such a pompous snot?"

"Ah, laddie, am sorry to disillusion ya, truly I am. Much as I kin understand yer attachment for our sweet lassies, 'tis time for you to recognize what's in store. Be no more romancing for any indentured once business gets underway and yer contract's fulfilled."

Marta took Danny's arm. "Not be angry, Danny. This way, walk me." She led him away, putting her arm around his. He melted.

Michael stood, transfixed by the strands of Moria's hair fluttering in the morning breeze. Each strand seemed to have a mind of its own. Moira's return gaze unnerved his. He turned to watch Danny and Marta wander. When he turned back, Moira was still staring at him. He flinched. She smiled. Like Marta, she took her man's arm. She led him off on a different tack, leaving Knob to fend for himself.

"Do I detect jealousy in your silence?" she asked after a tour of the deck.

"I don't trust that merchant. He rings false."

"That, my dear Michael, is rather plain."

"Then why the curtseys and smiles?"

They walked a bit more. "You surprise me, Michael. I sense you more boy than man when it comes to romance."

"Have I claimed otherwise?"

"At times, you seem worldly at so many things, music, doctoring, scheming. Yet you hide your true heart. I have readily shared mine." She slipped her hand inside his jacket sleeve and tightened her hold on his left arm. "But I can't be left waiting without some clue, Michael, some hint of the sense of yours."

He put a hand on hers.

"Surely, you're not still pining for Emma, are you? She is married, Michael. Why do you choose to ignore that reality?"

"It's not that," he said looking across the harbour. "Beware of that oaf. Am sure he's less than what he seems."

"How I enjoy your jealousy." She gave his arm a couple of soft squeezes. "Surely you must know it is enjoyable for a lady to receive a flattery now and again. As you don't seem to understand the concept, I'll take it from whomever is willing to offer, whether it be from our awkward but sincere Mr. Farrell or this pretentious merchant."

He put his other hand over hers. "Indeed, were I to compete for your attentions, in a fair field of battle, I'd hope to have more to offer than a pledge and a kiss."

"A kiss'll be a welcome start."

"Will build up me courage."

"When? While I'm here would be best. Certainly before we are parted out on our serving ways." She stopped walking and turned him towards her. "Any word from MacNeal?"

"Not as yet."

"Michael, where will I go? What will happen to us? I'll be lost without you, and ever so resentful. I'm scared."

He gave her cheek a soft kiss. "I am too, but we will find each other." She hugged his arm even tighter and let him continue.

"I'm not sure how to fight for you without a purse, without the means to care for you. I can only hope you'll not be led astray by the likes of a Mr. Royce." He didn't voice his fear, *I've lost that fight before.*

"Oh Michael, you must learn that ladies, though we may be fair and young, can readily pierce the thinnest foils and the evident failings of Mr. Royce and his type."

"A relief."

"But do not forget, Michael, the power a few easy flatteries can have. Ladies find receiving them most pleasant. Many's a girl who falls for easy promises made by red coat soldiers. Emma comes to mind."

That stung. "Do I need a rapier to clear the field?"

"Really, Michael, why do men always resort to weapons? Violence is not as attractive as you men seem to believe. Flattery 'tis much more welcome, and you don't risk an early grave."

"A grave risk indeed. Not sure I can even hold a sword." Then he was serious. "Four years seems forever," he said, squeezing her hand, "especially when one's heart is tormented with uncertainty."

Across the water, Michael could hear a terrible row. Royce had shed his veneer of refinement as soon as he returned to his launch. He kept up the abuse as his slaves rowed to the wharf. Moira seemed not to notice at first as they circled the deck.

"You see, Michael," she said without looking back, "such poor behavior is not a surprise. We barmaids know how to spot false flatteries. The trick is to enjoy them without taking the source seriously."

On their second pass by the quarterdeck MacNeal interrupted. "Mr. Shea, a word, if I may."

"We can twirl again later," Moira whispered as she let Michael go. "I'm off to have a goodbye with Marta."

As she climbed down the hatch, Michael bade her goodbye. "Adieu, Lady Moira, adieu," he affected an Elizabethan bow, "until the morrow or another bright day. If ever there was a truer promise, we'll walk one day along these streets that bear the impress of sweet Queen Anne's kiss, this fair city, of Annapolis."

She gave him a wave.

"A most touching display, Mr Shea," MacNeal said, "though I think the rhyme a bit forced."

Red faced, Michael gave a shrug.

"Perhaps you could expand on your poetic sentiments at my table this evening? A fare-thee-well, of sorts, from captain to ship's doctor? I have ordered some tolerably good Madeira."

"Thank you, sir, that would be grand." But Michael was wondering, *why the change of heart?*

CHAPTER 51

DINNER TURNED OUT TO BE A STAND-UP AFFAIR AROUND THE CAPTAIN'S table. Cook indicated a bowl of stew at the end plus fresh-baked bread, still warm, but that was all. Michael savored the first few bites. Captain MacNeal was true to his word about the wine. At a nod from Supercargo Edmund-Tell, Cook poured Michael a healthy tankard. MacNeal and Edmund-Tell offered obligatory toasts. "To the king, his health and kingdom, long may they reign." Michael shrugged them off. MacNeal chose not to respond to Michael's bad manners. He got down to business knowing he'd soon be relieved.

"We will embrace the dock in the morning, Mr. Shea." He put his Madeira on the table and paced a step or two, hands behind his back. "Once settled, we will move the sick bay on deck, as we discussed. However, there will be, how should I say this, a new arrangement," he stopped pacing and looked directly at Michael, "as to who'll attend to *The Delight's* medical needs." MacNeal watched Michael swallow, it seemed, in slow motion.

"Sir?"

"We have happy news for you, Mr. . . ." MacNeal handed Michael the indenture agreement he had signed in London. "By what name shall we call you?"

Michael grimaced as he glanced at the document. "That was the doing of the indenturing agent, Mr. MacNeal, a relation I believe. Was his idea to abandon Irish names to 'avoid a stir at Gravesend,' was the way he put it, as Catholics are not encouraged to travel to Maryland."

"It is heartily discouraged," the supercargo agreed.

"At yer brother's suggestion," Michael emphasized, "he wrote in new names for us. I will readily explain to the customs agent if you prefer. We thought it a temporary expedient. We were told it would be easier to sell our contracts."

"Indeed, this could be the case," the supercargo said.

"Could be?" Michael asked.

"Aye, depending on who knows how best to keep such things . . . in the hold, shall we say," MacNeal answered.

The supercargo continued. "Otherwise, we'd be obliged ta return the two of yas to London and report yer deception."

"Wouldn't it be better to just sell our contracts and be done with us?" Michael suggested. "Otherwise, we all lose."

"Aye, Mr. Shea," the supercargo said, "that we would, if we were found out by the Customs House. Therefore, to avoid such a pecuniary disappointment, arrangements have been made for disposal of your indenture. A Mr. Charles Carroll has accepted your contract."

"Has he now?"

"He has," the captain answered. "We found the letter of introduction in your indenturing papers." He handed them to Michael. "I sent a note when we went ashore. By his reply he readily agreed. Says he has need of medical assistance. Normally such transactions take place on deck as part of our daily business. However, due to your history on this voyage, we think it best to avoid any chance of another misadventure. We find it necessary to achieve the transaction this night. A private sale, shall we say, one that avoids making any false declaration or mention of papists reaching these shores. Mr. Carroll readily agreed. Methinks he's done this before."

"I'll get my fiddle and things and make my goodbyes, then."

"Alas, we don't have time for fare-thee-wells," Captain MacNeal said. "The launch is waiting. Mr. Carroll is at his dock now."

"What of Danny, sir? And Miss Baker? You promised to accommodate."

"We will endeavor to do what we can," the supercargo said, "once you're ashore and we have assurance you've not made any contact with the Customs House."

"Until that time," MacNeal continued, "Your associates are confined to quarters. I am tempted to retain Mr. O'Mara as ship's carpenter if he'd consider sailoring over servitude."

"May I say goodbye then?"

"Again, we don't have time, Mr. Shea. Mr. Carroll awaits."

"Miss Moira?"

"As she did not ship out under false pretense, we have more leeway to negotiate for her service."

"But Moira is not a Palatine."

"Obviously," the supercargo said. "Whether she stays with Brouchard remains to be seen. In any case, 'tis only yourself and Mr. O'Mara that have put us in a bind, so to speak."

"There may be . . . " Michael stopped himself from revealing that Moira signed her indenture under false pretenses. He remembered Farrell's comment about servitude for minor children lasting well past their majority. ". . . time for a letter?"

"No time. Mr. O'Mara and Miss Baker will be told how to contact the Carroll home once we conclude this business."

"I must have a chance to speak—"

Supercargo cut him off. "All is arranged. A boat awaits. Mr. Farrell has already stowed your belongings. Cook will escort you."

CHAPTER 52

ONE OF THE FIGURES ON THE CARROLL WHARF WAVED AS THE LAUNCH approached. Behind the silhouettes, up on a hill, a grand mansion lit by candle glow that revealed a finely built red-brick house with two roofs. A voice hailed, *"Bonsoir,* Michael, *si bon de vous voir. Bienvenue à Annapolis. Bienvenue chez moi."*

Michael recognized the voice. "Ahoy! *Les Irlandais ont survécu à la cruelle Atlantique."* When the launch bumped against the wharf, Farrell tossed a line to secure the launch. Carroll's slave tied it to a dock piling. "I'll takes yer baggage, sir." He reached for Michael's lumpy clothes bundle. Michael hesitated before relinquishing his fiddle to the outstretched hand. He caught himself staring at a dark brown hand stretching out of an off-white shirt sleeve, good quality, with ruffles. The hand steadied Michael during the transition from boat to wharf.

Michael's head was spinning as he got both feet on the landing stage. He turned to bid farewell to Farrell. "My regards to Miss Moira and Danny. Let them know if you could, Liam, I had no choice in this."

"Aye, Michael." Farrell saluted. "They will know you have not abandoned them." He extended his hand to shake Michael's. "Good luck, Michael, been a pleasure."

Michael's throat tightened, his eyes watered, he wobbled on the dock.

Carroll and his slave stood with Michael as Farrell and Cook rowed away. Then Carroll spoke. "May I say, my old friend, it is so good to see you. Even in the dark, I can see you're looking lighter than when last we met."

"Been a long time at sea. Horrible food and always in short supply. *Je n'ai jamais apprécié le ragoût de rat."*

Carroll grimaced at the thought. "Never fear, we can fatten you up. I hope you will embrace my household and consider it your home. I certainly would consider it an honor to have your talents grace our family's service."

"Will do my best." Michael thought he heard his name. He turned around to give *The Delight* a long look across the harbour. He thought he saw two shadows in the dark, dark bumps really, just above the rail.

"Memories." Carroll put an arm around Michael to turn him away from the ship. "They'll take a while."

"Two in particular." On a second look back, the shadows were gone. "I traveled with dear friends. One was Danny—he was with me when we last spoke in London."

"I remember him. A handsome look about him. A gifted singer, filled the room with his voice, as did the lady who danced."

"That would be Emma. You remember another girl who sang?"

"Certainly, exquisite voice as well. The blend of the two ladies was intoxicating. I shall never forget their enchanting performances."

"That was Moira, Emma's sister. She ended up on *The Delight* with us. I fear for her safety. She's nearly seventeen. She secreted herself to travel with us. Was more than a fortnight before I realized she were even aboard."

"A stowaway?"

"Bribed an indenturing agent."

"Did she now? A resourceful one, but why indenture yerself if you have the wherewithal to bribe someone?"

Michael paused. "She did it for love. For me. Truth be known, I had pleaded with her sister, Emma, to join me. I had mistaken desire for love. Instead Moira hid amongst pilgrims. It's a conundrum I've yet to settle in my mind."

"Where will this Moira end up then?"

"Precisely. Have you need of a beautiful singer who can enthrall your dinner guests?"

"Any other skills? Resourcefulness is certainly a start."

"Her family owns the White Lyon. She knows taverns. She also has a most steady hand for medical procedures."

"A female doctoring? Most curious. I can make inquiries."

"Would it be possible to act quickly? Moira is ill suited to be a milk maid."

"There is time. We have a day or two before Captain MacNeal's advert circulates."

"In the morning, sir?"

"Not to worry. Am quite sure we can find a spot for her. What about your friend Danny?"

"Danny can fend for himself. If he finds employ in Annapolis, we'll find each other. It's Moira that concerns me."

"In the morning, then." He waved a hand towards the house. *"Ma maison est à toi."* As the slave led the way up a steep little hill carrying Michael's baggage, Carroll asked, "The passage was tiresome? Was there much music making out on the Atlantic?"

"Hard to pull a bow when the ocean's tryin' to drown ya."

Michael wasn't ready to explain. He was captivated by the Carroll man, a tall black lad, about Michael's age. It was unusual enough to have someone else carrying his load, however light it might be, but even stranger to see his first black man close up in light grey linen hose, darker britches, and black leather shoes. Under his buttoned deep blue waistcoat, a white shirt with small ruffled cuffs. *So well dressed*, Michael thought. They followed a path leading up to a plateau with a sizable area for outdoor entertaining.

From the higher vantage point, Michael watched the launch disappear behind *The Delight*. He scanned the deck. No shadows. He turned his attention to his host.

"Was pressed into service as ship's doctor. Lost some souls."

"I hear you outdid yourself in service to Captain MacNeal."

Michael didn't answer right away. He studied the dark form of *The Delight* at anchor. *After all that turmoil, she's looks so peaceful now.* He finally turned to Carroll to broach an uncomfortable question.

"Ah, oh dear, um, how shall I ask this? What form of address will suit while I'm in your service?" Carroll raised a hand to put the conversation on hold.

"Mr. Shea will stay in the east dormer." The slave nodded and disappeared inside the house with Michael's baggage. Carroll joined Michael watching cat paw ripples ebb and flow across the harbour. "We must abide by formalities in public. In private, we can be Michael and Charlie, if I may call you Michael."

"By all means."

"But only in private. In front of the servants and slaves, in public and especially in the presence of my dear father, you should address us both as Mr. Carroll. I warn you, many find father cantankerous at first blush. He would not understand our intimacy, considering the gap in our positions, but then again, he wasn't aware of your efforts to save me from that butcher Oliver. I still thank the saints for sending you to my sickbed."

"Was my pleasure to wait upon you." He paused. "Charlie?"

"As we are alone, I can be Charlie." Carroll opened the rear door to the house and poked his head in. He waved Michael to follow as he put a finger over his grin. "Our cook has already retired," he said picking up a small lantern. "Our house has as well, and as you can see here, our kitchen fire is out. That's Lucy, our cook," he whispered, motioning to a form asleep on a cot. In the small hallway leading to the staircase, he continued. "She gets preference to sleep alone in the kitchen. Some other slaves bunk together behind the hearth." He gently shut the door and signaled with a nod for Michael to follow up a circular stairway. "Lucy's day starts well before sunrise. I'm too weak to wake her for a late meal." He led Michael to a parlor room on the next floor that was used for small meals during working hours.

"All I can offer you at this hour is some wine. The sideboard is bare for the night. We can find you some hot stew at Middleton's, if you have the energy."

Michael's stomach roared to life at the prospect of food. "Stew would be most welcome."

Carroll poured him a sip of wine and nodded to a chair at a small table. "Excuse me while I arrange for my carriage." He disappeared into a larger room facing the creek. When he returned, he set the agenda.

"Tomorrow we will discuss business. I'd like to show you around our fair city. There's much business and industry to see. I'm sure you'd like to visit our Assembly Room. A dance is organized most every week in season. Perhaps we can inquire as to how they're set for fiddlers?"

"Will I be able to seek employment outside of service?"

"We will find a way."

"What manner of work will be expected while I'm in your employ? Labor? Planting? Cooking? Thrashing tobacco?"

"Thrashing our tobacco?" Carroll stifled a laugh. "We'll find suitable duties. Certainly, Papa won't want you thrashing his tobacco. He'd have you whipped for mistreating his precious crop." He poured Michael another small sip. "The harvesting term is threshing. In any case, we don't trash tobacco, we dry it. 'Threshing' is what's done to grain."

"I have much to learn, then."

"Indeed." Carroll was still smiling. "I'm sorry, Michael, for laughing. I have this image stuck in my head of Father chasing you around Doughregan with his whip, his head all in a boil, after you 'thrashed' his tobacco."

"A friendly sort, your father?"

"Tobacco is money and money's not to be trifled with. Tobacco is the source of all our wealth in the Chesapeake. No planter would take kindly to losing even a leaf. We have problems enough getting a fair price once it gets to London. It's a constant struggle with factors and agents pilfering from our shipments."

"Your factors steal from you, too?"

"Stealing is a harsh word, but that is how it feels to all of us colonial planters, like Jonathan. The price delivered is always less than agreed, many times far less. Factors blame it on spoilage, damage at sea, evaporation even."

"Evaporation?"

"I've had more than one factor make such claims. We never get full credit for our crop. Lots of hidden fees, taxes, surprise commissions. Most planters feel powerless to prevent it. Many, perhaps most, end up indebted to merchants and traders. Our resentments simmer. I understand Jonathan's anger. It's a shame he could not moderate his passion. My family has learned that reliance on tobacco and trade with London is a dangerous way to secure a fortune. This is why we develop domestic markets. It helps to break the stranglehold London has over us. We could get better prices from the French and the Dutch, and much better terms, but of course we are forbidden from shipping on anything but an English bottom. The temptation to sail south is ever present."

"Is there much smuggling?"

"We are not so bold as New Englanders. There's nowhere to hide in Annapolis. Most of us are too genteel to openly smuggle like they do in Massachusetts."

Carroll turned to household business "Let's turn to domestic matters. We have male slaves who serve as valets to assist me with my duties. You'll join their ranks. You'll have your own bed with them, on the top floor, last door. Nice view of the harbour. Having only realized you were joining us this day, we have not discussed duties for you. I have written to Father to solicit his thoughts. I did emphasize your medical training."

Michael put his empty glass on the side table and waited for an explanation.

"I've proposed a medical role for you . . . to protect our labor investments."

"And?"

"If you don't mind, could you give me a day or two? I feel obliged to review this with Father as it concerns work on his estate . . ." Carroll let the idea trail off.

"As to your arrival, as I agreed with this Edmund-Tell person, it is wise to avoid the Custom House. It would be bad manners to reveal I've engaged yet another Catholic in the house." He smiled. "The king has his church St. Anne's. We Catholics have no church. They are forbidden. Have been since that wretched Dutchman took the throne. They may call it 'Glorious,' but of course we don't agree, now do we? William's laws against Catholics punish us here to this day. We celebrate a Mass in our home, when we have a priest. Father likes to host the Jesuits, even as he torments them. Most of the time, they are resident at Doughreagan. That's our family plantation north of here. Our family refused to make a pretense of changing churches as some cousins have done. Now, we have. . . ."

"No disrespect intended, Charlie, but I have another matter to discuss that is pressing on my mind, one that has tormented me since leaving England. It concerns your friend Jonathan."

"Ah, yes, Jonathan Clayborne, a rather impulsive but sincere Virginian. I trust he is well."

"Jonathan's dead, sir."

"Oh dear, Jonathan dead? The pox, a fever?"

Michael was about to tell the story when the front door opened and the slave who had carried Michael's things entered. "James is ready, masta."

"Thank you, Dominic. Let James know we're off to Middleton's."

CHAPTER 53

ON THE WAY, MICHAEL SHRUGGED OFF CARROLL'S ATTEMPTS AT CONversation by nodding in James's direction. "It is not necessary," Carroll said, but Michael rode in silence.

Once settled in a corner table by the fireplace at Middleton's, Carroll order a stew, bread, and an ale for Michael. Carroll enjoyed a brandy. They were an odd pair, a gentleman of highest order in the company of an emaciated effigy in a threadbare jacket that might once have been blue. The frayed cuffs looked like exploding dandelions.

Michael ate before talking. "Much appreciated, Charlie. Been a long time since we've enjoyed hot food." He turned to savoring the ale and then spoke. "I was transfixed by your driver. Those eyes, like tiny moons floating in the air. Quite a sight. Your driver's far better dressed than any servant I've known."

"James is a most trustworthy slave. Silence was not necessary."

"I'm sure."

"And he is discreet."

"He well may be. My experience is otherwise."

"You've been a servant before? Dealt with slaves?"

"Slaves, no. I tasted privilege before I fell from grace. And I've lived amongst the meaner sorts. You've not tred those streets. The rules, as you well know, are quite different for the social classes. Take this fine tavern, for example."

Carroll turned to give the interior a distracted onceover. "This is indeed a fine establishment. That's Sam Chase at the bar, the one with the ruddy face. Humble origins, son of a preacher, but he can't control his passions. A dangerous sort for a lawyer. He was the ringleader who just ran our newly appointed Stamp Act Tax collector out of town. Led a mob of three hundred to prevent Zachariah Hood from landing here, his hometown. Mob dragged a wagon to the dock with a gallows and Hood's effigy hanging on it. They lit it on fire. Mr. Hood took the hint, stayed on board, and escaped later on horseback. The taller one is William Paca, they're both rising lawyers. Chase, the mob leader. Paca is of the best of families."

Carroll waved a hello, but the men didn't take notice. He tried to hide his embarrassment.

"Why such a passion over taxes?"

"Parliament didn't consult with us. We all hate the idea of being treated as children, but that doesn't justify mob action. Mobs are uncontrollable. Dealing with Chase is difficult." He changed the subject. "That's Billy Creagh two tables over, facing us. He runs the shipyard we rode past."

Michael returned to his point. "Who provided our drink?"

"Mrs. Middleton, mistress of this tavern."

"I mean who delivered our drink just now? What color coat did he have on?" Carroll started to turn around. Michael stopped him. "No, don't go looking. What color?"

"Blue."

"He has no coat." Michael lowered his voice. "It's a shabby blue-green checked waistcoat under a dirty apron. No, don't turn around. Where is he now?"

"Not the foggiest."

"Setting a table by your ship maker. He's dallying about, polishing a plate that doesn't need polishing."

"Clearly, I'm not as observant as you. But what be the point? He's but a servant."

"Precisely." Michael took a sip. "You noticed your friends, Charlie, but not much else. Typical of high station, no offense intended. The server lingers by your friends. They chat away, oblivious to his presence. Why? Because he is 'but a servant,' as you just said. Had Jonathan played more my game, he'd be alive to defend his family."

"Your game?"

"Aye, my game. Patience. Observation. Listen. Learn. Jonathan was unable to restrain his passions. Action clouded by rage. A dangerous mix."

"Yes, a gentleman must embrace moderation, moderation in all things. There is no elegance with intemperance. What's this to do with servants?"

"I've made my way in taverns like this. I watch. I listen. I collect things said and done. Your peers suffer from the arrogance that comes with their class. They treat the lower sorts as if we're bugs in the night. You can't see well when your nose is held high." He whispered, "Let me tell you, Charlie, your friends' conversation, their thoughts are known."

"Eavesdropping on a private conversation? A gentleman would never do such a thing."

"Don't be so sure."

"Father would have the man whipped."

"No doubt. But the good ones are discrete. Your man tonight, he's good. Quite the stoic in his driver's seat. I doubt very much he were of empty mind, not with his skill with your horses. If I were in his place, I would do the same, pretend disinterest. For example, how many times do you think Mrs. Middelton's man needs to rearrange that table?"

"I hadn't noticed."

"Precisely."

"What's the point of this? I had expected to hear about Jonathan."

"My apologies. 'Tis all so new, my mind is racin', comparing the old and new, what's familiar, what's not." He toyed with his mug. "Murdered. Jonathan was murdered."

"How? What happened?"

"The night we last met, at the White Lyon, a dreadful night." Michael refreshed his memory. "There was an ambush, a fight, a confrontation. Jonathan was found outside in the tavern's courtyard, in the snow, with his throat cut. I was called to help. He knew he were dying. I did my best to help him."

"Who would do such a thing?"

"Officially, assailant 'unknown.' But Jonathan knew who killed him, and I think I now know as well." From under his jacket, Michael pulled out Jonathan's leather wallet and laid it upon the table. "Before he died, Jonathan gave me this."

Both stared at it for a time. "Money? Letters to a sweetheart? His family?" Carroll asked.

"Took a time to figure that out." Michael lowered his voice again. "Several letters, mostly to his father. Some notes to himself. Much is in a cypher. At first, it defeated me. Events didn't allow time to consider what these papers held. Jonathan entrusted to me, so I only hoped to deliver these papers somehow to his family. He had plenty of money in his pockets that night. Robbery was not the motive. I left the money with him. I took only what he gave to me."

"Of course."

"Could have used a few quid, mind you, but I feared his money."

"How do you mean?"

"A lad like me were found with a dead man's purse?

"But your hosts clearly accounted for your whereabouts."

"Yes, but how long will they remember the way events truly transpired? Many an innocent's hung on lies. I thought it best to remove myself from London before stories were forgot, or invented. To be carrying Jonathan's purse could only mean I murdered him."

"How much?"

"Near thirty pounds. More in his room."

"You were in his room?"

"It was terrible cold that night. We sheltered in Jonathan's room to sort things out."

"The papers. He entrusted them to you. Did anyone witness this?"

"We were alone."

"Was there an inquiry?"

"Briefly and not much of one, at least not while I was with Jonathan. I suspect collusion, sir."

"Collusion?"

"Jonathan was in London to confront those who swindle his family and his fellow planters in Virginia. I think he was murdered because of it."

"Over commissions?"

"People kill for much less."

"Who would do such a thing?"

"Those with much to lose, especially when it comes to honor. He confronted one factor, demanded restitution. The factor refused. Honor forced Jonathan to provoke pistols at dawn. Jonathan prevailed."

"Revenge, then, for the man he killed?"

"Perhaps. Jonathan was searching for three malefactors. After he killed the first, word spread quickly through London. The second quickly made amends when Jonathan confronted him. It's the third factor, I suspect, who is behind Jonathan's demise."

"Jonathan made no secret of why he was in London," Carroll recalled. "I know many a tobacco planter who shares Jonathan's ire. We all suffer the ill treatment in London and the traders, factors, and merchants seem to grow more brazen. The value of our tobacco is greatly diminished, the prices agreed to are reneged upon, and the goods we expect in exchange are vastly different, often inferior, to what was ordered and promised. We planters understand Jonathan's resentments, though dueling is not the answer."

"That was his mistake, his lack of restraint. The hunted knew they were being hunted."

"There is a clue then, in his papers?"

"At first it was hard enough to even read Jonathan's handwriting. His cipher made it ever more confusing. He offered a clue when he scratched this." Michael pointed to Jonathan's last communication, "miss v." "Assumed he meant a lady. His mother? Sister? Betrothed? What would you make of that?"

"A brother? I know of no sister. His mother, I believe, was a Diane and in any case, she succumbed to fever years ago. Perhaps a betrothed? Miss Veronica, Violet, Venus, Virginia?"

"He wasn't pining for a lady. I had little opportunity to consider this puzzle during much of our voyage. But after touching in Antigua, I had some, shall we say, private time, to consider his cypher. It was there that I realized he was giving me the antidote."

"Which is?"

"Simple really. His hasty scribble, 'miss v,' doesn't allude to a lady. He's saying, 'missing vowels.' Jonathan scrawled his most private thoughts with just consonants. The reader must add the vowels. Certainly awkward, but one gets used to filling in. With a bit of effort and practice, I could decipher his story. For example, what do you make of this?"

He pulled a paper from the wallet, slid it across the table, his finger on the salutation. It read: "DrtFr, nrpltrlstJn6."

After a moment of study, Carroll had it. "I'd say he means, 'Dear or Dearest Father, in reply to yours of June 6' or some such sentiment."

"Read on then."

Carroll studied before translating. "Without a doubt . . . 'the third, a concern,'—nice of him to spell this out, Matthew Broadbent & Son,—'a name on a sign. Behind this charade,'" Carroll paused to think. "He could mean chicanery, his scribble is hard to make, though it makes little difference." He resumed reading. "MB . . . gambling syndicate . . . two brothers . . . swindle across England . . . call themselves Broot. Pretend German extraction . . . the Holy Roman Emperor?" Carroll looked up at Michael. "Quite imaginative history."

Michael nodded.

Carroll skimmed the letter until something caught his attention that was plain to read ". . . business in Quacks, the Old Nose . . . With bribes . . . hunting for M. Broot," Carroll stalled. "I don't know these places."

"Molly clubs."

When the term didn't resonate with Carroll. Michael tried again. "'Disorderly houses' is the polite term in the newspapers."

"Oh, you mean for sodomites?"

Michael nodded, "They congregate with brothels near Covent Garden, Drury Lane, the Exchange and Lincoln's Inn."

"Nasty business."

"Some see it as an evening's entertainment."

Carroll frowned. "So, n-t-r-s f-p means . . ." he looked at Michael.

"F-p is fop." Michael jumped to the chase. "It appears Johnathan first encounters this M. Broot at one of these Molly houses. Later Jonathan begins to suspect that there's more to his new friend than just a fellow Molly. Through whatever means, Jonathan connects M. Broot to the tobacco scheme. They lose touch. Then fate reunites them at the White Lyon."

Michael paused to let Carroll catch up. "When we last met at the White Lyon, the night of Jonathan's demise, the big man attacking Jonathan was Marcellus Broot. Remember, he flouted about in flamboyant dress and affected effeminate manners," Michael offered.

Carroll finally deciphered it. "Must mean notorious." Carroll took a sip then continued. "A notorious fop . . . younger of two. The older calls himself Walter Bryan Broot." Carroll looked up. "At least he makes one name plain," then he returned to translating.

"By . . ." Carroll stumbled over n-s-v-r .

"By unsavory means," Michael offered.

"Yes, that must be it. By unsavory means," Carroll continued, "the Broots took over a respectable business." In an aside to Michael, Carroll looked up from the letter. "He must mean the aforementioned MB & Son." Then he continued. "The elder Broot courted and married widow MB, still grieving, and the MB fortune, now much diminished. The work of accounts falls to the younger M. Good with maths."

"He's referring to Marcellus Broot." Michael filled in the next line. "Jonathan says, 'prowling mollies in Mulberry Garden and Italian houses.' That was a tough line to cypher."

Carroll looked up. "Sounds like our Jonathan's a modern-day Captain Rigby, yes? Had you an inkling about Jonathan's proclivities?"

"Of course. But he was a fine fellow, very passionate about finances and honor."

Carroll continued his translation, "Let's see, ah here we are, Jonathan writes, 'discover this Marcellus, expose fraud . . . demand restitution . . . redeem family honor and fortune.'" Carroll looked at Michael. "So Marcellus was the one who pounded Jonathan's head on the floor."

"The same. And he had help, of that, I am sure. There was another who joined the Broot's party after dinner in a private room, where I learned, they scheme to cheat at cards. This man suffers from the gout. Walked with two canes. I'm sure it was he who dispatched Jonathan. I think you met him this morning: Sylvester Edmund-Tell, supercargo of *The Delight*."

"How could he? He can barely walk."

"Very handy with a razor. I saw him cut a Barbary throat. Very little effort, even for a man who can hardly stand on his own. I am sure it was he who helped Marcellus murder Jonathan."

"Why kill poor Jonathan?"

"Fear of exposure. The Broots are by nature dishonest. It's their way of life. The Broots would suffer terrible loss if they were exposed."

"Are you at risk?"

"Edmund-Tell doesn't know I was there, nor what I know. He didn't attend the dinner. He arrived later for a gambling table." Michael recounted the story Emma had told him about the gambling part.

"Why do you tell me all this?"

"Loyalty to my patient's dying wish. I trust you can help me make the final delivery to enlighten his family of his discoveries, and his demise."

"Will Edmund-Tell get away with murder?"

"Who will prosecute him three thousand miles away? How do I prove any of this?"

Carroll nodded, "You must be exhausted. Let's call this an evening and resume on the morrow."

It was a quiet carriage. Michael nearly nodded off on the short ride home where the house slave greeted them at the small front porch.

"Dominic will show you to your quarters. Michael, I bid you goodnight."

Michael nodded and followed Dominic up the staircase to the third level.

Chapter 54

Michael was nudged awake. It was well past dawn. The household was full of noisy activity in the levels below. The sight of a tall dark-skinned man at the foot of the bed startled him before he realized where he was, the servants' quarters at the Charles Carroll house.

"Mista Carroll says ta give ya dis." The house slave, Dominic, handed Michael a newspaper folded back upon itself to reveal a notice. It read:

JUST ARRIVED, In the Ship The Delight, Capt. Jas. MacNeal, from London, now lying at Annapolis, a Cargo of choice healthy INDENTED SERVANTS, to be fold for cafh, or good Bills of Exchange on Wednefday next, Men and Women (Freewillers & Redemptioners) amongft them many exceeding good Tradefmen, Houfe-Carpenters, Joiners, Cabinetmakers, Bricklayers, Black and White-Smiths, Tailors, Weavers, and other ufeful Tradefmen. Attendance is given on board the faid fhip, to agree and difpofe of their Times to ferve. The faid Ship will take TOBACCO and LUMBER to London by applying to S. S. Edmund-Tell.

Scrawled across the bottom of the advert, a note from Carroll. *When you're presentable, we will inquire about your friends.*

Michael looked up with a smile. "Let's get cracking, Mr. Dominic."

Michael found Carroll on this porch watching James drive his carriage roll up Duke of Gloucester Street.

"You mentioned visiting *The Delight?*" Michael asked.

"Alas, it is too late. I sent a servant this early morning to inquire about your friends. I'm sorry to report their contracts have been claimed."

Michael's shoulders slumped, his head as well, as if he'd just been punched in the stomach.

"Already? How . . . how could this happen?"

"Same as you, I suspect," Carroll said. "Shipping news has a way of getting around. This is a small town."

"She was with the Palatine party."

"Apparently she no longer is." Carroll turned towards Michael and realized his disappointment, but Carroll looked at him like the servant he now was.

"Sorrys to hear, suh," Dominic said, putting a hand on Michael's shoulder.

Carroll handed him an unsealed envelope. Michael withdrew the note.

Dear Sir,

As per our agreement, terms for Mr. O'Mara and Miss Baker have been agreed upon. Mr. O'Mara to the Owens family in Annapolis, four years. Miss Baker to the Royce estate in Chestertown until her majority. It is up to Mr. Carroll to arrange for any communication as direct contact between servants is not allowed outside permission of their masters.

I have proposed to Mr. Carroll to negotiate for your services to care for our sick while The Delight remains in port, if you would be so willing, and Mr. Carroll generous enough to provide your assistance.

Yours,

Capt. Jas. MacNeal

Michael wanted to scream.

"They are not lost, Michael," Carroll said. "The Royce family lease a warehouse from my family on the wharf. Their plantation's near Chestertown. We may find reason to visit. Mrs. Owens's Coffee House is but a short walk from here."

"You read my letter?"

"Not at all. A gentleman would never read another's correspondence. However, as you so plainly opened my eyes last night, servants do have a way of collecting information. Dominic says a sailor hobbling on a crutch extended his good wishes and related the news. Said he'd be most pleased to visit with you. You will soon oblige him."

Michael tried to weigh options he didn't have. "You're sending me back to *The Delight*?"

Carroll nodded. "You're to provide medical service. I will insist on a very good fee. Your supercargo insisted on an unusually steep price for your contract. I now have an opportunity to return his generosity . . . only the . . ." Carroll realized Michael wasn't listening.

Dominic watched a wave of gloom overwhelm the servant doctor. He could smell tears before Michael wiped his eyes with the cuffs of his jacket. Dominic put his hand on Michael's back. "It takes time, suh, more times than in a day, befores a heart kin find comfort in this land. Some never does."

THE END

About the Author

THOMAS GUAY HAS A COMMUNICATIONS degree with a double major in history from the University of Maryland and became a journalist because he enjoys writing and telling stories. After a career as a Capitol Hill reporter, he refocused on colonial history and started research-ing what would become this book by focusing on the plight of indentured servants, the *Peggy Stewart*, and other tax-related uprisings in the Chesapeake Bay region.

KAREN GUAY

Guay has also worked as a host at the Charles Carroll House in Annapolis. Currently, he is an eighteenth-century reenactor and tour guide sharing stories about the Golden Age of Annapolis, 1750–1783. He lives in Annapolis, Maryland; enjoys sailing on the Chesapeake Bay; and plays traditional fiddle tunes with the popular music group The Eastport Oyster Boys.

www.ingramcontent.com/pod-product-compliance
Lightning Source LLC
Chambersburg PA
CBHW022121160225
21802CB00003B/3